T0356718

Archangel's Ascension

A Guild Hunter Novel

Nalini Singh

BERKLEY ROMANCE
New York

BERKLEY ROMANCE
Published by Berkley
An imprint of Penguin Random House LLC
1745 Broadway, New York, NY 10019
penguinrandomhouse.com

Copyright © 2025 by Nalini Singh

ISBN: 9780593550038

First Edition: May 2025

Printed in the United States of America
1   3   5   7   9   10   8   6   4   2

The authorized representative in the EU for product safety and compliance
is Penguin Random House Ireland, Morrison Chambers, 32 Nassau Street,
Dublin D02 YH68, Ireland, https://eu-contact.penguin.ie.

For Illium and Aodhan
Adi and Blue
Sparkle and Bluebell

Archangel's Ascension

Today

1

Illium swept past the sleek skyscraper that pierced the white clouds of an early spring day, so close that his wing threatened to brush against black glass tough enough to withstand an angelic strike. It made sense that the innovation had come about in New York—born in the mind of a mortal who had been "sick and tired" of angelic battles leveling his beloved city.

No building, not even the most reinforced, would survive should an archangel turn their ire on it, but archangels had armies for a reason. War was fought on many fronts, and that mortal, his name and history immortalized in the records kept in the Refuge, had given New York a critical advantage: its buildings would not fall easily in any engagement, would instead provide cover for counterstrike after counterstrike.

As it was, in the hundreds of years since the invention of this new material, New York had come under only the mildest of attacks—in all cases as a result of Illium's asshole of a father being pissy that his son would rather serve another archangel. But even Aegaeon hadn't had the heart for a true

war, so New York hadn't fallen again since the end of the
War of the Death Cascade. But why be stupid and arrogant?
Better to build ever tougher.

A tall woman with striking facial bones ran to a window
of the skyscraper to wave at him. He dipped his wings in
acknowledgment. She'd worked in that corner office for
half a decade, was a senior associate as of two years ago,
and her face still lit up every single time he flew past. Because she was family. Part of the clan that Catalina and
Lorenzo had created when they fell in love countless mortal
lifetimes ago.

The most extraordinary thing of it all was that his beloved friends' little bakery in Harlem had survived the inexorable passage of time. The home of the city's famous
angel-wing alfajores thrived still in that old building where
the recipe had first been born—a building that had never
lost its warm heart, no matter how often it'd been repaired
and renovated. Because every generation of Catalina and
Lorenzo's family birthed a passionate baker who wanted to
carry on their legacy.

Illium had purchased the entire block piece by piece to
ensure the little bakery would always have a home, that it'd
never be forced out by progress or simple change. Harlem
might morph and alter around it like a chameleon forever
in flux, but even when that part of the city had gone dangerously gray for a period, become the haunt of vampiric excess and mortal pain, no one had dared come for the bakery.

The entire city knew that it sheltered beneath wings of a
vivid, unmistakable blue veined with fine filaments of silver.

Using those wings to ride the air currents coming off the
ocean, Illium flew through the crisp bite of spring. It whispered of snows not long past, was even more acute in the
fine mist that kissed his skin as he rose through the clouds
to fly at a higher elevation.

Other skyscrapers speared through the clouds around
him, and lush floating habitats appeared to sit atop the puffy
white, but none came close to the soaring wonder of Raphael's Tower. The tallest point in the sky at any given time,

built to offer clear lines of sight in every direction, it, too, had undergone many an iteration over the passage of time, but always, *always* it had been a beacon of power and light. No black glass for the Tower, its body a steel gray that glittered with metallic highlights. The windows were reflective at the top levels, the levels that would be the most important in any battle, and they intensely annoyed Illium the man, who was as curious as his pet cat.

First General Illium, however, well understood their facility and had been part of the team that had designed the Tower when it came time for a new build. He'd also made sure the entire building was technologically connected in ways unlike that of any other archangelic stronghold in the world. The one thing that had never changed, however, was the waterfall of railingless balconies from which angels took flight.

He caught sight of a pair of wings opening up in flight just then. Feathers the shade of dark mahogany, hair a touch lighter, the flight form of a warrior.

Andreja.

Seven and a half millennia of age or so—she'd forgotten her actual birthing day eons ago—she wore the amber of an angel far younger than her. She, who'd vowed never to lock herself to one lover. But even tough and battle-scarred Andreja wasn't proof against Laric's patient determination. When she'd told the healer he was too young to tie himself to her, he'd simply waited her out.

"He asks me every time he clocks up another century— and reminds me that *we've* clocked up another century together," Andreja had complained to Illium. "Man is relentless."

Illium's lips curved at the memory; he knew all about quiet, relentless types. He also knew that Andreja had been so terrified of commitment because of how much she loved Laric; she'd been scared he'd fly away after he was healed of his own terrible pain. But Laric was like Illium: they loved deep and true only once . . . and for always.

Sweeping down through the clouds with his own lover's smile in his mind's eye, he dropped to the first set of nonreflective windows, got a wave from a passing vampire with hair of liquid jet that reached her lower back.

Her black bodysuit boasted a jagged cutout over the shoulder and upper chest area that peaked at one shoulder, and her boots had chunky heels of clear glass so high that he had no idea how she walked so effortlessly in them. While her hair had been black this past century, Holly's eyelashes changed color with the day and her mood.

Venom green, came the laughing comment into his mind before he could ask the question, Holly's ability at mental speech excellent. Not every vampire developed that ability, but Holly had been Made by an archangel. An insane one, but one of the Cadre nonetheless.

I'm feeling mushy in love today. She blew him a kiss before vanishing around the corner.

Three floors farther down, a wing of angels took off, with Sameon at the head. Illium would recognize those brown wings tipped with black anywhere, as he would Sam's intense style of flight. The angel of some seven hundred years of age—give or take a few decades—had learned under Galen, but he was a much more contained flyer than the Barbarian—a direct contrast to his openhearted personality. Should the Tower hold a popularity contest, Sam would win.

Everyone loved the dark-eyed wing commander and loyal member of Elena's Guard.

Today, Sam took his wing out over the glass and metal of the city and toward the crystalline blue of the water. That hadn't changed, either—the glass and the metal that was New York. Different, yes, with more skyway bridges, the subways sleek with self-driving transports, and the buildings and floating habitats designed to be full work-life environments, including sprawling internal gardens brought about by the quiet influence of the Legion's green legacy.

But the soul of the city?

It beat loud and clear in the traffic that buzzed along the streets, and in the distinctive yellow color of the autonomous cabs. The technology could've long ago moved into private vehicles, but while vehicles with the *option* for autonomous operation were popular—with the driver in control of switching it on or off at will—there'd been no demand for fully self-driving cars after a few unfortunate incidents where the safety features had caused the vehicles to come to a halt due to sensing "pedestrians."

Said pedestrians had been frothing-at-the-mouth vampires driven by bloodlust who'd smashed into the vehicles and made a meal of the hapless passengers.

Turned out mortals could have immortal memories when it came to fear. Didn't matter how the manufacturers tried to push upgraded vehicles they promised wouldn't turn their drivers into sitting blood banks; no one was buying.

Illium, lover of tech though he was, couldn't blame them.

Flying cars, of course, had never stood a chance in a world populated by angels, the risk of collisions too high.

He grinned as, just then, he spotted two street vendors yelling at each other across a busy avenue, no doubt complaining about patch poaching. The cabdrivers might have been superseded by technology, but the people were still there—and they were still New Yorkers. Hot dog stands, coffee carts, vendors hawking tourist tchotchkes, the colorful parade continued unabated.

All that had changed was the way of it: the stands and carts were flight capable these days—the sole land vehicles that had an exception to the usual flight rules, but only to claim or leave their assigned spots on rooftops and in habitats. They also had a ponderous maximum speed, and were limited to highly specific pathways at assigned times of the day.

No one wanted a hundred superpowered carts blundering about in angelic airspace.

"Markets have existed since time immemorial," his mother had said to him during one of his visits to Lumia, as the two of them walked the bustling lanes of the local market accompanied by a gaggle of children who adored Sharine, the Hummingbird. "I cannot foresee any future in which they die a total death."

Neither could Illium. The age of online convenience had

been followed by a return to open-air markets—the young rediscovering that which their ancestors had disavowed—until the world now stood at a midpoint that had held stable for two hundred years.

One of the vendors saw Illium just then. The man's top half was painted a vivid glowing pink, his bottom half apparently clothed but who knew. Illium was all for self-expression but he'd never been tempted by the trend for paint-closets that decorated their users each morning. At least the Tower had put a "must wear actual physical underwear" law in place.

The painted man lifted up a hand in a wave before going back to his argument.

"Aren't you afraid that being so friendly with the mortals will make them no longer respect you?" a much younger Sameon had asked Illium after the then-youth was first stationed to the Tower, his dark curls atumble and his brown eyes painfully sincere. "You're the only battle commander I know who has mortal friends, and smiles more often than he scowls."

Awash in memories of friends who had laughed with him over the centuries, Illium had clasped the bright-eyed angel on the shoulder. "Respect, Sam, isn't a matter of fear. Respect is power used to protect and to shield—and to go on the offensive when needed. This city knows I have and will again spill my blood for it. I don't need to put on a grim mien to be respected."

He was still thinking of the cheerful, mischievous boy he'd watched grow into a powerful man when he flew over the Hudson—wider now, its path cutting away part of the city that had existed when Raphael first set up his Tower.

The river had already begun to do its slow, steady work by the time Sameon came to the city, wet behind the ears and with his whole heart full of devotion for Ellie, but it had eased up after a period, as if content with its new channel. So many years had passed since then. Funny to think that Sam was now older than Illium had been during the Lijuan years.

The years of horror and pain and a Cascade of Death.

It struck him, not for the first time, how awfully *young* he'd been at the time. Yet the Cascade had tried to shove him full of a power his mind and body had been nowhere near ready to control. It would've killed him had Raphael not interceded. Illium had been ecstatic when the world went back into balance, taking with it the threat of an early ascension—and he remained as happy when it became clear he'd been bypassed for ascension.

After stabilizing during the time now referred to as The Rise of Marduk, his power had never again spiked. He knew the spiteful in angelkind whispered that he must be disappointed in his "decline"—as if he wasn't one of the most powerful angels in the world outside the Cadre—but Illium had never *wanted* to ascend, never wanted to become one of the rulers of the world.

He loved this city, and he loved being one of Raphael's Seven, part of a tight group that had survived so long as a unit that they were legend even among angelkind.

No other archangel could claim to have warriors so loyal and so true.

Illium was content to serve millennia as Raphael's first general.

As he was content to live in the Enclave home he'd built with the man he loved beyond reason or sense. Situated not far from Elena and Raphael's own home, theirs was a simple thing of large glass panels and a soaring ceiling nestled in the trees, but beside it stood a much larger building designed to capture light from every angle.

The studio was, however, also engineered to ensure that Aodhan could create shadows or semidarkness as needed; furthermore, he had the ability to turn all the windows opaque, should he wish to remove from passing angels the temptation to peek at his works in progress.

Illium landed in front of the open barn-style doors.

And there was Aodhan in the center of that cavernous space awash in sunlight, the dazzling brightness of him scowling as he worked on a tiny sculpture that had him clenching his jaw and muttering under his breath.

A cat with fur of darkest gray and one white paw usually lay curled up on another part of his workbench, dozing in the sun. Shadow, of the line of Illium's beloved Smoke, was far more attached to Aodhan than she was to Illium—and Illium well understood that.

He, too, would choose Aodhan over anyone and anything.

Today, his lover wore a loose linen shirt of the kind he'd long preferred, with an opening at the neck and no buttons, the color a faded cream. He'd pushed both the sleeves hard back, the hem of the shirt flirting with pants of a fine brown canvas splattered with color from how often he wore them while painting.

While Illium had tested new styles and fabrics over the years, Aodhan knew what he liked and stuck to it. "It means I never have to worry about horrendous images from the time when transparent plastic was all the rage."

"Hey! Even I drew the line at that," Illium had protested. "Though I admit the puffball season was a bad idea on my part."

Truth was, he loved Adi for being so content in his skin and in his being.

His warrior-artist's shoulders pushed against the linen as he twisted to better see the sculpture, his thighs rigid against the canvas, and his hair—that pale hue coated with what appeared to be shattered diamonds—falling out of its rough queue to tickle his cheek. It almost reached his shoulders this season, and Illium knew he'd lose patience with it soon, but for now, Illium enjoyed playing with the softness of it when they kissed . . . or when they just lay on the grass together under the stars, their wings overlapping and fingers interlinked.

He'd never understood the perfection of a moment until he'd spent hours just watching the stars emerge overhead on a dark night in a hidden forest with Adi by his side. His entire being had been happy in a way that was the universe contained in his skin, the energy inside him in no hurry to be anywhere else.

It might've taken the two of them time to figure out who

they were to each other, then again to understand how to go forward not only as best friends but as lovers, but once they had, that had been it.

Two strong temperaments meant they'd clashed over the years, but love . . . love was a generous thing, each of them easy to forgive the other. And any moments of temper were but minor irritants in an eternity of love.

Illium couldn't imagine life without Aodhan.

Who looked up just then, his extraordinary eyes—shards of translucent blue and green shattering outward from a pinpoint black pupil—filled with storm clouds. "Tell me again why I'm making these ridiculously tiny fairies?" His skin was starlight, the beauty of him a wonder of muscle and power and hands careful enough to handle the delicate lines of the whimsical creature in his hand.

"Because they make people happy—and they always seem to find their way to the person who needs them most." The two of them had never discussed the whys and hows of that, but it was understood that Aodhan had an unknown power that he was able to impart into these artworks he made once every decade or two.

Tiny statuettes that brought wonder even in the heart of darkness. "Where's Shadow?"

"In the house." Aodhan put down his work in progress with infinite care, then shoved a hand through the diamond-bright strands of his hair. "She can sense that there's a storm coming, doesn't like how it feels on her fur."

The sky was a piercing blue topped by fluffy white, but Illium knew Aodhan wasn't talking about that. It was the energy that had begun to gather in an invisible tempest over the past few days, a prickling that made the tiny hairs on Illium's arms rise, his senses on high alert. "Someone's going to ascend."

It wasn't always forecast this way, with a rising tension in the air. The last ascension—Suyin's, straight after the end of the War of the Death Cascade—had been a sudden, violent thing, Suyin's injured body smashing through a wall of the Tower's infirmary to spear into the sky.

No buildup of power in the air that was a heavy pressure on the skin.

No taste of a strange and lovely metal on the tongue.

No whisper of a mysterious scent on the breeze.

Only a sparkling black rain that had lasted hours—and that had started even as she ascended.

"When I spoke to Mother yesterday," he added, "she said it happens this way sometimes. As if the world knows before any sentient being."

Aodhan's eyes met his, but there was no question in those astonishingly beautiful shards. Aodhan, more than anyone, understood that Illium hated the idea of ascension. He wasn't in the least jealous of the person who'd have to play Cadre politics and leave the people he loved to set up a whole new territory.

He began to step through the door just as Aodhan turned to walk toward him.

A distant hum. A rising wind. A sun exploding in his chest.

No!

2

Because they make people happy ...

Of course Blue would say that, Illium's heart the biggest of anyone Aodhan had ever known. Even now, when he was a seasoned first general who'd led troops into battle with gritty focus, Illium had managed to hold on to his heart with a stubbornness unparalleled.

Today, as he stood in the doorway, the wind riffled through the blue-tipped black of his hair, a lover as intoxicated by him as Aodhan. Sometimes, he felt so much for Illium that he was tempted to pull back, retreat from the power of it—such a tide could sweep a man under, bury him as Aodhan had once been physically buried by those who would own him.

But that was the thing with Illium.

He'd never wanted to own Aodhan. Only to love him. That changed everything.

His heart sighing at the feeling of being home now that Illium was nearby, he began to walk toward his warrior. Though Illium's body had gained another layer of muscle over the centuries, his biceps cut, he remained streamlined in form under the sleeveless leathers that had been a gift from Raphael a long time ago.

The black had faded under the sun, rain, and constant wear, and it bore more than one small tear, but it still fit Illium like a glove. The sword over his shoulder, however, was new. Thunder, to pair with the swords that made up his line of Lightnings. Aodhan had designed the hilt of Thunder—to Illium's exact requirements. Including a grip that mirrored the precise shape of Illium's fingers.

The woven metal of the design glinted in the rays of the sun that speared through the doorway just as Illium smiled . . . and burst into light golden and violent enough to shove Aodhan back with explosive power. Yet he hit the wall with far less force than he should have, and knew that Illium had managed to protect him even as he couldn't protect himself.

Because the love of Aodhan's life had blasted through the roof of the studio to become a blazing golden star in a sky gone the intense, unmistakable blue of his wings.

Debris cascaded around Aodhan, dust coating his tongue as he shoved away a fallen beam with a bleeding hand to run outside. "Illium!" He emerged into a world filled with a driving rain that was droplets of molten gold. It pooled in his palm like metal gone liquid in the forge, rippled off his wings in tiny balls.

The cut on his hand vanished under a line of gold that was a kiss.

Aodhan knew he should stay on the ground, that it was madness to get in the way of an ascension, but he tried to rise up anyway, tried to get to the man who was his heart, his chest painful with the pressure of not knowing if Illium was all right. The last time the power had tried to force itself into him . . .

Illium!

No reply to his panicked call.

Driven by fear for his lover, Aodhan managed to rise far enough up to see that the Hudson had turned liquid gold, a glittering beauty that wasn't natural except for this single moment in time when the entire world became attuned to this one being. For the gold wasn't shiny and new. It was aged with a haunting patina, the same dark shade as Illium's eyes.

Then Illium's power shoved Aodhan back to the earth.

And Illium, he was a supernova of gold against a sky suddenly devoid of clouds and turned the distinctive blue of his own wings riven with veins of glittering silver and gold. The shields around the floating habitats blazed a dazzling gold as they dropped to the lowest possible altitude in full emergency mode; their world was built for power that broke the skies . . . but still, no one had expected this, not after seven centuries.

This wasn't like before, Aodhan told himself, when the golden light had poured out of Illium's mouth and cracked his skin, bending his back almost in half.

This wasn't death.

This was . . . ascension.

Wet on his cheeks, but it wasn't from the startlingly beautiful rain. The wet was Aodhan's tears. Because while many dreamed of ascension and of power limitless, Illium had dreamed of being by Raphael's side through the eons, a first general loyal. Heart-friend to Elena, treasured member of the Seven, beloved by all in the Tower and adored by the citizens of the city, Illium had wanted nothing more. He'd been happy, had intended to stay true to his purpose through eternity.

But that could never again be his place.

As being one of Raphael's Seven could never again be Aodhan's.

Today, Aodhan became to Illium what Dmitri was to Raphael: second to . . . the Archangel Illium.

Yesterday

(Seven Hundred Years Ago)

3

Wet and bedraggled from the storm that raged around them, the sky roiling black and the ocean below full of turbulent white caps, but with joy and a nervous excitement emanating from his pores, Illium flew into New York side by side with Aodhan. And realized that they hadn't discussed a critical question in their time alone—how they'd tell the people closest to them of the fundamental change in their relationship.

Now it was too late. Illium could see Raphael on the Tower roof, waiting for them to come in. The rain beat down on the midnight of Raphael's hair, dripped off the white-gold of wings held with warrior perfection, and carved runnels of water down his well-worn and sleeveless black leathers, but he stood as if he noticed none of it, an archangel strong.

Illium landed in a wash of wind, his heart a huge ache as his feet hit home ground at last.

The sire embraced him with the arms of a warrior welcoming one of his own home . . . and the care of a man who had known Illium since he was a child. A man who had been more father to Illium than the waste of cells who was his biological male parent.

Theirs would never only be the relationship of warrior and liege, would never be the same as the relationship Raphael had with others of his Seven. Raphael was too young to hold the position of father . . . or he should've been. Inside Illium's heart, however, that was where he stood—as the man who had taught the boy Illium had been how to be a good man, a trusted angel, a loyal battle mate.

He'd also taught a brokenhearted little boy that his father's actions had *nothing* to do with him. He'd rocked Illium in his strong arms while telling him that he was a good boy, a good son, and the best kind of friend to Aodhan. "Any man would be proud to call you his son, Illium. Never ever forget that. *I* would be proud to call you my son."

It had taken Illium time to internalize those words, to accept that his father's abandonment said nothing about him as a person, but Raphael was the one who'd started him on the journey. As Raphael was the one who'd given him his first sword and taught him how to hold it.

He'd been an archangel with countless calls on his attention, but he'd made time for a shattered little boy until that boy saw nothing wrong with dropping by an archangel's Refuge stronghold to send word to his beloved "Rafa" of his latest accomplishment. It was also a testament to the people Raphael chose to surround himself with that his steward and other Refuge staff had solemnly recorded Illium's news, promising to send it with the next courier to Raphael's territory.

Raphael had replied every single time.

Now, the archangel broke the embrace to slap him lightly against the side of his neck in welcome. "Of course you had to choose to fly into a storm." Laughter and affection in the intense blue of his eyes, his archangelic power a vibration in the air that Illium could almost hear. Water dripped off the black of his lashes, both of them grinning at a homecoming too long in the making.

"Where's Ellie?" Illium asked, his nerves jumping even in the midst of his happiness.

A gust of wind hit his back just then, Elena coming in to land. "Bluebell!" She jumped into his arms, and he spun her around, neither one of them in the least fear of Raphael's wrath for Illium's handling of his consort.

Raphael understood what Elena was to Illium.

When he put her down, she laughed and ran her fingers through his hair. "Look at you. All wet." A glance at Aodhan out of pale gray eyes with an edge of true silver that hadn't retreated after the Cascade but instead bled into the gray in a seamless flow. "You too, Sparkle."

Aodhan scowled at the nickname, but stepped close enough that Elena's wing brushed his in a gentle hello. The other man was healing, but Illium didn't yet see a future where Aodhan would be as comfortable with touch as he had been before his capture by the monsters who'd scarred his soul.

The other man had never been as easy with touch as Illium, but with the people he loved and trusted? He'd not only been happy with it, he'd often initiated it. A small hand sliding into Naasir's as they walked in the Refuge while Aodhan was a child, the forearm clasp of warriors with his training mates as they grinned at each other in friendly challenge, the easy brush of wing against wing with friends as they sprawled on a mountain plateau sharing food and mead, his body languid.

Today, Aodhan didn't break the link with Elena's wing as they stood in a small circle in the rain. The water saturated their hair but ran off their wings to crash onto the roof in tiny splashes; with angelic bodies designed for flight at altitude, the cold mattered little to anyone but Elena. She was still too young—but even she seemed disinclined to break up this impromptu gathering in the rain.

His own body flushed with heat, Illium touched the belt buckle Aodhan had made for him, then took a deep breath. "Sire," he began, only to freeze.

He, a man known for his charm and ability to talk about anything with anyone, couldn't find the words to tell Raphael that he and Aodhan were more than the best of friends now, that they'd taken the first steps into a partnership far more intimate.

But Raphael interrupted. "Go get dry, both of you. We can talk more later—a few of us would like to gather tonight to welcome you home if you're feeling up to it?"

Relief flooded Illium's bones, because he still had no idea how to put the shift in his and Aodhan's relationship into words. Not even to himself. "I'm always up for a party," he said with a grin. "It'll be good to see everyone."

An indignant meow sounded from behind Raphael. When the archangel shifted, Illium saw a drenched Smoke scowling up at him. The stray kitten he'd adopted had grown into a sleek and healthy cat with fur like dark smoke, and eyes that seemed almost sentient in their directness. Right now, she was *most* displeased at having had to venture out in this weather to see him.

"Smoke!" Going down on one knee, he gathered her into his arms and against his chest. Where, despite her annoyance at the rain and at him, she began to purr, a happy little engine.

"I left her safe and warm in your quarters, but she clearly found a way out," Aodhan said with a shake of his head. "She watched for you every day."

Illium rose back up, Smoke cradled against him.

It felt natural to step beside Aodhan, overlap his wing with the other man's, and just be under the rain of their city while the sire and his consort stood with them. The rain, the wet, the cold, none of it mattered. He was home.

Aodhan and Illium both had suites in the level of the Tower dedicated to the Seven's private quarters, and today, when they exited the elevator, Aodhan sensed the emptiness in the air. None of the others were in their own suites.

When he glanced at Illium, it was to see that the other man remained shaken from the emotional shock of their decision to surrender to the love between them that was far beyond friendship. His fingers were in Smoke's fur, his expression pensive as his wet hair dripped water into those stunning eyes.

It would've been easy to push him, tell him they'd already made this decision in the storm over the ocean, but if the past had been about Aodhan, the present was about Illium—an angel with a heart so huge that he kept on forgiving those who hurt him, and who would give Aodhan anything he wanted if he asked.

Because Illium's love for Aodhan was as huge as that damn heart of his.

But Aodhan had *hurt* Illium by freezing him out for centuries. However long his Blue needed to trust him again the way he'd once done, Aodhan was willing to wait.

He cupped Illium's cheek. "Get dry, then have a rest before the gathering." He ran his thumb over Illium's cheekbone. "We have all the time in the world, Blue."

Illium swallowed hard and looked up to meet Aodhan's gaze with a familiar directness. Below the playful games and delightful charm, Illium was built of honor. "I don't know why . . ." He exhaled. "I've been counting down the days until I could come home to you, and now that I'm here, I'm so afraid, Adi."

Blue and Adi.

Names from a lifetime ago that somehow fit their new relationship.

"I'm not going anywhere," Aodhan said, his entire being heavy with the terrible realization he'd had in Amanat.

All but one of the people Illium loved—or had loved—had abandoned him in one way or another.

His father.

His mother.

Aodhan.

Raphael alone had never faltered.

Even Kaia, the mortal he'd loved as a youth, had left him. Her loss of memory hadn't been by choice, but it had been a terrible loss nonetheless.

Illium might never understand the wound in his heart, but Aodhan did, and he planned to do whatever it took to help it heal—even if that meant waiting another eon for Illium to believe in Aodhan's promise to never again leave him.

Turning his face into Aodhan's hand, Illium released another breath before giving a small nod and walking into his apartment with a purring Smoke in his arms. The cat had shadowed Aodhan since she'd arrived in New York on the cargo plane that had also ferried home Illium's few belongings—but Aodhan had known he'd be invisible to her the instant her beloved Illium returned home.

In this, he and Smoke were well aligned: Illium was Aodhan's lodestar, too.

His heart ached to see the other man's wings lowered as he walked through the door, his head downbent. Poor Blue. He didn't understand what was going on in that bruised heart of his, didn't know why he was acting with what—to him—would seem like a lack of logic.

Frowning, Aodhan walked into his own suite and, after quickly drying off and changing into a more formal tunic and pants, made a call he'd never thought he'd make.

The member of Lady Caliane's court who answered smiled at seeing his face on her screen. "Aodhan. Is all well in New York?"

"Yes," Aodhan said. "I would request a moment of Lady Caliane's time, if she is available."

A curious look, but the maiden said, "I saw her just before. I will go and ask."

The screen went into a holding pattern, and when it cleared a minute later, it was Raphael's blue eyes that looked out at him from a face both feminine and of a warrior even though Lady Caliane's black hair was unbound today and anchored with a circlet of silver, the clasps on her shoulders delicate silver leaves where they held up the white of her dress.

And though angels didn't appear to age beyond a certain point in time, there was a weight to her presence, a vastness of memories—of grief and love and pain—in her gaze, that made it clear that she was eons older than Aodhan or Raphael or anyone else in the Tower.

"Young Aodhan," she said with a smile that reached those ancient eyes. "I'm pleased to see you again, and looking more rested than when you visited Amanat."

He'd had only one real conversation with Raphael's mother the entire time since she'd woken from her more than a thousand years of Sleep. Prior to that, he'd dealt with her staff or—at most—exchanged only necessary words with her as part of his duties.

It wasn't that he didn't like her. Nothing so personal. She'd simply been an Ancient unknowable to him until he'd come to Amanat after ending his term as Suyin's temporary second. A short break where he could rest and rejuvenate himself for the long flight home. Instead, Lady Caliane had altered his entire understanding of his relationship with Illium.

We often don't see the hurt we put on those we love most. And he is so bright, Sharine's son, so full of life and laughter. He hides his bruises well, I think, your Bluebell, using that joyous self as an impenetrable shield.

"Lady Caliane, I thank you for your time." Then, though he wasn't a man who trusted many with his innermost thoughts, he spoke to her. Because she understood in a way no one else could—both because her closest friend was Sharine, the Hummingbird, and because her own losses and grief had given her a wisdom profound.

"Illium is struggling with his emotions," he told her. "He doesn't understand that deep inside, even as he wants to hold on to me, he doesn't trust me not to abandon him again."

"Ah." Lady Caliane's expression softened. "You want to

ask me if you should tell him? Expose his unknown scars to his eyes?"

Aodhan nodded.

"First, young Aodhan, tell me what your own choice would be?"

He frowned, but shook his head. "I think it'll damage him to know that he carries such wounds. Right now, he's handling everything other than us without issue—Lady Sharine's return to herself, his father's awakening."

He pressed a fist to his heart. "I feel it here that if I show him this wound, he'll blame himself for not being able to get past it, for not being stronger. Lady, he has already been too strong for too many years—I don't want him to just power through because he thinks it's what I need. He gives and gives and gives, has dealt with blow after blow."

His mother's absence of the mind, her shattered psyche.

Aegaeon's abandonment.

Aodhan's abduction and long recovery . . . and his choice to immure himself in a world of silence and distance.

Just dealing with it. One blow after another.

All without losing his smile or his ability to love, his beautiful heart bruised but refusing to callus over.

"He has done *enough*." Aodhan's voice was firm.

"There, child, you have it." A soft smile. "You know him better than himself in this—and perhaps for some things, that is as it should be. In time, he will be ready to see into these wounds, but not now. Not when he is in a phase of transition." A pause. "We are fragile at such moments, more breakable than we understand. Protect Sharine's son through this."

"Always and forever." Aodhan inclined his head on that vow. "Thank you for speaking with me. I know your time is valuable."

"Not so valuable that I do not have it for those who have stood by my son's side so valiantly all these years." Eyes of endless blue darkened. "I wish you both well, Aodhan. I would see joy for you both—for in your joy, Sharine will find her joy, too. Perhaps it will ease a little of my friend's guilt."

Then she shook her head. "But that is not for you to consider. At this point in the turning of the hourglass of eternity, you must be selfish on Illium's behalf. Sharine's bright, beautiful child does not have it in him, I think, to be selfish for himself. He is too much his mother's son."

4

Aodhan was still mulling over Caliane's words when there came a light tap on his door. He opened it to see a man with shaggy hair of a true silver, his eyes the same against skin of deep brown kissed by gold. Dressed in a gray T-shirt paired with black cargo pants, he would've passed muster as a vampire serious and strong with most people.

But Naasir wasn't a vampire. Neither was he an angel or a mortal.

Naasir was Naasir.

"You made it." Because it wasn't only a casual gathering tonight—*all* of the Seven would be at Illium's homecoming. With things still unstable at the time of Aodhan's return, no gathering had been possible, so this was the first time Aodhan had seen Naasir since Aodhan's term as interim second to the Archangel of China.

It was clear to him that the most primal member of the Seven wanted to haul him into a hug, but wild at heart though he was, Naasir had never crossed the boundary Aodhan had laid down over two centuries ago. Despite the fact that Aodhan knew his response had been a thing induced by trauma, not a conscious choice, he suddenly wondered why he'd applied it to this man who had only ever hauled him out of harm . . . and who'd introduced him to wonders untold.

"Come, small sparkles." A wicked grin that wasn't quite civilized. "Today I'll show you a snow tiger."

A memory from a lifetime ago that had him jerking toward Naasir. Who hugged him as fiercely as he'd done when Aodhan had been a "cub," curious and trusting. When a purr vibrated in Naasir's chest, far deeper and more of a rumble than with Smoke, Aodhan felt emotion lodge in his throat. Very few people knew Naasir could do that, but Aodhan had heard the sound before . . . when Naasir had been attempting to soothe the hurt of the child Aodhan had once been.

"Do you still think of me as a cub?" he asked as he drew back, a rasp in his voice.

Naasir's shrug was languid, his voice holding a growl as he strolled into Aodhan's suite. "No. Cubs grow. You've grown strong and dangerous." Then he paused. "But when you're hurt, I remember the cub you once were, so small and wild inside your skin. As I remember the wounded fledgling we found." A piercing look. "You're better. Not all better, but closer to it than before."

"Yes." Aodhan looked at the door Naasir had closed behind him. "Where's Andromeda?"

"Running a bath." Naasir's voice held the smug contentment of a man who adored his mate and was quite certain he was adored in turn. "I'll disturb her once she's in it." A grin as wicked as that from Aodhan's memories before Naasir stalked over to haul Aodhan into his arms again. "I have missed your smell so close, small sparkles."

"Big sparkles now," Aodhan said past the lump in his throat.

Laughing, Naasir drew back, then prowled into the kitchen, sniffing. "You have a cat?"

"Illium adopted one in China."

"Cats are the best choice of pet." He sprawled down in

one of Aodhan's sofas, as feline as Smoke when she was feeling lazy. "Suyin has invited me to visit her territory. Andi wants to go, write this part of China's history from experience. Is it safe for her?"

Aodhan poured the other man a drink. "Specialty blood from Elena's café," he said, holding up a small bottle of obsidian glass imprinted with the logo of the business. "I think you'll like it."

Naasir's lips curled in a dubious expression, but he accepted the glass of rich ruby-red blood, sniffed. He'd only just taken a sip by the time Aodhan sat down with his own drink—a glass of honey mead.

"So," Aodhan said, "about China—fair warning, I'm on Andi's side. This history should be recorded by someone on the ground. But danger remains." Then he told Naasir all he could, both from his own experiences, and from the knowledge Illium had shared with him through his letters. And despite the fact that Naasir had avowed his intention to disturb Andromeda in her bath, he stayed for well over an hour.

Their conversation was of two allied warriors sharing intel.

But when Naasir did leave, it was with a quicksilver smile, the ripple of a tiger's stripes emerging in the rich brown of his skin. "I'm happy to see you again . . . small sparkles."

Aodhan smiled as Naasir disappeared into another suite. With time yet on his hands, he then cleared up a couple of Tower matters he was handling for Dmitri—and all the while he thought of his Blue.

The night murmured a soft dark beyond the windows by the time of the gathering.

Word had come around a half hour ago that, with the rain having passed, Montgomery had dried the roof using secret Montgomery methods, so they could gather there, under the starlit sky. The clouds had faded with the rain, New York sparkling clean.

Exiting his room, he reached out to Illium with his mind. *I'm heading up. You can make a grand entrance. Everyone will want to be there to welcome you home.* The others had already done so with Aodhan when he returned home, even if those in the Refuge hadn't been free to travel to the city at the time.

Even had it been possible, Aodhan wouldn't have wanted a gathering. Not with Illium missing. Because they, each of the inner core of Raphael's team, played a different role in their group.

Illium wasn't only Aodhan's heart. He was the heart of the Seven.

Things didn't feel right when he wasn't around, and everyone had mentioned it to Aodhan in one way or another since his return from China. Even Jason, the quietest of them all, had said, "The city doesn't sing as brightly with Illium gone. Do you feel it?"

The spymaster's facial tattoo—a true agony to have made permanent—had been stark in the morning light, yet the blackness of his wings remained paradoxically soft enough to merge into that same light. "The wind carries a note of melancholy, a lover waiting for his return."

Aodhan didn't hear the winds, not as Jason did, but he knew his best friend was missed, keenly so. There was no one in the entire world like his Blue, and Aodhan wasn't such a jealous being that he couldn't share Illium with the countless people who loved him. All he hoarded for himself was that piece of Illium's heart that would only ever belong to the one he loved for all eternity.

Because come what may, he knew that piece was his, had been his for a long, long time. What remained elusive was Illium's trust in Aodhan's commitment to never again emotionally vanish from his life.

Wait, I'm almost ready, Illium protested. *I'd be fully ready if Smoke hadn't decided to hide my boot. She's mad at me for sending her ahead in the cargo plane even though I've explained that I couldn't carry her the entire distance home.*

Aodhan's shoulders shook, the urge to cradle Illium's face in a kiss a near-overwhelming wave. *Take your time and give her an extra cuddle. I'll be waiting for you up there.* He wanted Illium to have this moment, get a glimpse of just how important he was to the Tower and to the people who called it home.

Oh, great, I just realized she's dragged my forearm sheaths off the bed and to parts unknown. I was planning to wear those.

Chuckling quietly at Smoke's antics, Aodhan stepped out on to the balcony closest to his suite, and spread his wings for the short flight up. The night air had a biting freshness that came only after a storm, and the city sparkled like stars strewn onto the earth, the darkness concealing the continuing scars from the war.

The area Raphael had been forced to cleanse with angel-fire remained a dead patch where neither mortals, immortals, nor the creatures of nature wanted to go. Several skyscrapers were yet in the demolition phase, and certain roads were still being laid, and those were by no measure all the marks the war had left on the city.

New York, however, was taking it in stride. They'd all seen what had happened in China; compared to the horror of that silent landscape devoid of its people, its cities empty of life and its landscapes vicious with murderous traps, this was nothing. New York would rise again, and it would rise even brighter and more defiant.

After doing a wide sweep to take in more of the view, he ended up on the roof—to see that Montgomery had set up several strings of glowing bulbs across the roof, the ends anchored on heavy stands usually stored in a basement area. But the butler had been judicious—the lights were muted and created only a gentle glow in the corner set up for the party. The rest of the rooftop remained in shadow, lit up only by the stars.

Aodhan landed at the same time as Galen, who'd arrived from the other direction. Raphael's weapons-master was in formal leathers of deep bronze, his thickly muscled arms bared to reveal the amber amulet he wore around his left biceps.

Red hair tumbled from the wind and eyes of pale green awash in light, he looked far better than the last time Aodhan had seen him in person—in the direct aftermath of the war.

"Aodhan! At last I can welcome you properly home!"

"It's good to see you, my barbarian friend." Aodhan reached out to exchange the forearm grip of warriors with him, because in this, he had to make the first move.

No matter that he'd embraced Naasir and had been embraced by him, touch was still a complicated morass for him, but this was one of the Seven, a man who would die for him without hesitation. As Aodhan would for him.

They'd stood back to back in battle often enough, ready to ward off blows to protect each other. What then, was such contact, against the depth of their shared trust? The time would come when he wouldn't have to rationalize tactile contact—Aodhan was determined that would be so—but for now, it helped him to make a conscious choice each and every time.

There is a mortal saying, Aodhan. Keir's gentle voice, the healer's sensitivity innate. *A strange and lovely one for a species that lives but a heartbeat compared to our endless existence. They say that life is a marathon, not a sprint. In your case, endurance and thoughtful steps forward will win over reckless speed.*

Tonight, Galen accepted Aodhan's offered forearm with a grin, theirs having always been the friendship of compatriots. While Galen was older, he'd joined the Seven after Aodhan was full grown. "Naasir and I both have to head back after two nights, but neither one of us was going to miss this, no matter how short our stay. Trace's stepped in to cover, with assistance from Nimra and Noel, who happened to be on a visit to the Refuge."

Aodhan glanced around after they broke the arm clasp. "Where's Jessamy?"

"Walking up with Vivek—they had historical data to discuss. Jason's deputy has managed to dig up scans of books long believed lost."

A glimpse of silver in Aodhan's peripheral vision, Naasir walking out onto the roof hand in hand with Andromeda. He'd changed since he'd come to see Aodhan, now wore blue jeans and a black blazer over a black shirt.

Andromeda, in contrast, had chosen a knee-length and wide-skirted dress of a deep citrine that complemented the dark chocolate shade of her wings while closed. When opened out, the design on her feathers was far more intricate, altering in subtle nuances of color that culminated in a pale golden brown at the tips.

Curls wild around her fine-boned face, she ran over to welcome Aodhan, her smile startled when he took her hands. "Oh," she said, her fingers curling slightly over his. "This is wonderful, Aodhan."

He knew she didn't mean the party.

"Yes," he agreed with a smile.

They'd barely finished the exchange when Jason landed with Mahiya. He was in black as always, but Mahiya had chosen an ankle-length skirt of vivid magenta embroidered with golden thread, and paired with a close-fitting blouse in the same rich hue but without any embroidery. Draped over the set was a scarf of translucent gold that she'd pleated to appear like a sari. The same gold glinted from the fine rope she'd woven through her braid.

Her eyes crinkled as she laughed at something Jason had said.

Aodhan wanted to paint her and the spymaster just this way, mentally tucked away the image. As he did snapshots of each of the others on the roof tonight, he'd paint the entire scene, he decided, gift it to his Blue.

Dmitri and Honor arrived just then, Jessamy and Vivek right behind them. Jessamy's gown of soft pink brushed against the brown of Vivek's suit pants as they spoke intently. Vivek was in his most streamlined wheelchair, his hands partially covered by leather gloves that matched his sharp suit. Honor, meanwhile, had gone for a thigh-length and long-sleeved dress in dark red velvet, while Dmitri's suit was as black as Jason's formal tunic and pants.

Aodhan made note of the fine details like Dmitri's grin at a comment from Naasir, and how Andi hugged Honor with a delight that was reciprocated. How Galen clasped Vivek's arm the same way he would any warrior, and how the head of the Tower's tech command seemed to fall into easy conversation with the man they called the Barbarian, even as Jessamy broke away to take Mahiya's hands.

When Elena and Raphael landed on the roof, Raphael proved to be in formal leathers of a dark gray, while Ellie had chosen a fitted thigh-length dress in a vivid blue that she'd paired with black ankle boots, her hair scraped up into a high tail. When she turned, he saw that the side panel of the dress was an intricate lattice of sharply angled fabric that exposed not skin, but a shimmering inner layer.

"Only because I just had to fly up from our suite," she said with a laugh when Mahiya complimented her dress. "Otherwise I'd have flashed half the city. Raphael had to give me the all clear before I could come up as it was!"

As Mahiya giggled and lifted up her skirts to show Ellie the black tights she wore underneath while an intrigued Jessamy looked on, Venom ran up, Holly's hand in his. Elegant suit and a youthful dress at the height of fashion, they were both smiling.

The entire Seven was together, but for Illium.

Also on the roof were the Tower's chief healer, Nisia; Montgomery and Sivya; and angels like Andreja who had known Illium a long time. The younger crew would have to wait till the morning to see him. This wasn't the time for a huge, overwhelming gathering.

How late am I? Illium's clear voice in Aodhan's mind.

Not late at all.

Wings of blue appeared over the side of the roof . . . and then Illium was laughing as the gathered group sent up a cheer. "What are you all doing here?" he cried out as he landed, and was mobbed by hugs, and kisses on the cheek, and shakes of his forearm.

"It was a good excuse for a party," Venom quipped, but his hug was as tight as the others.

The other man could be cool and distant with outsiders, but never with his brethren. The deadly vampire with the slitted pupils of a viper had welcomed Aodhan home by re-creating his favorite dessert—one usually only available from a single baker in the Refuge. Not that he'd taken credit, of course. It had just appeared in a box on Aodhan's dining table.

Aodhan stayed back while the others spoke to Illium—he'd had more time than anyone with Blue of late, when their sojourn in China overlapped. It gave him joy to see the other man deluged with love and affection . . . and he felt a surge of possessive happiness when he saw that Illium wore the belt buckle Aodhan had designed and made for him.

Jessamy took Illium's hands and squeezed them, a deep smile in the soft brown of her eyes. "Well," she said in that gentle way of hers, "I wouldn't have believed it when you were a babe, Illium, but you have somehow managed not to fall into a gorge, get impaled on a weapon far too large for you, or fall off a roof while attempting to prove that you could fly even when the best you could do was imitate a drunken bumblebee."

Grinning without remorse at all he'd put their teacher through during his time at the Refuge School, Illium broke the handhold to wrap Jessamy up in his arms and lift her off her feet. She laughed, the sound as warm as her heart. There was more laughter in the time that followed, more conversation, and so much food.

Montgomery and Sivya had been told not to serve others at this gathering of friends, but they hovered over the food anyway, wanting to make sure everyone had what they needed. Raphael finally physically pulled his butler and cook away from the banquet table, then *he* poured them drinks.

It took time, but the two did relax at last and give up their duties for the night. And when Venom started up the music, Aodhan saw Montgomery draw Sivya into his arms in a shadowy corner of the rooftop, his hands at her waist beneath the drape of her wings. She placed her hands around his nape in turn, her fingers playing with the dark of his hair and her expression one Aodhan had never before seen, because it was for Montgomery alone.

He glanced away, loath to invade the privacy of their love.

Three songs later, Venom switched up the slow and easy tones to a pounding beat that had Naasir hauling Andi onto the center of the roof and spinning her around in a dance so fast and energetic that only Naasir could pull it off with a winged partner.

Afterward, Illium slammed down his tankard of mead in laughing challenge. "I refuse to be out-danced by our resident tiger-creature." Even as Elena shook her fist at him for taunting her about her continued lack of knowledge of Naasir's exact "species," he took off into the sky.

The others whooped and yelled, Naasir loudest of them all.

Illium was a firefly in the darkness, his speed dizzying, and his acrobatic moves dazzling. As Aodhan gloried in his skill and power, Illium's mind touched his own, the contact so familiar, it was a well-worn groove in his senses. *Do you remember, Adi?*

Putting down his drink, Aodhan stepped quietly to the edge of the roof while the others were preoccupied watching Illium. *I'm ready.*

Illium dived as if about to crash into the roof, and Aodhan took off at speed.

Two seconds later, Illium had reversed his dive in a maneuver very few angels could pull off, and they were "braiding" the air in quick-fire symmetry. Aodhan had never had Illium's ability to make hairpin turns, but this was a pattern they'd practiced and practiced again until they could predict each other's movements—and that Illium had designed to take Aodhan's range of winged motion into account.

It was music in the air, fast, beautiful music that sang through his bones and made him laugh in exhilaration.

When the two of them landed as one on the roof to rapturous applause, he couldn't help grinning and wrapping an arm around Illium's neck to hug him close. Illium didn't resist, their wings tangled as they waved off accolades on their performance . . . before Illium raised his hands playfully at the others to continue with said accolades.

Heart a rapid pulse and skin hot, his Blue by his side, Aodhan had never been happier.

Illium looked up, laughter bright in the aged gold of his eyes, and for a moment, the world seemed to freeze.

They didn't have much of a height difference—an inch or two. But at this angle, and how they were standing, it would've been so easy for Aodhan to lower his head and kiss Illium without thought, simply because he was there and he was Aodhan's everything.

Illium's pupils flared, his breath catching.

5

Raphael stood at the edge of the roof, his consort by his side.

They'd ended up just beyond the spill of golden light that was the party, the city a bejeweled dazzle at their backs.

Elena leaned into him, her arm around his waist as his arm was around her shoulders, their wings in intimate contact. "Did you see that?" A whisper, as Aodhan turned from Illium to reply to a comment from one of the others . . . yet the two stayed close, their wings overlapping at the edges.

"I wondered," he murmured. "When they returned home." He'd sensed an electric tension in the air that he might've put down to an argument if both hadn't been glowing with happiness.

"Do you think . . ."

Taking in the pair as they separated, with Illium pulling a laughing Holly into a dance, and Aodhan being waved over by Dmitri and Andreja, he said, "No, not yet. Neither is the kind to conceal a bond that's settled and firm."

He looked down at his hunter, the near-white strands of

her hair shimmering against the dark gold of her skin—as a random bolt of wildfire danced slyly through her feathers. A lingering mark of the Cascade and all that had come with it.

His arm curling tighter around her, he said, "Are you surprised, *hbeebti*?"

"I might've been before, when I figured Illium was still obsessed with the mortal he once loved."

Raphael frowned and realized he'd missed an important fact. "He hasn't reached for the pendant this entire gathering." It had become an unconscious habit with the angel, to play with the gift from his long-dead lover. "Then again, it's only been a short time since his return home."

But Elena shook her head. "That fight those two had at our Enclave house?" She shifted so that they were face-to-face, their bodies moving with sensual awareness in the mellow jazz that had replaced the previous pulsing beat. "I started to get a clue then. Because you don't fight like that with anyone but the person who means the most to you in the entire world."

He wrapped her up in his wings, her lithe hunter's body pressed to his, breasts against his chest and thighs oh-so-tempting under the short hem of her dress. "Yes."

Her fingers brushed his nape, her hip a sweet curve under his hand—and the sleek black cuff she wore around her left wrist a hidden garrote. Strong and soft, powerful and vulnerable, Elena was the most incredible enigma of his life. He could love her ten thousand years and still discover new facets that took his breath away.

"Honestly," she murmured after they came up from a kiss as languid as the music, wet and lush, "I wouldn't have been surprised if they'd headed that way earlier."

"I'm glad they didn't." He pressed a kiss to the curve of her neck, felt her nipples pebble against his chest. "Both needed to grow into their own skins first, become who they were meant to be."

Elena shivered, nuzzled into him. "We're going to get in

trouble if we keep doing this." A rise up onto the toes of her boots, a slide down.

Groaning at the subtle tease of the hard ridge of his arousal, he tugged her closer, shifting his hand up to lay it flat on her lower back. Despite all the work yet to be done to repair their city, Raphael felt freer than he had in a long time. There was no hovering threat on the horizon, no gathering army or insane enemy.

He could dance with his consort in unhurried pleasure—and he could give his attention to the happiness of his people. "When your Bluebell and Aodhan were babes, we worried that they'd become a society of two, so entwined that they merged in a way indefinable but damaging."

It had been Aodhan, so quiet and apparently willing to go along with Illium's schemes, who'd concerned the adults involved most; it had taken them time to realize that beneath Aodhan's quiet lay a nature stubborn and firm. He was no follower; he was a true friend who called Illium out when necessary, their friendship born of the deepest balance.

"I suppose," Elena said, "I've never thought about that because I've only known them as adults, each very much his own person." She put her head against his shoulder, her wings tucked neatly against her back, and the scent of her a familiar kiss in the back of his throat. He wasn't a hunter, didn't have his consort's enhanced sense of smell, but he'd know her even in the darkest room.

Now, she ran her fingers delicately over the inner curve of his wing. Sensation rocked through him as she said, "Are we supposed to pretend we see and notice nothing until they're ready?"

Raphael glanced over to the two—just in time to see Illium looking at Aodhan, who was deep in conversation with Dmitri. The blue-winged angel's expression . . . it held a torment of the heart that didn't make sense in the context of the unbreakable friendship that existed between him and Aodhan.

But then, Raphael reminded himself, Illium was no longer a babe about whom Raphael knew everything. "Yes," he said. "I don't think they themselves know what they are to each other at this juncture. We wait for them to decide." No longer could he wrench both out of trouble as he'd done when they'd been small angels up to mischief.

This time, Aodhan and Illium were in a maze they alone could navigate.

6

The party went on longer than anyone had expected—because none of them wanted it to end, it was so rare for them to all be together. When they did finally call it a night, it was closer to dawn than to midnight, and Illium yawned the entire way down to their suites.

"Get in bed before you fall asleep standing up." Aodhan nudged the other man toward his room.

As he went to head to his own, Illium closed that strong warrior's hand over his wrist, tugged.

Though his skin grew tight, his body aching with a need too long unfulfilled, he said, "You're so exhausted, you look drunk. And ridiculously adorable." He wanted to run his fingers through Illium's hair, nuzzle his cheek, just hold him tight.

"So we'll sleep."

"What about Smoke? I can go pick her up." Not wanting Smoke alone so soon after his return home, Illium had asked Izak to cat-sit—and for the young angel to bring her up to the party during a period of mellow music. After she'd been petted and gushed over to her heart's content,

Izak had taken both himself and a sleepy Smoke back to his quarters.

"Izzy dropped her off not long ago—he has an early shift. She'll be lazing on the bed if I know Smoke."

"He's building her a cat maze, you know." Aodhan pushed back strands of Illium's hair. "He's the reason she can sneak out of anywhere."

"No, my cat child is just a prodigy."

Amused and awash in affection, Aodhan didn't resist when Illium pulled him into the suite and shut the door.

Illium happy and in a playful mood was a delight.

Aodhan allowed the blue-winged angel to push him up against the back of the door, his hands on either side of Aodhan's head, and his body all muscled heat layered with the faint scent of sweat from the dancing. It altered his natural scent, turned it more raw, making Aodhan want to lick it up off his skin.

When he kissed Aodhan, it was all light brushes and little bites. The embers in Aodhan's blood heated, his hands going to Illium's waist to pull him closer, their bodies hard up against each other in a way that was unmistakably erotic. He could feel Illium's desire, his own a rigid pulse low in his body.

"You're too thin," he said to the softness of Illium's lips, before taking a nip of his own. "You didn't eat enough tonight to make up for what you burned flying home." Angelic flight burned an intense number of calories, and Illium had been battling storm winds on top of that.

"I ate every single alfajor in your last package." Kisses along Aodhan's jawline by the only person in all the world that he'd not only allow this close—but adore this close. "Didn't even share one. In my defense, they arrived at night. Smoke ate seven treats and went into a food coma, and I did the same with the cookies. It was one hell of a party of two."

Chuckling, Aodhan fisted his hand in the blue-black silk of Illium's hair and tugged his head up for a full kiss, slow and deep and luxurious, as he drew in the wild and primal scent that was Illium. Because he and his Blue? They *did* have all the time in the world now that they'd taken the first step, made the first decision.

Illium groaned as Aodhan massaged his nape, their bodies rubbing up against each other in a visceral hunger born of their love—a love that had worn the name of friendship for centuries and always would. Because before being lovers, they were and would always be friends, loyal to the bone.

Illium's clever fingers on Aodhan's white tunic with detailing in a glittering pearlescent white, his breath hot against Aodhan's jaw. Reaching around, he began to undo the buttons that kept the tunic snug around Aodhan's wings. Soon as he'd succeeded, Aodhan lifted the tunic from the bottom and peeled it off.

When Illium shuddered out a breath, Aodhan went to tease him that it wasn't as if he'd never seen Aodhan bare-chested before . . . but it hadn't been this way, he realized. Their decision to become lovers had altered a fundamental aspect of their universe, until this, too, was new.

Illium's fingers landed as light as butterfly wings on skin that suddenly had a million nerve endings, all of them erotic in ways unknown to him until this instant. Aodhan had always been annoyed by the shimmer that dusted his skin, the shimmer that made him so dazzlingly bright in the sunlight.

Today, that same shimmer reflected back on Illium, creating their own private sun.

"You are so beautiful, Adi."

A roar of ice smashing into Aodhan, sucking out his warmth as his mind disgorged a memory he'd done his best to bury and forget.

So beautiful, so unlike any other in our kind. My beautiful, precious prize.

He fought the spiraling panic with desperate fury, needing to be what Illium needed, to be the giver, not the taker. To be *present* in the here and now. But his body locked up, his breath shallow and fast as his heart galloped.

"Aodhan." Illium's hands leaving his body.

Another kind of panic fluttering inside him, Aodhan tried to push words out past a throat gone gritty and dry.

But Illium hadn't left him, was just moving his hands to cup Aodhan's face. "Focus on me, Adi," he said, his tone firm. "Listen to my voice, and to nothing else. It's me and you in this room, trying to figure us out, and I'm maybe a little drunk on that moonshine for which I gave Venom the recipe and with which he spiked the punch, but I mean, it isn't *that* strong."

Aodhan wanted to laugh at the confession, but his voice was strangled, a dark hand squeezing his throat. *Blue.* A fraught mental cry.

I have you, Adi. No one will ever fucking touch you without your consent again. I'll chop off their hands, and then I'll string up their bones in a necklace I'll wear like some barbarian out of myth, until they call me Illium of the Bones.

A splutter of laughter did leave Aodhan's lips then, summoned by Illium's unrelenting determination not to leave him in a lightless box, hostage to his nightmares.

There you go. Illium continued to speak into his mind. *That's my Adi. Keep on walking back to me, even if I'm drunk and might wear a necklace of bones, and may possibly have promised Smoke she could sleep cuddled up on my chest if she'd stop sulking.*

Aodhan's laugh was a deeper sound this time, the hands with which he clutched at Illium urgent. Gathering him close, Illium wrapped his wings around him and stroked his back while rubbing his cheek against Aodhan's own.

Around Aodhan's ankles twined a body soft and small, Smoke making little sounds that seemed to be an attempt to calm and soothe.

Even your cat knows I'm having a breakdown.

You are not having a breakdown—you're having a breakthrough. There's a difference.

A long squeeze, the hug held until Aodhan's muscles were no longer locked in stone, and he could breathe again, speak again. "I conquered this," he gritted through clenched teeth, breaking out of Illium's hold to stride to the huge living room windows that overlooked their glittering city. "I worked with healers to make sure I *conquered* this!"

Smoke at his feet again, the sounds she was making more impatient now.

He picked her up out of habit and she cuddled into him, once again a purring machine. He couldn't yell now that he was stroking her, his next words were low and hoarse. "I conquered this," he repeated, and beneath the anger was a plea.

Illium's heart twisted.

Aodhan was the strongest angel he knew—and that included the entire Cadre. None of them had survived what had been done to Aodhan, come out compassionate and free of cruelty. Aodhan could've turned twisted in the aftermath of his kidnapping and torture—instead, he made artworks of transcendent beauty, and he created small things designed specially for children's soft hands.

"*Mea lux*," Illium murmured, calling Aodhan his light in a language that had been ancient even when they were children; but it was no comment on Aodhan's skin or hair. No, it was an endearment that encapsulated Adi's heart—and who he was to Illium. "You beat those bastards a long time ago." Walking over to stand next to Aodhan, he spread his wing over the other man's back and wings.

"Not if I'm falling into the abyss at having you touch me. *You*, Blue." His voice cracked, shattered, splintered glass at their feet. "The one person I would lie down and allow to put a blade to my throat if you asked."

"I didn't realize you were into that type of kink." Illium rubbed his thumb absently over his belt buckle. "To be honest, I don't know if I'm into knives. Not in bed anyway."

"*Illium.*"

Lips kicking up on one side at his best friend's exasperated tone, he reached out to delicately stroke the arches of

Aodhan's wings . . . and saw it, the shiver that turned into a shudder, the weakened and aged tendrils of darkness attempting to take root once more.

But it was the lost look in Aodhan's eyes that cut him off at the knees. Since the day they'd crossed the boundary from friends alone to lovers, too—in heart if not body— Aodhan had been the stronger one, while Illium hesitated, scared in a way he couldn't explain. He'd loved that strange imbalance for what it meant for his friend's healing.

And he *hated* that the pathetic fuckers who'd taken advantage of Aodhan's inherent sense of honor had dared reach out of the past and hurt him again by making him question his own strength. Moving his hand to lie flat on Aodhan's wing, on those soft feathers that glittered as bright as diamonds, he said, "I spoke to Keir. While he was in China to work with Jinhai."

Aodhan's expression was a study in confusion at this apparent change in subject, but the compassion in him— sweet, haunting, a fucking testament to his refusal to bow down to evil—won over his pain. "How is Jinhai? I wanted to visit him, but both Keir and Suyin suggested it was better I wait, so that he bonds more tightly to Suyin and those others of her court who are looking after him."

"Yes, they told me the same." Illium continued to hold the shattered glass of Aodhan's gaze. "Keir says the boy came close to imprinting on us, like a lost chick." Because they were the only people in his shrunken world who'd not only seen *him*, but who'd treated him with kindness. "Better that he imprints on Suyin, so she can control him as he grows into his power."

Aodhan's expression turned stark. "He has so many strikes against him. What are the chances he'll make it?"

"At least now he has the opportunity to try." Illium moved his fingers on Aodhan's feathers with careful gentleness. "I spoke to Keir because he knows all of what happened to you—I thought you wouldn't mind. I didn't ask him about your private conversations," he clarified. "I wouldn't cross that boundary."

"I know." Aodhan stroked Smoke. "What did you ask him?"

"Well, while I was out there all alone obsessing about you, I realized that you haven't physically been with anyone for over two hundred years." Not since the rotting dead couple for whom no one mourned and even fewer remembered had taken that which was not theirs to take. "I asked Keir for general advice on how to do things right, so I didn't hurt you."

"There you go, looking after me again." A hard line to Aodhan's jaw.

Illium threw up his hands, not about to bend on this integral aspect of his personality. "You agreed I could."

Squeezing his eyes shut, Aodhan exhaled, then opened them again. "Yes, I did. I'm just angry and not at you. What did Keir say?"

"Nothing. He said he needed to speak to the two of us together so as not to betray any confidences." Frustrated as he'd been by that answer, Illium's respect for the healer had grown ever deeper. "But he gave me a book."

Going to his bedroom, he retrieved a small book bound in leather, its pages browned, and took it to the living area, where Aodhan yet stood. "It's old, from Keir's private collection. He lent it to me for as long as we need it." Throat dry, he said the most important words. "It's healers' wisdom from long ago, about how a person can reclaim their body after an experience where the choice to share that body was taken from them."

He held his breath when Aodhan went motionless. Never did he want to hurt this man who was his forever, but they had to talk about this. Illium had hoped all his preparation was for naught, that their kisses and touches in China evidenced that Aodhan was no longer in pain from the wounds that had stolen his light from the world for centuries . . . but China had been the beginning, hadn't it? Small, snatched glimpses of what could be.

Tonight was the first time Illium had touched Aodhan's bare skin with carnal intent. And while Aodhan's female abductor might have tried for kisses, Illium knew Aodhan had never given them to her. Her pressing her lips force-fully against his mouth didn't count, would *never* count. So Aodhan could kiss Illium, could hold Illium.

But the rest? Being touched in intimate ways that were only ever meant to be a gift given?

That had been stolen from him while he lay broken, having been made too weak to fight back, his psyche debased as his physical being was violated over and over again.

"I conquered the monsters who took me," Aodhan said softly, his eyes on the brilliant night of their beloved city, "but no, I haven't shared my body with anyone since. Before you, Sachieri and Bathar were my last experience of touch beyond that of polite contact or of healing."

Shifting to lean one shoulder against the window, Illium reached out to scratch Smoke on the head in the spot she liked. Her eyes went heavy-lidded, the rhythm of her purr that of a small engine. "The book says that often, such trauma only rears its head in an analogous situation."

"Blue, the one thing I can say for certain is that there is nothing in your touch that is like theirs." Pure anger in the hard glint of Aodhan's eyes.

7

Many people would've flinched from the taut bite of Aodhan's anger; it was a thing as controlled and deadly as a scalpel in a surgeon's hand. Slow though Aodhan was to anger, when he did give in to the emotion, it was with the same intense passion that he brought to his art. But Illium had been tangling with his lover's quiet but intractable temper near to his entire lifetime.

He stood firm.

"This is a bruise that goes to the soul, Adi. The healers' book also says that it only becomes apparent when there is infinite trust between both parties." Aodhan could allow the fear to rise *because* he trusted Illium not to take advantage of it.

His best friend's jawline didn't soften, but he said, "I'll read it," in a voice that was pure rough grit.

"Why don't we read it together?" Shoving aside his own rage at people long dead, Illium tried out his most charming smile. "While I'm snuggled up to you and you're giving me a shoulder massage."

Aodhan's lips twitched. "You just want a shoulder massage."

To see his Sparkle's smile return even that much, it made Illium's heart turn cartwheels. "I mean, two birds and all that." Reaching out, he ran his fingers through Aodhan's hair, fascinated as always by how soft it was when it glittered so diamond bright.

Smoke yawned just then, displaying sharp feline teeth, then jumped out of Aodhan's arms to pad into the bedroom. "She's probably on the bed again." Illium bit down on his lower lip. "I did promise."

Grabbing the side of his neck, Aodhan drew him close enough to kiss. "We're both too tired to read that book tonight, but I'll give you a shoulder massage."

Illium stole another kiss on the way to the bedroom. This time to the line of that stubborn jaw. Their wings tangled, biceps pressed together. "Have I mentioned that you're hot when you're angry?"

"I'll have to remember that." Aodhan smiled.

It was a punch right to Illium's heart, his entire being melting in ways that should've probably concerned him. But he was too drunk on Adi to care.

Smoke had indeed curled up in the center of the bed like the queen of the castle. Leaving her there, Illium took off the top of his leathers but tugged on a simple white tee straight after.

"It'll be uncomfortable for you," Aodhan murmured, nodding at Illium's leather pants.

Illium was about to say it didn't matter when he realized it did to Aodhan. "Wait a minute. I think I have . . ." Digging through his clothes, he held up a pair of pajama pants in pale green with chirping bluebirds on them. "Janvier's gag gift finally has its day."

Grooves around Aodhan's mouth, that deep smile one Illium had missed for an eon. "You're adorable."

Illium felt his own cheeks heat up. It wasn't that he didn't know how to handle compliments, but that this was Aodhan saying those words, looking at him in a way that did dangerous things to his self-control. No shields, no distance, just unadulterated want and a love that was a thing of warrior possessiveness.

His heart kicked.

Breathing shallow, he ducked into the attached bathroom to change even though they'd been naked around each other more than once in the way of warriors stripping off after a battle to bathe. Things had changed. They looked at each other with lovers eyes now, and tonight, this, was about comfort—not only of the body, but of the soul.

When he returned, it was to a room bathed in the soft glow of a small bedside lamp. Aodhan had activated the blinds, cocooning them in warm privacy.

Illium's Adi, his skin and hair ashine but not harsh in their glitter in this light, had taken off his shoes, but kept on the linen pants he'd worn to the party.

He already sat on the bed, his back to the headboard, one knee raised, the other stretched straight out, and his hand on a dozing Smoke. Illium, skin hot and body wanting to react in ways that weren't right for this moment, held his breath as he settled himself with his back to Aodhan's chest.

Smoke's head poked up.

Chuckling past the desire that choked his throat, he picked her up to cradle her against his chest. "Is this all right?" he asked Aodhan. "How I'm sitting against you?"

Aodhan's answer was a firm stroke of the arch of Illium's left wing. Having not expected the intimate touch, a touch that went straight to his cock, Illium jerked up, disturbing Smoke—who flounced off to curl up in her well-lined and plush basket with her back to them. "Adi." It came out a croak. "That wasn't the plan."

"You know what I just figured out?" Aodhan murmured against his ear, his hand gripping Illium's other wing arch. "I have no problem when *I'm* the one doing the touching." Another firm stroke on that part of a wing that was only ever to be touched by healers—or lovers.

Illium's body grew rigid, his pulse a drum as his back arched into the muscled heat of Aodhan, warrior artist and

blood-friend who'd refused to let Illium walk into battle
alone.

That was when he felt it.

A thick, dark heat against his lower back, the two of
them separated only by linen and soft cotton.

The realization that Aodhan wanted him as badly made
his toes curl, his abdomen clench.

But Aodhan didn't continue the caresses, instead nuzzling Illium. "Blue-mine, this won't be about you giving to
me. I forbid it."

"First of all, you can't forbid me to do anything. Even if
you just called me 'mine' in that deep voice and scrambled
my brain. And secondly," Illium rasped through a dry throat,
"why is it so sexy that you're forbidding me to do something in bed?"

Aodhan ran a finger down Illium's throat. "Because you're
a contrarian." His voice was a low hum against Illium's
body. "I want this to be give-and-take. That means I give of
my body as you give of yours."

Illium groaned. Whatever fears he had, they had nothing
to do with his physical attraction to Aodhan. "You're going
to be responsible for my sad and very aroused demise."

A chuckle . . . followed by a suckling kiss of his throat
that made Illium's body harden to near pain. *"Adi."*

Another nuzzle before Aodhan leaned back, tugging at
Illium so he lay supine against him. Reaching out a hand,
Aodhan switched off the lamp, then opened the blinds using the remote.

New York danced with man-made starlight beyond the
windows.

"I want this for us," Aodhan said, the words a rough
confession. "The soft and the playful and the dance before
the dance."

Illium's heart ached all over again. Lifting Aodhan's
hand from where it lay against his pectoral muscle, he brought
it to his lips, pressing a kiss to a palm callused by centuries
of both weapons work and the making of the art that was

Aodhan's lifeblood. "We'll have it," he vowed. "Starting with our first official date."

Aodhan's chest moved against him in quiet laughter. But his words were intrigued. "A date? Me and you?"

"Why not?" Illium ran his hand down Aodhan's forearm. "What should it be? A sunset cruise? No, too many people. How about a sunset picnic tucked away in the Catskills where no one can disturb us."

Aodhan was quiet for a long moment before he said, "Yes, let's do that." He ran his fingers through Illium's hair. "I'll speak to Keir alone about my reaction first. Later, we'll speak to him together."

"You don't have to include me, not if—"

"You have a right to be there," Aodhan interrupted in that firm voice of his that was really doing things for Illium. "You're going to be navigating this final fucking hurdle with me."

Aodhan didn't swear as much as most of the Seven. But when he did, he meant it. Illium kissed his palm again. "I'll be there, sir."

"Smart-ass." A rumble of sound but Aodhan continued to stroke his hair.

Smoke, who'd decided they'd been ignored long enough, came back over to jump onto the bed and, when Illium gathered her to him, cuddled into him without claws or hisses.

Neither of them spoke again.

Illium's eyes closed under Aodhan's hypnotic caresses, the other man's big body around him and Illium's wings tangled up in between in a trust he'd never before given to a lover. Always, Illium had been in charge. He didn't trust anyone else that much.

Except for the man who was his light.

Aodhan woke curled up behind Illium, one wing over him, and his arm tucking Illium close. Aodhan had remembered to close the blinds before he fell asleep, so the room was gray with shadows, no sunlight pouring in to turn him into an earthbound star. Sometimes, his tendency to sparkle was fucking annoying more than anything.

Smoke lay sleeping in the curve of Illium's body, but raised her head when Aodhan stirred.

"Shh." Aodhan used a finger to pet her back down; her fur was as soft as a cloud.

Yawning, she cuddled back into Illium's chest. Aodhan smiled. Because that was Illium: rescuing the lost and the broken, and holding them safe and warm.

His smile faded on the thought—because he was once again the one who needed tending, needed help.

"No," he said aloud, refusing to allow himself to go down that self-destructive path. He'd accepted Illium's need to care as a deep part of his lover's psyche—and so he would let Illium care and even hover.

The difference was that he intended to give the other man what he needed, too.

Pressing a kiss to the golden skin of Illium's shoulder, he slipped out of bed as quietly as possible. But Illium was a warrior honed in battle, one who'd spent a good chunk of the past year in a territory devastated by evil. He woke at once. "Time is it?" A mumble.

"Early," Aodhan said. "But I have a meeting with Dmitri in an hour. You rest." The two of them were old enough not to need the same amount of sleep as mortals, but Illium had flown halfway across the world. He needed downtime.

Turning over onto his back, Illium blinked those golden eyes slowly, before a smile curved his lips. "Hi."

Aodhan had painted Illium thousands of times over the centuries, but never this way. With his hair all mussed and that sleepy look on his face, his impossibly beautiful lashes shadowing his cheeks because he had them at half-mast.

All while he held a purring cat to his chest and stroked her with lazy movements.

"Really, you look at me like that and expect me to focus." Aodhan mock-scowled before leaning down, his wings spread over them, to brush his lips over Illium's.

Smoke reached up to bat at his feathers with one paw, her claws sheathed.

Used to her fascination with his feathers, Aodhan let her be to concentrate on the man who flat-out undid him. "I should paint you like this—except naked, with only a sheet to protect your modesty—and sell prints. I'd make a fortune." The only hitch was that he'd never share this intimate Illium with his drowsy smile with anyone; whatever he painted would be for their eyes alone.

Illium chuckled before reaching up to run his fingers along the underside of Aodhan's wing. The soft feathers there weren't anywhere near as sensitive as the ones at the arches, but a small shiver rolled over Aodhan nonetheless. Because it wasn't just about biology—it was about Illium touching him.

"As long as you do one for me of you shirtless and barefoot while you scowl at the easel. I love that intense look you get." His eyes glowed without warning, a thing impossible for anyone but an archangel.

Aodhan forced himself to maintain his composed expression. Ascension continued to be an unwanted shadow that loomed over Illium. Telling him of the fleeting energy surge would only ruin his day—and Aodhan didn't want to do anything to erase his smile.

All he could do was hope that the violent power of the Cadre wouldn't abuse the heart of the boy who'd been his best friend, a heart that had matured in the powerful man he'd become, but never lost its gentle, kind core. "I'm going to go before I surrender to your wiles and end up late for my meeting."

Illium's shoulders moved as he laughed. "I do have good wiles."

But he rose with Aodhan when Aodhan lifted himself back to his full height. And he got out of bed to walk Aodhan to the door. Smoke, who he'd put on the floor, stretched luxuriously, back arched and tail curling upward, before she padded happily at their side. "What's the meeting about?"

"Cleaning up the city. Lot of crime got ignored or obfuscated by the war." The aftermath had also been chaotic.

"The mortals are dealing with the mortal-on-mortal crimes, while the Tower is handling anything that might involve an immortal or almost immortal. Dmitri's got a cold case he wants me to look at."

Illium's eyes had grown sharper, more alert since the instant he woke, and now they lit up. "That sounds interesting."

Aodhan pointed a stern finger his way. "No. Get that look off your face." He scowled, once again confronted with how much weight Illium had lost, his bones pushing too hard against his cheeks. "You've earned a serious vacation. No one's going to expect you to do any work for at least a month."

"What I've earned is the chance to work in my own city," Illium muttered with as dark a scowl. "I'll see you up there—I'm going to horn in on your case and you can't stop me."

Throwing up his hands, Aodhan nonetheless couldn't squelch his pleasure at the idea of having Illium so close after their separation. "Smoke's welcome at tech command. Vivek and the others enjoy her company, and there's always someone there so she won't be lonely." He glanced at the clock on the wall. "I'd better go. Meeting's at eight thirty."

"I promised Mother I'd call her the morning after I reached home, so I'll be a little late, but don't leave the Tower without me."

"Tell Eh-ma I send my love." Aodhan couldn't help reaching out to brush his fingers over Illium's jaw, the tactile contact making his body clench . . . and Illium suck in a breath.

8

Illium's heart exhaled after Aodhan left, his muscles turning liquid—not in relief, but in sheer besottedness. You'd think he'd be over that stage after knowing Aodhan for five hundred years, give or take, but no, it looked like he was going to go through the whole besotted phase before he settled down into being a mature partner in love.

Grinning, he crouched down to give Smoke the scritches she loved. "Do you think he has any idea how soft it makes me to know he looked after you so well while I wasn't here?" He'd known Adi would, of course he had, but to have his faith evidenced in Aodhan's concern that Smoke not be lonely, well, it melted things inside him.

Smoke butted at his hand in demand.

"I have no idea where your food is, sweetheart." Aodhan had taken care of it yesterday. "I'll just ask—"

But Smoke was already bounding out of the living room into the small kitchen that was part of the suite. As always, Illium's was pristine. He never used it except maybe to heat up a snack—he'd much rather eat with other people, and there was so much good food in the city.

Smoke sat with her paw on a lower cupboard door.

"Of course you'd know." He bopped her on the nose. "And of course he'd put some in here." Because that was Aodhan, thinking ahead, doing small, thoughtful acts.

His heart sighed again. "What am I going to do, Smoke?" he murmured as he opened the cupboard. It had a latch that meant Smoke couldn't get into it on her own, but otherwise swung wide with smooth ease. "I have an image to maintain. Making heart eyes at Aodhan doesn't quite fit my battle commander status."

His pet was already at the sleek white food bowl that sat in one corner, next to an equally sleek water bowl. He knew Aodhan had hand-made them even before he got close. The man had put tiny golden sparkles in the material, then burned in Smoke's name in a darker gold.

She happily began to crunch at her dry food after he filled up her bowl. While she'd eat anything, she'd always had a preference for crunch over what many would call more deluxe meals. "You're a survivor, aren't you?" he said as he put away the rest of the bag. "And so are we, me and Aodhan. The rest of it, we'll figure out together."

Illium would let neither the strange fear that overcame him at times, nor Aodhan's nightmare memories, hinder their journey.

We have all the time in the world, Blue.

Yes, they did.

Illium, I forgot to tell you. Aodhan's voice in his head. *Smoke prefers to go outside when she needs the facilities so I set up an area for her and she's made a beeline for it every time. She's learned how to catch the elevator but never goes outside the Tower precinct.*

Illium's already soft heart turned ridiculously mushy. *I told you she's a prodigy,* he said, because he couldn't put the enormity of his feelings into words. *Also a bit feral after growing up on a building site and hanging out with me in a tent—or in the open air when it got too hot.*

Leaving Smoke to her breakfast on the feel of Aodhan's mental kiss, he wandered into the bathroom for a quick shower to more properly wake himself. Angels did better with switching time zones than mortals, but it did still take their bodies time to catch up—especially after a long span in another region.

He wasn't the least surprised when Smoke poked her head inside the open doorway after a minute, her suspicious form a smudged shadow against tiles of black riven with silver. "Still here," he said from the wide expanse of the tiled shower room. "Not murdered by water."

Smoke, for all that she'd spent her formative months next to the ocean, was of the opinion that water was the enemy, to be vanquished. The first time she'd seen him submerge himself in a pond, she'd jumped in after him in an attempt to drag him out.

He'd finally taught her that he didn't need rescue, but she continued to believe him dim-witted to get so close to water. Today, she gave him the feline side-eye from the door; it said that she was not amused by his decision to drench himself, but she still didn't return to her breakfast until he'd switched off the shower and was drying himself.

Did Smoke guard you in your shower, too? he asked Aodhan.

While Illium had a bath in his suite as well as the shower, Aodhan had only the shower. A deliberate choice on Raphael's part when he'd built this iteration of the Tower. The archangel knew that Aodhan hated baths—an aversion born of the torture he'd endured where he'd been buried in water that drowned him over and over again.

No. Smoke finds me acceptable, but she wouldn't pine for me if I died under the wrath of the shower. You're the only one she finds worthy of guarding while you undertake the idiocy of voluntarily subjecting yourself to sprays of water.

Laughing so hard, he snorted—damn but he'd missed Aodhan's dry humor—Illium finished drying off before pulling on fresh jeans along with a simple black shirt that had zippered closures at the bottoms of the wing slits. Shrugging it on over his shoulders, he did up the buttons down the front, closed the wing slits, then rolled the sleeves half-way up his forearms.

His hair he styled by thrusting his fingers through the strands.

When he walked out of the bathroom, Smoke indicated the desire to be let out. He opened the door, then called the elevator for her. "See you after you're done." No doubt she'd already trained other Tower residents to do her bidding when it came to summoning the elevator back up.

Leaving the suite door ajar for her return, he grabbed a cup of coffee and made short work of the croissant dusted with flaked almonds that had appeared in his kitchen while he was showering. Beside it was a plate of sliced fruit garnished with raisins and sugared cashews, all of it arranged around a small pot of his favorite blueberry oatmeal.

Illium's face went hot in a flush of pleasure, his body feeling weightless. Being spoiled by Aodhan wasn't anything he'd have ever said he wanted, but now that it was his reality?

Wow.

Stomach full and butterflies dancing in his bloodstream, he walked out to sit on the balcony railing he'd asked Aodhan to have installed before he came home. It made it harder for him to take off from this spot, but it meant Smoke could play safely here.

The city murmured with life beside him as he called his mother using the function that would permit them to see each other. After learning of that capability in modern technology, his mother hated audio-only calls.

Eyes of pale champagne against sun-kissed skin, hair ebony tipped with gold, and the wings that appeared behind her a wild indigo caressed by palest gold, his mother's face came onscreen within a single ring, and he knew she'd been waiting for him—but she hadn't reached out.

It wasn't a power play, rather the opposite.

She was very careful to treat him as an adult these days, hesitant at anything that might be considered an overreach. Oh, she still told him to listen to his mother at times when he was teasing her, but things like this? Where it might be thought that she was attempting to be the adult while treating him as a child, she tried *so hard* not to do it.

In her lost years, she'd often thought him a babe. She'd made him honey cakes and kissed his hair and told him to be good for his teacher. He'd gone along with whatever she said, and not once had he blamed her for her fractured mind. That would be like blaming the earth for being cracked after an earthquake.

The one thing that had never changed was her love for him. She'd drenched him in maternal affection even as she lost piece after piece of herself.

But his mother was a survivor, too. She'd come back strong and defiant . . . except for this one thing, this churning guilt inside her when it came to her son.

He'd never mentioned that he'd noticed how careful she was about not crossing any boundaries, and he never *would* mention it. That would hurt her, shake the foundations she'd rebuilt out of courage and determination—and pure spite at Aegaeon; Illium wasn't about to repay her endless love by causing her pain. He loved seeing her grow ever tougher and even a touch wild, Titus her willing accomplice.

Talk about besotted. The archangel who loved Sharine, the Hummingbird, was still in that stage. So perhaps it never passed when love hit hard, so real it spun you in circles.

Illium decided he was okay with that.

"Illium," his mother said, her gaze awash in infinite joy and shadowed by black lashes dipped in gold. "I heard there was a party last night. I didn't expect you to be up so early."

"You have better spies than most archangels," Illium teased, well aware that it must've been one of the people who worked under Titus's spymaster, Ozias, who'd passed on the information.

Archangels, even those who were allies or friends, spied on each other. Illium thought of it as a game between the friendly archangels, but it also made him worry for what everyone said was the growing power in his cells. He wasn't ready to play the games of the Cadre, might never be ready.

A vein on his arm glowed liquid gold at that instant, a silent reminder that the choice had never been his. Ascension couldn't be controlled. In his case, all he could hope for was that it would wait until after his first millennium of life.

He might survive it then.

"You're too thin." His mother frowned. "I know Suyin too well to think she wouldn't feed her people, so what have you been doing to get yourself in this state?"

He grinned. "Hollow bones, that's what you used to say." The truth was that he'd been running at full capacity the entirety of the time he'd been in China; Suyin had needed everything he had, and he'd seen no reason to hold back.

Suyin herself was as thin as a rail right now—and that took *serious* overwork by an archangel. "I would give of my blood if it would heal this land," she'd said during his last week in her territory, as she crouched down with her hand on the dirt of a newly plowed field.

"But even an archangel's blood can't turn back the clock of this evil, magically fix what my aunt polluted. Hers was a power corrosive. But it also limited her—she could've never understood the heart of the people who are now mine. Their courage humbles me." A glance up at Illium. "As does the power of the friendship shown to me by others."

His mother's voice broke into the echo of Suyin's poignant words. "I'm going to find out how to order you meals in your city," she said, then hesitated.

Wondering if she was going too far.

"I'd rather you make me a giant batch of your honey cakes," he said with a grin that told her it was all right, that he didn't see her need to care for him as an overstep. "I'm sure one of Titus's spies—ahem, *couriers*—will drop it off for you."

Her lips twitched. "According to my beloved, archangels don't do anything as pedestrian as spy. They *reconnoiter*."

Throwing back his head, Illium laughed, and when he met his mother's eyes again, she was smiling with every part of her. "How's my other boy?" she asked as Smoke called out to tell him she was back, then wandered outside to pounce on imaginary prey. "He came home too thin and exhausted, too."

"He's doing so well, Mother," he said, knowing she'd understand that he wasn't only talking about Aodhan's physical status. "He sends his love."

Sharine's smile softened into tenderness. "I'm glad you're together again. I never worry when you're with Aodhan or Aodhan is with you."

Illium's chest expanded, contracted. "Mother . . . I think we're changing," he whispered. "Becoming more to one another."

A tilt of Sharine's head, an even gentler smile. "Ah, my baby boy," she said, slipping unknowingly into maternal affection as Illium got off the railing to pace the balcony. "Life is complicated, is it not?"

Illium slumped back against the nearest wall. "Yes. I'm terrified."

Her nod was careful, considered. "Change *is* terrifying," she acknowledged. "But remember this, son of mine, your friendship with Aodhan is no glass bauble that will break if you mishandle it. It is a thing of steel and granite. Perhaps it will end up with a few dents or scratches if you make a mistake, but it will *endure*."

He swallowed hard, wanting desperately to believe her. Because the idea of damaging the most important relationship in his life was a visceral fear that nipped at his heels when he was alone and his thoughts had too much room to roam. But the alternative? Not even worth thinking about.

"I'm tough," he said, determined not to falter because he was scared. "I'm the son of Lady Sharine, who has tamed the great Titus himself and now has her own pride of lions that she rides every sunset!"

Sharine's laughter at his repetition of that preposterous rumor was a waterfall of sound. "You are an awful child," she said, her cheeks creased. "But we love you so. Especially Titus, who has told me that if we were ever to be blessed with a child, he would hope for just such a son."

She touched her fingers to the screen as she had a way of doing when she spoke to him and to Aodhan. "You *are* strong." A mistiness in her gaze. "You persevered through my shattered years—"

"M—"

"Hush now, Illium, let me speak." A firm tone. "You stood beside me with a strength and a compassion that couldn't have been expected in one so young. That kind of heart? It is a tremendous gift."

A wisdom to her that was a thing of age so profound that he had no idea when she'd been born, she added, "You were my light in the darkness. If you're afraid, Illium, it's only because your heart is so huge. Never *ever* forget its power."

She touched the screen again. "Spread your wings, my cherished boy. You no longer have to watch over me, watch over anyone. This time is *yours*. Fly to your happiness. Claim the love of the one person who has ever been your heart's mirror."

9

Dmitri was waiting for Aodhan on the balcony outside the second's office. He was dressed in a black suit with a dark gray shirt open at the collar, his black hair neatly combed, his shoes polished to a shine.

"Formal," Aodhan commented.

"Attending an event with Honor. New intake at the Guild—she's one of the speakers." Pride glowed in the darkness of his eyes. "How's our Bluebell? Still asleep?"

Aodhan's entire body warmed at the memory of Illium sleep-tousled and drowsy. "No. He's planning to join us after he talks to Lady Sharine."

"I thought so—he might've earned a rest, but he's not one to sit still." The vampire who was over a millennium in age and one of the most powerful people in the immortal world gave Aodhan an update on two other situations Aodhan had helped handle, before nudging his head at the entrance to his office.

Once inside, Dmitri went to his desk and turned the screen of his computer so Aodhan could see it. "This incident's just

shot to the top of the list after a fire investigator finally had
time to go through what little evidence is available."

Aodhan nodded, aware that the backlog was significant
even with everyone working as hard as they could. Priority
had been given to clear cases of murder or attempted murder, other violent crimes.

"The evidence we have," Dmitri said, "is mostly images
from the security cameras around the site, as well as photos
taken in the aftermath by the mother of one of the victims
once she returned to the city after the war."

Wings of wild blue on the balcony, visible through the
floor-to-ceiling window at Dmitri's back. "Illium's just arrived." Aodhan fought to keep his expression neutral as the
other man entered the office, all wicked grin and wind-
tumbled hair.

His breath speeded up nonetheless, his wings wanting to
shift and rustle, as if he were a young buck with his first
lover rather than an angel of half a millennium with the
man who'd been his best friend all his life.

"I'll put you on this with Aodhan," Dmitri said after the
two had greeted each other and Illium had made his case
for being allowed to help. "It probably needs two sets of
eyes on it anyway. But take a break if you need it." His
command held a weight Aodhan's never would when it came
to Illium—not only was Dmitri older and deadlier, he'd
also known both of them as ungainly babes.

"Will do." Having come to stand beside Aodhan, Illium
kept his wings tucked scrupulously close to his body—his
mind, however, was a whole different matter. *You look gloom-
ier than that picture Greta keeps on her desk of the being
the mortals call the Grim Reaper.*

I'm attempting to appear professional.

I will, too, then. Squaring his shoulders, Illium arranged
his face into an exaggerated grimace while Dmitri was distracted pulling up images on his computer screen.

I'm going to strangle you soon, Aodhan threatened.

Relax, Adi. A glint in those golden eyes as he tapped

absently at his belt buckle. *No one knows we were cuddling half-naked in bed at sunrise.*

Aodhan felt his cheekbones flush, could only hope the way light refracted off his skin diffused any visible appearance of color. It wasn't that he was embarrassed by what they'd done. It was that he wanted to haul Illium close and kiss that teasing mouth. He'd never realized how soft those lips could be, or how much he'd enjoy learning the shape of them.

"Got it." Dmitri's voice snapped the simmering tension in the air, turning them from playful lovers to dedicated members of the Seven in a heartbeat.

On Dmitri's screen were stills from a number of security cameras. All showed a burned-down building with street frontage. Most probably a business, given the signage on the buildings around it.

The fire had left a long black streak on the shop to the right, but that was the worst of the damage on that side; the closest building to the left was separated from the burned structure by an alleyway, which seemed to have saved it from any harm. The building in which they were interested, however, had been reduced to rubble—rubble that had still been smoking at the time the cameras recorded these images.

"Fire occurred right before the final battle with Lijuan," Dmitri told them. "A fire suppression team managed to get to it, but they assumed it had been torched as a result of the war.

"Since that entire block had been confirmed as evacuated, with the verification door seals visible on the other buildings, and they had multiple other fires to attend, they didn't spend any time looking over the debris—truth was even if they had found the bodies, no one could've attended to it at the time."

"Bodies?" Illium folded his arms. "Multiple victims?"

"Two, one vamp, one mortal," Dmitri confirmed. "Discovered by Giulia Corvino, the mother of the vampire—Marco—who died in the blaze. She's the reason we have the security camera images—she asked the neighboring businesses for them while they were still in post-war cleanup mode. Another week and they'd have been wiped."

He leaned forward with his hands on his desk, a tic in his jaw and respect in his tone. "Giulia is also why we have photos of the actual remains in situ. Otherwise, they'd have been packed up by one of the morgue crews for later identification."

Because war, Aodhan thought, did not allow for the niceties of peace. "She sent the photos to the Tower?"

"Via Navarro—he was Marco Corvino's angel." Dmitri named a senior angel of about three thousand years of age with whom Aodhan was familiar. "Problem is, Navarro sustained serious wounds in the final battle, so it took eight months for the file to even reach the Tower. His staff weren't sure what to do about Giulia's insistence that it was murder, just shelved it until he was up and running."

His eyes narrowed. "Must've killed her inside to see her son as bones, but she wanted justice for him and his girlfriend. Tough woman."

Aodhan looked at the photos with a new eye, seeing in their stark silence a mother's grief—and her determination not to allow this cruelty to stand unavenged. "Marco must've been very young if his mother's not only alive but capable of mounting an investigation."

"Kid was barely past his first decade under Contract." Dmitri's lips pressed tight. "We lost a lot of young angels and vampires in the war, but at least they all chose to be in the fight. If what Giulia suspects is true, Marco was murdered in cold blood, the war used as a cover-up."

"What was it?" Illium asked. "The shop? I assume he ran it for Navarro."

Nodding, Dmitri said, "Place sold liquor." He pulled up an image of the shop before the fire.

Illium leaned in for a closer look.

Dingy paintwork, faded signage, bottles lined up in the window, this wasn't the neighborhood shop where folks went to pick up a bottle of wine or a six-pack of beer. This was for serious drinkers. Not the kind of place Illium would've expected an angel like Navarro to acquire, but it might've been about holding the land rather than any particular desire for the shop.

"The way the fire's contained to the footprint of the targeted shop," Aodhan said, the sound of his voice rolling over Illium in a resonant wave. "Is that part of the reason for suspicion?"

"Not the containment but the ferocity of the blaze." Dmitri switched back to the still of the destroyed building. "While the fire crew managed to keep it from spreading, they remember it being a hard battle. That's part of why they thought it the result of an angelic strike—with all the alcohol on the scene providing the perfect fuel."

Illium nodded. While only archangels could create angelfire, the virulent flame that could end the life of another archangel, powerful angels could turn their power into energy. Both Illium and Aodhan could do it, and if they set flame to a place as incendiary as a liquor shop, it was possible it'd burn until it ran out of fuel.

"The buildings on either side and behind it are concrete," he murmured, working through the mechanics in his head. "Same as Marco's shop. Not easy to burn *without* assistance."

"A mortal could've set it up from the inside using additional accelerants," Aodhan suggested, "but it would've required being fatally close to the danger . . . whereas even a weak angel could ignite it from a safe distance using a weapon." Frowning, he went around to the other side of the desk so he could look more carefully at the photos and stills.

While Aodhan zoomed in on details, Illium said, "Why was such a young vampire in this part of the city during the war in the first place? Anyone of that age was given a relatively safe task out of the line of fire." Unlike Lijuan, Raphael hadn't been out to sacrifice the untrained.

"That's part of the mystery," Dmitri said, just as Aodhan stopped on an image of the remains taken by Giulia.

Charred bones, two skulls, colored glass melted onto them.

"No fangs on the right skull. The mortal."

"Yes." Dmitri pulled up a photo of a pretty woman with short black curls and skin several shades darker than his own. She wore black-framed spectacles and had a dreaminess about her that was echoed in the print of the blouse she wore—a watercolor of flowers rippling on water, the strokes deliberately smudged by the artist so that nothing was defined or sharp.

"We were able to identify her because Giulia was all but certain it had to be Marco's girlfriend, Tanika. While her dentist's building was obliterated in the war, he'd backed up his patient records in the ether."

"Cloud," Illium corrected because Dmitri had asked him to point out any such errors; the other man was one of the most technologically savvy of the other Seven, but every so often, he said something that reminded Illium that the second was over a thousand years old.

Dmitri nodded to acknowledge the correction, and Illium knew he wouldn't make that mistake again. "Marco's dentist had his pre-Making X-rays. Since only the incisors change in the Making, we were able to verify the vampiric remains as Marco's with ninety percent certainty. Add in the location and it's unlikely to be anyone else, but the forensic teams are running further tests."

"How old was Tanika?" Aodhan asked.

"Twenty-nine."

All of them went silent. Mortal lives were so short, and this mortal life had been snuffed out at a point where an angel would yet be a child, a being who'd barely even glimpsed the world.

"The pathologist who examined the remains found no signs of visible trauma," Dmitri said at last, "but it could've been a soft-tissue injury obliterated by the fire. I've authorized a forensic anthropologist to take a look anyway."

Illium took in the second's expression, realized they were missing something. "You're going to a lot of trouble for a case many people would've written off as an accident of war. Especially this long out from the deaths."

Jaw working, Dmitri slid his hands into the pockets of his pants. "Walk outside with me."

Once on the balcony, the crisp morning air brushing their faces, the other man said, "According to Giulia, Marco had gained a stalker sometime in the half year prior to his death. Giulia only knew of part of it, but I managed to touch base with Navarro.

"He's grounded in Europe due to a torn wing tendon," Dmitri continued, "but he told me Marco began to receive incessant calls approximately five months before his death and that was only the beginning. Gifts delivered to his mortal family home as well as his angel's household, handwritten letters in the mail, odd occurrences that made Marco feel watched."

Illium's heart jolted, but Aodhan's mind touched his before he could say anything. *I'm fine, Blue.* A firm resolve. *I asked Dmitri not to shield me from such things anymore. To heal, I must grow.*

Curling his fingers into his palm until he'd formed a tight fist, Illium held his silence even as his need to protect Aodhan roared within. "I'm guessing you don't have an ID on the stalker or you wouldn't have called Aodhan in."

"No, she was very clever about that." Staring into the wind, Dmitri seemed lost in his thoughts, shaking them off only when Izak flew by with his wing. "But she—and it *is* a woman from the self-references in the letters that Navarro saw—made one mistake. She dropped off gifts on the balcony of the apartment that housed Marco's mother at the time. That balcony was on the eleventh floor."

Aodhan's wings stirred. "Venom could climb that, but Venom's an outlier even among vampires. Has to be an angel."

"Especially when you add in a second incident." Dmitri's eyes followed Izzy's wing as they practiced above the city, but his mind was clearly elsewhere, his voice harsh in a way that was deadly.

"Giulia is convinced that Tanika was—a month prior to the war—hit by a projectile dropped from above while she

was crossing an otherwise empty football field. There were
no houses from which anything could've been thrown and
the lump of what proved to be melted plastic was too big for
a bird. Tanika said she looked around but saw no one, but
she was dazed so it took her time. Long enough for an angel
to vanish into the clouds."

"A warning rather than attempted murder?" Illium
couldn't see why not a chunk of rock otherwise.

Dmitri nodded in agreement before shifting so he faced
Aodhan. "I'm giving you Marco and Tanika because you
asked me to send this type of situation your way, but if you
don't want the—"

"I'll take it. No young vampire or mortal should be ter-
rorized by one of our kind."

The two men's eyes met, and Illium had the strange
sense that there was something he didn't know, but they
did. As if they were part of a club of which he wasn't a
member.

His heart ruptured, the psychic tear agony.

He could think of only one experience the two might
share of which Illium wasn't aware: being the target of the
ugliness of obsession.

10

Are you sure, Aodhan? Dmitri's mental voice was as intense as the darkness of his eyes. *There's no shame in walking away from that which is toxic to you.*

I'm sure. He held the other man's gaze. *I feel only a violent anger, not fear.*

Dmitri, a man who had an intimate understanding of violence, gave a small nod.

Aodhan had expected a question from Illium at the pause that had gone on too long, but when he glanced at the blue-winged angel, he saw that Illium was focused on Dmitri, his expression stark.

Of course he'd understood without explanation. Illium's emotional intelligence was one of his greatest gifts. Aodhan also knew that Illium would never ask him to betray Dmitri's confidence—a confidence he'd shared while Aodhan lay broken in the Medica. Not just in the body, but in the mind.

"You will survive, Aodhan." A primal command, the hand Dmitri clenched around Aodhan's emaciated one strong.

"You can't know that." Aodhan was able to allow himself to be weak with Dmitri because Dmitri had carried him when he was a babe; he was the dangerous older brother who had always protected. "What they did to me . . . it broke me, Dmitri. I breathe but I'm dead inside."

Dmitri's eyes flared, his rage a kiss of red on his cheekbones. "I was broken once, too. I thought I'd never come back from that. But I did. While she rots and is forgotten. That will be the punishment for your captors, too."

Then, while Aodhan lay silent, Dmitri had told him the story of a mortal who had loved his wife and children with wild joy, and who had been best friends with a young angel who would one day become an archangel. And he'd told the story of how an angel obsessed with the mortal had murdered his entire family and Made him a vampire without his consent.

The monster had forced Dmitri to watch his son suffer in agony so terrible and without end that Dmitri'd had to make the choice to end his beloved boy's life. "I had to snap my Misha's neck," Dmitri had said, his voice a harsh rasp. "My smart, loving boy who I'd promised to protect forever. I had only ashes to bury of my Ingrede and our sweet baby girl.

"I broke, Aodhan. Into so many pieces that I wasn't even a ghost in the world. I wanted only to do violence until the horror of it overwhelmed my anguish. I was a vicious thing bent on destruction and excess, whatever it took to drown out what I had done . . . and what I had failed to do. It took me centuries to become a whole man again.

"So I won't tell you it'll be an easy journey, but you'll survive. I did so on memories of the love I shared with Ingrede and our children, and the friendship of an angel who fucking wouldn't let go. I won't let you go, either." Dmitri's grip had been gentle but unrelenting on Aodhan's fragile bones. "And we both know Illium will follow you into the place the mortals call hell if that's what it takes to bring you home."

Aodhan had cried for Dmitri as he couldn't cry for himself, and Dmitri had held him, allowing him to find surcease in his sorrow for another. They'd spoken many times over the centuries while Aodhan was lost, and each and every time, Dmitri had been unshakable in his faith in Aodhan's internal strength.

"Not necessary," he'd said when Aodhan finally walked out of the abyss and apologized to the second for letting him down with how long he'd been lost. "In my lost years, while I appeared present, I was determined to surrender myself to every bad and terrible thing I could. We all heal in our own way."

Now, that same man gave a crisp nod. "Giulia believes the stalker angel murdered the mortal Marco loved"—a voice that was an unsheathed blade—"and that Marco got caught in the cross-fire."

"It might have been deliberate," Aodhan suggested through the gridlock of memory. "If I can't have you, no one can."

Hands braced on his hips, Illium hissed out a breath. "You know, there's a good chance Marco proposed to his girlfriend. A lot of that going around during the war. That could've pushed the obsessed angel over the edge."

"Yes, I can see that." Dmitri continued to watch the wing, this time without distance in his gaze. "Whatever the truth, we have no proof as yet. All we have is a dead couple in a burned-down building. See what you can do. If you can track down the angel, I'll take care of the rest."

I think you should go find Honor, Dmitri, and remind yourself that you beat the one who would've caged you.

Dmitri glanced over, eyes narrowed. *I'm not spiraling into the dark, Aodhan. I'm just pissed.* A pause, his hand flexing open. *But I will go find Honor.*

"I e-mailed the complete files to you both." The second turned to Illium. "Not quite the welcome I would've wanted for you."

Illium—who'd wiped the stricken look off his face before

Dmitri glimpsed it—shrugged. "This? Pfft, it's nothing. Did I tell you about the boiling pit of putrid black that opened up under a house in China and just swallowed it? Now it bubbles away, like some primordial soup from which Lijuan will emerge as a fetid slime monster."

Dmitri's lips curved. "I hope it's some distance from Suyin's citadel?"

"Thank the Havens." Illium made a face. "But yeah, compared to that, this is roses. I mean, how hard can it be to identify a random angel in a city full of angels—especially in the aftermath of a war that messed up the usual investigative processes and destroyed multiple databases. Easy. We'll be done by lunch."

Dmitri's faint smile turned into a grin. "It's good to have you home."

An angel who can bring laughter to the darkest time? Such a being is a gift, Aodhan.

Words Suyin had spoken to Aodhan in China. They held a keen truth.

Illium's light came from within, and it was a treasure beyond price to those who were lucky enough to be in its radius.

As they flew to the site of what was most likely a double murder, Illium tried to trust what Aodhan had said to him about being all right with this—but if he was being honest, it was hard. Really fucking hard.

It took conscious concentration on his part not to blurt out the question, not to attempt to shield Aodhan from that which might dig up the ugly phantoms of the past. The last time Illium had attempted that, it had led to the biggest fight of their friendship.

I'm no longer a broken doll who needs to be protected from those who might play roughly with me.

No, Aodhan wasn't broken anymore. Not on any level. He was a powerful warrior who was choosing to face the horror of his past head-on—and Illium had promised him that he wouldn't give in to his overprotective urges where the other man was concerned.

You're going to explode if you don't say something soon. Aodhan's voice, deep and resonant . . . and affectionate.

Illium groaned as thick gray clouds began to move in from the ocean on a biting breeze. *I thought I was doing a good job of hiding the ten thousand shrieking voices in my head.*

I know you, Blue. Aodhan angled his wings to the left to lean into a current. *And I appreciate that you're trying.*

Illium flew around in a wider arc, so that they were side by side. *Look at both of us, being so adult. At this rate, we'll be wise old angels in no time.*

Aodhan's smile was slow, the shake of his head exasperated.

Their lighter mood, however, stood no chance against the despair of the burned-down shop, which had been left as it was, caution tape fluttering all around it. While the shop'd had hard drinkers for clientele, the area wasn't a dead end or murky zone that came awake only at dusk—the places around it were doing a brisk business.

A kebab shop sent enticing aromas into the air, two people queued outside what looked to be a clothing alterations place, while next door to the scene was a neat and tidy electrical shop that boasted they could repair any small household electrical item in ONE HOUR OR YOUR MONEY BACK. GINO NEVER LIES!

"I'd have thought someone would've tried to clean up the scene," Illium said. "Seems like that kind of neighborhood."

"Navarro's staff likely put out the word that no one was to touch it until he recovered—and since he sent the file to the Tower, I'd say he took Giulia Corvino's concerns seriously."

Illium went to reply when someone bustled out of the electrical shop. A short, rotund man with a black mustache that had been oiled or conditioned within an inch of its life, and hair as thick and abundant. He wore crisp black pants paired with an equally crisp shirt in a pale pink.

"Angels!" He beamed at them as he hurried over. "Giulia, she said the Tower was going to send people to look at this terrible situation. God rest their souls, that wonderful boy of hers and his sweet girl."

Bowing his head, he muttered a prayer under his breath before he looked up again. "But I thought she's grieving, it's not a real thing. Hard to have this kind of a ruin in the neighborhood especially as we've fixed up most other things, but we all knew Marco, know Giulia. We can wait, we decided together, until she's ready."

That entire spiel had been directed at Illium, which wasn't exactly a surprise. Aodhan's Blue was well known around the city, not just for the flamboyant color of his wings, but because he could as often be seen on the ground as he could in the sky. Illium patronized mortal businesses, had mortal friends.

Aodhan, by contrast, most often flew high in the sky—where his looks wouldn't attract attention. He did have mortal friends these days, one of his closest being the hunter, Demarco, but he'd grown up being an anomaly even among angelkind, his skin drawing light as if it were a faceted diamond. His hair was the same, as were the filaments of his wings. Every part of him shone, until it hurt the eye for others to look at him in bright sunlight.

At least the clouds that had moved in over the past twenty minutes meant he wasn't a star standing on the street. He remained, however, a stranger to this mortal—while Illium, though he might've never before spoken to him, wasn't.

"Gino?" Illium said when the man paused to take a breath.

His eyes went huge. "How do you know of Gino, angel?"

When Illium pointed at the sign outside the electrical shop, the man slapped his thighs and laughed uproariously.

"For a minute, I thought you were in my head." He used a neatly folded handkerchief to mop at his perfectly dry forehead. "So you've come to see about Marco and his girl? I don't know her name, poor soul."

"Tanika," Illium told him. "Gino, since you seem to know the situation here, what's your take on the fire?"

The other man pressed his lips together, his forehead furrowed. "We had to evacuate, you know, because of the war. I knew Marco would have to stay—he was under Contract, but he had no reason to be *here*." Gino waved at the shop.

"His angel only bought it maybe ten months before the war, I think. Marco told me the plan was to gut it, make it real nice, you know? Fit the rest of the neighborhood. So the angel wasn't going to waste someone to safeguard it during the war; if it fell, what does he care? He can build new from the ground up exactly how he likes."

That was a piece of information they hadn't previously had, but it was also unlikely to be useful in unearthing the murderer.

"I helped the boy lock it all up," Gino continued. "He was having trouble with the burglar shutters—usually this neighborhood is safe. We all keep an eye out and most of us live above our shops or close by. But we thought with the city empty, maybe the riffraff would try their luck, so up went the shutters. I mean, possible bad luck from a war strike is no reason to get sloppy. Why let good stock go to waste?"

"Were any of the other businesses damaged?" Illium asked, while Aodhan continued to hold his silence.

"No looting or anything like that," Gino said. "A couple of us had damage to the roof from the battles in the sky, and two or three came back to a cracked or broken window. I got that burn mark on my wall, but I got asked by Marco's angel's people to leave it, not paint it over yet." A pause, his hand rising to make a religious symbol. "But yes, as for damage, we were lucky.

"Three streets over, all the shops were vaporized—just

poof, gone and only dust left—but the archangel is good. He promised to rebuild and now they have brand-new shops, and everyone got a payment so they could start restocking. That's being a good archangel, isn't it?"

"Yes. The sire knows how to care for the people under his reign." Illium's words held a formality that betrayed nothing of his own familiar relationship with Raphael—because to most mortals, Raphael needed to remain a powerful and distant figure. "Is there anything else you think we should know?"

"He was a good boy, Marco. Even after he was Made. Didn't forget us, put on any airs. Still brought his busted electronics for me to fix."

Aodhan spoke up. "So he was part of this community even before he took over the liquor shop?"

Gino shot him the barest glance before looking away and back at Illium, but didn't clam up. "Oh yes. Used to help out at Giulia's deli down the block—she hasn't reopened, hasn't had the heart to." His face dropped. "But that's why Marco ended up in the shop in the first place—the angel wanted this kind of location and Marco knew old Olaf had been wanting to sell, so he arranged it all.

"Got Olaf a real fair price, too. A nice boy, like I said. Worked hard, don't know why he wanted to be a vampire and drink blood, but . . ." A shrug, as if to say he couldn't explain the vagaries of people. "He never tried to suck anyone's blood around here, laughed like a lunatic when I asked him about it." A sad smile. "Had a good laugh, that kid."

"We've heard that another woman may have been interested in him." Aodhan kept it vague so as not to influence the mortal man in any direction.

"Pah, Marco didn't talk to old Gino about those kinds of things. You should ask his friends." A nudge of his head down the street. "Two of 'em hang out at the corner." His lip curled up. "I told Marco he shouldn't be hanging with them no more. Bums. Live at home, no job, pants halfway down their butts."

"Did he have other friends?" Illium asked. "People who'd know him well?"

"Giulia's the one to ask. They were close—she raised him all alone after his papa died when he was eleven."

They spoke to Gino for several more minutes before it became clear that he'd already shared all he had to tell them. When he saw a customer heading into his shop, he said a swift goodbye then ran off to do business.

Others in the street had come out and were sweeping the curb in front of their properties, or whispering to each other while shooting glances at Illium and Aodhan.

Turning deliberately to look at the scene, Aodhan gave them his back. *You're the better of the two of us at speaking to mortals*, he said to Illium. *Do what you do.*

Give it a few more minutes and I'm sure they'll come over—otherwise, I'll do the rounds. Illium shifted so that they stood side by side, their wings held tight to their backs.

No contact. No hint of their personal relationship.

It meant nothing except that they were both highly trained warriors maintaining discipline on the city streets.

Illium pointed. "From the photos, Marco and Tanika were pretty much in the center of the shop."

Aodhan's mind was on the same path. "The blaze started with their bodies." He glanced at the scorched wall of Gino's shop. "No windows on the side facing the fire, solid concrete wall. Confirms that the containment of the fire tells us nothing."

"Yeah. Fire had nowhere to go, no more fuel to consume after it ate through Marco's shop."

Aodhan shifted to examine the scene from another angle as a woman crossed the street to approach Illium—no doubt seeing Gino chatting to him had given her the courage to do the same, but she'd still had to build herself up to it. She was tugging her oat-colored cardigan around her, her thin face pinched but determined and her gaze pinned on Illium.

Already, Aodhan could see others readying themselves to do the same, all of them wanting to impart what they knew and willing to brave their fear of powerful angels to do so, because this, what had happened here, was wrong.

Illium moved to meet the first woman, graceful and strong and with a heart that refused to stop loving even when it hurt him.

11

Illium hadn't minded talking to the shopkeepers who'd
been determined to share what little they had out of their
respect and liking for both Giulia and Marco, but he exhaled as they landed in front of a small apartment building
only a fifteen-minute walk from the shop. "The idea of facing a mother who's lost her child . . ." His entire self throbbed
as if bruised from the inside.

Aodhan squeezed his shoulder. "Unless she finds it difficult to talk to me, I can do most of the talking here."

"You sure?"

Aodhan nodded. "Your heart is too soft, Blue. I've grown
a carapace."

The words wounded Illium—because Aodhan had been
the more softhearted of them growing up, the gentle boy
with an artist's soul. It would've been easy to mourn who
his friend had been—but that wouldn't only be an insult to
all that Aodhan had become, it would mean that Illium
didn't adore this version of his childhood friend.

They were *all* pieces of Aòdhan.

Today, he just accepted Adi's offer, and they walked into

the building one after the other. Per the details Navarro had shared with Dmitri, Giulia Corvino had moved from her eleventh-floor apartment to a ground-floor residence in this building six weeks before the war.

Her home was just to the left off the main entrance.

When she opened the door, it was with no surprise in her expression, her features drawn. "Gino called me," she said in greeting, her simple dress as dark as her pain, the cardigan she wore over it so oversize that it could've fit Illium. "I've made coffee."

A sudden frown, a glimpse of her mobile features when she wasn't being suffocated by the weighted blanket of grief. "Oh dear, I'm not sure your wings will fit through this door."

"It's doable," Aodhan said. "Awkward, but doable."

Moving back from the door, Giulia did them the courtesy of going into her living room instead of watching them enter. Because it was more than awkward, and required the cautious bending of their wings. Bending that could lead to a break if they weren't careful.

Aodhan went first.

Entry into the living area is much easier, he told Illium from up ahead, as Illium navigated the door. *It's through an arch.*

Such arches had gone out of fashion in mortal homes a few decades ago, but they were far more angel-friendly than doors. However, given that the majority of mortals never interacted with angelkind on that level, they didn't build for wings.

Finally inside, he shook out his wings to ease up the cramping, then shut the door behind himself before walking into the living area. To find himself facing a sideboard on which were arranged multiple frames featuring photos of the same boy.

A chubby toddler gripping the edge of a sofa.

A smiling boy of four or five with his hands on the straps of a daypack, his face painted like a lion's.

Taller now, sitting in between a younger Giulia and a

bearded man who had the boy's face with more maturity
to it.

Photos of what looked like a beach vacation, Marco and
his father running into the surf, followed by one of the boy
holding a sports trophy, then in a graduation gown beside a
beaming Giulia, other celebrating graduates in the background. Still later, an image of the boy become a man—
long face, handsome bone structure, thick black hair, eyes
the hue of bitter chocolate. He was flashing his fangs in a
wicked grin, his hands clawed in an imitation of a vampire
out of a mortal horror movie.

"He was always smiling." Giulia straightened a frame
that didn't need to be straightened. "I told him the fang
photo was silly when he gave it to me, but oh, it made me
laugh. He hugged me until I admitted how much I loved it."

Her lips trembled in a shaky smile as she ran her fingers
over the glass of the frame. "I know some parents don't like
their kids becoming vampires, but all I could think was that
our child would live forever now. His father died so young,
and I was always scared I'd lose Marco, too. Then he became a vampire. Safe, I thought."

"He should have been," Aodhan said bluntly. "For centuries, even millennia."

Giulia blinked rapidly before rubbing her eyes with the
crumpled tissue in her hand. She, at least, had no trouble
facing or talking to Aodhan. It helped that he was inside,
with no sunlight on him—but Illium thought it was mostly
because Giulia's grief and anger had numbed her to any
other emotion.

"No mother should have to bury her child." Her voice
was a rasp. "But I had to not only bury my child, but go to
the funeral of the lovely sprite of a woman he intended to
ask to be his wife." She swallowed. "Tani—that's what everyone called her—wasn't interested in being a vampire, was
too attuned to the seasons of the world to want to alter her
place in it. He knew she'd die while he lived on . . . but she
was the one for him."

A long breath shuddered through lungs that couldn't

bear the pressure. "At least he was young enough to sire children, he told me. He'd have a piece of his love in their children and their children's children long after she was gone from this world.

"I think, if he'd met her before he was Made, he would've never applied. He was a lively boy, but his sadness over the idea of losing her one day . . . he was distraught when my husband died." She ran her hand over the cardigan, playing with a button. "Marco understood grief in a way I never wanted for my boy. I could see he was already bracing himself for Tani's loss."

Walking away from the photos after another harsh inhale, Giulia took a seat on the sofa. "I should've asked you to sit. I'm sorry. Please."

None of her furniture was suitable for angelic wings, so Illium perched on the arm of an armchair, while Aodhan chose to do the same on the sofa opposing Giulia's. "Wings," he said gently when she looked from one to the other.

"Oh," she said. "I never thought." A lopsided smile. "Never thought to have two of the Seven in my living room. Marco would've asked me for every detail, would've told his friends—and they're not bums, like I'm sure Gino told you." An exasperated shake of the head. "One's in grad school and the other just got out of a young marriage and is putting his life back together. Gino has some old-fashioned ideas, but he's got a good heart."

She rubbed at her eyes again, but it was as if she'd cried so much, her body had nothing left to give. "When I began to make noise about Marco and Tani's deaths, I didn't expect anyone to pay attention, much less two of the archangel's closest angels." A penetrating look this time, one with a serrated edge to it. "Is it because the archangel knows something?"

Aodhan shook his head. "Raphael would never protect anyone who harmed a young vampire. Quite apart from it being a matter of honor, it's a matter of maintaining vampiric discipline in the city." He decided to be blunt with

Giulia because she seemed the kind of woman who'd appreciate plain talking.

"Vampires who believe they can be killed with impunity before they've even completed their term of service will no longer be willing to behave. No city wants to have bloodlust-ridden young vampires wreaking havoc. Yes, angelkind can control them, but the damage to the ecosystem of the city would be significant—not to mention the time cost to the Tower and the Guild."

The dark veil of Giulia's grief seemed to retreat under a crisp understanding. "Yes, yes, that makes sense to me. You don't want an angel to go around breaking the rules any more than you do the vampires."

"You see why it's important we end this here, for practical reasons. But for me, this is personal. I want justice for these two innocent lives."

Giulia was silent for a long time, her eyes locked with Aodhan's, as if searching for the truth of him. "Tell me what I can do to help," she said at last.

"Navarro informed the Tower that he returned all of Marco's belongings to you."

"Yes." Giulia's nod was jerky. "He has been very kind—when I first went to plead with his people, and they told me he was injured, I thought he was brushing me off. I tried to investigate on my own, but I didn't even know where to start."

She twisted the tissue in her hand. "Then one day, the phone rings and it's Navarro. I only found out later that he was still healing when he called me, that he'd taken a near-killing blow in the war. I could tell he didn't believe me, but he said he'd pass on my concerns to the Tower's investigative team. That you're here tells me he kept his word."

"Navarro told you no lies," Aodhan confirmed. "He took it straight to Dmitri, who handed the file to a fire investigator for a first look, then to us after the investigator determined it likely to be arson."

Giulia's exhale was jagged.

"Do you have the items the unwanted suitor gifted Marco?" Illium asked. "Small or big. A letter, a card, an actual physical item, all of it will be useful."

"I couldn't go through the boxes," Giulia whispered. "I just couldn't bear it. It felt like truly accepting he was gone. Any packages she left for him on my balcony, I handed to him without opening, so I don't even know what was in them." Rising, she motioned them to follow. "It's all in here."

They managed to get through the narrow entrance opposite the arch and down a short hall to a room at the back, which had a window, a bed, and a spotlessly clean carpet. An empty vase sat on the windowsill, while someone had strung fairy lights around the top of the ceiling.

"This is my guest room." Her arms around her thin frame, her hug so tight it was as if she was trying to hold herself together. "I could've shifted to a one-bedroom when I moved out of our old apartment, especially with Marco living at his angel's residence, but I wanted him to know he could always come home. So I got the two-bedroom, and after moving me in, he put up his lights again. Wherever I lived, he used to stay at least one day a month with me, on his days off from his duties.

"Later, he brought Tani with him, and she was such a sweet girl, she'd refuse to spend the night one out of every two times. 'This is Mama and Marco time,' she'd say." Giulia's voice hitched. "I loved her, too, was looking forward to having her as my daughter-in-law, to babysitting the grandbabies they planned to give me."

A trembling laugh. "I was even looking forward to the unusual names I was sure she'd give them, ready to have a little Leaf or Sunshine running around. She was so innocent, Tani. I don't mean she didn't see reality. She did. But she also saw wonder in the everyday world, made it feel new and beautiful."

Like Kaia, Aodhan found himself saying to Illium, because Illium's mortal lover was a part of his history, not to be swept under the rug or willfully forgotten. *I might not have been her biggest fan, but I did appreciate her ability to find delight in the smallest wildflower, or in the perfect blue of a cloudless sky.*

I'm glad she had the life she did, Illium responded, an affection in his voice that was akin to what you might feel toward a distant but good friend. *Full of children and grand-children. I couldn't bear to think about that for a long time, but now I look back and I'm happy that the girl I loved once lived a life awash in love, including grandchildren who adored her for her sense of wonder. Tanika deserved the same chance.*

"Is it possible that Tanika was the main target?" Aodhan asked aloud. "We don't wish to fall into the error of assumptions that blind us."

"The only enemy she had was the woman obsessed with Marco." Giulia's skin flushed, her neck stiff with anger. "Otherwise, she was just a sweet normal girl who loved her parents, loved Marco, and had a job she enjoyed at a fashion boutique."

Aodhan made a note to double-check that view with Tanika's intimates, because there were countless things a woman wouldn't have shared with her future mother-in-law. But given the location of the murders, that Marco was the fulcrum and the reason remained the strongest possibility.

"Those are Marco's things." She pointed to a stack of four neatly taped boxes.

"That's all?" Illium asked.

Giulia's smile was faint. "He wasn't much of a collector of things. Not even at the age when most kids collect rocks or toys or special cards. He was content with just one—but it'd be one that was unique or sentimental. With clothes, he stuck to black. 'It all matches *and* looks amazing,' he'd say when I scolded him over it.

"He got even worse after his Making. Said he'd seen a couple of overstuffed houses when he visited older vampires who'd become mentors to him, and while he respected them as people, he had no intention of spending eternity the same way."

She shook her head. "I told him he was in danger of living in a monk's cell, but he laughed and hugged me off my feet and said never, because he'd always have the colorful blanket I made for him, and the photos of the people he loved, and the fairy lights he liked to string up wherever he slept. 'I don't need much more than that, Mama.'" Tears choked her voice on that final sentence.

Aodhan, despite his complex emotions when it came to touch, felt compelled to take her hand. It was soft, worn with years of life in a way the hands of immortals never became. She clenched her fingers around his, and in the delicate warmth of her, he sensed her mortality like a flicker at the corner of his vision.

How do you bear it, Blue? he asked, not for the first time. *These mortal lives are so fragile.*

Illium's eyes met his, a tender empathy in the gold. *The day I distance myself from mortals is the day I lose a piece of that thing mortals call a soul. I don't want to live in a walled city, my heart protected from bruises . . . and from the wonder of knowing extraordinary people who exist only for a single moment in time.*

Love overwhelmed Aodhan in a storm surge.

Illium's courage and grit were legendary, but this? This was an altogether different kind of valor.

He curled his fingers around Giulia's, careful of his strength . . . and suddenly aware that touching her had caused no subconscious recoil inside him, no flinch. He didn't know if it was because he was healing on a level deeper than he understood, or if it was because of Giulia. Her love for her son, her refusal to just accept his death, her willingness to go to Marco's dangerously powerful angel himself for answers—they all showcased a spirit as extraordinary as Illium's.

"I won't rest until I find out who did this to your son and his beloved," he promised her. "It doesn't matter how long it takes—I'm immortal. I will find an answer for you."

"I believe you," Giulia whispered. "And I'm glad Marco and his Tani have you in their corner."

"May we take these boxes with us? It'll be easier to examine them in a larger space. We'll bring it all back, I give you my word."

"Yes. But if you find anything that obsessed murderess gave him that he kept for some reason, then get rid of it after you use it to find her. I don't want it polluting the rest of Marco's belongings."

Aodhan inclined his head in a small nod before releasing her hand.

Given the space constraints in the apartment, he and Illium decided it'd be too difficult for them to maneuver both their wings and the boxes out at the same time, so they told Giulia they were calling friends to assist, then stepped outside her apartment to wait close to the main doors. She came with them . . . and squinted as the weak sunlight that poured through the doors hit Aodhan, transforming him into dazzling white fire.

Before he could apologize, she gave him a smile incandescent in its joy. "Marco'd be so proud of me right now," she said. "Standing here with the angel who always flies so high that mortals hardly get a glimpse of him. Hold on while I go get a pair of sunglasses."

Aodhan looked after her as she vanished back into the apartment. "She is extraordinary."

Illium, who stood across from him, the open doorway between them, smiled. "I think, Adi, you're about to make another mortal friend."

The thought was terrifying for all the pain it would one day entail . . . but no less beautiful for it.

12

"That's better." Giulia walked out wearing black sunglasses and with a plate in hand. "Here, I wasn't thinking before. I hand-make these savory pastries. Marco's favorites even after he became a vampire. He'd eat one half a day because that was all his system could handle so soon after his Making, but he'd finish them.

"Now I have too many when I bake but I can't stop. Eat, eat." A frown at Illium that was pure maternal disapproval. "Especially you. You never used to be that skinny."

So they stood there and ate several of the little pastries heavy with mozzarella and finely sliced meat and other things that all added up to delicious. When Janvier and Ransom walked inside after pulling up on their motorbikes from two different sides of the city, the vampire and the guild hunter cleared off the plate.

"I wish I could process more," Janvier groaned after he'd finished his second one. "*Merde*, but no one ever told me how much I'd miss eating when I became a vampire." His Cajun accent was thicker than it had been prior to his recent visit to his family in Louisiana, the moss green of his eyes languid, and his brown leather jacket soft with how long he'd had it.

Illium had met his family, the vampire having invited him along to more than one *fais do-do* over the time they'd known one another. Descendants of Janvier's adored little sisters, that family was a rowdy bunch that absorbed people into it with a warmth that was disarming. Illium had ended up full of Cajun moonshine, good food, and plenty of numbers slipped into his pocket.

Shy, Janvier's family wasn't, he thought with an inward grin.

"Marco felt the same." Giulia's smile was real and all the more poignant for the agony written in the swollen grittiness of her eyes. "He had a little book where he'd write out all his favorite things to eat, and then he'd schedule them. Said he had no time for bad food. Only the best. These were in permanent rotation." The last words were a near-whisper.

"I don't suppose you sell them?" Ransom said as he finished the last bite of his. "I'd love to take a box home for my wife and our little boy." A charming grin. "I'd be the favorite forever."

Giulia's whole face softened. "I'll make a new batch for you." She waved off his surprised response. "It's so nice to have young men around again. Marco's friends, they always filled up my house. They still come, but . . . we're all so sad." A rough exhale. "We don't know what to do with each other without him."

Turning toward her apartment at that, she invited Janvier and Ransom inside to shift the boxes. Once the two had carried them outside, Aodhan took one, Illium the next, and they flew them to the Tower before returning for the remaining two. Ransom and Janvier were still there, waiting just outside the main entrance to the building—a position from where they could keep an eye on the boxes.

"Giulia got a call from a friend." While Ransom still had long hair he wore in a queue, was sleek with muscle, and had weapons close at hand like any hunter, his eyes bore a few more lines at the corners than they had when Illium had first met Elena's hunter friend.

His new laugh lines, however, far outnumbered those.

The other man had fallen in love, sired a son with his beloved wife, Nyree, and was content in his skin as he hadn't been back then.

Janvier wore the same air of contentment. He'd always been laid-back with strong family ties, but after winning the heart of the hunter with whom he'd been in love since the moment he'd met her, Janvier was just happier. While he remained as unhurried in speech and manner as always, his eyes lit up when his Ashblade was nearby.

"There's my *cher*," he'd murmur, before strolling over to talk her into a kiss.

Illium wanted that kind of settled forever with Aodhan, the kind that sounded boring on paper . . . but that was multiplying laugh lines and eyes that glowed with happiness, picking up treats just because and coming home to arms beloved today, tomorrow, and all the days to come.

But his and Adi's ground was rocky yet, their path uncharted.

"Thanks for swinging by when I called," he said to both men.

Janvier shot him a lazy salute while Ransom straddled his bike, his arms braced on the handlebars. "We were discussing putting the word out on the streets about Marco and Tanika."

Illium would've been a fool to turn down the offer. Between the two and their associates, they had the gray heart of the city covered. "Appreciate that. We're working with limited material."

"We'll send you anything we discover." Rising to a seated position, Ransom bumped fists with Illium, nodded at Aodhan.

To Illium's surprise, Aodhan held out a fist, too.

Eyebrow raised, Ransom bumped his fist to Aodhan's, then inspected his own knuckles with a frown. "I half expected the shine to rub off . . . Sparkle."

While Janvier tried to hide a laugh by ducking his head, Aodhan made a rumbling sound in his throat and turned to Illium. "Sleep with one eye open, Bluebell," he warned solemnly.

"Smoke'll protect me," Illium replied as the other two laughed, even as his heart kicked at this further sign that Aodhan was dead serious about overcoming his dislike of touch on every level. Adi was *done* with the past, would allow no nightmare to anchor him in time.

The realization opened a door inside Illium he hadn't even known was locked.

Despite the pastries they'd inhaled, they were both hungry by the time they got the last of the boxes into a large conference room at the Tower. Leaving Marco's belongings there for the time being, they locked the door, then headed out to one of Illium's favorite rooftop vendors. The morning clouds had drifted farther inland, New York once more doused in sunlight.

Spotting the crowd around the vendor from above, Aodhan said, *We eat on the bridge.*

I'll get the hot dogs, Illium responded at once—because there was a big difference between one-on-one contact and being stared at by fifty people who weren't used to you.

I should— Aodhan began in a teeth-gritted way.

Nope. I'm putting my foot down. Illium wove steel into his voice. *You've never liked crowds, Adi. Not since you were a kid. Don't torment yourself just to prove a point.*

Aodhan's glance held not anger, but relief intermingled with affection. *That's an avatar I haven't seen for a while. Ball-busting Illium.*

Illium bowed even as his entire body melted at the open affection in Aodhan's tone. *Now stay put and look pretty while I—*

He dove out of the way before Aodhan could throw a bolt of power at him, was still grinning when he landed.

Several of the junior wing he often trained were waiting

for orders, and it ended up an impromptu gathering after he'd placed his and Adi's orders. He'd been planning to drop by their training area later today regardless, but it was good to see them whole and healed from their wounds.

"It's a plan," he said when one of them suggested a proper gathering after another member of the wing returned from the Refuge. "I'll bring the moonshine." He rose up into the air to the raucous sound of their cheers.

After he'd handed Aodhan his food, the two of them flew to one of the massive bridges that spanned the Hudson, and took a seat on the top girders, where New Yorkers had become used to seeing the two of them. It was also far enough up that no one could stare at them in close proximity.

As for binoculars, neither of them was worried about that. Aodhan was so dazzling in this kind of light that he basically couldn't be seen, and sitting close to him obliterated Illium's image, too—though he didn't much care if people looked.

They ate in quiet, basking in the sun, just watching the water and the cars.

No pressure to talk. No pressure to do anything.

No peace was as deep as the one he found with Adi. His best friend had always had the gift of quiet, could spend hours, even days, working on his art in silence. But until the kidnapping, Aodhan's silence had welcomed Illium in— he'd never closed himself off even at his most intense. He'd look over now and then to where Illium sat polishing his weapons, or doing exercises to increase his strength, or reading lessons designed to take him from simple warrior to wing commander and beyond, smile, then go back to his work.

Illium, in turn, had never interrupted him except when he'd seen Aodhan work too long without fuel. Aodhan would take the food from him with an absent-minded glance, eat it without noticing what it was, and at some point much later, Illium would get a "Thanks. What did I just eat?" as his brain caught up to what his body had been doing.

It had always made Illium grin. "Jellied squid," he'd say. "No, wait, I think it was crushed grasshopper sprinkled on a bed of pungent river moss."

This . . . it felt like them again in a way Illium couldn't explain to anyone else. He just knew that the long-locked door hadn't only been unlocked, it was gone, destroyed from the inside out.

But tempting as it was to linger, they were both too invested in Giulia's anguish, and the lust and obsession-driven murder of two young lovers. And Illium, he was viscerally focused on what this case meant to Aodhan. Would it dredge up memories better left forgotten? Would it cause harm or do good? There was no way to know until it happened; the only thing Illium could do was fly by his side.

That afternoon, it was to Tanika's distraught family.

"All she wanted was a normal life," her mother sobbed through her tears when they confirmed that the deaths were apt to have been murder, her ebony skin ashen. "A husband, couple of kids, a small place of their own. A nice apartment with a window box where she could plant flowers in the spring. She was a happy girl, our Tani, content with a normal life, not always searching for more."

"Not like Marco." Tanika's father's face was flushed red under the bluish paleness of his skin, his jaw working. "This thing, this evil? It came from him."

His barrel of a chest heaved. "I got no problem with Giulia. She lost her boy, too. But *he* chose that life, chose to go into a world that isn't for mortals. Chasing immortal life, chasing future things so far away that it don't matter to no one now. He should've never taken my daughter into that world with him."

"She had her own mind, Stavros." His wife's chiding was soft, the hand she curled around his bunched biceps gentle. "When was the last time she asked your approval on a boy, hmm?"

Stavros closed his palm over her fingers, the back of his hand nicked and scarred by life. "I told her, didn't I? That she shouldn't date a vampire, that it would all end in tears?

Why didn't she listen, Norma?" A roar of anger . . . but below the surface rage was a shivering pain that was tears contained in amber. "She was so small when I held her after she was born. Remember?"

"I remember. That funny smile they told us was gas, but she was always smiley, wasn't she?"

Stavros's nod was jagged, his hand tight on his wife's.

Unlike many Illium had met over the years, these two had been glued tighter by their loss. But though they had love aplenty for their child, they had nothing to give Aodhan and Illium when it came to their daughter's murder—just their certainty that the trouble had come from Marco.

"She was a good girl," her mother said. "A bit too 'head in the clouds,' as her nonna used to say, but it just made her all the more fun to be with. She was never into anything dangerous—her favorite thing was to go to those fairs where they dress up like in medieval times."

"She had no enemies," Stavros reiterated.

Tanika's friends were of the same mindset. Her coworkers, too.

"We get creepers sometimes," one of the other clerks at the fashion boutique said. "You know, men who come inside here not to buy for their ladies, but to chat up the clerks and customers, or fondle the lingerie." Her lip curled. "But Tani had what we called her Stavros side—no-nonsense, exactly like her dad. Don't think he ever figured that out, though; to him, she was just his baby girl."

A wet laugh. "But I never saw a creeper approach Tani—and just so I'm not giving you the wrong impression, we don't get that many overall. Maybe one or two every six months." A pause. "I miss her so much. She just . . . she had this happy inside her that infected everyone around her. You know?"

Despite the coworker's belief that Tani hadn't been bothered by a "creeper," Illium asked for any saved security footage. He wasn't expecting a positive response, not given the passage of time—but they got lucky. The owner was a cyber-packrat, and the war had helped with retention, too.

"We were online-only until last month," the lanky man told them. "Our building was vaporized in the war, and shops weren't a priority rebuild, not like hospitals and schools." A smile accompanied by a damp sheen to the eyes. "If you see the archangel, please say thank you. We figured we'd be forgotten in a war between archangels."

Illium knew the man was referring to the system set in place to ensure that those who had to wait for a rebuild didn't lose their homes or businesses in the interim.

"Most of us have more money than we'll spend in our entire immortal lifetimes," Dmitri had said when they'd been working on the post-war plan. "No point in allowing parts of the city to turn derelict—or to have the same happen to the people who make it what it is."

Not every archangel's second would've said the same. And not every archangel would've agreed with his statement. But meeting Elena had forever altered the trajectory of Raphael's life; there'd been a time when Illium was scared of who his archangel was becoming under the twin forces of power and age.

He'd also known he could do nothing to stop it—he was too young, didn't have that relationship with Raphael. Dmitri did, but Dmitri's dark past, of which Illium had only now gained a true glimpse, had put him on a similarly cold and violent path. Then had come Elena and her stubborn mortal heart and an unstoppable cataract of change.

This was the end result—a vibrant post-war city with a people who were blood loyal to their archangel. "I'll pass on your words to the archangel," Illium said to the owner. "Thank you for your cooperation."

"We loved Tani." The damp was a thickness in the other man's throat now. "She was just one of those people who made the world a brighter place."

Illium's fingers curled into his palm, his neck stiff with tension.

"I'll go over the security footage," Aodhan told him after they left the shop. "I know you want to see Catalina and she'll be waiting for you."

Despite Illium's desperate need to watch over Aodhan—and wouldn't that piss Adi off if Illium said it aloud?—he didn't demur. Catalina was an important part of his life, one half of a treasured friendship that had created an enduring groove in his heart.

At times, Illium could still feel the weight of Lorenzo's coffin as he helped carry his friend to his final resting place. So heavy he'd been, when in life, he'd been light on his feet, a man who'd twirled Catalina into a dance while flour dusted the air and Catalina laughed and told him she was halfway through mixing a batch.

Illium, tell him to be sensible!

When Catalina went, too . . . Illium's heart would hurt for a long time.

"I'm glad you've gotten to know her," he said to Aodhan, his throat dry. "I don't want to be the only one who remembers her in the eons to come." Mortal lives went by so fast, ancestors remembered in the heart for but a few generations. "I wish you could've known Lorenzo, too. So many hours we sat together over a glass, talking about nothing and everything."

He rubbed a fisted hand over the aching in his chest . . . then spoke a truth he could no longer shy away from, not if they were to build a relationship honest and deep. "You were gone for so long, lost to me in a way I didn't even understand until you started to come back. Without Lorenzo and Cat . . .

"Lorenzo knew my sorrows and my joys, as I knew his. Catalina understood my pain and my triumphs, as I understood hers. Lorenzo was mortal but his shoulders were as strong as yours or mine, able to bear the weight of what I entrusted to him. And Cat? You've met her. You know."

He'd felt disloyal at the start, that he was building a friendship so profound with anyone but Aodhan, but after a while, it would've been a disloyalty to Lorenzo, Catalina, *and* Aodhan to compare them in any way. Each friendship was its own living, breathing joy. And Aodhan . . . his Adi . . . was stitched into his very being.

Aodhan shifted so that his wing just brushed Illium's, the whisper of contact an act of painful intimacy. "I'm happy you had them," he said, his voice rough with emotion. "And I mourn that I can't tell Lorenzo how much it means to me that he was there for you at a time I couldn't be."

His best friend's expression turned stark. "Catalina will break my heart to pieces one day but to know her is a gift. Go, Blue. Spend the time with her."

13

Aodhan's heart had birthed a new crack in the past few minutes, and it only grew and settled into permanency as he watched Illium take flight, a stunning blue butterfly of courage and power. "Thank you, Lorenzo," he whispered to the spirit of the man who'd been there for Illium at a time in his life when he'd needed a friend true and faithful.

As for Catalina, bathed in the warmth of her bright, beautiful . . . and achingly transient mortal flame, he'd already said what he had to say in person. And as he'd sat with her, he'd felt the weight of the sorrow to come—because Catalina deserved to live eons, her heart and honor a match to any revered immortal.

But Cat didn't want to be immortal, and so she would go too soon. In doing so, she'd leave behind two angels who would miss her friendship and wisdom all their days.

You were gone for so long . . .

Aodhan and Illium, they'd never stopped being friends, not even during the worst times. Illium had refused to allow it. But there had been ruptures. They both knew it. Today, by exposing one of the deepest to the light of day, Illium had given Aodhan hope.

"I can take the truth, Blue," he murmured to that dazzling dot in the sky. "All of it. No more hiding. *Ever.*"

14

Catalina spotted Illium the instant he landed outside the little bakery in Harlem.

Her face—far more lined now than when they'd first met, but still as beautiful—became a small sun. Her embrace was warm and strong and *her*. He hugged her as tight, wrapping her in his wings and wishing he could stop her body from aging, time from passing—but even if he could, she wouldn't want it. No, Cat was ready to join Lorenzo when it was her time, her faith in a world beyond the veil unshakable.

Do angels have gods, Illium? Do you believe in a life after this existence?

One of many questions she'd asked him during those long nights they'd all spent together around the table in the back of the bakery, her curiosity opening his eyes to facets of existence he'd never considered.

"Go sit," she said today after they drew apart. "I have a big order about to get picked up. We'll talk after."

As familiar in this place as he was at the Tower, he

slipped through the swinging door to the kitchen. It was Lorenzo who'd installed that door soon after they first became friends, so it'd be wide enough for Illium to pass through with ease.

The kitchen was quiet and clean, all the cooking done for the day, the steel countertop spotless. Catalina's granddaughter and baker-in-training was also gone, her after-school hours in the bakery limited by her grandmother's decree. Soon as the clock hit five p.m., off went the apron.

"One day," Catalina had told Illium, "our Adriana'll do bigger things. She thinks she wants this bakery and her heart is in a good place, but that child has a bright mind and dreams big enough to power the moon. She'll need more, and for that, she needs to focus on her studies."

While Catalina finished out front, Illium set about making himself a coffee and Catalina her favorite fruit tisane doctored with a liberal dose of honey. He had both ready by the time he heard the ring of the bell over the shop door.

It sounded again a minute later, was followed by the click of the lock. He imagined he could almost hear the flick of the sign being switched to CLOSED.

Catalina was pressing a hand to her lower back when she walked in. "Why I do this, I don't know." She groaned. "I should be at home, watching *Presa del Cazador*, not on my feet all day."

It gave Illium great delight that Elena's most muttered-about show had not only been renewed again, but now had a Spanish spin-off, complete with a "hunter" who spent more time romancing vampire beauties than he did tracking.

He loved watching it with Catalina, so they could cackle together.

As for Catalina, he'd offered to fund his friend's entire telenovela retirement—one as luxurious as she wanted. Cruises across the oceans, travels around the world, as much gentle adventure as she could take. Because while he didn't have the wealth of those millennia of age, he was a senior member of an archangel's team—and he'd been working since the day they'd let him. He had more money than he could ever imagine spending.

"Ah, Illium," Catalina had said with a poignant smile, "I don't need to work. Lorenzo did our investments, made sure I'd be all right. I work inside this bakery because I loved Lorenzo here. He's in the walls, in the recipes we created together, in the memories at that old table."

Recollections untold in the brown of her eyes, her once dark hair now liberally laced with threads of silver. "*Mi corazón*, he'd call me while wrapping his arms around me from behind while I was trying to knead dough. I'd scold him for the interruption, but I never minded—and he knew. How could I leave him?"

Today, however, seeing that she was walking more stiffly than before he'd gone to China, Illium said, "You should rest."

He pulled out a chair for her at the small table tucked into the far-left corner, then placed her tea in front of her, his coffee on the other side. "Lorenzo wouldn't want you here only because you built this place with him."

He understood the true extent of her tiredness when she didn't immediately shake her head. "I saved you a box of treats," she said instead. "I knew you'd come today. It's in that top cupboard."

After retrieving the box, he put it between them, then selected a cookie dotted with sugar crystals. "I'm serious. You and Lorenzo always planned to travel. He wouldn't want you to give that up—I'm sure his ghost will follow you wherever you go, regardless. He was always possessive."

Throwing back her head at his scowl, Catalina laughed that husky laugh that was of the sensual young woman she'd once been. Illium saw that in her still, this friend of his whose outer self had softened and become more rounded—but what did the outside matter? Unlike her family, he knew that well before she'd been their *mamá* or *tía* or *abuela*, she'd been Lorenzo's Cat.

To Illium, she always would be.

"Oh, Illium, he was, wasn't he?" she said, her laugh lingering in the curve of the lush lips Lorenzo had so loved, a dance of light in her eyes. "So good-natured, but that man could turn dark when a customer dared flirt with me." A playful shake of her head. "Never with you, though—and you were the worst flirt of all!"

"Because he knew that *I* knew you were madly in love with him. You didn't even notice my beautiful eyelashes." As she snorted, Illium nudged the box toward her. "Eat the one with dark chocolate. That's your favorite."

"No, today all I want is pasta."

"I'll make it for you." Thanks to her and Lorenzo's liking for the dish, it was one of the few at which he wasn't only serviceable but excellent. "Give me a few minutes to get the ingredients from Levi." The grocer down the street had started his shop not long after Catalina and Lorenzo, was familiar with Illium.

When Catalina said, "Fresh tomatoes and garlic," instead of waving away his offer, he knew she was having one of those days when she *missed* her husband and didn't want to do so in the company of her daughter's family, who lived just above her apartment and would be expecting her for dinner. They adored her, and she loved them in turn.

Tonight, however, she wanted to spend time with a friend who had known Lorenzo as a young man, who had drunk mead late into the night with him and Catalina while they played cards and laughed and were young together.

"Call Sofia," he said, kissing her on the cheek. "Tell her you're having a date with me."

Though her lips curved again, her eyes now held an old and worn grief.

Leaving her to inform her daughter that she wouldn't be home for dinner, he ducked out to grab the supplies.

"Pasta today, huh?" the white-haired grocer said as he checked out the items. "I tell you what, I have fresh basil in my planter out back. I'll give you a bit. Trust me, it's delicious."

While waiting for Levi to return, Illium reached out to Aodhan with his mind. *I won't be home for dinner, Adi— I'm eating with Catalina. She's missing Lorenzo tonight. Will you look after Smoke?*

Of course I will, Aodhan said at once. *Ask her about the meal I cooked for her.*

You never told me you cooked for her!

I decided to keep it a surprise.

It's always the quiet ones, Illium said in a grim tone, but he was grinning. *Are you staying in?*

I just got a message from Demarco saying he's back in the city and on his own as his beloved is at a mortal wedding function for women only. I'll invite him for dinner.

Have fun. It made Illium's heart overflow with happiness that Aodhan had allowed this friendship into his life, even though with it came the promise of future pain—for like Catalina, the irreverent Demarco had no desire to live for eternity. *Don't let him lead you astray into a tattoo.*

I'm more interested in which part of his body he's talked his mate into marking—she believes him a pristine canvas and, to date, has only ever agreed to tattoo him thrice. The first was her name on a part of his anatomy I have no desire to see, the second is the guild mark on his inner left forearm, and the third I'll see tonight—he assures me it's in safe visual territory.

As Illium chuckled, Aodhan said, *Enjoy your time with Catalina, Blue.* A caress in the words that was a kiss against Illium's mind. *Smoke and I will be here when you return.*

"So," he said to Catalina once he was back in her kitchen, "Aodhan says he cooked for you."

Catalina put both hands to her heart with a gasp. "So beautiful he is, Illium. Like a star fallen to earth—and such compassion in that heart. It pours out of him brighter than his physical beauty. But"—a groan, her hands going to her face—"he cannot make a pasta!"

Illium snorted, his shoulders shaking so hard that he had

to grip the counter to keep himself upright. "None of us are perfect, Catalina."

"I ate it." A whisper. "I couldn't hurt his feelings, he was so proud of his gift to me."

The idea of two people he loved being so thoughtful of each other warmed Illium to the very depths of his being. "I'll only tell him the terrible truth after you're with Lorenzo," he promised with a wink. "Then I'll teach him how to make proper pasta, like you taught me."

"I never spoke to your friend before you were in China." Catalina took a long sip of her tea, sighing with her eyes closed as the heat sank into her bones. "Then he started to come in for the *alfajores* for you, and what could I do but fall in love with him? He's so distractingly beautiful that it's easy to overlook the tender heart inside, but I see it. That man knows how to love."

Her eyes drilled into Illium.

Who felt his cheeks begin to redden. Of all the people to figure this out, he hadn't expected it to be Catalina.

"I knew it!" Catalina slapped her hand on the table. "The way he speaks about you, and now you, looking like a kitten that got its tail stuck in a door. Why are you trying to keep it a secret?"

"It's new, Catalina." Illium chopped up tomatoes for the sauce, having already pulled out the spices Catalina kept stocked for just this purpose. "We've been friends forever— he was my first true friend and he will always be my best friend. The rest . . . it's . . ."

"You're terrified of destroying your friendship," Catalina said bluntly. "Don't look so surprised. I've been around a long time." Another burst of laughter. "For a mortal anyway."

Illium found himself wondering once again at the wisdom of some mortals who'd lived such a short life in comparison to his own. Was it only that angels were designed to mature at a far slower rate, or was it that mortals were designed to do the opposite, their brain and heart cells conscious of the inexorable passage of time in a way that made every moment portentous?

"Do you want to go back to how it was?" Catalina asked with the forthrightness of a friend who'd known him for decades—though she hadn't always spoken to him thus. She'd been a touch reticent at the start, though he'd never minded whatever she said to him, but it was as if she'd said to hell with filters after a certain birthday and he loved her all the more for it.

His answer was instinctive. "No. I—I can feel who we can be, like this huge and glorious sunrise on the horizon, if we can only make it there." The need to stand inside that sunrise hurt, it was so intense.

Instead of asking him what was stopping him, Catalina paused to sip her tea and to think over his words. He busied himself with reducing the sauce.

"I suppose," she said at last, "in such a long life, my friend, this decision could impact a thousand years."

"More," he whispered. "All the eons of my existence, Catalina. He's the only one I've ever loved or will ever love this way." A simple, inevitable truth. "Our healer refers to him as my heart's mirror, and I as his."

Pressing a hand to her heart, the gold of her wedding band catching the light, Catalina blinked rapidly. "What a thing you say, and yes, I understand." A roughness to her voice. "My Lorenzo was my heart's mirror. I had a knowing with him that I've never experienced with any other my whole life. That comes only once, Illium. Only once. Even for an immortal, I think this must be true."

"That's why it's so precious and so terrifying." Pressing both hands to the edge of the counter, he pushed back, his spine rigid. "I freeze at times, not knowing what to do—and I've never been like that with us. If anything, I've been the one who takes chances, gets us into risky spots." He wouldn't speak of Aodhan's past, wouldn't share what his friend chose not to share with everyone.

But Catalina surprised him again. "That night he cooked

the worst pasta in the history of pasta? He told me things. Enough to make me understand that he has no idea of court-ship beyond that of light, youthful things." Her eyes held his. "He hasn't had small loves to prepare for this big love, and he never played the games youths play in matters of *amore*."

Illium's heart kicked.

Leaving the sauce to simmer and thicken, he dragged out a chair and spun it around to straddle it. "He told you?" Aodhan never told anyone his story, not really.

Catalina closed her hand with its strong baker's fingers and fine mortal skin over his. "For you. He told me because he wanted my advice. He says I'm the oldest friend of yours that he knows—I don't know if he meant that in time, for I'm sure you have far longer friendships." A quick smile. "You're like Lorenzo, constantly making friends."

"But none like this," he rasped, devastated to realize all over again that this friendship wouldn't follow him into his next century of life. "None like you and Lorenzo."

Her hand squeezed his with conscious gentleness, as if he was the more fragile of the two of them. "Living forever isn't all roses, is it, Illium?" A tender smile, the age in her as vast as those of the Ancients he'd met, even though such was a thing impossible. "Aodhan told me so that we could talk without walls between us. He's such a *good* man, com-passion and a painfully deep ability to love woven inside the fabric of him, but a man bruised in ways I don't think either of you understand."

"I see the warrior, and I see his stubborn spirit, and I want to believe him healed," Illium admitted. "It hurts me to think he might not be, that he's still in pain."

Catalina frowned. "I'm not sure it's as conscious as that. He *is* strong and determined and I think he has conquered his demons—but only the ones he can see."

Illium thought of Aodhan's flinch at a loving touch, and at how appalled he'd been at his own inability to stride past that ugliness.

I conquered this.

Such anguish in that statement, but there'd been confusion, too, a sense of the ground becoming unstable under his feet.

"There are softer bruises that hide beneath the scars," Catalina said. "I think the problem with the two of you is that you're moving too fast. The touch on the hand comes first, Illium, not the passionate kiss. Those soft bruises hurt terribly—let them fade while you seduce him."

I want this for us. The soft and the playful and the dance before the dance.

Illium decided then and there that he'd find a way to make their date happen while not taking Aodhan away from Marco and Tanika. Because this case, at this time, meant far more to Aodhan than anyone but those closest to him would ever understand.

Illium would not get in the way of that.

Neither would he steal from Aodhan all the experiences his best friend had missed while locked in amber at a time when Illium was playing the games of a young angel with those who were inclined to play with him. However, he had no fear that Aodhan wanted to experience those things with anyone but Illium—he'd had myriad offers and approaches since his initial arrival in New York, and had no doubt fielded many more in China.

Truth was that his best friend had always been far more judicious in his relationships than Illium, no matter if it was friendship or a bond more intimate. He took time to make his decisions and stuck true to them—and got irritated if questioned over those choices.

Illium was the one he wanted; on that score he'd been clear.

The touch on the hand comes first, Illium, not the passionate kiss.

Lifting Catalina's hand to his lips, he pressed a kiss to her knuckles. And though it was his wont to make a joke, be playful, he held her gaze and said, "I have to get this right, Catalina." Even if fear was a constant whisper at the back of his brain.

Catalina's smile was gentle. "Oh, *mi amor*. Don't you see? You *don't* have to be perfect, don't have to get everything right. Not with the person who is your heart's mirror. All you have to do is love."

15

A day after they'd spoken to Tanika's parents, Aodhan walked toward Illium's Tower suite as the smudged curtain of night settled over the city. He felt as if he was stuck in mud as far as the case went, his body and mind grimy from even this tangential association with a being who thought they could own another, treat them as an object.

You are mine, pretty one. Always mine. Only *mine. I have branded you.*

He'd never told Illium about Sachieri holding a glowing red iron to his chest, searing her motif of ownership into it in an agony of scalding flame that burned his nerves and slapped blackness over his vision.

Not just once.

Over and over again, each time his immortal cells healed the scar. She either hadn't been clever enough to learn the technique that gave Jason his permanent tattoo, or she'd just enjoyed hurting Aodhan because he refused to say what she wanted to hear, refused to give her words of love and devotion.

Say it! Say it! You are mine! That is your only future.

Confess your love, my pretty one, and I'll make it nice for you here, gilded with your every desire.

The only desire Aodhan had had was for freedom.

The sire knew about the brandings—he'd torn open Sachieri's and Bathar's minds, uncovered every horrific detail, and then he'd punished the two until there could be no more punishment. But he'd never told Illium of that horror, as aware as Aodhan that their Bluebell's heart could take no more.

The last brand had already healed by the time he was found—and even Sachieri had begun to realize that she was pushing him closer and closer to true death. Only . . . in his mind, the torture hadn't stopped after his rescue; he'd woken up screaming to the burn of a searing brand day after day in the Medica.

The irony was that he'd refused to scream for Sachieri. Weak, starved of light, his wings useless, and his strength stolen, his reactions had been all he could control in that hellhole. He'd gone inside his head, to a place where no one could hurt him.

And he'd stayed there after his period of pain madness in the Medica.

But there was to be no more retreating for him—he'd made that decision after he finally realized the damage he'd done to himself and to others around him. Most of all to Illium, the man who had loved him even when Aodhan hadn't loved himself.

Wanting to see his best friend and lover, he opened Illium's door and called out his name.

Silence greeted him, no Smoke bounding over to examine him and decide if his presence was acceptable.

Shoulders dropping, he closed the door and went to his apartment instead. Illium wouldn't mind if Aodhan waited in his suite, but Aodhan would only miss him more if surrounded by his things, his scent embedded into the walls.

The door opened to the low murmur of music and the golden glow of candlelight. It sparked off him with a muted softness that was sunlight turned liquid. He'd liked the time of candlelight, appreciated its gentleness, and now his entire living area—which flowed into an open-plan kitchen—glowed with it.

"Blue," he murmured when Illium moved out of the candlelight clad in a simple cream tunic open at the neck, and jeans, his feet bare. "What are you up to?"

Instead of answering, Illium cupped one side of his face and nuzzled him. The other man's hair was soft against Aodhan's cheek, the scent of him so familiar that it made a sob catch in Aodhan's throat at the sense of coming home. "You look tired, Adi."

"Body and heart," he admitted, because this was Illium. "I also need a shower." Turning his face into Illium's palm as he put his own hand on the other man's hip to hold him close, he pressed a kiss to it.

"I've already prepared everything for you." His fingers wove through Aodhan's hair, his gaze tender. "I had my spy watching for you, so the water should already be at the perfect scalding temperature you like."

"Really?" Once, Aodhan would've been annoyed; now he felt caressed by the love that Illium gave so generously. "You asked Vivek to track me?"

"Only when you were within visual sight." Taking his hand, Illium tugged him to the bathing chamber. "He's always keeping everything in sight anyway. He thinks I'm playing a prank on you."

"Where's your little shadow?" Aodhan had become used to Smoke pouncing at him in welcome.

"Hanging out with Vivek while he does night shift. I figured Smoke and candles weren't a good mix." A brush of fingers against Aodhan's jaw. "Tonight, we play, Adi. I didn't think you'd feel like flying to the Catskills, so I brought the picnic to you."

Body and spirit sighing at the pleasure of being here, with this man, Aodhan let his lover draw him to the bathing chamber he'd bedecked with candles, in the center of which would normally sit an enormous tub designed for a being with wings. But Aodhan hadn't been able to bear baths since his abduction.

He didn't mind diving into ponds and lakes and the ocean, even enjoyed it. But a tub . . . a bath was too small, too tight, the walls too close even when he knew he could stand up at any time. He'd tried over and over again, hated it each and every time.

As a result, his bathing chamber was a huge space without any internal walls and with multiple jets of water directed to a central point, below which the floor curved gently down to allow the water to drain away. As promised, that water was steaming, the jets creating a heated rain that floated tiny water particles into the air. Those particles caught the candlelight in luminous beads that turned into a froth of sparkle.

A scent that he couldn't quite pin down, delicate and light, floated among the beads, brushed his skin, was a luxury of kisses on his senses.

Aodhan groaned. "I can't wait to get into that."

Dropping Illium's hand, he reached down to pull off his tunic and throw it aside.

He was beautiful.

Illium had seen Aodhan shirtless and even naked many times over the years. The exigencies of war and battle— and a lifetime of friendship—meant that none of it had ever really registered. They'd just been wild youths going skinny-dipping, or warriors dousing themselves with water between battles.

Just bodies that fought together, bodies as tools, nothing remarkable.

But this . . .

The candlelight caressed Aodhan's skin to a shimmering softness, his hair sending a kaleidoscope of light around the room. His wings intensified the effect, until Illium stood in the middle of a rain of light born of Aodhan.

But when he spoke, he didn't use the word *beautiful*. Would never again in the intimate space between them until Aodhan told him it didn't hurt him any longer. "You were made for candlelight, Adi."

Aodhan glanced over one muscled shoulder and his smile . . . it was one Illium hadn't seen since they were those wild youths. Before Illium's entanglement with a mortal and resulting punishment, before Aodhan's kidnapping, before the years of silence. "Are you seducing me, Blue?" He shifted so that they faced each other.

Illium's toes threatened to curl at the tone of Aodhan's voice, so low it was near to a purr. "You'll have to wait and see."

Eyes of shattered glass bright with fires intimate, Aodhan dropped his hands to the waistband of the rough brown pants of the kind he tended to wear for everyday things. They hugged his thighs before going down to be tucked into combat boots. Plain, unadorned, like most of what Aodhan chose to wear.

He'd been trying not to draw attention to himself for a lifetime, and that was part of it, but it was also just Aodhan. Even when they'd been young enough that Aodhan hadn't realized what his looks did to others, he'd preferred the simple over the ornate, had found as much pleasure in a smooth rock that he'd scavenged as another child might in a toy created by a master crafter.

Illium's eyes fell to Aodhan's hands, his heart kicking.

"I forgot my boots," Aodhan said, and—that wicked smile still on his face—twisted to sit on a bench built into the wall, above which was a shelf that held several folded towels.

"You're in a mood." Illium grinned, loving that this side of Aodhan was stirring to the surface—the side that held as much playfulness as Illium.

There was a reason they'd been friends since childhood.

After setting his boots and socks under the bench, Aodhan frowned before turning to look at the shower. "Rose petals, that's it. That's what I can smell." The words were startled, a hint of color on his cheekbones. "Really?"

"You deserve rose petals." He deserved every softness, every tenderness. "I saved the actual petals for the bed, found scented candles for here."

"I'm a warrior," Aodhan muttered, but he rose and moved to play his hand through the steamy fall of water.

"You're also an artist," Illium said. "I can't paint you, Adi, and I can't make you things like this belt buckle of mine." He touched the quiet emblem of Aodhan's love. "But I can give you rose petals and candlelight, and I can take you dancing on rooftops—or over a desert rave if you feel like it."

Aodhan's expression was difficult to read at that moment as he looked at Illium. But then he turned and, their eyes still locked, took off his pants.

Illium's heart was a drum by now, but he never broke the eye contact, never allowed his eyes to go south. He let Aodhan see that much as he wanted to dance with him in the intimate way of angelkind, what he wanted most was to just be with him.

Moving with the muscled fluidity of the warrior he was, his wings white fire in the candlelight, Aodhan walked into the fall of water. His sigh made Illium's entire body throb, but he stayed in place, just watching as Aodhan allowed the water to drench his hair before sleeking the strands back as he shifted to look once more at Illium.

The water turned the strands dark, cut back their shimmer, but only by a fraction. Aodhan was still Aodhan, the droplets on his eyelashes tiny diamonds.

"Are you coming in?" A husky question.

"I've decided to take the scenic route," Illium murmured past the stranglehold of desire. "Hold on."

Ducking out of the room, he went to the kitchen and returned with a tray on which stood a small bottle of champagne, a bottle of honey mead, two glasses, and a plate of sweetmeats: sugared figs, dried apricots, dark chocolate, candied almonds, and slices of mango cured with chili. He'd never in his life understood what Aodhan loved about the snack that burned Illium's tongue to cinders, but the man could eat a whole box of the stuff.

Aodhan laughed when Illium placed the tray on the simple black counter speckled with gold that was part of the single-piece sink, the dip in it a smooth flow that looked as if it had been created that way. "I see the limits of your love—not even for me will you drink champagne."

"Some things are a step too far," he said as he popped the champagne cork, then poured out a flute for Aodhan. "For my warrior artist."

Again, that hint of pink on Aodhan's cheekbones as he switched off all the spouts but the two that hit his shoulders and body from either side while leaving his head in clear air. "You're impossible."

"That's exactly how you like me." Putting down the bottle after handing Aodhan his champagne, he poured the mead into a matching flute, then picked up a sugared fig and walked to the edge of the spray.

When he held it to Aodhan's lips, the other man's pupils expanded, the dark pinpricks shockingly visible against the shattered blue and green glass of his irises. His lips parted, his lower lip soft and plump under the pad of Illium's thumb as he drew it out after feeding him the sweet morsel.

"I want to bite your lips," Illium murmured, feeling his way, watching Aodhan to see what would trigger bad memories.

Aodhan's breath caught, his pulse fluttering in his throat.

So Illium used his thumb to trace the curves of Aodhan's lips all over again before he drew back and picked up a candied almond to put to those same lips. He'd been so close to Aodhan all his life that he took the other man's looks for granted. All he saw was his Adi.

But today, he also saw how striking his eyes appeared when his lashes were dark with water, how candlelight made his irises less shattered glass and more a lazy river of refracted light. He saw the way his lover's biceps pushed up against the glory of his skin, and the way his wings had a powerful arch even when he was relaxed.

Teeth scraped his thumb when he withdrew it this time. His own breath shallow, and his pupils no doubt as dilated as Aodhan's, he put his fingers under Aodhan's jaw and leaned across and *just* a hint up to sip a kiss from those lips dusted with sugar from the candied almond.

It was a kiss unlike any other they'd shared, soft and sweet with an edge of delicious anticipation. It felt like a first kiss in many ways, the two of them finding out who they were in this private space different from any they'd ever before experienced.

They parted on a hushed lick of sound.

Aodhan's eyes were closed, his eyelashes throwing shadows onto his cheeks, his skin flushed . . . and his entire body languorous in a way that made the possessive, protective core of Illium's nature happy.

He liked knowing he was looking after his people as they needed. And Aodhan? He wasn't just one of Illium's people, he was Illium's *person*, his everything, the being without whom nothing would work quite right.

Those exquisite lashes rose. "What are you doing, Blue?" A rough whisper.

Illium ran his knuckles over Aodhan's cheek. "Courting you, Adi." He leaned in till their foreheads touched and the water hit his body from either side. "Let me."

Let me.

Aodhan's skin was too tight and yet relaxed at the same time, his entire body dreamy with pleasure. No one had ever touched him like this, ever treated him as infinitely precious in a way that wasn't about ownership, but about devotion.

Not the slavish devotion of those who wanted to worship him—he'd kept a wide berth from those so inclined over the years—but the passionate devotion of a warrior as powerful as Aodhan who had both stood with him and taken him to task when required.

Equals. They were equals here, as they'd always been in every other aspect of their lives.

"Shower with me," he whispered.

16

Already barefoot and a little damp, Illium stepped back to pull off his tunic, popping the wing closures in the process. He had a habit of doing that—Aodhan had quite the collection of buttons from when those had been the preferred closure. These days, Aodhan's Blue mostly broke zips, and kept the seamstresses in the city busy with his repairs.

His body was too lean, his muscles stark against the lines of him, and his skin a burnished gold that told Aodhan he'd spent countless hours shirtless while he was in China. Unlike Aodhan's skin, which might take on a golden kiss at best, Illium could tan to this rich dark gold that made him even more startlingly beautiful.

Those blue wings were an intense pop of color against the glory of his skin, his dark hair falling into his eyes as he threw his tunic aside. Shoving the strands back afterward, he stepped straight into the full path of the jets while still wearing his jeans.

"Illium!" Aodhan laughed as the angle of Illium's body sprayed water onto his face. "Have you forgotten how to take a shower?"

"No, but this shower is for you. Turn around, lean on the wall, and I'll clean your wings."

Angel wings were self-cleaning, but on this romantic night, Aodhan was willing to give Illium anything. He moved to brace himself with his forearms against the back wall, while Illium changed the jets so that they coated him in a gentle spray rather than a torrent.

His best friend and lover shifted so that he was still in Aodhan's peripheral vision . . . because he knew that while Aodhan could grit his teeth, bear it, he didn't like having anyone at his back when he was in such a vulnerable state. Then, jeans still on, he reached into a small alcove in the back shower wall to retrieve a tool, and began to detail Aodhan's wings in a way Aodhan hadn't even known was possible.

He hadn't spotted the array of tools until then, either, now realized they were brushes and combs designed to sleek feathers and separate filaments. It was long, painstaking work—and given the sensitivity in an angel's wings, it was also the most luxuriant thing Aodhan had ever experienced.

It soon became clear this was meant to be done in a bath, so that the recipient could turn pretty much boneless, but Aodhan was willing to stand there as long as it took. The wall was holding most of his weight at this point anyway.

Eyes heavy-lidded ten blissful minutes into it, he said, "Will I regret asking where you learned to do that?"

"Four-thousand-year-old angel decided to use me as a boy toy one summer when I was about a hundred and seventy. She was terrifying and knew all kinds of things and I barely got out with my life."

"Why don't I know about her already?"

"I did probably tell you—but I might've left out the more, shall we say"—a pointed cough—"interesting parts. She was an experience for innocent young Bluebell. Half the time, I felt as if I was in danger of being eaten alive, but for some reason, I liked it?"

Aodhan's cheeks creased at the slight shiver-shudder that rippled through Illium's body. "Is she still awake?"

A shake of Illium's head that he caught out of the corner

of his eye. "I like to think I wore her out. She went into Sleep only a month after that strange and enlightening summer. Or maybe I was her last hurrah." Illium's grin was in his voice. "I like that. What shall we do for our last hurrah when we're old and grouchy and ready for Sleep?"

Aodhan couldn't imagine a lifetime of such length. "Disgraceful things like gorge dive naked. Set all the proper old angels' hair on fire."

"Hah! I *told* Mother that you came up with our most devious pranks but she refuses to believe me to this day."

Face aching from smiling and body lazy from the intimate pleasure of having his wings attended to in such exquisite detail, Aodhan dropped all his defenses, stopped thinking, just let his Blue be in charge. He was aware of Illium moving, of the other angel controlling the temperature of the water when the heat became too much for even Aodhan, and he was aware of the candles burning down, but he felt no urgency to be anywhere else or do anything else.

He'd physically and mentally done all he could for Marco and Tanika this day, would start again tomorrow. Tonight was for him and this man who loved him enough to find ways to give him pleasure that no nightmare could touch.

Illium was working on the final of Aodhan's primaries when he realized his lover was all but asleep despite his upright position. He'd pillowed his head on his crossed forearms, and his wings had lost their warrior arch, his shoulders no longer tense in the way of a man ready to move at any minute.

Heart aching with all he felt, Illium finished up, then pressed a kiss to the top of Aodhan's spine—after deliberately making enough noise that the touch wouldn't be a surprise. "Out, Adi." He switched off the water. "Or you'll turn into a sparkly prune." Angelic skin didn't shrivel up at the same speed as mortal skin, but it *did* eventually do so.

A long sigh, followed by a stretch that would've done Smoke proud.

Groaning inwardly at all that muscled glory, Illium got himself and his sodden jeans out of the shower. At which point he stripped while Aodhan was still in the midst of his stretch, then wrapped a towel around his waist. He'd grabbed a big towel for Aodhan by the time the other man turned toward him.

"Fucking marble statue," Illium muttered. "It's ridiculous how you're built."

Aodhan's smile was deep, his eyes sleepy. "Ah, such romance."

Illium scowled. "Out. I slaved over ordering your favorite meal for you and you need to eat." Aodhan had been running himself ragged for the two victims he'd claimed as his own, and Illium knew he'd continue to do so.

Still smiling, and still proudly naked in a way that would've been impossible for him mere decades ago, Aodhan walked straight into the towel Illium held up. He let Illium wrap it around his hips, then stood quiescent while Illium rubbed him dry using another towel.

"I feel like I melted," he said at one point, draping his arms around Illium's shoulders and rubbing his nose against Illium's.

Illium's damn *heart* melted at that. Right into goo. He hadn't known it could do that.

After nuzzling Aodhan back, he used the towel to catch a couple of rogue droplets on the other man's chest, then deliberately dropped the towel to the floor.

"You know I hate dropped towels in the bathroom," Aodhan grumbled without removing his arms from around Illium's shoulders.

"I know." Illium was unrepentant. "I wanted to wake you up. I'm not letting you sleep until you eat." With that, and no matter how tempting Aodhan was with his skin warm and dry, his body lax, and his eyes drowsy, he took the other man's strong, callused hand and dragged him to the bedroom—where he'd set up a picnic on a folding table beside the enormous bed.

Beds made for their kind had to be enormous, especially

if they ever intended to share their sleeping space. While Tower staff had sourced the basic furniture for the Seven's suites, they'd each chosen their mattresses, and mentioned if they'd prefer any changes to the standard building plan—hence Aodhan's bigger kitchen and custom shower.

All the decorative personalization had been left up to them.

Aodhan's home was beautiful in its quiet touches—like the bedspread of white on white with just the barest blush of blue rising from the edges, and the elegant water jug on a corner shelf that Aodhan had found in China and asked Suyin if he could keep.

The archangel had looked befuddled, her surprise enough to trump her bone-tired demeanor of moments before; the latter was a face she showed only to her most trusted people. For the rest, those who looked to her for hope, for a reason to go on, she was an archangel without vulnerability.

"Aodhan," she'd said, while pulling her long ice-white hair back from her face with a tie she'd borrowed from one of her warriors, "you can take buckets of diamonds and rubies should you desire. But are you sure you want to bring this energy into your home? We're in an area dark with my aunt's influence."

"Objects can be cleansed of bad energies." Solemn words from Aodhan. "This work created by a gifted artisan shouldn't be abandoned or forsaken because of another's evil."

Now here it sat, physically cleansed by a concoction of Aodhan's designed not to damage the delicate paintings on the jug, and spiritually cleansed by a mortal holy man from China. Angels had no holy men of their own, not in that way. As Illium had told Catalina when she'd asked him, angelkind had no religions—perhaps an inevitable thing in a race of immortals for whom a life beyond this one was an academic thought at best.

The closest they got to it was talking about "the Havens" and life "beyond the veil" but even that was a nebulous concept with no structure behind it. Simply an acknowledgment that perhaps there *was* another plane of existence; that acknowledgment was enough to offer them a painful comfort when angels died young, as had happened in the war.

Then there were those of their kind who had become . . . different over time. Wise in a form that was transcendent, their minds and bodies apart from this world in a way that Illium couldn't explain. But to talk to them was to know you spoke to a being who was so present in the instant as to be a guiding star in your world . . . and so much in another place that you would never reach them.

Illium's own mother often showed glimpses of that, though he had the feeling she'd taken a deliberate step off the path of late, wanting to live life full throttle in the world in which they stood.

Illium also saw the promise of such transcendence in his best friend and lover.

Aodhan had always had a level of empathy beyond words. It was part of what made him an artist whose portraits caused his subjects to cry with all he saw in them, and it had only intensified after his kidnapping. As if the horror of it had ripped away a layer of protection, allowing him to see a world others never would. If the time did come that Aodhan walked that path, Illium hoped he'd take him along on the journey rather than leaving him behind.

Even the idea of it was a knife to his immortal spirit. He'd follow Adi anywhere, but there were some places he couldn't go without a hand reaching back to tug him through the divide.

But Aodhan's possible transcendence was a prospect eons into the future.

Today, his friend remained earthbound, his spirit hurt in ways profound; he needed tenderness.

There are softer bruises that hide beneath the scars.

With Catalina's wisdom in mind, he nudged Aodhan onto the bed he'd scattered with rose petals.

Not the rich red of seduction, but the pale blush pink of flirtation.

The other man sprawled with his back to the headboard, and his towel in real danger of falling off. As it was, one muscled thigh glittered under the candlelight when Aodhan shifted to sit with his left knee bent, his arm braced loosely over it.

Picking up a rose petal with a faint smile on his lips, he rubbed it between his fingertips before looking at Illium all lazy-lidded and content. "This is a good date, Blue." Simple words that made Illium feel ten feet tall.

"I'm just getting started," he managed to get out.

Yet playing with the petal, his expression vulnerable in a way Illium knew he'd show no other being, Aodhan said, "Who did Smoke spend the day with while we were out?"

Illium loved that he'd thought of their pet even at this moment. "Holly. Ingrate basically jumped on her from my arms. I was on my way to drop her off with Laric since he told me the patients love it when she comes by. Anyway, I swear they were talking."

Aodhan nodded solemnly. "No surprise. Holly is mostly a cat after all."

Illium laughed at the apt description of Venom's vampire mate. With her quicksilver nature and wry sense of humor—and changeable moods—Holly did have certain feline characteristics.

He was smiling at the thought as he shifted the plates off the table and onto the bed itself—on which he'd placed a special tray that was designed to stay in place and contain anything that slipped. He'd bought it especially for tonight . . . and all the nights to come when he intended to lavish Adi with affection, with care.

"You're the beautiful one in this relationship, Blue," Aodhan murmured, his voice quiet but resonant in its depth. "You know that, don't you? You're built to perfection, every sinew and muscle in flawless proportion. That's before you get to the most extraordinary eyes I've ever seen, and those firm lips that own mine."

Illium's cheeks heated. He went to make a joke about it, brush it off, but the way Aodhan was looking at him made that seem a cowardice. "Why don't we agree to disagree?"

he said instead. "Because I look at you, in the light or in the dark, and all I see is pure gorgeous man."

"In the dark?" A confused angling of the head. "I don't sparkle in the dark."

"You don't need to sparkle. You just need to be you." He continued to speak before Aodhan could reply. "The Aodhan who walked hand in hand with me for literal weeks after the asshole called my father decided to go into Sleep even though he had a kid who thought he hung the moon and who kept watching the skies for him.

"The Aodhan who, though his heart is of an artist, picked up a sword and learned how to be an elite warrior so that I'd never walk into battle alone.

"The Aodhan who doesn't get angry with me even when I confuse myself with why I'm so scared about us, why I take three steps forward only to stumble backward without warning. That's the man I see in the dark, and it's his wing I feel lying over me, protecting me in my sleep."

Aodhan's throat moved, his eyes wet. "Come here."

Unable to deny that husky request, Illium shifted to stand beside the bed next to Aodhan. The other man took his hips, rubbing the pads of his thumbs over the vee-line created by Illium's lean musculature.

Sensation shivered throughout Illium's body, along with a crashing wave of love so deep, it hurt.

If Aodhan ever left him again . . .

Before he could complete the agonizing thought, Aodhan shifted to press his lips to Illium's abdomen, just above the edge of the precariously knotted towel. Warm breath, sure lips, the barest touch of wet. Sucking in a rough inhale, Illium went to clench his hand reflexively in Aodhan's hair before a surge of protectiveness had him placing that hand on the other man's shoulder instead.

Never would he make Adi feel trapped.

The shoulder under his touch bunched as Aodhan shifted back, locked his eyes with Illium's . . . and tugged at the knot in the towel, his knuckles brushing Illium's abdomen.

The tug wasn't enough to dislodge it, just enough for a question. In answer, Illium didn't step back, didn't break the contact between them.

His heart was in his throat, his skin so tight, it felt as if it would burst.

Part of him—the part that had been looking after Aodhan for centuries—wanted to tell the other man that this was too fast, that it might rebound on him. But the Aodhan who looked at him, square jawed and with desire an inferno in his gaze, wasn't afraid or held hostage by nightmare. He was a warrior in control of his desires—and *this* was what he wanted.

Illium was who he wanted

Another tug, this one stronger.

The towel pooled to the floor . . . and Aodhan's gaze lowered.

He brushed his knuckles over the last inches of Illium's abdomen . . . lower . . .

17

Illium's entire body went rigid at the first contact of Aodhan's skin against his aroused flesh, his breath locked in his chest.

"Look at me, Blue." Only at Aodhan's murmuring order did Illium realize he'd thrown back his head and clamped his eyes shut, his hands curled into bloodless fists at his sides.

It took conscious effort to return his gaze back to Aodhan, the intimacy of it blinding.

His breath kicked in, rapid and shallow.

"Those eyes," Aodhan murmured, his knuckles yet grazing Illium in a butterfly caress that might as well have been a hot poker for what it was doing to him. "Those eyelashes. That skin. All mine."

Illium could barely think, every cell of his being focused on Aodhan. Except for in his days as an impetuous youth with his first lovers, he'd always been able to maintain a degree of control in intimate relationships. Never in a way that put him above his partner—that wasn't how Illium functioned. He didn't use people so cynically. When he shared his body, he did so with generosity and sincerity.

He'd just . . . never become lost in those past lovers.

Today, he was so lost that he felt unmoored.

Then Aodhan brushed the bunched muscles of his thigh with the fingers of his other hand. "Breathe, darling." A dazzling smile. "Or you'll give me the ego to end all egos."

Illium muttered a curse from their childhood, in a language no longer spoken even by those who'd grown up with it—but its creative curses lingered. This one had no direct translation into English.

Aodhan's laughter was full-bodied and so unrestrained, it made Illium's very being ache.

And his hands . . . they were those of an artist.

Today, Illium was his clay.

To be shaped with caressing strokes, to be squeezed just so for the right response, to be *handled*, until every nerve and pleasure cell in Illium's body was focused only on that point of contact. *"Adi."* A groan, a demand, his fingers digging into the taut muscle of Aodhan's shoulder without his conscious volition.

Aodhan didn't even seem to notice, his attention on shaping his living clay with a precision unbounded. "Let go," he commanded in a low growl. "It's my turn to look after you."

The words, that fucking low *voice* . . . Illium's world fractured into stars as bright as Aodhan, his tendons tense enough to snap. All while Aodhan stroked his thigh with his free hand in a touch so tender, it took this far beyond the primal and sexual.

Illium's knees threatened to buckle in the aftermath. As it was, he barely managed to stumble sideways onto the bed, somehow managing to avoid the tray of food; then he just lay on his back, his chest heaving and his wings limp. He was aware of Aodhan moving, stepping into the bathing chamber.

He was back moments later—with a kiss and a warm damp cloth, which Illium grabbed off him, his face flushed. After he took care of himself, he threw the cloth in the direction of the bathing chamber and had the satisfaction of hearing cloth hit tile.

Aodhan chuckled as he came down beside him after moving the food back to the table. "My Blue." He brushed his fingers over Illium's cheekbones. "I never thought you'd be shy."

"Neither did I," Illium muttered, because despite his flaming cheeks, this, just lying here with Aodhan's wing over his body while the other man touched his shoulders and chest as if discovering him for the first time, it felt good.

Felt right.

Felt like exactly where he was meant to be.

Aodhan wondered what it said about him that Illium's befuddlement restored something fractured inside him. He'd been off-balance since he'd frozen that first night, had felt as if no matter how far he came, he'd always be the one at a loss.

When he'd reached for Illium, it hadn't been with any conscious forethought. He'd just wanted to touch him, love him in the physical way that he knew was important to his Blue. Illium would never say it, never push Aodhan, but where Aodhan had become so familiar with physical aloneness that it had become a way of life, Illium had always been a creature of touch. The boy who'd hugged his friends and who'd cuddled into his mother's side, then Raphael's, while they read him stories.

"What are you thinking?" Illium asked, the aged gold of his eyes searching Aodhan's face. "I can almost see the gears turning."

Aodhan could've obfuscated it, hidden what must surely be a selfishness, but that wasn't who he and Illium were to each other—who they'd ever been to each other. So he told him. "Not with intent," he said afterward. "My only intent was to touch you, pleasure you, possess you."

Because it turned out that Aodhan had a deep streak of possessiveness when it came to Illium, this angel who had a thousand people—*more*—who all adored him and thought they had some private relationship with him.

"You've always worried too much," Illium said with a lazy smile. "It's fine. I had the same thought before—that between us, power has always ebbed and flowed. Sometimes one stronger, sometimes the other. It all equalizes in the end."

Aodhan shifted to lean on his elbow, his wing lying even more heavily against Illium—who began to play his fingers through the feathers as candlelight glittered on the blue tips of his eyelashes. And Aodhan knew he'd paint his lover this way, boneless and pleasured and with a smile flirting with his lips.

He fell asleep while planning out the brushstrokes, his head tucked against the side of Illium's neck, and his arm over Illium's chest, the two of them still crosswise on the bed, which was just big enough to provide them a comfortable sleep in even that position.

He didn't feel the kiss Illium pressed to his hair, or hear the emotion-drenched words the other man whispered in the candlelit glow. "I'm so glad you've come back to me."

They spent the entirety of the next day going through Marco's belongings.

Illium had already managed to access and read through the files on Marco's laptop—with no useful results. They'd set today aside for examining the other items, hoping for a better outcome.

The task was as grim as Aodhan had mentally predicted, but he felt more centered today than he had the entire time since the beginning of this investigation . . . the beginning of his decision to consciously confront the phantoms of his past. He'd woken up warm and rested, with his wing thrown over Illium as the other man lay flat on his front. Somehow, they'd moved ninety degrees on the bed during the night— probably due to Illium.

The other man had a gift for movement in his sleep.

But Aodhan hadn't woken at any point before morning, had apparently just gone with him—much as he'd done when they'd been children who'd fallen asleep together.

"Flying together even in sleep," Eh-ma used to say when she woke them of a morning after Aodhan had stayed over. "My two peas in a pod."

This morning, he'd woken with his face tucked into the crook of Illium's neck, his hand on his lover's rib cage, and his breath full of the scent of Illium. A scent that was home to him in ways beyond explanation; he just knew he could spend countless immortal lifetimes waking with his face nuzzled against Illium.

The other man had been over his shyness by the morning, had grinned and kissed Aodhan, called him "my adorable cuddle bug," then told him that, at one point, he'd had to "snake shimmy" his way out from under Aodhan to douse the candles and put away the food. "Then I slid back into bed, and you threw your wing right over me, and mumbled something about 'perfect shade of blue' and went back to sleep."

A smug grin. "Of course, then I knew you were dreaming about me."

No one else in existence would *dare* call Aodhan a cuddle bug, but from Illium when he was so happy and vibrant and full of unbounded affection . . . Aodhan kind of liked it.

He wanted to smile even now at the memory of Illium's infectious joy, but he'd just picked up a photo frame that held an image of Marco with his mother. The smile whispered away before it could form.

It was one of those images mortals got in their malls. A few of the angels and vampires in the Tower had them as fun souvenirs . . . but this was no joking souvenir. It was an artifact of love: a teenage Marco in his high school graduation cap and gown, his mother in what had to be her best clothes.

Giulia had her arm around Marco as she looked up to her taller son with an expression of utmost love, while he clasped his rolled-up diploma, a huge grin on his face. His hair had been longer at the time, two dark curves that brushed his clean-shaven jaw.

It was a more formal pair to the candid graduation photo

Giulia had on her sideboard. Had she chosen to display that one because it felt more real, more like her boy? How hard it must be for a mother to choose photos of her child from a lifetime of them.

"Giulia will like having that, even if she has her own copy," Illium murmured.

"Because he kept it," Aodhan said with a nod. "Long after he went from boy to man, he kept this photo of a moment of celebration with his mother."

"We can put things like that in one box," Illium said. "Good things for when she's ready to remember the happy times with her son. She can ignore the rest of his belongings until she's ready."

Aodhan set the frame aside—but only after opening up the back to ensure Marco hadn't tucked anything in there. There should've been no reason for the young vampire to hide items—it appeared he'd been up front about his stalker to his lover, family, and angel, but people also hid things as insurance or to spare a loved one from hurt.

The frame proved empty.

"I've gone through this small notebook." Illium held up the simple book with its cardboard cover that featured a low-slung car, its lines reminiscent of a jungle cat's. "Looks like he used it to remind himself of things on a daily basis."

He flipped open a page to show a crossed-out list. "Marco went to the effort of splitting it into months, had future notes about various important events including when Tanika's favorite band was going to be in town, and his mother's birthday—he planned to order her a special cake."

Illium traced Marco's scrawled handwriting with a careful finger even as his body grew taut, his voice harsh with anger at a life stolen. "He was a good son, a good man. The kind of man who remembered to pick up groceries for his girlfriend even though he only needed a bottle of blood, and who made a note to remind her of her parents' upcoming anniversary."

Aodhan's own fingers curled into his palm, his back rigid. "Someone took that man, and the woman he loved, away

from everyone because he wouldn't agree to be her toy."
Rage was a cauldron inside him. "I want to *hurt* them."

Illium's chest pounded at the open rage on Aodhan's
face. His best friend hadn't allowed himself to feel rage for
a long time. He'd been too badly wounded after he was first
rescued, and later, he'd pushed it all down so deep that it
had turned into a bone-scarring poison.

Illium knew the other man had spoken to Keir, had always hoped with every ounce of his being that the healer
had lanced the poison in private, but he wasn't so sure any
longer. Because Aodhan was the more stubborn of the two
of them—he was quieter and less inclined to temper, but he
held things deeper and longer.

"So do I," he said, not sure if it was the right thing to say,
but wanting Aodhan to know that his anger wasn't a response to be judged, that he had a *right* to rage, a right to
be furious at the kind of narcissism that had led to the loss
of two innocent lives. "Sometimes, rage is the only possible
response. Rage fuels us."

Aodhan's eyes glittered with the heat of that rage as he
picked up a pair of leather gloves from among Marco's belongings. Illium had already bypassed them, but Aodhan
frowned, stared. "These are too fine." He flipped the top of
one glove to reveal a furred interior. "The leather's as soft
as butter, and I think that's real rabbit fur."

He glanced around. "Look at the rest of Marco's clothing."

Now that Aodhan had pointed it out, Illium saw at once
what he meant: while Marco'd had a polished wardrobe, all
the items were in line with the kind of income he would've
had as a young mortal only a few years into his working
life. The same kind of income he'd probably had as a junior
vampire with a good angel—above the baseline require-
ment, but not by much. It would've increased as he rose in
seniority, but at the point where he'd died? No, he wouldn't
have had money to burn on fancy gloves.

"A gift from Tanika?" Illium suggested, then shook his
head. "No, remember what her mother said—she was a
lover of animals, didn't eat flesh in any form." The two of

them had privately wondered how she'd made her peace with Marco's need for blood, but it wasn't a question they could ask those who'd loved her.

"I agree. She would've never gifted an item that utilized both tanned hide and fur." Aodhan stared at the gloves. "Marco doesn't strike me as the kind of man to keep a gift from another woman, but perhaps he was tempted by the luxury of the item?"

Taking the gloves, Illium examined them with care. "I don't see any scratches or other marks that say these have been worn, but we wouldn't see that if he took care of them."

"Is there a maker's mark?"

Illium flipped both gloves halfway inside out, found no silken tag.

Frowning, Aodhan considered the luxurious materials and what looked to be painstaking hand-stitching. Not a mass-produced object. An artisanal creation. And no artist would mar their work with what they'd see as an unsightly label. "There." He tapped the inner part of the wrist edging, which, unlike the glove itself, was a deep, almost black-green; the thread used was a contrasting pale green. "That's the mark."

"Really?"

"I can't believe you're questioning me on the subject of gloves. You, the man who refuses to countenance wearing them." His chiding words were soft. "Even if you're in danger of frostbite."

"I'm a warrior angel. I'll wear gauntlets and wrist guards, but I draw the line at gloves." Illium turned the gloves the right way out again. "You know who it is? The maker?"

"Céline," Aodhan said, having placed that particular mark in the interim. "An angel of around six thousand, if I'm recalling correctly. Last I knew, she was based in Bordeaux."

Illium already had his phone out. "Two boutiques in the city stock her gloves. It's a place to start. We strike out, we go wider."

Aodhan agreed. "Unless she has changed her method since I last heard, Céline makes each pair by her own hand, has no assistants in the work itself. So even if we have to trace every pair of gloves made just prior to and during the time since the stalker began to importune Marco, it won't be a high number."

He considered it further. "Given the stalker's obsession, I don't think these would be hand-me-downs—they would've been bought specifically for Marco."

"We visit the boutiques in person?"

"Yes. No clerk wishes to anger a wealthy client, but they won't dare lie to the faces of two of Raphael's senior people." Aodhan scanned the other items laid out around the room. "We should go through the rest of this first; it's possible we won't need to rely on the gloves."

Nodding, Illium continued on from where he'd stopped—and found a small box full of bejeweled men's rings. He held one up to the light. The green glowed with a piercing luminescence. "Real, I'd wager."

He picked up another ring inset with a stone that could've been yellow or orange, depending on the light, but held more clarity and depth than either color on its own, and showed it to Aodhan. "This is a sunset diamond; I'd stake my wings on it. So named because no one could agree on whether to call them orange or yellow—and because of how the hues turn changeable depending on the light. Priceless after that archangelic tantrum a millennium ago that destroyed the area where they were most often found."

"Did you take up a new hobby and forget to tell me?" Aodhan raised an eyebrow; neither one of them had ever been the kind to bejewel themselves or to take much interest in such fashions.

The crease in Illium's cheek made his breath catch, his chest swell. Because this man with his wicked smile and playful heart, this man strong and loyal and kind in ways most of the world would never understand, was *his*.

"An art enthusiast gifted a stone like this to Mother three centuries ago when she decided to create a portrait of his family of her own volition. The color is distinctive—there's no other gemstone like it in the world."

Family portraits by Eh-ma were even rarer than these stones; perhaps she'd taken commissions when young, but that time was so long in the past that no one remembered it. Today, the Hummingbird created only what she wished.

"She set the diamond into a chunk of stone and uses it as a paperweight to this day." Illium's shoulders shook. "My mother makes her own rules."

Aodhan's eyes widened. "I've *seen* that paperweight. Eh-ma told me she just liked the way the stone sparkled in the light. I never even considered it might be a diamond." Squeezing his eyes shut, he fought back his own laugh, glad for this small moment of light in the darkness. "What's a sunset diamond worth?"

"All I know for certain is that it'd have been well beyond Marco's budget," Illium said. "I think it's out of *our* budgets, too. The person who gave it to Mother was eons older and wealthier than us, and even he treated the stone like a treasure equal to the value of a portrait by the Hummingbird."

Illium's mind flashed to the portrait that hung in his apartment of two small angels in jubilant if wonky flight over a field of bluebells, their faces wreathed in grins and their wings too big for their bodies.

It was one of his all-time favorites.

He and Aodhan had never had to worry about portraits; they had a collection of them through time, created by the most gifted artist among angelkind. An artist who loved them both. She'd painted an adolescent Aodhan at work on his easel, a frown line between his eyebrows, and she'd painted a "teenage" Illium practicing his sword drills, and those were just two examples of their solo portraits. She'd also sketched and painted countless images of their entwined lives.

But for a rare few exceptions, all of those pieces were either with her subjects or in her private collection. The exceptions were Raphael and Naasir for the most part, both of whom had received countless sketches over the years of Illium and Aodhan's childhood, as part of the letters Illium's mother had written to them while they were away from the Refuge.

"My favorite of Eh-ma's portraits," Aodhan said at that moment, "is that one of you in full battle mode, right after you were accepted into your first adult wing."

Illium's heart stopped, tight and hurting in a rush of emotion. "She was still lost in her mind then, but she found a way to see me." The painting was both a testament to love . . . and a reminder of grief. "I love it, too, but I could never hang it in my home."

Aodhan closed his hand over Illium's nape. "I know. That's why I never hung it up in your presence after she gave it to me."

Illium blinked, stared. "When did she give it to you?"

"When I was lost, too," Aodhan said, his voice husky. "Anytime you left the Refuge as part of your duties, she filled my home with portraits of you. Safety lines for when I began to fall into the abyss—I think that's what she saw them to be . . . and she was right. How could I surrender to the yawning maw when I knew you'd dive in after me, you stubborn, beautiful fool?"

The last word was so tender, it hurt.

18

Always, Illium said into Aodhan's mind even as a part of his heart cracked open at not only the gift of memory that was his mother's love for him and Aodhan both, but at Aodhan's continued refusal to shy away from the most devastating period in their history.

No more silent ghosts. No more words unspoken.

He and Adi, they were on this journey for the long haul.

His heart pulsing back into rhythm, his wings spreading in an exhale that was centuries withheld. "Hang it up," he said roughly as he slid his wing over Aodhan's closed ones.

A frown.

"It's different now," Illium said. "You just changed the context of how I'll look at it."

Aodhan squeezed his nape. "We'll see." Releasing him on that "don't argue with me" tone, he took the ring from Illium. "Why did Marco keep this and the other jewels? There's an infinitesimal chance they came from anyone but his stalker—so why did he keep them?"

Shelving their discussion for the moment because when

Aodhan got stubborn, importuning him got you nothing but a sore head, Illium glanced again at Marco's paltry belongings, recalled what Giulia had said of her son's habits. "He wasn't acquisitive, so it can't have been about wealth."

Aodhan's jaw worked, storm clouds in those astonishing eyes.

"People are complicated, Adi." Illium ran a hand down the steel rod of Aodhan's spine. "It changes nothing about his choice to say no. A gift given and accepted doesn't mean a contract made."

A shudder rocking his spine, Aodhan wove his fingers through Illium's. "Sachieri and Bathar never gave me gifts, but there were others who did when I was young and naïve. I thought people were being kind when they brought me rare pigments or special brushes, that they'd just thought of me when they ran across those items. Like you and Eh-ma, even Imalia and our parents."

Aodhan's parents hadn't quite known what to do with him, befuddled by the quiet-eyed child with a shining spirit who'd been born long after his sister Imalia was a full-grown angelic adult, but Illium knew his best friend had never doubted their love. They'd often brought Aodhan the wrong brushes or unsuitable pigments, but that they'd thought of what might make Aodhan happy while just living their lives had been enough—as had seeing their excited faces at having so successfully found what they believed to be the perfect thing for him.

Illium could still remember the day Menerva had presented her son with a handcrafted set of sculpting tools far too delicate for Aodhan's preferred medium when he sculpted. The handles of each had been inset with a stylized *A*. "I put your name down for a set two years ago when I first saw one," she'd murmured in her quiet way, her eyes smiling. "It didn't seem right that you not have the best tools for your art when that art brings us all such happiness."

That was why Illium loved Menerva, Rukiel, and Imalia. Because inept as they'd often been, they'd *tried* with their whole hearts—and they'd never attempted to stop Aodhan's attachment to Illium's mother, a woman who understood him so much better.

"It makes him happy to be with you and your son," Menerva had said to Sharine once within Illium's hearing. "I am joyful at that for him."

"Raphael, Naasir, the others," Aodhan continued, "they were the same with their random gifts. Just sending me things because they thought I'd appreciate it."

Naasir, for one, had shipped him a slab of clay from a distant corner of the world because it was the most astonishing pink he'd ever seen and he'd figured Aodhan would find a use for it. "I accepted gifts from others outside my circle of trust in good faith, gifting them back in kind with a piece of art."

With Illium and Naasir and the others in that circle, there'd been no need to pay them back—they'd all been a constant part of each other's lives, no one keeping track of such kindnesses because it flowed from every direction. "Then a supposed friend walked into my studio expecting a whole different kind of payment."

"Why's this the first time I'm hearing about this?" A muscle ticced in Illium's jaw.

"I told you about the first gifts, I think. When I thought people were just being nice." He closed his fingers over one of Illium's primaries. "Later, after I understood, I was embarrassed to have been so naïve."

"Did that—"

"He tried, but as soon as I realized what was happening, I shoved the pigment he'd 'gifted' me into his fucking mouth after pinning him to the earth—he'd forgotten I was in warrior training because of you. Then I grabbed a pot of stain that was nearby and threw it on his face. Let that asshole explain why he'd turned a splotchy frog-green—stuff clung to his pasty skin for an entire week."

Illium's mouth fell open before a snorting laugh escaped him. Wings drooping at his sides, he bent over, literally crying with laughter. "I can't believe you never told me *that*!" A light punch to Aodhan's abdomen.

"You might have been on one of your longer courier runs at the time," Aodhan said, his own lips twitching as he patted a breathless Illium's back. He'd forgotten how good pure, deserved anger felt, and he allowed the memory to settle into his cells now, reclaiming that fiery piece of the youth he'd once been.

"I did rant to Naasir, who went out and—unbeknownst to me for literal *decades*—made the asshole sit down and 'allow' Naasir to shave off his glorious fucking mane of hair. Naasir made him return for the same treatment for years." The one and only chimera in the known world could be terrifying when anyone hurt those who were his own.

"Good." Illium's smile was as feral as Naasir's. "I hope he made the ass piss his pants."

"After that incident," Aodhan continued, "I returned every gift except those that came from my people." He stared at the rings. "I don't only wonder why Marco kept these, I wonder what the angel stalking him believed it to signify."

They had no answers to that—and they found no further items that appeared out of place in the belongings of a young vampire. Neither did they unearth any of the letters Navarro had mentioned seeing to Dmitri. But as the stones in the rings were as unique as the gloves, they now had two threads to tug.

"The rings will be more difficult," Aodhan said. "The gemstones could've been purchased long ago, only the setting made for Marco—or the band resized. Still, immortal jewelers should remember a rare diamond of that size and clarity."

A glance at Illium. "Do you know any in the profession who'd be willing to ask around for us?" Jewelers who dealt with senior angelic and vampiric clientele were tight-lipped and secretive, but they were also the only ones apt to have an answer. Aodhan didn't think the stalker would've trusted anything of this caliber to a mortal, no matter how skilled.

"One of Charo's three beloved—Isiel—is in jewels." Illium grinned as he named the youngest of Titus's sisters. "He adores Mother and she just designed five pieces for him that have made him the envy of his peers. I'm liked by association so he should be amenable."

Aodhan glanced at the clock on the wall. "We have time enough to start this today. I'll take the first shop when it comes to the gloves. You take the other after you've made the call to Isiel."

Illium could've argued that there was no rush, that Marco was long dead, as was Tanika, but he'd never do that for the same reason that Aodhan couldn't just let this go: this wasn't about time, but about justice . . . and about memories.

Aodhan had never before walked into a boutique that sold such goods. In truth, he basically *never* walked into shops. As soon as the facility became available, Illium had taught him how to order any goods he wanted online.

He also had a longstanding network of tailors, cobblers, and other solitary makers who could supply him with what he needed. They were all immortal, so he didn't have to worry about changing to a new maker unless one of them decided to Sleep or otherwise withdraw from the world.

For one-off items that were easier to get in person, Illium was happy to pick those up for him—though strangely enough, Blue also didn't much like to linger in shops. That was despite the fact that when they'd been youthful warrior trainees, they'd often gone to the mingled mortal/immortal markets in large cities across the world, with Xi'an and Marrakech being favorites.

While Aodhan had flown in and out as quickly as possible, Illium had spent as much time chatting with the stall keepers and shop owners as he had looking at the actual goods. He'd forged such bonds in a single visit that he was welcomed like a long-lost friend on his next visit, with many an invitation to share a cup of fresh mint tea shouted his way.

"Markets are different," the other man had said to him when Aodhan had mentioned the discrepancy. "Usually open air—and even with the narrow corridors in the oldest ones, they take care to leave the top open so we can fly in and out. I never have to walk into a shop, either; the staff are always hovering outside ready to talk up their wares.

"Malls and department stores, on the other hand . . ." He'd shuddered. "They're so enclosed that often the only way to get out in a hurry would be for me to explode through the nearest skylight."

He'd thrust a hand through his hair, and even then, when Aodhan had only seen him as his best friend, he'd found himself wondering why he was the one who drew the most attention when Illium was so extraordinary. Especially when he smiled. And Illium almost always had a smile on his face.

Of all the highly skilled warriors of Aodhan's acquaintance, he was the one most apt to laugh.

"Boutiques are a bit better," Illium had added. "Just one shop usually, with wide doors if they expect angelic clientele, but still not where I'd choose to spend hours."

"You should've told me earlier." Aodhan had scowled. "I'd have asked someone else to do my pickups." Holly, for one, loved fashion and often browsed boutiques to stay up to date on the latest trends.

Illium had waved that off. "I don't care about short visits. But talking of shopping, we should go to the night markets in Marrakech again."

With all the political upheaval of the past years, they never had made it to those markets or to any other, but Aodhan made a promise to himself that, once this case was complete, and Illium had rested from his long flight home, he'd take his Blue to the markets.

He'd buy Illium the freshly churned ice cream served in small watermelon halves that Illium had always loved for their whimsy, and they'd play the games on the edge of the market to win inexpensive trinkets—for no reason but that it was fun.

Today, however, as the city began to flow out of high-rises

and into the subways at the start of rush hour, he steeled his shoulders and walked through the automatic glass doors of the exclusive Manhattan boutique that sold Céline's gloves. Per their website, they were currently out of stock, with shoppers welcomed to add their name to the waiting list.

The air inside was cool—and perfumed with a delicate scent that he recognized from the Refuge. The essence of a rare flower that bloomed only at the higher elevations for two months of the year.

Thankfully, the place was set up for angelic visitors, with a wide central space around which were placed pedestals, each lit with its own small spotlight. Each pedestal displayed one item.

The décor was white on white, the only touches of color coming from the items on display.

Perfume in a faceted crystal bottle no bigger than Aodhan's thumbnail, its top a bead of true gold.

A scarf so delicate, it was air, woven of material he couldn't guess at a glance, the colors a cascade of sunrise.

A pair of gloves clearly designed for masculine hands, and bearing the leatherwork stamp of a maker Aodhan knew well. He hadn't realized the maker offered such artistic items as well as the working gloves he made for warriors.

A tiny, frivolous handbag of black into which were woven the preserved feathers of various angels—all of them distinctive, but in a palette of blues fading to iridescent white. He recognized one of Illium's as well as one of his own. Each feather tiny, shed from the inner surface and each filament preserved with utmost care.

Oh, there was one of Raphael's and another that he was certain came from Yindi's dark blue wings. She'd been with Suyin since her ascension, was still in China. Add in the chaos of war, and it must've taken the craftsperson years to gather the feathers.

Aodhan appreciated both the vision and the work involved. It also made him wonder if there were other bags, each a singular creation with a different harmonious array of feathers.

"Sir." A woman with skin of ebony, her lips cherry red and her tightly curled hair cut close to her skull, beamed at him from his side. "I am overcome to have you in my shop."

She was breathtaking in the way of certain very old vampires, her cheekbones striking and her eyes unearthly in their size. Her body was willowy under her figure-skimming and ankle-length black dress, her shoes glittering silver heels that still only brought her up to his shoulder.

Her power was a deep hum beneath the surface.

19

Aodhan didn't have to interrogate the proprietor; a vampire old and savvy, her voice a rich thickness with a lilting accent, she gave him what he needed at once. Their entire inventory for the relevant time—five pairs—had been bought by Pierre St. John, a vampire with whom Aodhan was well acquainted.

"The gloves were gifts for his most senior staff," the proprietor told him.

She also shared that the other boutique in the city that sold Céline's work had received only two pairs during the time period in which he was interested. "I have had the pleasure of meeting Lady Céline," she told him. "It is my great honor that the lady favors us with her work."

Aodhan completed his task in a matter of minutes, but then voluntarily spent five more inside purchasing that artwork of a bag with the intent to send it to Eh-ma. It felt like a loosening of shackles that he could enjoy this pretty thing designed only to delight the eye, the maker's painstaking work deliberately concealed under a creation of cheerful frivolity.

His purchase sent the proprietor into such a paroxysm of delight that, for a moment, she wasn't a being old and perhaps jaded, the girl she'd once been surging to the surface. "To have the patronage of the one member of the Seven who is almost never seen anywhere but in the skies?" She spread her fingers over her chest, her nails painted a red to match her lips. "I shall be the envy of every single entrepreneur in my group chat!"

Her smug delight made him laugh—and that had her eyes going huge. "I almost believe I am hallucinating," she whispered.

After returning to his suite with amusement yet alive in his veins, he stored the gift, then flew over to Pierre's through the sepia tones of dusk. As he'd expected, the affable vampire gave him the list of names without problem—and every one of the giftees, baffled by the request though they were, produced their gloves when asked.

"Took a while, but I tracked down the other two buyers," Illium said when he returned from his own hunt. "One's in Europe right now, but his housekeeper was able to find the gloves in his closet, while the other located them stuffed into the pockets of his winter jacket. So we have no missing sets from the seven that came into the city during the window of time we decided on as reasonable."

They'd been generous with that window; increasing it seemed the wrong way to go.

"We'll have to widen the geographic search," Aodhan said at last, and even though he'd been braced for this possibility, it was still a blow. Especially because they both knew many angels were highly mobile; the gloves could have been bought in Spain or Singapore as easily as New York.

But it was all they had.

"I have Céline's contact details," he added. "We can get the names of all her clients directly from her."

But when he called, it was to be informed that she was at a gathering and out of contact for the duration. Aodhan could guess at the type of gathering—held by vampires and angels of a certain age, it was about rejecting the modern world. No phones, no access to electricity, basically nothing that hadn't existed five hundred years ago.

Candlelight balls, intellectual salons, a bloom of artists who wanted to inspire each other and work in a space filled with artistic energy, or a tangle of hedonists bent on an orgy, the type of gathering depended on the participants and their desires.

"There is a peace in creating without interference," Aodhan murmured to Illium after telling him that Céline was currently out of reach. "In prior times, I could work for days, weeks, *months* without interruption if I wanted."

"Yeah, but I don't think most of these candlelit types are like you, Adi." Illium bit into a crisp red apple he'd grabbed from the dining area before flying up to join Aodhan in the office he'd used in his attempt to contact Céline. He'd also picked up two pastries for a pre-dinner snack, and now handed Aodhan his favorite.

Glad to see Illium eating, Aodhan made short work of his own pastry.

"At the core of the movement," Illium continued after a satisfying crunching of the bite he'd taken, "is a dislike of the fact that mortals have so much agency now. Five centuries ago, a large number were either in small villages or in cobbled-together cities, under the rule of angels to the extent that they'd never even think about building their own towers of steel and glass."

Another bite. "On another point," he said after swallowing, "I've sent word to Isiel about the jewels, but he's out stone hunting—and while he's not the candlelit type, he doesn't carry a phone."

Apple finished, core and all—Aodhan was, as always, fascinated by how Illium could accomplish that fact with zero trouble—Illium bit into his pastry. It was a pleasure to watch him eat, his throat muscles moving with purpose and strength.

When a fleck of pastry dropped onto his chest, Aodhan picked it up from the soft gray of his tee and fed it to him, got a kiss on his fingertips for his trouble. Even as warmth spread through his wings at the affectionate touch that was pure Illium, he could see that the other man was tired. And why not? He'd been going full steam since returning from China—where he'd worked himself down to the sinew.

Aodhan didn't blame Suyin for his condition—this was all Illium. When he gave, he gave everything and all of himself. "I think," he murmured, "tonight we rest, and I make you a meal." They'd done all they could on the case at this juncture; there was no point in chasing their tails . . . and Aodhan wanted to look after his Blue.

Illium's smile was startled . . . and sweet. "I'm all yours."

No, Aodhan thought, the other man wasn't all his yet, seeds of fear and worry still holding him back from a final commitment, but he was well on the way . . . as Aodhan was well on the way to conquering the nightmare that had once had a stranglehold on him.

No more.

Smoke bounded out at them when they neared the office of Dmitri's chief administrative officer.

"There you are!" Crouching down, Illium cuddled and stroked his pampered feline. "I thought I dropped you off with Vivek's crew downstairs? Have you been bothering Greta?"

Having come to loom in the doorway, the grouchy admin at least a foot shorter than Aodhan peered at Smoke through the half-glasses perched on her aquiline blade of a nose. Black framed, they matched her severe black jumpsuit with fitted long sleeves.

Aodhan had never seen Greta in anything else, had often wondered if she slept in those jumpsuits, too.

Also, the vampire, with her dark red bob, emerald green eyes heightened by vampirism, and translucent skin was so old, she was petrified; she didn't need the glasses.

But was Aodhan going to mention that?

Oh no. He wasn't an imbecile.

Greta was Dmitri's right hand on the unseen end of Tower work for a reason.

"Your cat has a fascination with seeing angels take flight," she told Illium. "Spent most of her time on the window ledge, watching." It was crystal clear that she'd rather watch paint dry. "But she's a smart cat otherwise. Knows how to catch the elevator so she can move around the Tower."

"Thanks for looking out for her." Illium scratched Smoke between her ears. "She's so inquisitive, I worry she'll decide to head out into the city and not be able to find her way home."

A thawing of Greta's expression as a message pinged on the computer system at her back—which was complex enough to rival Vivek's. "Smoke is excellent company—and I wouldn't worry about her wandering. She seems to have decided the Tower is her territory."

Having heard her name, Smoke spoke up, then padded over to nudge at Greta's dark green ankle boots until she bent and petted the cat. An emerald ring circled her pointer finger, what appeared to be pagan runes on the titanium band. It made total sense to Aodhan that Greta had been a sorceress in her mortal life.

"Yes, yes, you're gorgeous." She gave Smoke one last luxurious stroke. "Now off you go so I can get some work done."

Aodhan held his silence until they were safely behind the closed doors of the elevator. Then he crouched down to scratch Smoke on the top of her head. "Just like your master, charming everyone in sight. Including a woman who looks at me like I'm a lizard that's dared crawl into her vision. A diseased lizard."

Illium snorted a laugh, while Smoke butted at Aodhan's hand for a firmer scratch just as the doors opened on their floor.

After getting out, Illium went to his suite to feed Smoke, while Aodhan entered his and changed into simple pants in a loose linen, and an equally relaxed shirt of the same fabric. Only the color differed, with the pants a rich brown, the shirt a dark cream. After folding back the sleeves to his elbows, he padded barefoot into the kitchen to see what he could throw together from the ingredients on hand.

Part of his prescription for healing from Keir had been to start taking care of himself from the inside out. That meant nourishing his body with things that both tasted good and were good for him.

"Not every angel cooks, but for you, Aodhan," the healer had said, "I think making a ceremony of cooking yourself a good meal at least twice a week is important. A way of saying to yourself that you are worth this time, worth this goodness."

Aodhan hadn't much been in the mood to hear Keir when the healer had first said that, but the farther he walked out of the dark, the more he understood the importance of Keir's wisdom. Since returning from the rigors of China, which had permitted no such time, he cooked as much as he could.

"There's a difference between fuel and nourishment," he said to Smoke, who'd beaten Illium over and was now looking up at him as Aodhan sliced various vegetables into thin strips. "And the same applies to the people we love." He wanted to nourish his Blue, wanted to care for him from the inside out. "Where's our favorite person, then?"

"Right here," came the answer from the vicinity of the front door. "Reye called as I was heading over, wanted company for dinner," he said, naming a member of his wing. "I told him I had a better offer." He walked into sight, lean and sun-browned and with a wickedness that glinted in the eye.

"You know he'll think you're with a lover?"

"I am."

Aodhan's heart punched into his ribs at that easy acceptance, even though he knew that it could never be so simple between him and his Blue. Still, it was a step, another move in their dance. "Sit while I prep. Tell me about what you did in China between your last proper messages to me, and your flight home. We haven't really talked about that."

While Smoke prowled around the suite, as if checking that no one had dared claim her territory while she'd been out, Illium settled at the kitchen table, his wings pouring down either side of the chair designed for angelkind, and told Aodhan of his final week in China. It wasn't that he'd gone silent or otherwise shut Aodhan out, just that his missives had been the quick ones of a man with little time on his hands.

"Mostly, we worked on the final touches to Suyin's citadel." He nibbled on the bowl of salted peanuts and cashews Aodhan had set out in front of him. "The more decorative elements, the things that are her trademark when it comes to architecture. It's a symbol, you know? For her people. Of hope and of the better future to come."

Aodhan nodded, content to just listen to Illium's voice as the other man detailed the build, then moved on to update Aodhan on the people with whom Aodhan had worked side by side during his more than a year as Suyin's temporary second.

"Arza's doing an excellent job as second, but everyone misses you—Arza included. Her respect for you goes to the bone. You ever go back and ask her to step down and she would."

"That's why I can't visit. Not yet." Suyin wasn't the right archangel for him, and he wasn't the right second for her. "Arza deserves the time to settle into her position until she *won't* even consider stepping aside."

Eating more nuts, Illium told him about a wedding over which Suyin had presided—it had been the citadel's first official celebration. "Complete with sky lanterns blown over the ocean, and musicians picking up instruments once thought forever abandoned."

"Describe it to me in detail." Aodhan rarely painted from anything but his own memories and experiences, but this was an event that should be immortalized.

"I took photos, too," Illium said. "I'll show them to you after dinner." For now, he began to color in the images with his words . . . and Aodhan's entire being felt anchored in a way that wasn't about chains but about freedom from all that had once held him down. This anchor gave him safe ground and, with it, the ability to take every chance.

There was nothing unusual in this night, this situation—he and Illium had eaten together plenty of times. Yet it felt different. Quieter, more intimate somehow.

The feeling intensified once he joined Illium at the table to eat, as Illium teased him about his penchant for a particular spice. When the other man bumped into him while they cleaned up afterward, his wing sliding over Aodhan's, Aodhan didn't move away. Instead, putting down the dish he'd been drying, he curved his hand around Illium's nape and stroked his thumb over the other man's pulse.

Illium's eyes were sleepy, his pupils dilated. "Adi." A single word that held so much. A lifetime. Of love. Of loyalty. Of sacrifice. Of patience. Of a bond without boundaries or endings.

"Come to bed," Aodhan murmured. "Keir gave me homework a long time ago."

"What did he suggest you do?"

"Become easy with touch by starting small with people I trusted."

"I'm afraid we're far beyond that," Illium whispered, as if making a confession. "Your hands quite undid me, in case you've forgotten."

Aodhan stroked Illium's pulse again, the staccato beat of it an addiction. "No, Blue, touch on *my* skin."

The sleepiness retreated, the gold of Illium's eyes liquid fire. Both of them silent, their rough breaths the only sound, Aodhan tugged him out of the kitchen and to the living area. The lights of the city sparkled beyond the huge windows, but since the post-war repairs, the view here only went one way—the windows were glazed in a way as to negate spying, inadvertent or not.

It meant he could tug off his shirt and drop it aside without worrying that someone was staring at him without his consent, coveting him. Making him feel less than a sentient being with his own hopes and dreams.

Just an object that could be owned.

But there was no danger of that here, with this man who had seen *him* from the first. And it wasn't only about his privacy. Because when Illium pulled his T-shirt off over his head, Aodhan didn't have to worry that others were looking at the man he loved when he was so vulnerable, so exposed.

They'd both discarded their shoes once inside the suite, and their toes brushed as they came close, closer. Aodhan placed his hands deliberately on Illium's upper arms. Giving the other man permission. Because that mattered to Illium, his lover tautly muscled and dangerously trained.

Their eyes tangled in a visual kiss, Illium placed one hand over Aodhan's bare hip.

20

Illium stroked up the merest breath, then down. "How's this?"

Every one of Aodhan's senses was focused on the skin-to-skin contact, on the slight roughness of Illium's touch, on the warmth and strength of a hand built to carry a heavy blade in winged combat. So different, he realized, from the hands that had viciously stolen the touch that should've been his alone to give.

"The ones who took me," he found himself saying, "were greedy. Weak. Cruel. You're not greedy. You're not weak. And you're *never* cruel."

Though Illium's expression darkened, his jaw clenching until his skin lost blood flow over bone, he didn't tell Aodhan that this wasn't the time to bring up his torture. His best friend in all the universe understood that this was no longer a wound to be kept in the dark inside him, where it could fester. It was time he exposed it to the light once and for all, and burned it to cinders.

"I'm nothing like them." Illium stroked his hip again, infinitely gentle despite his fury. "I'm also alive while those fuckers are dead and erased from existence. Keep that thought in your head anytime the memories try to claw back into you."

Aodhan gloried in Illium's anger, in the vibrant life of him. "You know how you fidget with things?" It had become clear to him since Illium's arrival home that the other man had switched from Kaia's pendant to using the belt buckle Aodhan had gifted him. Tapping at it when he was in thought, rubbing his thumb down the polished metal at times.

But, aware of how much Illium liked to play small objects through and over his fingers, he planned to make the other man a metal disk perfectly weighted for just such play—while stamping it with their entwined initials.

"You mean like this?" Illium took a small triangular piece out of his pocket with his free hand and played it around and over his fingers, his other hand never breaking skin contact with Aodhan.

Distracted, Aodhan stared at the paint-splattered object. "That's the broken tip of my palette knife." He'd snapped the narrow tool in the midst of an intensive painting session. "Blue, it's sharp."

"After I stole it from your easel, I filed down the edges." He slipped it back into his pocket. "It's mine now."

Aodhan had no idea how he'd gotten lucky enough to call Illium his own, but one thing he knew—he was never letting him go.

"As you're mine now," he said firmly. "I'm making *you* my fidget—the mental image on which I'll focus anytime I start to backslide. Because if there's one thing I know, it's that you'll never let me fall."

"Not even if you want to." Illium slid his hand up to spread it over Aodhan's ribs. "You're a stubborn bastard, but I've decided to never again play nice when it comes to your nightmares—I'm hauling you back from the abyss even if you try to take my head off."

"Call me beautiful again," Aodhan rasped, his abdomen

tensing. "I want to remember only you when I hear that word."

He could all but see Illium fighting his overprotective impulses when it came to Aodhan. "Beautiful," he murmured roughly. "Beautiful Adi with the artist's hands and a spirit made of steel fire."

His kiss was firm, demanding, his hand on the back of Aodhan's head.

Aodhan sank into it, into Illium, and into the words that Illium spoke into his mind. Of beauty, of adoration, of sensual promise. The things that his abductors had taken from him by making those words things he associated with cruelty and pain.

Today, his Blue rebuilt his entire understanding—with Aodhan's full cooperation. It was conscious, that cooperation, Aodhan anchoring himself in Illium each time he felt the wolves of darkness begin to gather, to howl.

When Illium put his fingers on Aodhan's waistband, Aodhan sucked in a quick breath before falling into Illium's kiss again as Illium tugged on the cord that was all that held up his pants.

The fabric pooled at his feet, Aodhan stepping out of it with conscious will.

No more flinching.

No *more*.

"My beautiful man," Illium murmured, his fingers tracing Aodhan's lips as he kept on rebuilding the joy in the words that had been stolen from him. "Look at all that ridged muscle"—tracing his abdomen—"those powerful thighs." His gaze dropped.

Aodhan's throat worked, his shoulders bunching. The thighs Illium had admired grew rigid.

"All for me." When he looked up, Illium's eyes glowed with a power they shouldn't, tiny suns that spoke of cells changing, morphing. "You became this so I'd never be alone on the battlefield. Your body is an act of love, Adi. Don't you ever forget that."

More walls cracked, crumbled, vanished into nothing. Because Illium was right. Aodhan had this body, these muscles, this strength *for* him. He'd never been interested in becoming a warrior, could've spent his entire immortal life in a studio or out sketching in a field, his muscles loose and relaxed instead of defined and cut.

But that would've meant watching from safe ground while Illium flew out to battle. And that, he could simply never do. So he'd carved out time from his art instruction under Lady Sharine—such precious time—to attend lessons in swordcraft, ground grappling, and winged combat. He'd begun to run to each of his art lessons in order to build up his strength. And he'd taken up flying on long routes with Illium to increase his endurance.

All of it because he loved Illium more than he loved the art that was a constant melody inside him.

None of it had ever been a sacrifice.

How could he have forgotten that? Forgotten that his flesh was a testament to his love and devotion? That his body was a love song to Illium? "I love you," he rasped. "More than air and sunlight, more than the sky or art."

"Aodhan." Another kiss, as fierce as it was tender as Aodhan tugged at the waistband of Illium's jeans.

The rasp of cloth over skin, the brush of skin on skin, the motion of two bodies in perfect sync.

"Beautiful," Illium said again in a breathless caress before they fell tangled and naked into bed.

Their aroused bodies pressed into each other, their wings overlapping as their thighs did the same. And Illium's eyes so full of a violent power that wanted to devour him, they were on Aodhan's face, his body, as he mapped Aodhan's love for him with his hands and his lips and his words.

A warrior's callused hands, but that same warrior had lips that sipped at Aodhan's and fingers that played over him with delicate grace as he showed Aodhan that his body wasn't just a vessel for agony, that it could bring pleasure beyond compare—not only physical, but of the heart.

"My beautiful, beautiful Adi with his skin like starlight." Silken strands of black hair tipped in blue brushing over his chest. "Hold on, *mea lux.*"

Tears streaked down Aodhan's face as Illium showed him what it was to trust a lover and have that trust rewarded a million times over.

An erotic kiss made tender.

A primal act laced with love.

A powerful body that treated his own with care, such infinite care.

Light sparked behind his eyes, brighter than sunlight on his skin, then he was breaking apart into endless tiny motes, a constellation of dazzling steel fire.

"I have you, Adi." Words he heard through his bones, a vibration to his innermost self. "I have you." Arms that wrapped around him, wings of silver blue that became his world.

He cried into the crook of Illium's neck, sobbing out the pain held deep inside his soul, until it had taken root, twisting him up in ways he'd thought nothing would heal.

He hadn't counted on Illium.

Who didn't tell him that he was ruining the night with his pain. Arms locked around Aodhan, he said, "Cry, Adi. Cry the poison out, every last drop."

Blue, they hurt me in ways I never told. A confession torn out of him before he allowed the memories to surface, allowed them to fill his mental voice as he told Illium his darkest secret. *I was so ashamed at being turned into that, at being unable to stop the degradation.*

His body continued to tremble with his tears. *I didn't want anyone to know. Not even you.* He'd been able to bear Raphael's knowledge only because of who Raphael was to him, to them.

"I knew." Illium's voice was crushed rock. "You had a nightmare in the Medica about a month after we brought you home, woke up screaming things that hinted at it. I decided to wait for you to be ready to talk about it."

Two hundred years, his Blue had waited. Two hundred years he'd continued to love him.

Love unconditional.

Emotion racked his entire body, until he could no longer identify the different strands.

A warmth at the small of his back, a softly furred and tiny body curling into him.

Illium and Smoke held him between them as he cried himself to exhaustion with the only beings in all the world to whom he could be this vulnerable.

He didn't dream that night, his sleep endless and deep.

Illium continued to stroke Aodhan's hair and back long after the other man had fallen asleep, Smoke's purr having gone silent as she joined Adi in sleep. His heart had fucking shattered with each one of Aodhan's tears, but he'd found a grim happiness in them, too.

Because, for a long, *long* time, Aodhan had refused to cry.

It was as if he'd decided that he'd had enough time to recover from his torture and abuse, that he must now be stoic, his pain locked up in the most impenetrable part of his psyche. He might've retreated from the world, but he'd also retreated from himself, refusing to even acknowledge his scars.

Raphael alone must have known the entirety of it, because he'd stripped the minds of Aodhan's abusers. Illium had no doubt that the sire had tried to get Aodhan to open up to the healers, but not even an archangel could make a savaged young angel speak of his horror if he preferred to encase that horror in stone and shove it away out of sight.

Raphael also wouldn't have dishonored the trust between them by forcing the issue. Especially not when Aodhan had been so fragile, body and mind held together by the gossamer cobwebs of hope and will. Later . . . well, Illium's lover was too strong, too stubborn, too determined to just *conquer it.*

Tonight, Illium had felt the stone casing not only crack but fall away. Because Aodhan hadn't retreated after speaking of the crimes against him. He'd curled impossibly closer, his own wings folded back so that Illium could enclose him in silver blue.

"You are extraordinary," Illium whispered, pressing a kiss to the diamond-bright strands of Aodhan's hair as heat stung his eyes.

I love you. More than air and sunlight, more than the sky or art.

Illium's entire being felt as if it had shifted this night, undergoing a fundamental change from which there could never be any return.

He'd never been jealous of Aodhan's art, or his affinity to sunlight, or anything else that brought him joy. This wasn't about that. Neither was it about a declaration of love. He'd never doubted that Aodhan loved him—that fact was a simple and inexorable part of his existence.

It was . . .

He couldn't break it down, couldn't put the emotion into words. He just knew that he was no longer the same man he'd been before this night.

I love you. More than air and sunlight, more than the sky or art.

The hours past reverberated inside him, his very cells stamped with the sparkle of stardust that was Aodhan.

21

Aodhan had never personally spoken to Céline prior to the call she made to him the following morning. He had, however, long been aware of her as an artist. A woman who worked in creative bursts, she hadn't produced anything he'd term *art* for the past century—to him, the gloves didn't qualify, for well made as they were, they broke no boundaries of design. However, prior to her latest fallow period, she'd sculpted breathtaking pieces in clay, and prior to *that*, she'd worked with stone, and so on.

Far older than him, she had a much deeper artistic history. But for all her undeniable talent, she was no Hummingbird, whose art seemed to transcend time itself. Céline's work had never quite hit that master-level edge—most likely because she never invested the time to take her raw talent in each discipline to the next level.

Had she stuck with the sculptures, for one, she *would* by now be Eh-ma's peer.

"Celi is like a butterfly," the Hummingbird had said to him with a sigh. "I have two of her pieces in the gardens of our southernmost home, and I love them for their naked energy, but I also see that she became frustrated and didn't push through to the next phase, to that which would have taken a good piece to a brilliant one."

Aside from that small bit of insight, Aodhan had no idea of the personality of the angel he was about to meet when he answered the call in the living area of his suite.

The screen cleared to show an elfin face with huge blue-green eyes, a nose dotted with freckles, and masses of honey blond hair pushed back with a metal band coated in fine gemstones. Behind her arched wings of the same honeyed tone. Her skin glowed the shade of cream mixed with sunlight, her cheeks dusted with a powder that made them gently sparkle. She'd painted her lips a sweet pink.

If he hadn't known her age, he'd have taken her for a much younger angel.

"Lady Céline," he said.

She pressed her hands together. "Oh, it really is you! When Sataki told me you'd called, I was sure he must be mistaken. I hate to say it, but he is a bit of a dunderhead." A whisper. "Pretty to look at but not much going on between the ears, I'm afraid. My worst failing is hiring staff based on their decorative nature. And you must call me Celi. I insist. I'm no lady!"

It would've been easy to take her at face value, to accept the bubbly personality and the bright eyes and the delight . . . but Aodhan felt as if he was viewing a painting. A meticulously constructed facade designed to obscure Céline's true self.

That could mean nothing, this an affectation that amused her, her outward personality and tone elements of herself she changed from time to time as other angels changed their hair color or style of dress.

"Thank you for your time," he said, keeping it polite.

"Of course, *mon chéri*! What can I do for Aodhan himself? Perhaps you want to make a joint artwork, *oui*?" She giggled at her own words. "You must excuse me. I am as giddy as a schoolgirl. I have long been a follower of your work."

Her accent had morphed from vaguely New York to heavily French between her words of greeting and this. An artifact of age or another mask? Just playing with altering herself. Perhaps that was the truth of it—that Céline's greatest artwork was Céline.

"I wished to ask you about your gloves," he said, and explained what he was after.

"Oh, Fia keeps track of that sort of thing." She waved a hand. "I'll have her send the list to you at once. One of my few sensible hires—fully functioning gray cells." Turning her head, she called out the name of the assistant.

A low murmur in the background soon afterward, with Céline asking the other woman to send Aodhan what he needed *tout de suite!*

Another murmur, before Céline turned back.

"There," she said, "it is done." A beaming smile. "How diverting, to be involved in a mystery all the way in Archangel Raphael's territory. What has happened?" She held up a hand, showcasing nails painted two shades darker than her lips. "*Non, non!* Do not tell Celi. I will make up far more interesting stories in my head."

"I appreciate your help," Aodhan said when she finally paused for breath. "If I may ask another question—have you made any direct sales in the past year or given pairs to friends?"

"I do not do direct sales," she said at once. "As for gifts to friends—not for a decade at least. My cherished intimates are heartily sick of my gloves as gifts, have threatened to gift them back to me if I dare offer them another pair." Another burst of laughter, her eyes dancing . . . and still, Aodhan couldn't quite make himself buy the insouciant affect.

"I thank you," Aodhan said, his intention to cut off the call after a polite goodbye.

But Céline leaned forward. "What is it like, to work under the Hummingbird?" A shimmer in her voice that might even have been real. "I thought once to importune her to be my mentor, but alas, it struck me that I have not the staying power she requires of her protégés. Is that not true? It's what I've heard. But honestly, it's all gossip and conjecture from what I see of those she's mentored."

"She is a brilliant artist, and a teacher beyond compare," Aodhan answered with utmost honesty.

Céline sighed, her hands pressed to her chest. "Perhaps one day, I will have an audience with her. I wonder if she'll even see me."

Aodhan could've told Céline that the Hummingbird had two of her pieces, but he couldn't make himself be friendly to this woman who wore a mask so jarring to his senses. "I cannot presume to speak for her" was all he said. "I will leave you to your work now, Lady Céline."

"No, please," she said with a little pout that soon dissolved into a smile. "Do stay and let us speak a touch longer. You are quite the most interesting person I've spoken to in literally *years*. Bordeaux is beginning to lose its charm, become a bore of old buildings and terrible soirees."

No French accent anymore. Her voice was that of an old angel who had grown up speaking so many languages that her accent was a mélange—though this, too, could be a facade, it seemed apt to be closer to reality than the rest.

"I'm afraid I must get back to my duties." He kept it polite though he could've pulled rank—in strict angelic hierarchical terms, he outranked her by a considerable margin. He was in the inner circle of an archangel, held more innate power—*and* was still growing and developing—while she was an angel of a certain age and power who would never progress any further.

But strict hierarchies weren't how the angelic world worked. Céline was connected by sheer dint of having been a social creature for centuries upon centuries. She no doubt had the ears of seconds and archangels through their courts, and if he made an enemy of her, she could decide to become a snake in the grass who whispered against Raphael for spite.

It might come to nothing, but there was no point in creating an enemy when he could as easily create a contact for future informational needs—because Céline would always be a social, connected creature.

"But I will convey your admiration of her to Lady Sharine," he said before she could interrupt. "She has been weighing up the idea of hosting a gathering of artists in Titus's territory once our world has settled better into this post-war peace. Maybe toward the end of the next decade, though it may take longer. Shall I inform her that you would be interested to attend?"

Her eyes glowed with a joy so earnest, it cut through all falsehood. "My dearest Aodhan—may I call you that?—my heart would stop should I receive such an invitation. It does not matter what I have on my schedule, I will wipe it all off the very day I receive word of this event. A decade or two is nothing, will fly by in but a heartbeat."

Her hand fluttered up. "Oh, I *must* prepare." A sudden intensity to her expression that cut away all artifice to reveal the burning core of a woman with a passion. "I will make a piece of art, a gift worthy of the Hummingbird."

Leaving her on that happy note, Aodhan signed off.

Her assistant had already sent through the list of dealers worldwide, neatly separated by country and region. He forwarded parts of the wider local section through to both Illium and Janvier. He'd apprised the vampire of the situation, and Janvier was more than willing to assist. "To lose family," he'd said, "it is an anguish, but to have them stolen? The grief becomes a spiked spear that shreds."

That done, he sent Lady Sharine a message about Céline's desire to attend the planned gathering and her intention to make art for Eh-ma. No reply, but he didn't expect one quickly. While Eh-ma had embraced technology after her "waking," she wasn't tied to it, would see the message when she saw it.

Then he dropped by Dmitri's office to give him an update on the investigation.

"Navarro's home," Dmitri told him. "Just landed. He shouldn't have been traveling but he wasn't about to stay away now that we know it was murder. He's ready to see you at any time."

So it was that Aodhan's mind was on the questions he

might ask Navarro when he left Dmitri's office, his thoughts heavy with the reminder of the crime that had stolen the lives of two innocent people.

His phone vibrated with an incoming message only a few steps down the corridor.

When he checked, it was to see a message from Illium: *Love you, Sparkle. Even if you did make me eat bran muffins for breakfast. (I'm staging a mutiny next time. I was blinded by love hormones today).*

Aodhan's smile felt as if it would crack his face.

"Well, wow." Honor, who'd exited the elevator while he was standing there, gasped and clutched at her chest. "I can see why people have written literal odes to your smile." Her grin was affectionate. "'Sunlight diamonds that cause heart's flutter' indeed."

Sliding away the phone, he said, "That's it. This time, I'm seriously going to strangle him." Because he could think of only one person who would still remember that ridiculous poem.

Laughing, Honor held up her hands, her uptilted green eyes as warm as the honey brown of her skin. "No, no, it wasn't our poor Bluebell. He actually groaned when I showed it to him. The Seven Fan Club dug it up out of some archive."

Aodhan made a pained sound, head in his hands. Illium had told him that a mortal had set up an "Unofficial but Loyal Fan Club for the Seven!" It apparently featured an online chat board where members posted photos, and shared tracts called "fan fiction" featuring members of the Seven.

"Don't read it, Adi," Illium had said solemnly, because of course he'd had to make a fake profile and go poke around. "They have us doing things with Dmitri that I'm not sure are anatomically possible. Also, there's an entire subforum that believes Venom can shape-shift into a snake and, well . . . let's just leave it there."

Smoke pounced out from the open door of Venom's empty office at that very instant.

Aodhan's frown vanished, his face creasing into a huge

smile; he hadn't realized Illium had dropped her off on this floor today. That, or Smoke had been catching the elevator again.

He had a sudden thought.

Head jerking toward Honor, he stared. "Why do you know about what's in the fan club?"

The hunter, who was dressed in sleeveless black leathers today, her dark hair pulled severely back, a gun strapped to her thigh and a couple of blades in arm sheaths, said, "I spy to make sure there are no dangerous loonies."

Crouching down to pet Smoke, she added, "I'm not interested in the ordinary folk—mortal and vampire and I'm pretty sure a few disguised angels—who are just starstruck. I mean I get it—my husband *is* hot." A grin. "And the rest of you clean up okay, don't they, Smoke?"

Gathering Smoke up into her arms, she rose. "My focus is on the ones who are obsessed to a level where they think Dmitri is *their* husband and Galen is sending them dreams every night. They need watching. Because no psycho is going to hurt any of you on my watch."

Aodhan knew fragments of Honor's history, enough to understand that this generous and vibrant member of the Tower could comprehend his scars better than most. It was an awful, terrible bond he wished they didn't share. "Thank you." He touched the back of his hand to hers, saw her pupils flare, vivid black against green so deep, it was a quiet forest pool. "I'm working on the touch thing."

Her smile was gentle and maternal in a way that reached deep into his heart. In strict terms, Honor was a baby in comparison to his age. She'd been a mortal of less than three decades when she'd become a vampire, was nowhere near even the halfway point to official angelic adulthood.

Yet the hunter had a sense of age to her that was at times a heaviness in Aodhan's bones akin to what he felt around much older angels. As if Honor had lived entire lifetimes before he'd ever met her.

"You'll make it," she said today, and it was a simple statement. "You'll never be who you once were, but what's wrong with that?" A shrug. "Change is a constant. Survivors adapt and thrive."

Her words lingered in his mind as they parted ways. She was right. Even if he hadn't been abducted, he would no longer be the youth he'd been at the time. That was an impossibility.

Survivors adapt and thrive.

Survivor was a label he'd railed against, because it implied the horrors done to him. But today, in Honor's eyes, he'd seen that he could own it, both what had been done to him, *and* what had followed—what he'd done, what he'd become, all the love that had surrounded him.

Coming on top of his emotional catharsis in Illium's arms, Honor's statement settled inside him, downy feathers coming to a gentle landing in spaces within that had opened up after centuries of silence.

Well, wow. I can see why people have written literal odes to your smile.

He paused on the balcony, the wind pushing at his hair. He had it all at once, why he hadn't liked Céline despite her charm and artistic spirit. When Honor had said those admiring words, it had been with teasing affection and genuine delight and absolutely zero desire to possess.

A friend who'd been happy to see him shine.

Céline, on the other hand . . . it had been there, in the eyes behind the mask. An avaricious glitter. She'd wanted him, but not in the healthy way a person attracted to him might want him. He'd experienced the latter over the years, more so since his shift from the Refuge to New York. Other angels as well as senior vampires had been open in their desire for his company.

"I figured why not try my luck," one had said after approaching him. "I'd kick myself if I never asked and you might've said yes." A smile. "So how about it? Coffee date?"

He'd felt awkward to be on the receiving end of such invitations, but had never reacted with a visceral dislike—and at least three of those same people had ended up becoming trusted colleagues. It had been different with Céline. Where the others had looked at him with genuine attraction and even flustered desire, Céline's gaze had held the clawing want of a being who wished to put him in a box and keep him for herself.

A wash of air, powerful wings closing next to him as Raphael landed on the balcony. The sire was wearing faded leathers of dark gray, had a streak of dust on his cheek and a rapidly healing cut on his jaw.

"Aodhan," he said. "I could see your scowl all the way from the stratosphere."

Aodhan should've asked him who he'd been sparring with since it couldn't have been Dmitri, but his mind was elsewhere. "I spoke to someone today who wanted me as Sachieri and Bathar did," he said, the words stark in the morning light.

Raphael's amused expression turned stormy, the intense, impossible blue of his eyes going frigid.

But Aodhan shook his head. "Oh, they'll never have me, won't even try. That's the point."

A raised eyebrow that was very much of an archangel.

"I'm too strong now," Aodhan explained. "She wants me, but she pretended not to—because I'm not prey any longer. I'm not young and untried and a little naïve. If I was shot through the heart with a crossbow today, even if they destroyed my entire heart, I'd still have enough power to blast them out of existence before I fell."

Aodhan's entire body filled with breath. "I think the only person who could take me down now is an archangel— and with Her Evilness dead, I don't think anyone else in the Cadre is collecting angels. Also, who would pick a war with you, Lady Caliane, *and* Suyin?" Because he knew all three would bring down the fury of the ages on his attackers' heads.

Raphael because he loved Aodhan.

Caliane because he was one of Raphael's Seven.

Suyin because of their personal friendship.

Raphael's lips kicked up. "Indeed, Aodhan, you have powerful allies and friends. However, Titus will be gravely insulted you didn't add him to the list—you are his 'step-son's' beloved, and so you fall under his umbrella of protection as much as mine."

Sound telescoped into nothing but the rasp of Aodhan's own shallow breathing, the words after "beloved" fading into a buzz of angry bees in his head. "You know?"

22

Raphael's answer was simple. "I've known you two your entire lives." Eyes of cerulean blue, endless in their depth, held Aodhan's. "If you have need of it, you have my approval. I'm happy that you've made your way back to each other after the turmoil."

Aodhan exhaled, unaware of how much he'd needed to hear those words of approval until they were spoken. It wasn't about permission—Aodhan would ask no one for permission when it came to loving Blue. It was about seeing the quiet pride in Raphael's eyes, in being reassured their sire saw no problem with two of his Seven being so entangled . . . and that the angel they'd once called Rafa saw their relationship and celebrated it.

"Illium is afraid," he said, the words no betrayal when it came to this man who was more father to Illium than Aegaeon would ever be. "I left him once, so lost in my own pain that I didn't see past his bright mask."

Raphael didn't break the searing eye contact, the midnight strands of his hair flowing back in a dark wave. "That you understand that is the first step." A careful touch on Aodhan's shoulder. "He waited two hundred years for you, Adi." A gentle reminder that Raphael had known him through all the seasons of his life. "How long are you ready to wait for him?"

The answer took no thought at all. "Forever."

A smile, Raphael's wings aglow. "Then trust will come, his fear buried under the weight of decades of having you by his side." He looked out at the city, its thousands of windows reflecting the sunlight to create a living fire. "I saw him after he helped carry the bier of his mortal friend Lorenzo. His heart was broken—and yet Illium cherishes his friend's widow even knowing that she, too, will break his heart one day."

Raphael's lips kicked up in a smile awash in affection for the boy he'd helped raise to manhood. "Our Bluebell's will to love is stronger than any fear. Especially when it comes to you."

Shifting, Aodhan held out his forearm in the grip of warriors.

Raphael took it, his hold firm.

No words spoken, the contact enough. Aodhan had never shut Raphael out when it came to necessary touch, but he'd rarely ever initiated it. Not even when Raphael was the one who'd carried him out of the hellhole of his imprisonment, Aodhan's broken, emaciated body cradled in his arms.

"Thank you, sire," he said today, as they stood with their forearms linked. "For carrying me home." His throat was thick as he said the words he'd never before vocalized. "For taking vengeance when I couldn't, for making it so I never had to fear those monsters again, and for keeping a place for me in your Seven even when I lost myself."

Raphael tugged at his forearm in a question.

Aodhan flowed forward into the other man's embrace.

Holding him tight, warrior warmth and archangel heart, Raphael said, "Never do you have to thank me, Aodhan.

You are mine, will always be one of mine even should you fly far from me one day. Vengeance was my right, and my protection yours." His voice was rough. "I'm only sorry I wasn't able to protect you from them."

So many wounds, Aodhan thought, hearing the raw pain in his archangel's voice. So many scars created by two vicious beings who'd wanted without reason or conscience. "They're the only ones to blame," he said. "I've come to accept that. Now you and Illium and the rest of the Seven who were there at the time have to accept it, too."

They drew apart, two men who at this instant weren't archangel and warrior, soldier and liege, only people who had indelible places in each other's hearts. Because as Raphael would consider him his even should he fly from the Tower, Aodhan would consider Raphael an integral part of his family for all eternity.

"You always were wise," Raphael murmured. "Do you remember the sketch you gave me the year after Aegaeon's abandonment?"

Aodhan cocked his head in a silent question.

"An image of people wearing festival masks. It was excellent work for a child, but what has always stuck with me is your frustrated little face as you told me that you couldn't draw all the masks." A glow of power in his wings. "'Some of them you can't see, Rafa. They're there but they look just like faces.'"

Aodhan felt his lips curve. "What an odd little child I must've been."

Throwing back his head, Raphael laughed. "A most fascinating conversational companion." But his gaze was serious when it locked with Aodhan's again. "What happened knocked your confidence in your ability to spot those masks, but you've always had it. It's good to see you trust in yourself again, Aodhan."

"It feels good from the inside, too . . . Rafa."

This time they laughed together, and if a passing wing of angels did a double take at the sight, well, Aodhan was starting to be all right with that kind of ordinary attention.

* * *

Navarro was waiting for Aodhan outside his home in the forested interior of the Enclave. A gracious dual-level building of warm golden brick, it was quiet, with no hint of staff moving about inside. The drive out to the road was a long and gently curving line shadowed by trees older than many a young angel in the Tower.

Navarro, too, had a sense of age and maturity that Aodhan had noticed from the very first time they'd met, his handsome face with its high cheekbones and angled jaw framed by long dark hair that went down to his waist. He often wore beads in that hair, or—as today—had a thin braid on one side around which was wrapped an intricate stack of threads in shades of red and black.

It should've made him look young, but his mien was too serious for that, his muscles used to being held with utmost control. In battle, he wasn't a showy fighter, rather a man who made every motion count—and once, long ago, he'd trained both Illium and Aodhan close to the start of their journey as warriors. He still returned to the Refuge for a decade every century to do the same for each new intake.

Navarro was a teacher patient and calm.

"If you don't mind," the angel said, "I'd like to walk along the drive rather than go inside. That's what I was doing prior to your arrival, but my wings are yet cramped from stuffing myself into that plane."

He flexed his upper body, the wings he'd referenced akin to those of a red-shouldered hawk, the topmost feathers a distinctive reddish-brown shade that morphed into a repeating black-and-white pattern lower down that was breathtaking in flight. "The healers were stern in saying that I shouldn't risk jostling them, and the trees on my land grow close to one another—else I'd suggest we walk among them."

Despite the pragmatic words delivered in a gruff tone, his expression held both sorrow and anger.

"Thank you for making the effort," Aodhan said, warrior to warrior, the two of them having long moved past the

student-teacher relationship. "I've had the same wing injury—
I know how much it must have pained you to sit for the
journey, quite apart from the feeling of confinement."

Navarro gave a clipped nod. "I'd already given my staff
leave prior to my decision to return home early, so I can't
offer you much hospitality."

"There's no need." Aodhan caught sight of an eagle sweeping in to land among the trees, but his attention was on the
other angel. "That you came so far while injured tells me
you valued Marco."

"I would have come regardless. While under Contract,
he was under my protection." Then Navarro exhaled, his
eyes focused into the distance. "But yes, Marco was a favorite."

The angel took several quiet breaths before continuing.
"He had a stable nature that's rare in young vampires, a
kind of innate balance. I saw him going far, and was much
saddened when I first heard of his death, but then I thought
him a casualty of war. A sorrowful thing, yes, but in a sense
to be expected. War does not spare anyone."

"Yes," Aodhan said. "War follows a well-trodden path
for all its violence, while this, what took Marco, came out
of the shadows, unseen and unknown."

Navarro's long hair gleamed in the sunlight, its rays revealing the strands of red and bronze hidden among brown
so dark, it was a breath away from black. "Marco was fresh
faced and eager and ready to explore the world of immortals. But . . . there was a goodness in him."

The angel halted in the shadow of a tree with a spreading
canopy in which songbirds gossiped, unconcerned with the
winged beings below. "Some people—mortal and immortal—
seem to have a heart that does not darken no matter what.
A resilience that is profound in its determination to stand
strong against all attempts to alter them for the worse. Do
you know what I mean?"

Aodhan met the other man's gaze. "My best friend is
Illium, Navarro."

A warming of the rich brown eyes that had the slightest

tilt at the corners. "Ah, I must be tired indeed to forget that—especially when Illium's nature used to concern me when he was a fledgling. How, I thought, could a boy with such a heart survive the rigors of life?"

Hands behind his back, he clasped the wrist of one with the other. "It was much the same with Marco. So young, he hadn't yet grown the warrior encasing necessary to guard his heart. I felt protective of him." A tightening of his lips. "I didn't favor him in any visible way—that would've only led to problems with his peers, but I did keep a closer eye on him."

Aodhan didn't interrupt.

"I only picked up that liquor shop because I intended for Marco to manage its future refurbishment and upgrade," Navarro continued. "It wasn't really my type of investment as it stood. I thought to have him manage it for a year or so in order to strengthen his administration and finance skills before I put him in charge of the upgrade."

That the angel had been so thoughtful in his oversight of Marco's development didn't surprise Aodhan. Everything Navarro did was tempered and thorough.

"You knew he had a stalker."

Beginning to walk again, Navarro frowned. "I knew he had an unwanted admirer, but her attentions seemed to peter out before the war. I assumed the infatuation had run its course.

"Prior to that, Marco did come to me to say an anonymous admirer had sent him gifts and letters. He didn't want to keep them as he was much in love with his chosen partner, but with the giver refusing to reveal her identity, he couldn't return the items."

"What did you advise?"

"That he give them to me. I placed most in the safe, but I—with his permission—wore one of the most distinctive rings for over a month, at a time when I was mingling with angelkind at various events."

"A silent statement that the gift was unwanted, had been passed on to his angel to curry favor."

"That was my intent in wearing it—but it appears his admirer took it as a sign that I was appropriating Marco's gifts. He received even more jewels, this time sent to his mother's home. He continued to pass everything on to me to store in the safe until such time as he could return them. He was sure the admirer would approach him in person soon enough, as was I." His muscles locked. "Neither one of us foresaw that it would be in murderous violence."

One question answered at least. Marco hadn't kept the gifted items. They'd been in his effects because Navarro had considered them part of Marco's estate.

"We didn't find any love notes or letters among his belongings."

"No, I didn't pass those on. Marco hadn't wanted the attention, so why make his mother worry about his honor? The jewels and gloves, I thought she could sell. Marco always spoke about buying his mother a luxurious apartment once he held a more senior position with the attendant income."

Aodhan wondered what Giulia would say when she realized the jewels had been purchased with her son's blood? Then again, did she have to know? Could this not be a gift from a son to his mother, a mother who had no one else left? "Will you tell a lie for me, Navarro?"

The other angel looked at him, his gaze rich with empathy. Navarro might not see it, but his more solemn personality aside, the angel wasn't so different from Illium and Marco. His heart remained defiant and unjaded.

Navarro's next words confirmed Aodhan's belief. "Marco's mother. The jewels are a gift from me in honor of her son's exemplary service. It is agreed."

"Why aren't you part of the Tower's senior team?" Aodhan asked in genuine interest, because Navarro was far too stable and wise not to be more heavily utilized.

"I was once," Navarro said, to Aodhan's absolute astonishment. "Back when Raphael first ascended." Clearly noticing Aodhan's surprise, he smiled. "Raphael needed a transition team, and as he'd been one of my favorite students once, I volunteered. I don't regret doing so, but I also don't regret stepping down when others became available. I am not made for politics and an archangel's senior court cannot avoid it.

"But I have a feeling I won't be able to sidestep being recalled to the Tower much longer—Dmitri keeps threatening to haul me in kicking and screaming." A scowl marred his expression. "Each time we meet for a drink, I warn him I'll insult everyone and cause a war, and he tells me he doesn't believe me."

"Neither do I." Aodhan could see the angel as the calm head of the negotiating table instead. "Thank you for agreeing to dissemble for Giulia. She'd never accept jewels touched by her son's blood, but I think she'll accept a gift from an angel who valued him. Even then, she'll likely not accept the entirety of it."

Navarro considered that. "Perhaps I will buy her that luxurious apartment when she attempts to return the jewels. I will say that it is what Marco wished to do, and I feel it my duty as the angel who failed to protect him." His expression was grim. "I *do* feel that responsibility. All that time, all those gifts. I thought it a foolish old angel with too much money and not enough sense, and didn't treat it as seriously as I should have."

"Did Marco tell you about a possible assault from the air on Tanika?"

A sharp glance. "No. When did this occur?"

"In the lead-up to the war."

Navarro sighed. "He likely didn't want to distract me from battle planning. Regardless, he should've been safe. He was to remain in the underground weapons repair area during the war—as safe a location as there can be in a conflict of that size. He had no real skills at repair; he was tasked with organizing the movement of weapons in and out, and doing anything else required by the armorers."

"Something drew him out. A threat to Tanika?"

"Yes. I can think of nothing else that would've caused him to abandon his post—Marco was the kind of man who kept his word. His mother had already evacuated. I believed his young woman had as well, but I think now that she must've never gotten the chance."

Taken, Aodhan thought, used as leverage. "The notes and letters? I would see them."

"I am truly sorry, Aodhan. I destroyed them when I believed Marco lost in the war."

23

Aodhan had steeled himself for disappointment for this very reason, but the confirmation hit like a blow nonetheless.

"I recall the general timbre of the messages," the other man added before Aodhan could respond. "She called Marco her beloved, and said she intended to be with him for eternity. Generic inanities. Not an original thought in the bunch."

"Did she ever threaten Tanika?"

Navarro paused for a long moment, his wings held with warrior motionlessness—an act so innate that even an injury couldn't halt it. "I recall only two mentions of Marco's young woman. The first was contemptuous. She said she understood he needed a blood donor and that things might go too far during a feed, but to never get emotionally attached to his food."

A tic in his jaw, Navarro began to walk again. "Marco was angry. He never wanted Tani—that's what he called her—to feel like she was only a blood donor, and would often drink bottled blood so their every date wasn't about him feeding on her. From what he said of her, I don't believe she minded but it was important to him.

"Now, the second note . . . it held more vitriol—and I did put one of my senior staff onto tracing that one because it struck me as crossing a line, but she had no success even though she's my best tracker. There was simply no trail to follow—the letter was hand-delivered by being dropped onto the drive during a high-traffic time in the sky. And I have none of the recording eyes of mortals."

Whatever Navarro might believe, it appeared to Aodhan that he'd done all he could to get to the bottom of what had, to that point, appeared a disturbing but not dangerous infatuation. "What did it say?"

"It was written in a jagged script, the fountain pen pushed so hard that it had broken through the thick parchment in places. She referred to Tani as a 'blood whore' who should know her place, and intimated that if she didn't, it wouldn't end well for her. That was where the writer betrayed herself another way, too—she said, to the best of my memory: 'I am the caliber of woman you should call lover.' Until then, we had suspected but hadn't categorically known the gender of this person."

Navarro's boot landed on a fallen branch, the crunch loud in the greenery-draped landscape. "That is the last contact of which I'm aware, and it came some month and a half before the drums of war began to sound. I believed the writer had flounced off."

Pain scored his features. "When Marco's and Tani's remains were found at the shop, I believed he'd met her there after she missed the evacuation, that it was a temporary shelter while he worked out how to get her away from the fighting."

Turning, he faced Aodhan. "It still doesn't make sense to me, the obsessed one murdering Marco, too. I would've expected her to take the chance to abduct him—no one would've known of it, Marco listed as missing in war."

A horrific scenario. A victim so cagily trapped that people didn't even know they were alive. Rescue would never come. Once, that would've made Aodhan's gut churn, his nightmares claw awake.

Today, it just intensified his rage.

"Something went wrong," Illium said when they met up that night on the Tower roof, the area swathed in shadows while New York fell away around them in a glittering carpet.

None of them had had any luck with the gloves, so they focused on what Navarro had told Aodhan. "I think he's right," Illium added. "Abduction was likely the point, Tanika's the only planned death."

"The perfect crime." Aodhan flared his wings, only to snap them closed with a hard movement. "Except as I knew you would look, Raphael would look, Naasir and Galen, Dmitri and Jason would look, we both know Giulia would've looked. She would've dug and dug and dug."

Illium found a primal joy in Aodhan's rage. He knew that psychic wounds such as those Aodhan had experienced never truly disappeared, but he also understood that scars could form over them, that the wound could age until it was a faint echo rather than a throbbing pulse.

It was Keir who'd told him that many months after Aodhan's rescue, when he'd still been in the Medica healing from his physical injuries. "His heart is cut and bleeding. But as his physical injuries will eventually scab over, then heal, so will the wounds to his spirit. Their timeline, however, is far slower—and where immortal skin is rare to scar, even we cannot escape scars to the spirit."

Keir had run his hands through Illium's hair as he sat slumped on a large stone, the cold winter wind at his back. "I would not say so for all angels, but Aodhan? Your friend has an inner sun that powers him, a spirit unlike any I have ever seen. Even more, he has his heart's mirror to reflect that light back to him, further intensifying its strength."

More gentle strokes, a warmth coming from him that had nothing to do with heat. "He will come back to us, Illium. This I believe with everything I am."

You were right, Keir, he thought this beautiful New York night, his heart so full, it ached.

Out loud, he said, "Yes. Giulia would've searched and searched until she found an explanation for her son's disappearance."

"The angel miscalculated in more ways than one." Aodhan clenched his hands on the roof edge on which they sat. "Does Venom still have that punching bag in the basement?"

"Feeling murderous, are you?" Illium's blood ran hot. "How about we strip off and spar?"

Aodhan shot him an assessing look. "No, you're still too thin."

"The insult!" Shifting, Illium poked him in the chest. "I can take you any day of the week, Sparkle-pants."

"Sparkle-pants?" Narrowed eyes glinting, Aodhan rose to his feet and strode to the center of the roof. "Now I'm mad." He put his hands to the bottom of his tunic to pull it off and throw it aside.

Illium's heart thudded as he followed Aodhan up. "Oh, look how scared I am." Grinning, he stripped off his own top, then they both got rid of their boots and socks and began to circle each other. "That the best you can do? Cassandra's grandmother could move faster."

"The roof is a very hard surface," Aodhan murmured, the muscles of his shoulders glinting under the faint moonlight that diffused in through the puffy night clouds. "Sure you can handle it, my little blue flower?"

His gut clenched at the roughness in Aodhan's tone, the way his eyes moved over Illium. "Oh, we're trash-talking now, are we?"

"I do believe you started it." Aodhan moved in a blur of speed that had Illium hitting the rooftop hard on his back before he rolled up and away with the bounce of a honed warrior—and retaliated with a kick.

Anyone watching them would've thought they were in a fight to the death. And there *were* people watching by now, their movements having caught the eye of passing angels. What those angels didn't see in the darkness was the flashing grin on Illium's face, or the equally amused and infuriated mental muttering from Aodhan.

If you dare use "Sparkle-pants" in public, I will release a painting of you dressed in a romper and ruffled shirt such as the ones some mothers inflict on their angelic toddlers.

I could pull it off.

That got him a growl. Which honestly, was ridiculously hot coming from his contained lover. *This is the only time I wish I were an archangel.*

A rapid-fire exchange of blows and kicks that turned them into a diamond-blue blur.

Aodhan's chest was heaving when they faced each other again, as was Illium's. *Why?*

So I had glamour and could turn us invisible. Then we could take this dance to the sky. His body throbbed, blood molten at the idea of tangling wings and limbs with Aodhan high up above the earthbound starlight of the city.

Aodhan managed to capture him in a hug-like grip as he said, *I hear there are blind spots all over the place. Somehow, the satellites never quite get any images in those areas at relevant times.* His breath was hot against Illium's ear, his body slick with a faint layer of perspiration.

It took serious effort—mostly because he'd rather lick Adi up—for Illium to twist out and away. *I had to do something when surveillance cameras and satellites that could capture images in high definition became a thing.*

Angelkind had thought about banning the technology, with a strong push from the older sector of angels, but the Cadre had decided it was useful to them, too—as long as it was in their control. The leash of that control might be long, but it was still a leash. *My team wouldn't hear the end of it otherwise.*

They'd worked it so certain remote areas went "dark" on an unpredictable basis—unpredictable to outsiders and anyone looking to exploit a security hole, that is. All senior Tower angels knew where to get the list of the planned blackouts.

The juniors had to get creative, or wait until they were in the safe zone of the Refuge. Such was life when you were a young angel with amorous intentions. *The oceans are still safe. Not much pinpointed on vast swathes of open water.*

Conversation stopped as they came into contact again, both of them flying into kicks at high speed, which were, unbeknownst to their growing audience, part of a routine they'd practiced as youths until they could pull it off at an insane velocity.

Silence surrounded them when they landed on their feet on opposite sides, each focused grim-eyed on the other. Only Illium was close enough to spot the amusement in Aodhan's eyes.

Have you ever had to do cleanup after a couple in the throes didn't check for technological watchers, and got caught?

Illium groaned inwardly. *Let's not go there. There's a reason there are so many mortal artworks that show angels "falling in agony" from the sky.* For some reason, mortal minds seemed to have trouble computing that angelkind might be up to more illicit things in the air, but at least it made life easier when dealing with the inevitable slipups.

Also, forget about a couple, he muttered. *One day I'll tell you about a quartet that decided to get creative. If I have gray hairs, it's because of those four—even I learned things when the images first showed up on our monitoring system.*

Aodhan's shoulders shook . . . but he blocked Illium's next strike with a superb show of brute strength that made Illium's cock throb in ways that had nothing to do with combat . . . at least not this kind of combat.

Will you two stop pretending you're fighting to the death? came a dark voice in their heads. *I've fielded at least five panicked reports so far and I am not in the fucking mood.*

Yes, Dark Overlord, Illium replied to Dmitri.

Aodhan, please kill him so I can enjoy a moment of peace.

Eyes squeezed shut, Aodhan was clearly fighting not to

laugh. *Consider it done.* He opened those eyes of shattered glass. "Truce, my little blue flower?" he asked in a voice so quiet, it barely reached Illium.

"Truce, my pretty Sparkle-pants," Illium replied in as low a volume before they separated and bowed to each other in the way of warriors formally ending a sparring session. It seemed necessary in light of those panicked reports.

When they rose back up, then clasped forearms, the silent crowd began to clap and whoop at what had been, Illium knew, a display of skill they rarely got to witness. That kind of speed in angelic ground-sparring could be achieved only between two high-level warriors who'd been training together so long that they could predict each other's moves to a hairbreadth.

Broken wing bones had never been a possibility.

After giving the others a good-natured bow that clearly delighted them, Aodhan snapped out his wings . . . and took off into the night sky in a seamless vertical ascent that turned him into a streak of starlight.

More than ready to be alone with his Adi, Illium took off after him.

No one else was fast enough to follow them, even had they tried.

Illium was the faster where he and Aodhan were concerned, but Aodhan was stronger, which meant he could brute-force things in a way Illium couldn't as quickly— such as just powering through the headwind that hit them as they were striking out over the ocean.

Illium played with the currents instead, and ended up to Aodhan's back left not long afterward. A tanker piled high with shipping containers erupted with tiny waving figures as they flew past at low altitude, so Illium circled back at an even lower altitude to "buzz" them.

He was close enough to hear their delighted shouts.

Rising again, he caught up to Aodhan with ease now that the wind had dropped. His heart thudded as he flew almost wingtip to wingtip with the other man. He had no idea what Aodhan was thinking, but given their playful midfight conversation . . .

His mouth dried up. *Where are we going?*

Angling his wings left, Aodhan turned toward the endless horizon. *We're just flying.* A wicked glance. *I am way too big a sparkling target to dance that dance anywhere but in the protected skies above the Refuge.*

Illium found himself saying, *I swear I'll black out every single recording system in the entire region. Strange, inexplicable failure, so sorry.*

Laughter in his mind, the Aodhan of yesterday a bright echo in the Aodhan of today. For this man, Illium would do anything. Even just fly wild and free . . . until they dove into the ocean far from land and from any oceangoing vessels.

It was under the waves that Aodhan took his face and kissed him with a raw passion that had him groaning and wrapping himself around his half-naked lover . . . as his wings created a glow around them that he ignored with every fiber of his being.

The Cascade was over, ascension no longer a possibility.

Their upper bodies collided, hard muscle to hard muscle, firm lips to firm lips, hands in hair and wings working to keep them under. Because angels could go without air much longer than mortals.

And this kiss . . . it was a kiss that spoke of a dance hundreds of years in the making.

They parted only when their lungs hurt from the lack of air, and even then, they lingered, looking at each other in the glowing blue-green of the ocean, the merest handspan of water between them.

When they erupted out of the waves, it was as a pair.

There could be no dance here, not without protections in place to shield an act Illium would not have visible to the world . . . but when they tumbled into bed together after drying off, they did so skin to skin.

Mea lux? Are you sure?

I changed inside today, Illium. I understood my power

for the first time and it is a dividing line between past and present.

Illium had no more questions, not when he saw the determination in his lover's eyes. From that point on, there was only them and this joyous moment in time.

Hot breath against the curve of a neck.

A callused hand skimming down a flank.

Fine strands of hair against a ridged abdomen.

Knowing caresses at the arches of wings held with precision.

Kisses raw and untamed as perspiration broke out over their bodies, arousal a pumping beat in the blood.

"You taste of salt and want." Words that only amped up the need thick and humid in the air.

Gasps, tugs on hair, and the taut strength of one flipping the other, the chest of one pressed to the bed as his lover took control. Thighs thick with muscle pushed apart in a tussle that had no loser. Bodies rubbing together with a roughness that was natural for two warriors.

Wrists grasped. Demands made.

Laughter deep and intimate wrapped in love endless, kisses that were never enough . . . and wings that arched open until they became a feathered sky.

24

Isiel, Illium's jeweler contact, came through the next morning. *At least two of the pieces in the collection of images you sent belong to an angel named Lailah out of Northern Africa*, he messaged. *Last anyone saw them was on her at least. They're of a caliber that word would've got out if they'd changed hands.*

"Why do I know that name?" Aodhan murmured as they lay naked and warm in bed, Illium's head pillowed on Aodhan's shoulder as the blue-winged angel looked at the message while Smoke dozed curled up in a patch of sun lower down the bed.

Aodhan couldn't imagine a more perfect moment.

"Lailah is Andi's mother."

Aodhan blew out a quiet breath. "I keep forgetting her bloodline." He stroked the fingers of his free hand over Illium's chest, his other arm folded behind his head. "She's so unlike anyone I could imagine coming from Charisemnon in any form."

"Lailah used to be part of Charisemnon's court but I have no idea of her current whereabouts." Frowning, Illium put his phone aside. "Titus doesn't keep that style of court—and even if he did, I can't see him trusting Charisemnon's daughter."

"No. Even without the problematic blood connection, she's not the type of person Titus would consider for a position."

Aodhan had enough memories of Lailah—now that he'd placed her—to know that she was a beautiful dissolute, an angel who'd been powerful and dangerous in defense of the part of the territory she'd once held on behalf of her father, but who'd otherwise lived a life of . . . nothingness. His memories brightened as he continued to focus, until Lailah emerged full-fledged, the images from the rare times he'd run across her.

Overtly sensual, with invitation in hauntingly lovely eyes of a near-translucent brown intermingled with gold, she'd oddly not repelled him—because Lailah looked that way at everyone. Aodhan had been no different. She'd have coupled with him if he'd shown an interest, but she'd had no particular desire to seduce or entrap him.

If anything, he'd felt sorry for her.

"I always had the feeling that Lailah didn't care," Aodhan said, his eyes on the ceiling of the suite and his mind on the last memory he had of Andromeda's mother; it was from at least a century ago, when she'd visited the Refuge. "For all her dissolute ways, it seemed to me that she felt nothing. That she was just going through the motions."

Illium lifted himself up on one arm—careful not to disturb Smoke—to look down at Aodhan. "When did you meet her?"

"The odd passing conversation in the Refuge during the time I was based there." He spread his hand on the heat of Illium's back. "She and Andi's father, Cato, used to run Charisemnon's Refuge stronghold for short periods and I dealt with them as part of my duties."

Eyes of aged gold grew darker. "Have you ever noticed the pattern of Andi's wings when open?"

Frowning, Aodhan thought back. "A dark brown with

delicate gradations to a pale sunlight shade. I never really thought about it, but they're not similar to Cato's or Lailah's. But Charisemnon had brown in his wings."

Illium nodded. "That's what I always thought—that she got his genes on the wing coloring. Only I saw Dahariel training with her when she first came to the Refuge. That remote training area on the western edge."

"Ah." Aodhan saw it now, what Illium's quick mind had done at once; in flight, Dahariel's and Andromeda's wings would be all but identical. "Dahariel doesn't do favors for baby angels." The ruthless angel was an excellent warrior, but he had a vein of cruelty in him that meant Aodhan had always kept his distance.

"I've never mentioned it to anyone else," Illium said. "None of my business."

"I won't, either," Aodhan promised. "Our poor Andi didn't have the best of luck, did she? In either the man she calls her father, or the one who may be her blood father?"

"I don't know too much about either Cato or Lailah."

"Cato is . . . faded, that's the best word I can find to describe him, and it has nothing to do with the pale blue of his eyes, or the soft blond of his hair, even the mist gray of his wings. His presence simply doesn't leave a mark. Lailah is different."

Aodhan thought back to the single conversation he'd had with the other angel that had nothing to do with his duties as one of the Seven. "She looks like Andi and yet she doesn't—that's why I never quite link them together. Andi is . . . vibrant, alive, fascinated by the world." Not only was Naasir's mate a scholar intrigued by everything around her, she also had an inner wildness and a sense of unjaded wonder.

"I once ran across Lailah seated in a small grove near where Eh-ma used to live." He had a vague memory of helping his mentor plant small bushes there, his hands flecked with dirt and his heart happy. "The morning fog was thick, and I was simply walking and there she was."

A lovely creature seated on a stone bench, her curls sleek and glossy where they fell down her back after being pulled partially back by a diamond comb, and her airy gown a misty green that reached her ankles. Her wings—a rich cream with primaries of gold—had flowed with as much grace, while an emerald as deep a green as the forests of Tanzania sat between her breasts, aglow against the dark honey of her skin.

"My apologies, Lady Lailah," he'd said. "I did not mean to disturb your contemplation."

Lailah had looked at him with those eyes that had become even lovelier in her daughter, and said, "No, Aodhan, I am sorry for all the people that look at you like you are an object to contain and hold. They don't understand that the best gifts are given, not taken."

Then she'd glanced away, her gaze turning inward.

Today, he repeated to Illium the words Lailah had spoken in the haunting quiet of that morning. "It was so strange because we'd never had a conversation about anything but minor territorial matters until that day. I always thought of her as a touch vacant even if she was strong in terms of angelic power. But after that morning, I began to wonder what it was to grow up as Charisemnon's child."

Illium's gaze turned distant. "Sometimes, I wonder who I would've been if I'd grown up as Aegaeon's son. It gives me nightmares." Quiet words; not a joke.

Aodhan reached up to squeeze Illium's nape. "You didn't," he said. "You grew up as Sharine's cherished son, as your adored Rafa's little shadow, and as my best friend."

A slow smile, but the darkness remained. "You've made me look at Lailah in a whole different way. I dismissed her, too—except for on the battlefield. There, she can fight. But otherwise, I've always thought of her as a useless courtier."

He spread out his wings until all Aodhan saw was Illium-blue. "Do you think she'll have done anything with her life after being freed of her father's influence, or do you think it's too late for some people?"

Aodhan stroked Illium's nape. "I honestly have no answer to that. I haven't lived long enough yet. But today, we speak to Lailah and find out the path she chose to take."

* * *

First, however, they had to track down Lailah's whereabouts. Which turned out to be far easier than Aodhan had expected.

"She's still in her father's former territory?" He raised an eyebrow at Dmitri. "I'd have expected Titus to eject her." It wouldn't have been malicious, just expected politics—Lailah was a reminder of the previous archangel, and while Titus didn't want Charisemnon's territory, the simple fact was that, with only nine archangels in the post-war world, there was no one else to take over that devastated land.

"I can see Titus's reasoning on the point." Dmitri took a sip from a black mug emblazoned with the emblem of the television show *Hunter's Prey*. A gift from the youngest wing in the Tower, who were all, for whatever reason, addicted to the show, which bore no resemblance to reality whatsoever.

As for what was in the mug, it was either Dmitri's breakfast or the single triple espresso his vampiric system could handle daily.

"Lailah never had any political power," the second pointed out. "Charisemnon certainly never used her as his mouthpiece. She was seen as just another courtier for the most part. As far as I know, she's in the same palace she occupied prior to the war."

But when Aodhan made the call using a wall screen in the office set aside for the use of those of the Seven who didn't need a permanent presence on this level, with Illium just out of visual range, it wasn't the jaded and dissolute courtier who appeared on the screen.

This woman had the same bone structure, the same skin, but not only was she thin enough to have lost the curves of her face, her once-glossy curls were pulled back into a rough knot, and she wore not a drop of cosmetics. No jewels adorned her ears, dotted the side of her nose, or sat around her neck.

Neither was she wearing a gown, but what looked—oddly—like a gray T-shirt.

And was that a streak of dirt on her left cheekbone?

Her expression was . . . no expression. Not the jaded nothingness of their prior meetings but a whole different thing altogether. A wariness of showing herself?

"Aodhan." A break in the wall, a smile that warmed her eyes until they were almost like Andi's, her unembellished face suddenly startlingly young. "It has been many years."

"Yes," he said, not sure how to read this woman who was so unlike the one he'd once known. "Thank you for taking my call."

"Of course. Is it to do with Andromeda?" A hard swallow, her gaze searching his. "Is she well?"

Aodhan had the sudden thought that Lailah truly didn't know. Which one of them had created the distance? Mother or child? "Yes," he said. "I saw her not long ago. She told me of her work on translating a language long thought lost." Even an immortal race couldn't beat the inexorable march of time in such matters.

Lailah's face lit up in a way resplendent. "She was always the cleverest of children. And her mate? That wild creature who loves her so? He is well, too?"

"He remains as wild and loves her as much—or even more."

"Your words are the best gift anyone could give me." Her thin face continued to glow; she was more beautiful in her guise as a proud mother, Aodhan thought, than she'd ever been as a bejeweled courtier. "Thank you."

"Lady Lailah," he began.

"Just Lailah," she said firmly. "I don't claim Charisemnon as kin any longer and am no high-ranking courtier, nor have I earned the appellation through my work or habits. I am Lailah . . . or I am trying to discover who Lailah is meant to be." That last was spoken almost to herself.

"Lailah," Aodhan said. "I wish to ask for your assistance in solving a mystery in my city."

"Oh yes?"

Aodhan brought up images of the jewels on one half of the screen. "Do you recognize any of these?"

A frown, as she took her time examining the photos. "My memories from huge chunks of my past are blurry, but I do remember the sunset diamond. Charisemnon gifted it to me on my majority." Flat words without tone or timbre. "I haven't seen it for centuries."

"An expensive piece to lose."

"I hated it." No equivocation, her eyes devoid of anything— so empty that Aodhan wondered at all the things she didn't want to feel. "Shoved it in some corner and forgot about it. Likely several of the other jewels are mine, too, for I know they are gemstones found in this region, but I couldn't tell you. I was . . . not well then, Aodhan."

Tiredness now, her fingers rubbing at her forehead. "I didn't want to remember, and so I made myself forget."

Aodhan understood in a way that would escape most people—and he had no fear that she was prevaricating. This woman had stripped herself down to the bone, was rebuilding a person she didn't even know yet. So he kept his voice gentle when he said, "Do you have any idea how it might've vanished from your home?"

"We hosted many people over the centuries." Lailah looked around with an emptiness in her gaze, as if searching for memories of those guests. "I called them friends at one time but we were never friends. I don't know if I have any friends aside from Cato." No sorrow, no attempt to gain sympathy, nothing but an unvarnished statement of truth. "But wait . . ." Deep grooves formed in the center of her forehead. "There's something I *do* remember."

25

Lailah looked over to the left. "Cato!"

A male voice sounded in the background.

"A moment, Aodhan. Cato is dealing with one of the animals. I will go speak to him then return. I want to make certain of my memory and Cato is often better at the details of that time."

Aodhan muted his end of the feed after she'd disappeared from the screen. "That is *not* the woman I met in the Refuge."

Arms folded, Illium was leaning back against the wall. "I like this one better than the one I've always heard about."

"So do I," Aodhan said.

Lailah appeared on the screen again, and he unmuted his feed.

"Yes," she said, sounding a touch breathless. "I did remember correctly. An angel who used to linger here was obsessed with that diamond the rare times I wore it—exclusively when my father was visiting. She has had many names over the years, but Cato says the last one he recalls is Bijou."

A name that translated to "jewel" in French. An affectation? Or how she saw herself?

The name rang no bells in Aodhan's head, but he didn't run in courtier circles. Jason or one of his people would be more knowledgeable. They made it a point to watch everyone, even those who appeared to be pointless pieces of fluff. Many a spy had hidden in those ranks. "Do you think this Bijou might've taken it?"

"I would not accuse anyone, but she was the one with the most avaricious eyes when it came to that particular stone."

"Can you describe her?"

"She changes her hair color often—and I think these days, she would also change her eye color, but her natural shade is a hazel green that is startling in its paleness. It's part of why I remember how she looked at the stone; her stare is disconcerting. In all honesty, I'd have *given* her the cursed stone if Charisemnon wouldn't immediately have noticed should it have appeared on anyone else."

"So if she took it, she knew not to display it."

"I can see her hoarding it, pleased with her secret. Bijou had that way about her, a sense that she was always watching, ready for any vulnerability that she could either utilize—or gloat over knowing. She's old but not particularly powerful, so she grasps for power in other ways." No judgment or anger in Lailah's tone, the words nothing but a description.

Bijou didn't matter to her. Not as Andi mattered.

"Her hair, it has always been long and straight anytime I've seen it," she added. "She was proud of that. Her skin is like Cato's—so pale as to look bloodless." A faint smile. "Though Cato is at last gaining a hint of color after all his time in the sun."

"Her wings?" Those were often the most distinctive things about an angel.

But Lailah said, "Cream, with no other elements. I believe that's why she plays up the cosmetics and clothing so much—I thought her wings lovely and elegant, but she couldn't bear having what she called 'pedestrian' feathers.

She used to color parts of her wings, too, but you know how difficult it is to get color to last on angelic feathers, so she gave up on that."

Aodhan could've ended the call then, but he found himself curious about this woman who appeared to have stepped out of centuries of bondage of a kind unknown to most. "You're different, Lailah," he said without artifice. "You're not lost any longer."

A smile so haunted, it hurt. "Oh, Aodhan, I am still very much lost—but I'm trying to build myself a road that takes me out of this black maze in which I find myself."

She wrapped her arms around herself. "Please don't mention our conversation to Andromeda. Our child has found her wings, and I would that she fly in freedom without looking back. There's nothing good for her here, no joy in what I or Cato represent."

"I won't mention it." Even as he spoke, Aodhan wondered if Andi was as ignorant of her parents' current state as Lailah believed. A scholar did not blind her eyes. But this scholar had also been a child in a household tainted by Charisemnon, so perhaps this was the one subject on which she wished to remain ignorant.

Aodhan would not gainsay whatever decision it was that she'd made.

"Will you tell me what you do now?" he asked. "I am curious only, so if you'd rather it remain private, I will not importune you to speak."

Her expression softened. "Our home has always been a haven for animals, and now that is our focus. We have let it be known that we will care for wild orphans, for wounded creatures, for any such being that needs us. We did much the same in the war, attempting to protect the wildlife against the scourge of the reborn, for animals played no part in that atrocity and yet it was their drinking water that was fouled by the dead, their land that was infested."

Passion pumped fire into her cheeks. "You do not know the depth of our gratitude and respect for Archangel Titus, he who has allowed us to retain oversight of these lands. He has said that we are to think of ourselves as guardians of the wild, tied to his court under that duty."

Those lovely eyes so like Andi's, but with such terrible pain in their depths, met Aodhan's. "I would like to live that title until it erases what I once was, until it is all I am. So would Cato. And so we work here, in our small slice of the earth, watching over the animals.

"We have few staff—none for the house. We've shut up most of it. The staff we do have help with the wounded beasts. A mortal even! He is a physician of animals, a wondrously clever man, and Cato is learning under him, for Cato, too, is proving clever in ways he was never allowed to know.

"He grew up under Charisemnon, too, you know. We were . . . companions in our strange exile." A love in those words that was a gentle creature with wobbly legs. Because Lailah and Cato had only ever, Aodhan realized, known each other as the ghosts they'd become to survive Charisemnon's court.

"I didn't know that," he said.

Lailah's smile was sad. "Most don't. The man who sired me never allowed Cato, this beautiful child of a favored courtier, to be anything but a pretty ornament. You should see him now, Aodhan—he helped birth a rhino calf yesterday!"

"And you, Lailah?" he asked, his heart aching for the child hidden within Lailah, the one who was so proud of her companion in pain—and survival.

"My task is protection of the animals"—her face glowed again—"and of the lands. I've also been showing the mortals near us that they can look to us for help should they have need. They will bring us their wounded animals now, and no matter if it's a humble goat, we turn no beast away."

Aodhan found himself hoping that she'd make it out, that the whispering dark wouldn't pull her back under. And though it was presumptuous, for they barely knew each other, he said, "Don't allow the shadows of the past to steal your future bright, Lailah. Remember, what was taken was done so without your consent." She'd told him so on that strange foggy morning in the Refuge; never could she have understood so well otherwise. "You bear no blame."

Eyes shimmering, Lailah inclined her head. "I will fight, Aodhan. Perhaps one day, I will feel worthy enough to reach out to the child I failed over and over again. That is the bright goal that drives both Cato and me."

When Aodhan turned to Illium after ending the call, the other man said, "Jason's out of touch for a few hours so I sent the description of Bijou to both Dmitri and the sire. Neither recognized her."

"Let's ask Jessamy before we track down one of Jason's people." The spymaster's agents were scattered through various territories, a number deep undercover, and Jessamy had a steel trap mind when it came to angelkind.

Closing the distance between them, Illium brushed his fingers over the edge of Aodhan's left wing with a tenderness that undid Aodhan. How, he thought, had he ever lived without this?

"You were very kind to Lailah," the other man said.

"Speaking to her, I gained a fleeting glimpse of what it must've been like to grow up as Charisemnon's child—and I realized that my nightmare was but one of many." He pressed his forehead to Illium's. "It isn't a thing of comparison."

He tried to find words to say what he wanted to say.

But it was Illium who did. "You have the experience to know that while she did things to Andi that have caused the gülf between them, she was also a child once, a child raised in the grip of evil."

"It makes me wonder how many wounded ones walk the earth," Aodhan said, the knowledge a quiet sorrow within. "And it makes me realize how lucky I am." His nose brushing Illium's. "I was never alone in the fight, not even in that box they put me in."

Illium stopped breathing. "Adi," he murmured, cupping the side of his neck with one hand, his lover's tendons strong against his touch. "You don't have to talk about that."

"I know." Aodhan pulled back only enough that they

could look each other in the eye. "But proving that I can is important to me. I'd like to show you something after we talk to Jessamy."

As it was, Galen was the one who answered their call. "She's sleeping," the weapons-master said in a gruff tone. "Was working on an ancient script till all hours for days. Finally went down today." Scowling, he shoved a hand through the deep, pure red of his hair. "I used to think scholars were soft and gentle creatures." A snort. "No one warned me about their refusal to back down when on the quest for knowledge."

After leaving a message with him, they decided to go over everything they had so far, to ensure they hadn't missed a critical clue and to make a plan for their next move. They were just finishing up when Jessamy returned their call. Her chestnut hair in a loose braid, and her face marked by sleep lines, she held a large mug of something that was emitting curls of steam.

The mug was misshapen, no doubt created by a student.

"Galen said you called." Her voice, husky from her recent sleep, put Aodhan in mind of a hundred childhood pranks, a thousand happy moments of her holding his hand as she walked him to the playground or just crouched down to talk to him, those kind brown eyes a gentle horizon. The same eyes had watched over him in the Medica.

She'd brought him his favorite sweets from childhood, and a book of stories of wild imagination. Stories to give him escape. It hadn't worked, not then. But he'd read the book in the darkest part of night three decades later, found peace for a few hours at least.

"You didn't have to call straight after you woke." Illium threw up his hands. "Galen will have our heads."

A grunt sounded off-screen. "You're safe. It's all her doing."

A soft smile on Jessamy's face, she murmured something to Galen in a language Aodhan couldn't understand. When he glanced at Illium, Illium shook his head. But it was clear Galen knew exactly what she was saying, because he growled back an answer in the same language.

"Hey, no secret love messages in front of the children," Illium protested.

Jessamy's smile made her eyes crinkle. "What did you want to ask me, small sparkles and small blue wings?"

Aodhan laughed. If anyone had earned the right to tease them thus, it was the teacher they'd tormented with their rambunctiousness. "We're trying to trace an angel once called Bijou."

Jessamy sipped her drink as he repeated Lailah's description of the angel, her eyebrows drawing together to create a pointed vee. "She's not using that name now, and her hair is an ice-white, her eyes sharp green, but I'm certain it's the same person."

A small nod to herself. "She likes altering herself in whatever way is available in that time period. She once told me she would do the surgery that mortals do to change their faces if angelic healing wouldn't override the changes within two or so years."

"Two years," Aodhan murmured. "Lailah did say she was old but not powerful."

"You spoke to Lailah?" Jessamy's gaze was suddenly opaque, her fingers tightening around the mug. "How are she and Cato?"

"Both seem to be doing well. They're focusing on the animals that live around them. Lailah asked me not to mention her to Andi."

"I won't, either," Jessamy said at once, with no attempt to hide her protectiveness where Andi was concerned. "The decision to reach out or not must be Andromeda's and hers alone. As for your Bijou, if it's the angel I'm thinking of, her current name is Vixen."

"Vixen?" Illium rolled his eyes. "She has a high opinion of herself."

"I don't know her well, but I think part of her problem is that she *doesn't* have that high opinion," Jessamy countered.

"About four centuries ago, her long-term vampiric partner left her rather cruelly. He'd found a younger lover—an angel of barely a hundred and three. An adult by angelic law, but the tryst made distasteful by the difference in their ages. He was well over two thousand by then."

Big age gaps were common in the world of immortals— Galen and Jessamy were the perfect example. The same could be said for Dmitri and Honor, or Elena and Raphael. The critical difference was that they'd all been fully adult at the time, both biologically and in terms of their mental and psychological development.

Had Elena been *born* an angel, however, it would've been an entirely different story.

There was a line you did not cross with born angels, an age *before* which they simply weren't mature enough to be considered equal partners to anyone but their peers. Their kind matured slower, and the decade after they first left the Refuge?

Vulnerable didn't begin to describe it.

In the Tower, young Izak, though several years senior to the girl Jessamy had mentioned, was still treated as a fledgling. Not in a way that was condescending, rather with the awareness that he was at a critical stage of his development, and that it was their responsibility to nurture him to his full adult strength.

"A predator." Illium's statement was clipped.

"Just so," Jessamy said. "I was worried about the girl both because of her youth, and due to the disturbing depth of Vixen's rage. However, the girl's parents were senior courtiers in Uram's court at the time, and they ensured she was soon separated from the predator—and he knew never to try the same again.

"Vixen, too, was smart enough not to make an enemy of an archangel. Instead she found her own young lovers and began to parade them around." Jessamy sighed. "Her concerning rage aside, I felt sorry for her for a time. She did have good reason for her anger after all—and if she'd turned it on her former lover, I'd have felt no ambivalence about my response, but as it was . . ."

A long pause before she continued. "Her lovers continued to drop in age until it became a distasteful morass where those of us who were aware of her proclivities began to warn young angels of her predatory nature. She never tried for anyone under a hundred, but that's the best I can say about her."

"She turned into the person who hurt her," Aodhan murmured.

"Sad, isn't it?" Lips turning down, Jessamy shook her head. "I have seen it again and again through time, and I'm certain those close to Vixen attempted to warn her of her descent—she was never a loner, that one—but she either would not or could not listen, her brain chemistry forever altered."

The angelic librarian tapped a fingernail against the mug. "She's well aware of the ill feeling toward her in the Refuge, near our most vulnerable. I haven't seen her walking these pathways for at least a half century, perhaps more.

"My present description of her is from a letter I received from a scholar in Elijah's region some eight months before the war—yes, I'm sure I have the time right. He mentioned her peripherally as part of a group he met for lunch, but he's a sketcher, and he sketched her in color. I'll send you a copy."

Aodhan thanked her. "Even if she's changed her hair or eye color since, it'll be much easier to trace her now that we have a name and starting point. Now rest before you drive Galen to distraction—because as far as I can tell, either you adopted a wolf and forgot to tell us, or that's our Barbarian growling off-screen."

Jessamy's laughter merged with Galen's grumbling before she waved goodbye.

"Our quarry was in Elijah's region eight months prior to the war," Aodhan said to Illium. "Not difficult for her to make it to New York, be resident here during the period covering Marco's stalking and murder. As far as we know, the stalking began approximately six months before his death."

Illium's phone rang. Glancing at it, he said, "It's Jason," and threw the audio-only call onto the big screen so they could both hear it better.

It turned out the spymaster had unexpectedly flown into a zone with reception.

When they asked him about Vixen née Bijou, he said, "I've run across her here and there over the centuries. Hold on, the signal's improved." A flicker on the screen before his face appeared. "She attaches herself to the fringes of an archangel's court, but the closest she ever made it to the inner circle was her acquaintance with Lailah."

He turned, seemed to be listening—and that was when Aodhan realized Mahiya must be with him. A fact Jason confirmed with his next words. "Mahiya says she spent a few years hovering around Neha's court in the period after she left Africa, but there's a gap in my knowledge of her after that time. We only have her on a specific watch list, and if she doesn't run foul of that, she gets to live her life."

"Targeting all but underage angels?" Aodhan guessed.

Jason nodded. "Jessamy sent out an alert about the situation. And my people don't forget their tasks, so if she hasn't come to our attention, it's because she's kept her nose clean there."

"Could she have switched to young vampires?"

Jason angled the camera so they could see Mahiya, her braided hair ashine in the sun.

"Yes," Jason's princess said. "When she was in India, I saw her with a vampire who was yet under Contract."

As vampires were mortal adults when Made, their brains and psyches fully mature in comparison to immortals of the same age, such relationships crossed no ethical boundaries unless that vampire—per their Contract—happened to be under the control of the other party at the time. The latter was considered distasteful.

"We've had word that she was last seen in Elijah's territory," Illium said. "But we suspect that she moved to New York before the war."

The tattoo on the left side of Jason's face stood out in stark relief as he turned slightly in the air. Long strands of his unbound hair waved across his face at the same moment.

After pushing them back, the spymaster said, "I'll send a message out to my people. If she is in the sire's territory, she might've attempted to insinuate herself with one of the powerful angels in the region. Check with Vivek, too."

The Tower's chief intelligence officer, however, struck out on the topic of Vixen. "Must not have poked her head above the parapet," he muttered as he continued to search his databases. "Gap could also be a result of post-war chaos. Balls did get dropped even by me."

Leaving him with a scowl on his face, Aodhan contacted Janvier to ask if he and Ashwini could plumb the gray heart of the city for any details of their target, to the Cajun vampire's easy agreement.

"We should check out Erotique, too," Illium suggested, the two of them having walked out to stand on the railingless balcony outside that level of the Tower. "Vixen sounds like the kind of person who'd want to be seen at the hottest club in town."

Aodhan shuddered. "Being closed up inside a small space filled with discordant music and erratic lights is not my idea of enjoyable."

Illium smirked. "Come on, Sparkle. I'll protect you from the googly eyes of the other patrons."

Aodhan smacked him in the back using his wing.

Having not expected it—it was a thing done among children in the Refuge, not adults—Illium tumbled off the balcony with a startled shout. Aodhan's shoulders shook as he walked over to watch the other man straighten himself out, then shoot back up to scowl at him.

"Really?" his friend said in a stern voice, hands on his hips. "Are we younglings now?"

"You're just mad you didn't think of it first." The only way to succeed in that particular game of one-upmanship was to take your target unawares. With Illium, that was close to impossible. "Admit it," he said, aware of their audience of amused angels nearby.

"Grr." Illium did an excellent impression of the Seven's resident chimera. "I won't forget," he threatened. "A century or nine after today, long after your memory of this insult has faded . . . bam, off you go."

26

Aodhan's laughter filled the air. "I await your vengeance, my Blue."

Illium's heart burst with hope, love, happiness. To see Aodhan laughing so hard, with his head thrown back and his eyes alight, to see mischief in those eyes that had been solemn too long—for that, Illium would forgive any ignominy.

Especially now that he'd heard Aodhan's chuckle deep in the night, against the curve of his neck. The man was lethal and Illium was so susceptible to him that it was his greatest weakness.

"As I was going to tell you before you attacked me," he said on a huff as Aodhan's laughter faded into a deep smile that would've caused heart attacks had he been on the street, "the club's not open right now. You're safe."

Aodhan narrowed his eyes. "Or maybe you're plotting something." Then he grinned again before sweeping off the balcony, his next words in Illium's mind. *Whatever it is, bring it on. I'm ready for you.*

At last, thought a long-buried part of Illium's heart, a

part that had waited with loving patience for centuries. *You've come back to me at last. All of you. Every beautiful fragment.*

Giving a battle cry of untrammeled joy, he raced after Aodhan and the two of them flew an acrobatic path to the club—and perhaps they took the long way, because this was pure delight. They rose, they fell, they cut each other off, and they took corners at dangerous speed.

Illium grinned when he caught startled faces at high windows, and flat-out laughed when Aodhan buzzed a group of shocked pedestrians—who then screamed in delight and grabbed for their cameras at having been so close to an angel no one ever saw at ground level. One of Aodhan's feathers floated off at the same time, and a car came to a screeching halt, doors flying open as the people inside raced to grab it.

Then the tableau was past, the two of them racing to another section of the city. They weaved through residential high-rises built with the minimum permissible gap—still wide enough for an angel to fly through, but it took skill not to veer and scrape their primaries on the walls.

It took even more skill to do that while racing up, then diving down.

You're just showing off now.

Illium grinned at that disgruntled statement, but he could feel Aodhan shadowing him. His friend and lover had to work harder to pull off the nimble movements, but he was perfectly capable of each and every one.

They emerged into clear skies before racing back over the city.

When they landed in front of Erotique side by side, slamming down onto the ground at the last second after pulling up from a high-speed dive, it was with their chests heaving and hair tumbled. "That was fun." Aodhan's grin was wild and of the boy who'd joined Illium in every one of his harebrained schemes as a child.

Cheeks hurting from the force of his happiness, Illium shoved a hand through his hair just as Dulce threw open the club's door. "Oh, thank the Havens!" Her eyes were huge, the irises an intense purple possible only in a vampire who'd started out with eyes a specific shade of blue. Their color was stunning against the raven black hair she currently wore in a shoulder-length mass of waves.

Pressing a hand to her heart, her ring finger encircled by a band of gold, she said, "When I saw the speed of your landing through my office window, I thought I was going to discover you both slammed into paste on the sidewalk."

"You wound me, Dulce." Illium clutched at his own heart with both hands. "Are you going to let us in? Sparkle here is attracting attention—hey!" He'd been ready to catch Aodhan's wing at his back again, had a trick up his sleeve for that, but Adi had just doused him with a bottle of cold water. "Where did you even *get* that?"

Aodhan capped the bottle with a smile as Illium shoved back his wet hair. "I like to be prepared." He turned to Dulce. "We haven't formally met. I'm Aodhan."

Her lips were twitching. "Dulce, and I think we're going to be fast friends," she said. "I've been trying to take Illium down a peg the entire time I've known him and never yet succeeded." She held open the door. "Come on in."

Aodhan was curious about this place that he knew Illium had frequented on a regular basis for a number of years prior to the war.

Dulce, while relatively young for a vampire, clearly had a familiar relationship with him. "Nice to see you, stranger," she said as she threw him a clean towel from behind the bar. "I thought you'd forgotten us."

"I've taken up crochet," Illium said from under the towel he was using to dry his hair. "Swallows up all my time."

Rolling her eyes but smiling, Dulce reached up to retrieve a glass.

"I meant to ask," Illium said as she added two others beside it, "how did the owners lure you back? Last I heard, you were happily managing your own place."

"Fifteen percent stake," Dulce said with a grin. "Turned

out business dived without my magic touch. I have good people managing my own club, but you know me—I keep an eagle eye on all operations."

Illium whistled. "Next thing I know, you'll be *the* club boss in the city."

Dulce's smile made it clear that was her goal. "I know Illium's drink of choice," she said with a glance at Aodhan. "What'll you have?"

Many a senior angel would've been annoyed—even angered—by Dulce's familiarity, but Aodhan liked being treated as just another angel. Even a friend. He knew it was all because of Illium. He was the one who was friends with Dulce . . . and perhaps had once been more. The way they teased each other, it implied a depth of connection that went beyond friendship.

But Dulce wore a ring now, and Illium was Aodhan's.

In an immortal's life, jealousy could be a thing corrosive. Especially jealousy with no cause. Whatever had happened between the two was long in the past, as were Aodhan's youthful love affairs.

"Do you carry honey mead?"

"I have an artisanal batch that just came in from a new supplier. I'd be interested to hear what you think of it."

As she poured, he looked around the club. The walls were a gleaming black, noon sunlight slanting in through the high windows. It should've looked dingy, a place that came alive only in the night, but the club was both scrupulously clean and elegantly styled.

The glossy black walls worked as well in daylight as they did in the night, and the polished concrete floor added a hard edge that felt deliberate. People didn't come to Erotique for soft—but neither, from what he'd heard, was it akin to the seedier flesh clubs of the gray district.

It straddled a fine line not many establishments could manage.

He looked up to the domed ceiling. "Are those swings up there, past the central drop lights?"

"Yes, new addition—the dome, too," Dulce said. "We got hit in the war, figured why not build better? Customers love it. Too much." A husky laugh. "We had to hire an angelic bouncer to kick off angels who were just sitting up there people-watching and not buying drinks.

"Now it's a VIP section with a cover charge, which works nicely. Special mood lighting for that section, too, and flying bar service from young angels who want a risqué job on their résumé." Amused affection in her tone. "I draw the line at under a hundred and fifty, though. You winged players are just babies before then."

Ironic that this young near-immortal understood that truth better than Vixen or her former lover.

"Never in my life," Aodhan murmured, his attention still skyward, "would I have imagined angels on swings in a club in New York, and now I want to paint the scene."

"Come one night," Dulce offered. "I'll sneak you in the back—you can see everything on the security cameras if you don't want to be on the floor."

"Perhaps I'll take you up on that." He accepted the mead she handed him, while Illium—the towel draped around his neck and his hair tumbled and damp—wandered past the neatly stacked-up tables and chairs to look at a large mural on the back wall.

"This is new, too," he said. "Are those cavorting nymphs?"

"Keep looking." Dulce laughed, the sound throaty and low. "We told Sujata to create it as if she was high on mushrooms."

Aodhan hadn't heard of the artist before, but her work was eye-catching. Walking over, he pointed out a satyr twined with a snake creature wearing a tiara.

"Are you sure she wasn't *actually* high?" Illium called back.

More laughter from Dulce, who was leaning on the bar sipping on a glass of blood that might well be her first meal of the day, given the working hours demanded by the club. "Knowing Sujata, it could go either way. She was impossible as a mortal and that hasn't changed in the time she's been a vampire except to grow more talented."

"I would meet her," Aodhan said, stepping back so he could take in the whole work. "While her style is different from mine, it's bold and intriguing." Yet in flux, but very much its own creature.

"Oh dear, mortal ancestors." Dulce groaned. "Woman'll be insufferable at hearing that, but I'll pass on the word nonetheless. The things I endure for my friends."

Smiling, Aodhan took a sip of the mead, allowed the flavor to settle. "This is excellent," he told Dulce as they walked back to her. "Thank you for introducing me to it."

"My pleasure." She shot a glance at Illium, back at Aodhan. "So, spill. I know this isn't a pleasure jaunt."

"No," Aodhan admitted. When he described the angel they sought, Dulce made a face. "Yes, I know her. She comes across as polite for an angel—no offense but some of your kind, especially the older ones, are utter nightmares."

"Trust me, we know," Illium muttered, his scowl so dark that Aodhan knew he was thinking about his arrogant asshole of a father. "Why don't you like her?"

"Because it's all an act." Dulce put down her glass. "That sugar-sweet thing folks do to hide vile hearts. Pure calculation behind the eyes. She was up in the swings three days after she first appeared in the city—that's how fast she insinuated herself into the top echelons of the club, the people who know the floor hosts and can always get a booking."

"Social climbing wouldn't be enough for you to dislike her," Aodhan guessed.

"No, hell, I'd admire her if it were that alone—I mean, you have to be smooth to talk around the warriors who come in here and she managed it," Dulce admitted. "And I clearly have a soft spot for charmers."

Illium grinned at her pointed look.

"But," Dulce continued, "she hit on one of my staff—a vampire not long out of Contract—and that's a strict no-no.

Staff are off-limits. If people hook up outside the club and get something going, it's not my business. But the club is their workplace, and they deserve to feel safe doing their jobs.

"*Everyone* who frequents the club knows that. I cut her some slack because it was her first visit, even went and personally explained the policy. She came off sincerely apologetic and didn't do it again inside the club . . . but the staff member spotted her hovering outside his window two nights later. Creeped him the fuck out."

"She was showing off her ability to track him." Illium slammed his glass down on the counter. "And scaring him for daring to deny her."

"That was my take." Dulce's tone was as cold as Aodhan's anger. "No proof, though, since she wasn't caught on any cameras. Majority owners of the club said I couldn't ban her, especially since she had so many socially influential friends."

A curl of her lip said Dulce didn't plan on being the minority shareholder much longer. "But I could and did ensure he had a powerful escort home each and every night. All our bouncers are good people, stepped up. I also asked one of my Tower friends—Zia—to do regular flybys if she had the time."

"You should've told me, Dulce." Illium's voice was tight. "I'd have handled it."

"You were my next stop if she kept escalating—you're the nuclear option I save for worst-case scenarios. But Zia did the flybys, even roped in a few of her squadron to join in, make it clear he was under angelic protection.

"It must've been enough to scare Vixen off, because she stopped paying him any attention at all—prior to that, she'd used to watch him when she thought she was unobserved. Could be she doesn't actually understand cameras. Some of the old ones are like that. Anyway, it was eerie how totally she ignored him afterward. As if he didn't exist."

Either Dulce was right and the show of dangerous angelic

oversight had scared Vixen off, or she'd already found and fixated on Marco by then. "Do you know if a vampire named Marco Corvino frequented this club? He was young, still under—"

"Marco?" Her face turned pale, her fingers tight on the glass she'd picked back up. "Of course I knew Marco. We were from the same neighborhood—two and a half centuries apart, but I still have descendants there, drop by now and then.

"He wouldn't normally have been allowed into the club because the entry prerequisite for vamps is post-Contract, but I let him in during the quiet nights. Kid was so fresh and shiny, he might as well have been polished. He thought Erotique was the wildest place in the city."

"Such innocence." Illium's joke was gentle, the hand he touched to Dulce's compassionate. "I'm sorry you lost him."

"Yeah, fucking Lij—" A pause, a sharp look at Illium. "Vixen?"

"Looking likely. Could she have met him here?"

"Yes. She's a regular from before the war, here almost every night." Her jaw worked. "I knew I should've booted her!"

"You did what you could," Aodhan said. "She's responsible for the rest."

Dulce's eyes gleamed with an edge of red, but she said, "Bitch is still in the city. Looks different than before the club shut down during the war, but she was in here two nights ago. Yellow hair, can't recall the current contact lens shade, but I'm pretty sure I can get you her address—night she was here, she took home a vamp whose name I remember."

Pulling out her phone without waiting for their response, she made a call, was blunt in her request. "Don't ask me why I need Vixen's address, and I won't mention your tryst to your wife. And don't you dare warn Vixen or you'll never enter this club again."

A pause.

"Pleasure doing business with you." She scribbled the

address down on a piece of paper after hanging up. "What a slime. I thought they deserved each other. As for his wife, she's smarter than him by a country mile, knows he's a serial cheater, but their relationship is their business."

She pushed across the paper. "Get that bitch."

27

The fine-boned angel of about five feet five inches who called herself Vixen was wrapped up in a silken robe, her feet bare and her hands around a mug of coffee, when Illium and Aodhan dropped onto her seventh-floor balcony an hour later.

The open doors gave them a clear sight line to where she stood by her kitchen counter.

Eyes devoid of contacts—and yes, a distinctive and pale greenish-hazel—grew huge, her lips, stained a soft pink, parting on a gasp. "I did not ever expect to gain the notice of the Tower," she gushed, abandoning her coffee to run toward them.

The hair that streamed behind her was a rich and false yellow akin to marigolds.

"You must excuse how I'm dressed." Pretty words, an even prettier smile. "I have only now risen. The clubs in this city are astonishing—I go for an hour or two and end up staying till they close their doors."

Aodhan had been afraid he'd strangle her the minute he

came within sight of her, but while the rage remained, it was a cold, cold thing. He saw her . . . and he saw weakness and guile and evil, the smiles and the words nothing but window dressing.

Céline without the subtlety or talent.

While the mask would've frustrated the child he'd been for his inability to paint it, Aodhan had gained that skill over the years, until he could paint this woman with her smile and outward prettiness and have it radiate cunning and viciousness.

But no matter how covetous and murderous her nature, she was no threat to him or Illium or anyone else of their ilk; the only reason she'd been able to harm Marco and Tanika was that they'd been so heartbreakingly young. Against stronger foes, Vixen was a coward.

He'd wait for evidence to convict her, but he had no doubts on his conclusion of her guilt.

"The angels of the Tower have been aware of you for some time," Illium said in that light way those who didn't know him often took as flirtation. It wasn't. It was a mask for his own anger, because masks could be used for good as well as evil.

Vixen, however, wrapped up in her grandiose plans of rising to the apex of angelic social hierarchy, was oblivious. Blushing right on cue, she invited them inside. Aodhan felt Illium's body tense, reached out with his mind: *We should accept, or it will be a show for her neighbors.*

Marco and Tanika deserved better than that.

Stop me if I give in to the urge to wring her neck, Illium responded before crossing the threshold.

Inside, the apartment was wide and spacious, decorated with an elegance that was about the finest things. Artwork, the furniture, even the mug that held her coffee, it was all from well-known designers and artists across time.

"I have never been able to acquire one of your pieces," she whispered to Aodhan in a tone that was perfectly modulated to flatter without appearing servile. "But I hope now that you know of my interest, you will put aside a sketch for me."

She fluttered a delicate hand to her chest, her nails painted a translucent yellow and her eyes huge orbs of innocent wonder. "A small thing, perhaps even a piece you might otherwise discard. I'd never presume to ask for a work on canvas or for one of your sculptures."

He'd always thought evil intelligent, but cunning wasn't the same as intelligence. This woman truly thought two senior Tower angels had come to her home because she was a dazzling drawcard.

"I have heard that you collect gems," he said instead of answering, because they must have concrete proof. "I'm currently working on a piece that requires many different gemstones." He kept his tone remote because he knew that would compel her to do whatever she could to get in his good graces.

Aodhan hated playing such games, but here? With this woman who'd murdered two good people out of spite and envy? Yes, he was more than willing to make an exception. "Several of the gems I need are rare."

Vixen's eyes fairly blazed. "Oh, indeed, I've had many dazzling finds over time. You have come to the right person. If you will give me but a moment!"

Neither he nor Illium said anything aloud while she was gone from the room, but that didn't mean they were silent.

She's very stupid, Aodhan said with an unkindness he reserved for evil. *Her avarice and desire to rise to the top blind her to reality. She seems to have no concept of the fact that we're in a post-war reconstruction period, with no time for inane social calls, even were either one of us so inclined.*

I really want to slice off her head. Illium's mental tone was as grim as his expression was light. *Get blood all over this white carpet. How mad do you think Raphael would be if I did that?*

I think the sire would be exasperated but never angry. Not after what had happened to Dmitri, then to Aodhan;

there were some trespasses the Archangel of New York was incapable of forgiving.

Eyes as familiar as his own breath held Aodhan's, the understanding in them a testament to his Blue's huge heart. *What do we do with her? We both know she's the culprit.*

Aodhan had already considered that question, come to the only possible answer. *First, we must have proof. Our instinctive certainty isn't enough, because any action we take reflects on Raphael.*

Illium exhaled slowly. *At least one of us has a calm head.*

Once we have the proof, we take her to the sire. She'll fly with us of her own accord. This execution must be done in front of witnesses after she has confessed her crime— and I think Giulia should be there. Marco's mother would not rest easy until she knew her son and Marco's love had been avenged.

Illium nodded just before Vixen emerged dressed in a gown of rich orange vibrant against her pale skin. She was too clever at the game of seduction to flaunt cleavage, but the dress was cut in such a way as to hint at her curves, invite the eye.

The angel held a small but not insignificant box made of golden wood polished to a shine and closed with a steel clasp that she'd already unlocked. "I have more stored in a vault in Istanbul," she said breathlessly, "but these are the best of the best of my collection. I never travel without them."

Aodhan allowed her to show him jewel after jewel, waiting until the very end to say, "I was hoping you'd have a sunset diamond. It is the gem I wish to make the centerpiece of my work—I'd heard that you had one in your collection, though you wear it but rarely." A calculated risk, that statement, but he was certain Vixen wouldn't have been able to resist flaunting Lailah's diamond, even if only to a small group of intimates.

A rapid flutter of lashes, a kick to the pulse in her neck. "I'm sure I can locate one for you—I patronize many jewelers who save special stones for me. Unfortunately, I gifted mine to a lover who was most ungrateful for it." Pinched lips before she smoothed them out into a soft smile. "Alas, I do not know what he did with it."

That she'd called Marco a "lover" when he'd refused all her overtures said even more about her personality and ethics. "He must've been a dazzling being indeed," Aodhan murmured, "to be worth such a stone. Anyone I know? Perhaps I can persuade him to release it to me."

A flick of her hand. "Oh, he died in the war."

"Our sympathies," Illium said, flowing into the conversation. "We lost so many good people. And then there were the countless injured to the point of near death." He casually mentioned several names. "Talking of which"—he turned to Aodhan—"I forgot to tell you Navarro is back in the city. Figured you wouldn't want to be surprised."

Seeing Vixen go motionless, Aodhan said, "A pity that we could not choose who lived and who died." His ambiguous words paired with Illium's familiar conversational tone had the desired effect.

Vixen took it for a sign of intimacy. "Navarro *steals* things from the vampires under Contract to him," she shared in a hesitant tone, as if afraid of their reaction. "Can you imagine? He just appropriates their gifts. I find that repugnant."

Aodhan tilted his head. "How do you know this?"

"My lover was, unfortunately, tied to him. Navarro not only took from him the tokens of my affection, but had the gall to wear the items in public."

It was enough to solidify his certainty to stone, but Aodhan wanted her to admit it, wanted her to show the blood on her hands. Gripping her throat with one hand, he smiled.

Vixen's pulse skittered, but not in fear.

That came when he lifted her off the floor with that same hand, his grip firm. "This is tiresome," he said, using words and a tone that would penetrate her self-absorption.

"Tell me to whom you gave the gem. I do not play games when I want something."

Her legs kicked as he began to cut off her air.

"A vampire!" she rasped out. "I tell the truth! Just a vampire under Contract I was foolish enough to fall in love with. He died in the war. In a fire. Navarro may have the jewel!"

"The name of the vampire?"

"Marco Corvino." Her fingernails dug at his hand in a futile gesture. "If you don't find the diamond with Navarro, then perhaps Marco gave it to the whore with whom he thought to betray me." A slow spread of red in her irises, fine blood vessels beginning to burst. "He asked her to marry him! He could've had *me*, and instead he asked *her* to marry him."

There we go, Illium murmured. *The trigger for Marco's murder.*

"That a vampire yet under Contract, scrawny and young, threw you aside," Aodhan said, squeezing harder, "makes me believe we've made a mistake in thinking you suitable for Raphael's court." Raphael had no court, had never had a court as such. His Tower was filled only with people who played a useful role and had no time for petty intrigues. "You are weak, pathetic."

"No, I'm strong!" Vixen coughed, her face bulging— and he thought it fitting that her outside now matched her inside.

"I can prove it." An attempt at a shout that came out barely audible.

Aodhan released his grip the slightest amount, enough that she could speak.

"I showed Marco that he couldn't betray me without consequences. I burned him alive," she hissed. "But first, I made him watch as I cut the throat of his whore." Her eyes glittered. "I am worthy of the Tower. Worthy of you."

Aodhan's fingers threatened to spasm to crushing tightness. The part of him that had once been Marco, hunted and abused, wanted to watch as she scrabbled at his hand, her feet kicking helplessly and her wings fluttering . . . but that would be a step into the abyss he'd fought so long to avoid.

So he smiled and put her feet back on the floor. "You are who we believed you to be," he said, while she gasped and choked. "You will accompany us to the Tower."

Her expression was dazzled.

28

Raphael felt nothing but a cold anger at the sniveling creature in front of him.

With her own confession to hang her—which she'd admitted to again in front of Raphael, this time driven by terror of an archangel's violent power—there really wasn't much more to it.

Vixen's ending was a quick, brutal thing that came the next eve, held in a clearing deep in the Catskills with a somber group of witnesses: Illium and Aodhan, Navarro, Elena, Honor and Dmitri, and one steel-spined mortal. Tanika's parents had declined to attend, but Giulia had turned up, her face stone.

All three of the parents had requested the execution not be public.

"Justice for our Tani shouldn't be a display," her father had said to Aodhan when this member of Raphael's Seven went to tell them of Vixen's apprehension. "She was a private person. And . . . he was, too. Not his fault he attracted that evil creature."

From what Aodhan had passed on, Stavros continued to

struggle with not blaming Marco for his daughter's death, but at least he was trying. Raphael hoped that, together with his wife's love, it would help him avoid the inner rot that came with bitter rage. Perhaps so, too, would the knowledge that while his child had been killed by an angel, she'd also been avenged by angels.

Now, Aodhan and Illium flanked Giulia, Navarro on Illium's other side, while the rest of the witnesses stood slightly back in a sign of respect to Giulia's grief, as Raphael undertook the execution. He'd asked Marco Corvino's mother if she wished for Vixen to suffer the same torture as had been bestowed upon her son, a burning alive. For an angel, that could mean hours, even days, before true death. But Giulia had shaken her head.

"Marco was a gentle boy, a gentle man. I won't desecrate his memory by lowering myself to her level. But her death is necessary. Evil can't be allowed to linger in this world—especially immortal evil."

Raphael had given her a small nod. For an archangel to speak to a mortal thus, it was unusual, but when he looked at her grief, he remembered Dmitri's. Who stood in this forest clearing today, as did Honor, her hand in his.

Obsession that takes, that steals, Dmitri had said privately to him, *is an evil without end, never satisfied. I agree with Marco's mother—she needs to be removed from this world before she destroys more lives.*

Now, as the skies began to fade into deep oranges and pinks above the Tower, far from this grove shadowed by forest giants, Vixen begged for forgiveness. Her face was blotchy with tears. Tears she hadn't shed until it was her own life on the line. Tears she'd never have shed had they not uncovered her crimes.

No, she had taunted Tanika, then Marco—for this, too, she had confessed.

Raphael didn't bother to respond to her begging before he ended her in a single bolt of archangelic energy. She was ash between one breath and the next, her entire existence reduced to a pitiful pile of dust, which Raphael then used his power to lift dirt and bury, so that it would not linger in the air.

"It is done." He glanced at Dmitri. "Send a notice to Jessamy. Make sure both the crime and the punishment are recorded in our histories."

His best friend held his gaze, what passed between them a haunting whisper of memory. "I'll do it today," the vampire said before moving so he could look at Giulia. "I'll also ensure that Marco's and Tanika's names are noted in our histories, along with their biographies. They will not be forgotten."

As Misha and Caterina and Ingrede haven't been forgotten.

Words unspoken, but Raphael heard them all the same. The names of Dmitri's murdered family were in no history book, but the vampire held them close to his heart, as did Raphael. He'd eaten at Ingrede's table, played with little Misha, visited with a rattle he'd carved for the new babe when Caterina was born. He missed them, but he knew that he would never miss them as Dmitri missed them.

Honor's hand squeezed Dmitri's just then, and Raphael saw raw anguish in the green of her eyes as she turned to her husband. When Dmitri allowed himself to lean into her, Raphael exhaled quietly. This execution and all that had led to it must've stirred awake the worst memories of Dmitri's life, but Dmitri wouldn't spiral, not if he was allowing Honor to be there for him.

Elena slipped her hand into his. *Are you okay, Archangel?*

Yes, executing Vixen took nothing from me. She would worry about that, his hunter. *It was akin to removing vermin from a storehouse of food: a necessary act.*

I agree with you. Her anger was a taut, vibrating thing. *It's like when I execute a bloodlust-driven vampire. I don't enjoy it, but neither do I wallow in guilt about it. It has to be done.*

"What does haunt me is the why of it," he murmured, while Aodhan held a sobbing Giulia in his arms. "Why do we seek to take that which isn't ours?"

"*We* don't." Firm words. "There are always bad actors in any society. The test is how we deal with them." Her eyes were silver blades, clear and sharp. "This was justice. You didn't let it slide because Marco was 'only' a young vampire, and Tanika 'only' a mortal. That matters."

"Yes," he agreed. "It matters." He wove his fingers through hers. "Let us fly, *hbeebti*. I think Giulia will feel more at ease with just Aodhan and Illium and Navarro." Marco's angel was the one who'd escorted Giulia from the car to the execution area, Giulia's hand locked tight around his forearm.

Dmitri caught Raphael's eye at that moment, motioned that he and Honor were heading down to where he'd parked his Ferrari.

Raphael gave a small nod before touching his mind to Illium's. *How is Aodhan?*

Standing as strong as these trees. Golden fire in Illium's gaze. *He is unshakable.*

29

Giulia had asked Illium and Aodhan to stay with her following the execution, "so we can spend the night hours talking about Marco and Tani." While she liked Navarro, she'd shared that he intimidated her, while they reminded her of her son.

Yet this same woman had taken her quest for justice to Navarro's very door.

But when they reached her apartment, she said, "Stavros called," her eyes tear-reddened and her voice raw as a result of her earlier heartbreaking sobs. "Invited me to join him and Norma in a private memorial to our children."

"Would you like to go?"

"Yes." A maternal smile at Aodhan's question. "It's all right. I know Stavros wishes his daughter had never gotten mixed up in the immortal world, but he didn't sound angry today, just sad. A heartbroken father. I think it will be good for all three of us to be together."

It took no time at all to recall the Tower car and driver who'd taken her to and from the Catskills. After opening the car door for her, Aodhan made sure she knew she could call them at any point should she have need. "Whether to-night or any night to come," he said, his voice that beautiful quietness that wrapped around a person like a hug.

Giulia squeezed his fingers with her own. Her eyes were wet again, the tears that fell silent. "I will," she said. "And for so long as I live, I plan to call you both my friends." A shaky smile. "Don't make a liar out of me."

"Never," Aodhan promised as Illium nodded in agreement. "I cherish your friendship, Giulia. We'll talk soon."

They escorted the car from above, flying high in the night sky. Though they couldn't hear the conversation when Stavros and Norma stepped out of their small townhouse to welcome Giulia, that it was a welcome was clear.

The three hugged in a huddle of grief before moving inside.

"Will you come somewhere with me, Blue?" Aodhan asked as they hovered above the city. "I know it's been a hard day, but it feels like the right time for this."

"You never have to ask," Illium said. "Where are we going?"

"To what I wanted to show you before we broke the case and time got away from us. A storage locker on the outskirts of the city that I've been using to keep some of my work."

Illium whistled as they stretched their wings in flight. *I'm guessing no one knows that or the place would've been robbed ten times over by now.* Fans, unscrupulous dealers, art enthusiasts, the list went on.

It's in Beth's name.

Illium fell a few feet, he was so startled. *Ellie's sister?*

Yes. I asked Ellie for help when I wished to hire the facility, and she was with Beth at the time. Her sister was happy for us to use her name as a shield. They set it up online then and there, but Beth knows nothing of what's in it and doesn't wish to know. She asked me to please change the door code she had to input as part of the rental process so that she's never even tempted to peek.

Illium wanted to smile at the idea of Elena's younger

sister hiring a locker for one of the Seven, but his stomach was tense. He couldn't imagine what it was that Aodhan stored in that locker—they had plenty of other locations to keep their things. *You never told me about this locker.*

It would've hurt you then, was the firm answer. *If you can protect me, Blue, then I can protect you.*

Illium scowled, thinking of their conversations in China, of how Aodhan had accepted Illium's need to look after him. Not just accepted, Illium admitted to himself, but embraced. No longer did his best friend see Illium's care as an attempt at control—he understood that this was how Illium loved his people.

And Aodhan?

Aodhan was his everything.

I don't like this place already, he muttered as they overflew the pulsing night beat of the city.

Cars flowed on the streets where they weren't backed up in a sea of red brake lights, angels flew cross town to clubs or to meet up with friends, all under a moody charcoal sky where clouds had blotted out the stars. It didn't matter. New York created its own stars in the thousands of points of light dotted around the city, along the streets, and strung up on rooftops.

I love the city at night, Aodhan said at that moment, before taking a deep breath of the cold air this high. *The streets become rivers of light, the skyscrapers jagged mountains under an endless sky.*

He'd always been good at that, Illium thought, painting scenes with his voice as well as his hands. *Will you paint New York for me just that way?*

I'll do it in black and white with only flickers of colors, so the light appears to move. His hair rippled back in the wind, his wings glinting in an errant spotlight that had been pointed skyward.

A few more minutes of flight found them over quieter residential areas, then even those fell behind.

How did you get stuff into the locker without being noticed?

I did it in the darkest part of night when the sky was cloudy and starless much like today. Part of the reason I chose this facility is because it's run-down and doesn't have much security. No cameras. It's also in an industrial area that's all warehouses. No street activity after night, for it's too remote and, as Beth put it, "creepy."

And you chose this place to store your art?

The actual storage lockers are tough, and I placed a strong lock on it. As for the work inside . . . let's just say I had a complicated relationship with it at the time.

Though tension gnawed at Illium's gut, he didn't badger Aodhan for further details. It had to be bad if the other man hadn't told him all this time . . . and he'd know the full extent of it soon enough.

There it is. Aodhan angled over an area that was dark but for a few anemic lights, which barely penetrated the gloom.

I think we're in danger, Illium said in an ominous tone, taking it in from above.

The facility appeared even worse than Aodhan had described—cement walls with peeling paint, the roof pock-marked with rust, the driveway cracked in so many places, it was almost a grass lot. He spotted no movement around the storage facility, but someone was working a forklift at the warehouse across the road.

They waited until the operator was on the far side of that warehouse before they landed. It took Aodhan only a moment to key in the entry code.

The door locked behind them with a hard snick.

"This way." Aodhan began to walk down the cool cement hallway filled with endless doors that ended at a vanishing point into eternity.

"You know, in those movies you watch with Ellie," Illium said darkly, "this is where you both start yelling at the innocent future victim to run."

"Stay close. I'll protect you from the monsters."

"Funny." Illium's scowl hid the rapid pulse of his heart—not at the environment, but at Aodhan's teasing words.

Whatever this was, wherever they were going, it didn't hurt Adi any longer.

His locker proved to be halfway down the hallway on the left.

When he input the code, Illium said, "The day of my birth." Angels didn't often celebrate such things after their majority, and many of the old ones had no idea when they might've been born, but Illium had come into the world at a time when Jessamy was the Librarian; she kept a neat list of all angelic births.

Aodhan's smile carved his cheeks, turning him from handsome to devastating. "I had to choose numbers I'd never forget."

Illium wanted to haul him close and kiss him until neither one of them could breathe. It took serious effort to keep it contained, but this wasn't a moment to interrupt.

This, whatever it was that lay in the locker, was important enough to Aodhan that he'd first hidden it, and now wanted to share it with Illium.

Once they were past the coded lock, the door opened to reveal *another* door, this one barred with a huge padlock. "I'm starting to get why this facility hasn't gone out of business despite its less-than-personable appearance."

"Ransom told me about it," Aodhan said. "I was talking about finding a place to store some of my art, and he said the most secure place he knew looked like an abandoned building and was surrounded by chain link with holes in it. A facility no self-respecting burglar would even think about wasting his time on."

Taking a key from a small pocket in the front of his pants, he unlocked the padlock. "Close both doors behind us."

Only after Illium had done as ordered did Aodhan turn on the light.

Canvases sat in piles across the majority of the space. Not stretched over wooden frames, not even rolled up in cardboard tubes. Just flat, paint-heavy sheets that had been placed one on top of the other . . . and still, despite the lack of anything to bulk them up, the piles reached halfway to the ceiling and filled up three quarters of the room.

Illium could see none of the work, the canvases stored face down.

"Where did you find the time to paint all these?" It wasn't as if Aodhan hadn't been creating art Illium *had* seen in the interim, and his work wasn't slapdash. A single piece could take months if he had dedicated time to spend on it, while a number had taken years.

"Here and there over two centuries." Aodhan pulled one off the pile. "It was almost a compulsion for the first century. Then it became a way to try to understand my own scars." He placed the canvas on the ground, face up.

Agony seared Illium.

It was a self-portrait of Aodhan as he'd been when they'd found him, his body emaciated, his face hollow, his eyes devoid of the light that was Illium's Adi. And his wings . . . Illium wanted to fold over in anguish, only stayed upright because Aodhan was looking at the painting with an expression of interest but no pain.

Almost as if he was examining someone else's work.

"I never saw you do these," Illium whispered.

"I never did them when you were near." Aodhan spread his wing over Illium's in a sweep of heavy warmth. "It was my secret thing for a long time, a kind of inner flagellation to punish myself for having been so naïve."

Illium struggled not to interrupt; he hated Aodhan talking about himself that way, but this was the past, unchangeable even by the Cadre.

"I did eventually tell Eh-ma—and even lost as she was then, she never revealed my secret. Instead, she used to sit there sketching while I painted feverishly, then she'd critique my work."

He chuckled. "Took me a pitifully long time to work out that it was her way of taking the emotion out of it. She turned an act of anguish and rage into a thing mundane." He pointed at his own painted face. "I think on this one, she told me I got the cheekbone shading wrong because I was working too fast."

Illium loved his mother, adored her for being kind and generous and a loving pair of arms all his life. Today, he found himself aching to hold her tight, make sure she knew how important she was to him, to Aodhan, to the world.

"I'm glad you showed someone." His eyes felt gritty, his emotions hard and brittle. "Are they all . . ."

"Like this?" Aodhan shook his head. "But there are only three variations. It's either me, the box, or this." He dug through the pile to show Illium a painting so black that that was all it appeared to be at first glance. A square of nothingness.

But a closer look and he began to see the screaming faces hidden within.

A horrifying vision of nightmare.

"The inside of my brain," Aodhan said in a pragmatic tone. "Once." Raising Illium's hand to his mouth, he pressed a kiss to his knuckles, that beautiful starlight hair falling over his forehead as he did so.

"I know it's a shock to see these, but I wanted you to before I destroy them all. I haven't done one for the last three or so decades, but I couldn't let go of them. To the extent that I boxed them up before I first left the Refuge, and every so often I'd ask the stronghold staff there to ship me a few boxes. No pattern to it, a way to keep from drawing attention."

A noxious secret, Illium thought, a shadow Aodhan hated but couldn't shrug off.

"Now, at last"—Aodhan took another canvas, scowled, dropped it atop the others he'd shown Illium—"I feel nothing when I look at them except annoyance that I was working so fast that I did nothing close to my best work. Eh-ma was right about the cheekbones on that first one. And this one, the definition's awful. It's fit only for the rubbish heap, all of it."

Illium swallowed hard, his hands in brutal fists. "I feel

like I should be a good citizen of the world and stop you, tell you this is a priceless collection of work for all that you're able to find flaws with it, but fuck that. I want to burn it to cinders." It was a physical representation of Aodhan's pain, and Illium hated its very existence.

His hand glowed with power. "Can I do it now?"

"Blue, you'll blow up the building," Aodhan chided, his eyes flicking to Illium's wings. "Especially when you're glowing like that."

For once, Illium didn't care about the lingering symptom of archangelic power that wasn't his, would never be his if he had his way. "How else are we going to do it?" He wasn't leaving until he'd erased this pile of hurt and terror from existence.

"I never really thought about it." Aodhan rubbed his jaw, scanned the piles. "I threw away all the boxes after I laid out the canvases, so we don't have those to reuse."

Illium's rage was fuel for his brain. "I'll get someone to drive a large truck here, and we'll load up every last canvas, take them out to a remote location, and have the bonfire of all bonfires."

It was Dmitri he decided to ask to drive the truck—because Dmitri had been there when they brought Aodhan home, Dmitri knew all of it, and he had no wings that made driving a truck awkward at best.

Despite the fact it was after midnight by now, he made the call, got a husky-voiced Honor on the line. But though it was clear both had been asleep, Dmitri didn't tear Illium a new one for his request. The second knew Illium would've called him only if it *had* to be Dmitri who drove the truck. "I'll be there soon as I can requisition a truck from the Tower garage," the other man said before hanging up.

"Do you want Dmitri to see these?" Illium asked. "Or shall we carry them in a way he can't?"

"The latter," Aodhan said at once. "I want no more memories of these than already exist. They were a cleansing of my soul, stroke by stroke. Now it's time for the detritus to be removed."

* * *

Dmitri just nodded when Aodhan refused his offer to help carry out the canvases, then stood watch over the truck in the moonless dark. Clad in black jeans and a black T-shirt, his hair roughly brushed, he should've looked young and careless. Except this was Dmitri, a vampire of such power that even senior angels treated him with wary respect.

His presence was a pulse in the air, dark red and viciously controlled.

Illium had the feeling that Dmitri knew what Aodhan had been doing. But if he did, he said nothing about it, and—once they'd emptied the storage locker—Illium and Aodhan flew overhead while Dmitri drove the vehicle over two hours north out of the city, to a remote area inland from the Hudson River.

No city to warm the air with particles of light here, the world pitch-black.

"Thank you," Aodhan said to Dmitri after they'd emptied the truck of its cargo.

A nod from the second.

But Aodhan had more to say. "Did you know?"

"No." Dmitri shrugged. "But I figured something like that had to be going on. You're an artist, Sparkle. It's what you do."

A gentle slap to Aodhan's face that held the affection he'd shown them when they'd been baby angels. "I, meanwhile, spent my rage getting into every fight I could, got beaten to a pulp more than once because I took on far older vamps.

"Only reason they didn't rip off my head is because, one, Raphael kept hauling me out before it got to that point, and two, even the most infuriated old ones felt sorry for me— they thought I'd had a bad Making, was half-insane. I think you took the better route."

The hug between the two was initiated by Aodhan, but Dmitri's hold was tight, the fisted thump on Aodhan's shoulder one of brotherhood. He murmured something to Aodhan that Illium didn't catch before they broke the embrace.

"Don't linger too long," the second said. "Forecast says there's a huge storm coming." Jumping into the truck on that, he turned it around for the drive home.

And Illium set fire to the stack of canvases after a nod from Aodhan.

The flames were a dazzling blue that sent curls of black up into the atmosphere.

30

"Showing off?" Aodhan teased, even as the blue flames altered to a more prosaic yellow-orange.

"I think it was just my pissed-offness coming out," Illium muttered, circling the bonfire to ensure it ate up every tiny fragment of every canvas.

Aodhan let him circle, let him pace, his own presence peaceful as he told Illium more stories of Eh-ma, of how she'd chided him for covering the canvases in black without thought to how much depth he'd need for the images hidden within, and how she'd once argued with him that he hadn't been that thin when he came back.

Aodhan laughed, a glittering candle set incandescently alight by the flames. "I was healed enough by then that I argued back that I most definitely *was* that thin, and we quibbled until she drifted away into the fog of her mind. But she always came back, always found me at the times I needed her most." His voice grew thick. "We should go see her."

Illium fell in love all over again with this warrior artist with all his shades of being. Looking up at the sky as fine motes of ash floated up against the pitch dark, he recalled all the technical data in his head. "Adi, there are no satellites passing overhead. No security cameras in any direction." A rasp of sound. "There are no people living nearby, and even if someone has chosen to wander the wild . . . there's no light. No moon. No city bright. Stars hidden by heavy cloud cover. You don't sparkle in pure darkness."

Aodhan looked at the skin of his hands. It glittered in the firelight, but should he step back into the heavy shadows of the trees, he'd become just another shadow. His skin needed light for life, drew it to him, but it couldn't draw what wasn't there.

"Then," he said, "let's hope this fire burns fast."

Illium immediately threw more power at it, sending the flames ten feet high.

Laughing, Aodhan went to drag him close, but Illium resisted. "No, I have to see this through."

Aodhan had already made his peace with what burned in front of them, but he understood his lover, so he let Illium babysit the fire until the last ember had cooled. Then he lit up the space using his own power, so that Illium could poke about with a stick to ensure nothing of any canvas had survived. It'd be a miracle given the intensity of the fire caused by Illium's dangerous energy, but Aodhan accepted Illium's need.

"It's all gone," the other man said a good ten minutes later, then blasted the earth with another strike of power just in case.

Aodhan allowed his light to go out when the earth stopped glowing red.

Allowed himself to be cloaked in the lush black wings of the night.

Illium shot up into the sky.

Aodhan rose behind him after a short delay, the game one of reading air currents, of listening for Illium, because neither of them could see each other in this utter lack of light. When they met midair, they kissed by feel, their wings threatening to tangle as they spun in the sky.

I would know you by your kiss, Illium.

Dropping his head to the curve of his lover's neck . . . he brought Illium's hand to his bare hip. Because before joining his best friend and heart's mirror in the sky, Aodhan had removed his clothing and laid it in a spot he could find again in the night.

Illium's gasp was a whisper in the air, his other hand tangling in Aodhan's hair as they both held the hover with the skill of warriors honed. "*Mea lux?*" A question in the endearment.

"I've never been more sure." Aodhan had shed the chains that had weighed him down for too long, would brook no interference from the past. "And you, my darling Blue? Do you wish this?" He kissed his way back up Illium's neck and along his jaw, until their lips were a hairsbreadth apart. "It must be a symphony of two. I'm ready to wait as long as you need for your song to join mine." This dance of angelkind was the ultimate intimacy—and between them, a declaration undying.

Illium's kiss held his entire huge heart, those strong hands cupping Aodhan's face as his lover's wings shifted the air currents so that they spun faster and faster. Without warning, Illium shot up into the sky, but this time he took Aodhan with him.

Releasing a shout of glee such as he hadn't in eons, Aodhan folded back his own wings, giving control to his wild and nimble lover. Who took them so high that the air turned thin and ice-cold, and they were hidden in the thick mist at that extreme elevation.

Ice crystals formed on the blue-tipped black of Illium's lashes, a delicacy of fragile diamonds.

"Ready, Adi?" A wicked question, Illium's lips against his ear, his breath hot, licking heat up the shell of it.

"Always, Blue."

They fell at reckless speed, the rushing air a frigid counterpoint to the heat between them. As reckless as his fall,

Illium tore off his clothes and threw them about without losing contact with Aodhan.

"We are never going to find them again!" Aodhan was laughing as he said that, even as he took over the fall while Illium undressed.

"I'll fly back naked! Imagine the headlines! Finally, everyone will have the answer to the question of whether my cock is blue!" With that laughing statement, Illium snapped out his wings again and Aodhan closed his.

This was who they'd always been—equals. Control flowing back and forth. No leader. No follower.

Just Illium and Aodhan.

Sparkle and Bluebell.

Adi and Blue.

They shot up again, but this time, their bodies were aligned, the heat between them a tactile creature aching and wanting. Ripe, full, a promise of limitless pleasure. Interlocked, their lips voracious, they flew higher and higher.

When they fell, it was locked in a kiss, their legs tangled with carnal intent.

Powerful thighs pushed against powerful thighs as Aodhan's hands, then Illium's, clenched on flesh taut with muscle. Neither one of them felt any need to temper their strength. Two warriors whose bodies were strong and whose trust in each other was absolute, their dance was no delicate ballet but a hotly desired clash, rough and hard and raw.

They fell and rose and fell again.

Until their skin was slick with sweat, their pulses aligned in a staccato beat.

And though they hadn't prepared for this, it didn't matter. Pleasure came in many forms, and this night, they found the pleasure available only to two winged beings who knew each other's most sensitive spots, two combat-ready fighters who understood their own bodies inside out, two lovers who were ready to touch and adore and learn, two aroused men who had no limits with each other, two friends who loved above all else.

It was love, and it was transcendent.

* * *

Aodhan lay spent and sweat-damp on the soft grass, while Illium leaned over him, stroking his chest and dropping an occasional kiss on his jaw or lips. One of Aodhan's wings was pinned under his best friend and lover . . . and Aodhan didn't care. There was trust, and then there was what he felt for and with Illium.

"You feel like Smoke right now," Illium said, a smile in his voice. "All drowsy and relaxed."

Aodhan ran his fingers lazily over Illium's wing. "She's going to be mad we didn't pick her up from Izzy." Having realized early on what their day was going to entail, they'd asked the young angel to collect her from tech command at the end of the day and make sure she got her dinner.

Izzy had promptly stated his goal of "catnapping" Smoke for the night.

"I'll buy my way back into her good graces with the special treats I ordered for just such an emergency." A kiss pressed to Aodhan's pectoral, Illium's other wing sweeping over him in a silken blanket before Illium laid his head against Aodhan's shoulder, turning so that he lay on his back, too.

As they lay there, sated and happy, the dark clouds above began to move.

A cool wind whispered through the trees at the same moment.

The storm was coming, but its leading edge pushed the clouds aside to reveal the stars.

Aodhan smiled even as his body began to glimmer at that far-off hint of light. It felt right, that they should lie here under the stars on this stormy night when his life had begun again in all its facets wild and astonishing.

Today

31

No one had ever described ascension to Illium. In truth, he'd never thought to ask. It had seemed self-evident: a massive surge of power into an angel's body that forever altered him into something *other*, even among angelkind. He'd thought he'd experienced an aborted ascension when the Cascade attempted to force power into him.

How foolish he'd been.

The first punch of that violent energy, it was as he'd imagined—but it didn't come from without. It came from *within*. As if a closed door in his mind had suddenly blown off with a force so vicious that it sent him to the sky without his conscious volition. Resisting it was an impossibility. To be an archangel was to be remade by the forces of the world itself. It was agony and it was beauty and it was all he was and all he could become and it was eternity.

As he hung in the sky, held up by nothing but the power of ascension, he felt it begin—the alteration of his cells. Each and every one in his body beginning to change in an unstoppable cascade. Every particle that made him Illium was reshaped in this endless time that was his ending and his beginning.

Intellectually, he knew it wasn't endless. He'd witnessed Suyin's ascension, read about others in their histories. But in this space that he occupied in the universe, time had slowed to where a breath took an eon, and his heart didn't pulse so much as wait in echoing silence, the pause between beats was so long.

In that forever, he saw himself being born, a red-faced infant his mother cradled to her breast with infinite tenderness while tears streamed down her face. He cried, too, at the beauty of her love for him, her child that she'd nurtured in her womb.

Next to her stood Aegaeon, his face awash in a wonder that made him seem a wholly different man. The hand with which he touched his son's head was proud, the kiss he pressed to Sharine's cheek one of utmost love.

Another man. Gone now.

Illium mourned the loss even as his heart overflowed at being loved by a mother luminous and full of joy . . . and old, so, *so* old. He felt it now, the weight of her years, the countless scars on her soul, the fine fractures that had spread outward in a slow creep until they broke her. And still, she was this being radiant who grew ever stronger. To be the son of Sharine, the Hummingbird? It was the greatest honor he could imagine.

He saw every moment of his childhood, from birth to toddlerhood.

His heart cracked at his first glimpse of Aodhan, reformed again with rivers of glittering brightness within that was his love for the boy who ran with him in his memories, racing him to the gorge so that they could get up to mischief.

Eyes of infinite blue looking into his as Raphael crouched down so that they were eye to eye. There was an amused affection in his smile and his expression held a care that Illium felt down to his bones. He had always known that Raphael loved him. But today . . . today he saw into the heart of an archangel, and he knew that he had always had a father even after Aegaeon's abandonment.

In his mind's eye, he held out his hand to the man he called Rafa, and his Rafa took it before rising, and they walked together through the Refuge, a boy with too-big wings that trailed on the ground, and a warrior strong and tall who had never lost his ability to care for the most vulnerable among them.

The hand altered, became dark-skinned, with the golden stripes of a tiger beneath, and when he looked up, the man who walked with him had eyes of liquid silver and hair the same. He showed Illium a huge white spider that hid against the snow, then pulled him onto his back and went running through the craggy edges of the Refuge where Illium wasn't permitted to go on his own.

Screams of boyish delight, the crisp bite of snow.

But the back wasn't Naasir's now. It was that of a deadly vampire who swung him around into his arms and gripped his jaw as he told Illium not to do that again lest he hurt himself. Dmitri's eyes were dark and intent, his hold gentle. But only now did Illium see the agony hidden in the dark, the anguish that Dmitri had never shared with him, and he understood that Dmitri had once been a father.

His mother's voice as she made him honey cakes to take with him to sword training and asked about his day at school. Sharine racing out from their home to wave the wrapped packet at him because he'd forgotten it in his rush. Her arms holding him tight and moving him from side to side against her as he laughed and squirmed, saying he'd be late . . . but delighted by her affection all the same.

She smelled of sunlight and joy and home.

Then there *he* was again. A young man of radiant light, so bright and strong that he stopped Illium's heart. Especially when he smiled.

They flew together, finding new routes, making their own paths.

Shadows. Grief. Loss.

He wanted to turn his face, not look at those parts of his

life, but ascension demanded everything. He couldn't turn away. So he saw his father go into Sleep. He saw his mother forget him. And he saw Aodhan leave him without ever moving away.

The agony crushed him.

Yet despite his pain, he stood firm, stood strong, his hand held out to them.

And one by one, they came back to him . . . even the one he didn't want. He did turn away from Aegaeon, because that thread was done, cut. No pain at that, no second thoughts.

His mother's laughter again, her hands on his cheeks.

His Aodhan's smile, dazzling and ever brighter.

Raphael. Dmitri. Naasir.

The others who had come before and after. Jason, so silent and quiet, his facial tattoo a bare curve on his cheek, but there he was, handing Illium a toy he'd lost as a child and been distraught about. Jason had found it for him, even though the Jason of that time had been swathed in a silence born of another child's terror.

Venom, so young and wild. Galen, barbarian ways and loyal heart.

Elena, stubborn new spark in eternity and owner of a piece of his heart.

Jessamy, both slender hands on her hips as she groaned while a tiny mud-splattered Illium stood in front of her doing his best impression of being sincerely remorseful.

He laughed in his ascension, cried, too, was angry, all of it at once.

A thousand faces. A million names. He saw and heard all of them in a kaleidoscope that spun and spun without ever overwhelming him.

Keir, patching him up over and over again, his hands ever gentle.

The Primary playing chess with him while seven hundred and seventy-six others watched through translucent eyes defined by a new ring of mountain blue.

Lorenzo, beating him at cards while Catalina laughed at their competitiveness.

His beloved Smoke curling up against him in her final days, when he'd just sat with her against his chest for hours, stroking her fur as she slept.

Lijuan staring at him in battle from across the field. Dead eyes. Cold eyes.

Kaia so happy and sure of herself, the sweet taste of young love, new and untried.

War, fire, loss, battle, victory.

Raising his sword for his archangel and going down on one knee as Raphael appointed him his first general. Such pride he'd felt that day and every day since. It rolled over him in a primal wave tinged with a heavy sense of grief.

Never again would anyone call him Illium, First General to Archangel Raphael.

Kissing Aodhan, the two of them tangled up in the sky, wings and limbs and spirits. A moment of clarity and unbounded peace, the knowledge that this was where he was meant to be, and who he was meant to be with.

Aodhan was his moonlight and his sunlight, his air and his heart.

Now . . . for the first time since they'd met, they were no longer the same. A stutter in his heart, his mind, a worry unknown. But there was no stopping this. The cells in Illium's body had almost completed their transition into another form. The power within him . . . he could no more describe it than he could the wind or the air.

He could reach in his hand and scoop it up and it would overflow.

Then it did, pouring out of every cell in his body until he was nothing but light, nothing but an incandescent golden fire that burned across the entire world.

32

Raphael had blasted out the *Land!* order the instant he realized what was happening. Accidents did and could occur during an ascension, angels scorched out of the sky if they lingered too long after the energies spiked. Even major structures like the floating habitats would've been destroyed if they hadn't descended and attached themselves to their allocated anchor points.

Illium couldn't stop that. Neither could Raphael. The forces of ascension were their own.

His fingers curled into his palm as he stood on a skyscraper of black glass on the eastern edge of his city, a city he'd seen rise and fall and rise again through time. But today, even his beloved New York couldn't hold his attention, not when Illium burned up in the forces that had once captured Raphael in their irreversible grasp.

He wondered what Illium saw, what he felt. He'd asked his mother about it once, asked Uram, too, and both their stories had been different from his own. Only on one thing had they all agreed: ascension made them *other* in ways incomprehensible but unequivocal.

Archangels weren't extraordinarily powerful angels. They were whole different beings.

It's Illium, isn't it? Elena's mental voice was strong, his consort no longer the just-born angel she'd once been.

Yes, hbeebti. *The energies we believed had set him free were but waiting.*

Grief and pride roared through him in an agonizing fury.

Grief that he would lose Illium from his territory, and that the boy full of laughter and joy he'd watched grow into a man of heart and honor would now have to tangle with the politics and power plays of the Cadre.

Pride because Elena's Bluebell had not only survived but thrived after going through in the first five hundred years of his life more than most immortals did their entire lifetime. Illium had a spine so strong that nothing could or would break it, and a mind so intelligent that he could bend without considering it a blow to his power. He also had a heart that meant his rule would be honorable . . . would be glorious.

The rule of Archangel Illium would one day be legend; this Raphael believed with every fiber of his being. *I always knew he'd fly high.* In his mind ran a laughing little blue-winged boy shouting, "Rafa! Rafa! Watch what I can do!"

That time was gone forever now, Illium's ascension creating a stark dividing line between past and present. From this moment on, the two of them would no longer be able to be in the same place for long periods without giving in to an aggression that couldn't be controlled, for it was an impulse born of the physical changes in their bodies. An impulse linked to the energies of the world itself.

Raphael would never again go flying with Illium except when they visited each other's territories. Illium would never again sprawl in an armchair in Raphael's home and have a drink while Raphael did the same, their interaction having nothing to do with politics.

To be Cadre *was* to be a political creature.

I will miss him with my every breath, he said to his Elena, his throat thick and his heart aching as the golden sky cracked with a rain unnatural and unearthly in its jeweled beauty.

I want to hold him in my arms and protect him from the world of archangels, Elena confessed in a shaky tone. *But I'm so fucking proud of him at the same time. He was fine with not ascending, never got annoyed with the idiots who whispered that he was a failed ascension, had the confidence to just shrug it off. He's lived life on his own terms.* Anger threaded her words now. *The forces of ascension are ripping that away from him.*

Yes. It is a paradox that in order to become one of the most powerful beings in the world, we must at the moment of transition be utterly powerless. Perhaps there was meant to be a lesson in that, but no archangel appeared to have learned it.

Our task now, he added, *is to be his friends as we have never before been.* Raphael lifted his hands, his palms and fingers coated with Illium's golden rain, his skin a gloaming of mystery. *You know we will lose them both?* They were a pair, had always been a pair.

Illium and Aodhan.

Sparkle and Bluebell.

Archangel and Second.

I know. The rest of the Seven are going to be devastated.

I've been lucky beyond compare. He had to acknowledge that, had to focus on the gift and not the loss. *No other archangel has had such a devoted group of warriors with him for centuries upon centuries. One or two, yes, but never an entire united group that functioned as a seamless unit. I'll tell Illium to take others from my troops if it'll give him a first court that he trusts.* It wasn't the done thing among angelkind, but theirs was no ordinary relationship. *I will give him every advantage.*

I always knew that, Archangel, said the woman who was the reason for his eternity. *Tell Jason to spy extra hard on him until we know he's all right, that he has good people around him.*

Jason won't need my instruction, Elena-mine. If I know him, he's already putting the pieces in play.

Soft laughter wet with tears.

He swallowed hard, the lump in his throat a raw chunk of pure emotion.

Illium sucked the light back into himself with a sonic boom of sound, and when he landed, it was in front of Raphael. Cracks went out in every direction on the roof, as they stood, archangel to archangel.

That was how it always was when an angel ascended in the territory of another. They came face-to-face once the ascension was complete. Right after the war, it had been slender Suyin who'd stood shell shocked in front of not just him, but the rest of the Cadre, too—for the others had been near him at the time of her ascension. The white of her hair had been electric with a dark power that glittered like shattered gemstones and made her eyes glow from within.

"Raphael," she'd said once they were alone, an echo of the power of ascension in her voice, "I am changed. I am become not what I once was. There is a violence within me that never before existed, and it is focused on you."

At times, Raphael thought the enforced dynamic between archangels a thing perverse, one that *wanted* to urge them to war, but if that was what the voracious beast wanted today, it would be disappointed.

Raphael would not war with this boy become a man over whom Raphael had watched for centuries. A man who had stood with unshakable fidelity beside Raphael his entire adult life.

"Sire," Illium said, his eyes shining with a power that would take time to settle, and the blue-tipped black of his hair crackling with fine threads of gold.

Raphael shook his head. "No longer that, Illium."

A jerk toward him before Illium stopped himself—but then Raphel saw the stubborn set to his jaw with which he was intimately familiar, and the angel with blue wings was hugging him with a tightness that would allow no retreat.

Having already thrown up glamour around them the instant Illium landed, so that no one could spy on this moment between an archangel new and his sire past, Raphael clenched his own arms as tight. "My pride in you is boundless," he said, his voice rough. "You will be the best of archangels and I will be proud to call you my ally and friend."

Illium's arms tightened even further around Raphael, and there were tears in his voice when he said, "I will be your ally till the day my end comes, sire. This I promise on my blood."

There was that stubbornness he'd first seen in the bright, intelligent boy who'd called him Rafa. "Never call me 'sire' in front of the others, Illium," he said roughly after they pulled back and were face-to-face again. "Archangels are predators and you *must* be a predator among them." He cupped the other angel's face as he had when Illium was a child. "I know in my heart what you are to me, and what I am to you."

A shuddering breath, before Illium inclined his head. "The glamour is up?"

Raphael nodded. "I can drop it—"

"No, let me do this one last time." Then Illium went down on one knee after drawing his sword from the scabbard on his back and laying it across his knee. His wings were draped with precision for a formal bow, his head lowered, and his fist at his heart. "For all that you have done for me, for all that you have *been* to me, for all that you have taught me, there are no words enough to thank you, but thank you I do, sire."

Raphael didn't fight his own tears. "I will always be there for you, Illium. Never will I raise my hand or my sword against you, come what may. This is my promise." Perhaps a rash one, but Raphael knew himself—if he ever hurt Illium, he would no longer be the man Elena was proud to call her consort; he'd have become a monster.

Eyes shining wet, Illium raised his head. "Never will you have to fear me as an enemy. This bond between us, it is forever. I will come to your aid should anyone dare raise their hand or sword against you."

Raphael held out a hand.

When Illium took it and rose to his feet, they both knew it was the last time he'd ever call Raphael "sire" out loud. And the last time he would ever bow to another archangel. That was as it should be, his growth a thing of destiny.

"No tears," Raphael said, and used his forearm to wipe off his own as Illium did the same. "You must now wear the face of an archangel to everyone but those you trust to the core of your heart." He hated that he had to teach Illium to create a facade, when Illium was the most openhearted of them all.

Sighing, the blue-winged angel slid his sword into its scabbard, then placed his hands on his hips. "I really fucking hoped I'd avoided this whole ascension business." A scowl. "Maybe I'll just change the Cadre instead, si—Raphael." A smile full of a wildness that was pure Illium.

Raphael had the sudden thought that the Cadre had no idea what was about to hit them. Laughing at the wild blue storm to come, he dropped the glamour as Illium rose into the sky to head in the direction of the Enclave.

Dmitri, he's still our Illium. My trust in him is absolute. Though they all knew it already, he had to say those words now that Illium was an archangel. Dmitri would pass them on to Jason, Venom, Galen, and Naasir. Elsewise, the remaining members of his Seven would be torn between their loyalty to the both of them.

Dmitri's voice was gritty in his mind. *Fuck, I'm going to miss them.*

Them, because they all knew where Illium went, so would Aodhan.

Now, Raphael watched Illium drop from the sky over the Enclave, and he wondered how it would play out . . . because for the first time in their entire existence, Aodhan and Illium were no longer equals in power.

Yesterday

33

Twenty-five years after the end of the war, and Illium and Aodhan were at a celebration thrown by Lady Caliane.

India had been devastated both by the reborn children Lijuan had created during the war—and the price the terrible heartbreaking scourge demanded of the people who'd had to deal with it. It had crushed the spirit of this vast and ancient civilization.

Then had come Neha's decision to go into Sleep a mere decade later, leaving her yet-mourning territory without an archangel.

It could've broken this land.

But Lady Caliane, with her wisdom gained from mistakes so dark that she was forever altered, had stepped in and cherished India as if it was her beloved city of Amanat. So much so that she hadn't left its soil since taking over as Archangel of India but for short visits to check in on Amanat, and visit her son. It had still taken this long for the territory to get to its feet, even begin to heal. Their unwilling involvement in Lijuan's ugly murder of thousands of children was not an easy burden to bear.

The process would take many more decades yet.

These week-long celebrations, to be held across the entire country, were a gift from an archangel to her tired people—telling them that they could claim happiness, that joy was not a gift forever stolen from them.

Illium hadn't been there when Caliane spoke to Raphael, but the sire had mentioned it to him. "She wants her people to remember that life is more than pain and rebuilding and grief. For one week, India will effervesce in all its glory, and it is her hope that the memory will take them through the next year, when the celebration will reoccur. She intends for this to be a high point everyone looks forward to each year."

Illium and Aodhan had arrived three days into the celebrations, after Dmitri and Venom left to return to New York. Galen and Jessamy had also just left, with Naasir and Andromeda arriving in their stead. A flow that meant Raphael's territory as well as his Refuge stronghold would never be without one of its senior people.

The same applied to Illium's mother and Titus. As Caliane's best friend, Sharine had been in India for a week prior to the celebrations, with Titus flying in right before it kicked off. They'd both stayed for two additional days before returning to Africa, with Zanaya and Alexander taking their place in India. The three archangels worked well together as allies, each keeping an eye on the territories of the other.

The sole exceptions to the constant balancing of senior people in and out were Elena and Raphael, who Caliane had requested stay for the duration—and Jason. The spymaster had asked Raphael if he could remain in India throughout. Illium could guess that the spymaster wanted to be by Mahiya's side as she returned to her homeland—a place where her life had been a thing of quiet torment.

Mahiya herself had said so to Illium once, when he'd dropped by for dinner while near their home. He hadn't given her advance notice, but she'd welcomed him with a delighted hug nonetheless, then plied him with foods literally fresh from the pan, while Jason made droll remarks about Mahiya reinforcing the foraging instincts of certain uninvited guests.

The spymaster had become far less remote in the decades since he'd fallen in love. His ability to become a shadow remained unparalleled, but the Jason of before would've never made such a dry joke while filching a fresh samosa from his lover— because it *had* been a joke, his own embrace of welcome as fierce as Mahiya's.

For the Seven were as much a brotherhood as they were warriors under the same liege.

"My aunt," Mahiya had said when the conversation drifted to India and Archangel Neha, "wasn't the best of foster mothers is about all I can say politely." Her peacock's wings still, her face holding a distant look as she rolled out a fresh roti. "But I would be lying if I said I didn't miss the colors and scents and wonders of the place that was my home for most of my lifetime."

Today, Mahiya danced in the street below with a number of other women, mortal and vampire, all in jewel-hued skirts and tops embedded with tiny mirrors that reflected the light of the setting sun. The dancers had tied their long scarves— the colors matched to their skirts or tops—cross-body to keep them out of the way, their bangles making fine music as they raised their hands.

Four of Mahiya's bangles—one on each end of the stacks of color that covered her wrists—had bells on the end; she was so delighted by them that she'd come over to show Illium before she left the palace. "Look what Jason got made for me!" She'd moved her hand, her skin decorated with an intricate tracery of henna, to release a delicate cascade of music. "Aren't they so beautiful?"

Jason himself was difficult to see below, hidden as he was against the shadow thrown by an ancient building of pink stone pitted by time, but when Illium did finally spot him, he also spotted the smile on his face.

He glimpsed a far different expression on the face of the angel with wings of peacock blue and green who stood on a facing rooftop. Over three thousand years of age, Nivriti had within her the ability to hurt an archangel—but only *one specific archangel*. Neha, her twin. Now gone into a Sleep from which she might not return for eons, if ever.

He'd never seen Nivriti in anything but warrior leathers, but she'd softened enough for the celebration to have donned slim silk leggings of a pale purple paired with a thigh-length tunic in a more vivid shade of the same hue. Silver embroidery ran thick on the hems and along the neckline, that silver echoed in her bangles and in the thread woven through her single braid.

That Princess Mahiya Geet had inherited her wings from her mother was not a question.

Today, Nivriti watched her daughter with pride and love tempered by an old anguish . . . and also frustration. As used to getting her way as Neha, Nivriti was clearly still struggling with the unalterable truth that any relationship she had with Mahiya would always be on Mahiya's terms.

Asshole parents, Illium thought, never quite got it.

Mahiya might disagree with that description of Nivriti, given that Neha had imprisoned her twin and stolen Mahiya. Illium accepted that Nivriti hadn't abandoned Mahiya out of choice, and that her love for her daughter was true. On the flip side, all three people concerned in the love triangle that had led to Mahiya's horrific time at Neha's court had been selfish assholes.

Mahiya didn't much talk about it, but Illium had heard enough through the grapevine to draw his own conclusions.

Aodhan, crouched on the rooftop beside Illium, said, "I have no idea how Mahiya's managing to do that dance without tangling up her wings."

"It's like combat." Fascinated by the same, Illium had watched the movements with intense focus. "I could do it. So could you."

His features kissed by the red-orange glow of the sun, Aodhan shot him a dubious look. "Go on. I dare you." A grin as roguish as Illium's—and one that had once again become a normal part of their life after being absent so long.

"Oh, you think I won't." Illium's blood heated. "Dare taken. What do I get if I succeed?"

Aodhan rubbed his jaw. "I'll let you teach me the dance. *And* I'll do it in public before we leave."

"Done."

With that, Illium flared out his wings and flew down to join the dancers. Waiting until one of the women broke away to sit for a while, he flowed into the rhythm. Laughter feminine and delighted rose up around him as he began to move his hands and his body with the near-liquid fluidity of the others.

It was, quite frankly, a lot harder than it looked, but he'd never been one to give up.

"Wings like a babe!" Mahiya called out from across the circle, her cheeks flushed and eyes bright under the dusting of gold on her eyelids. "Triple fold!"

A triple fold was *extremely* difficult for an adult angel to pull off. Illium managed it, but had to keep concentrating to hold the position for any longer than a split second. But he saw what Mahiya meant at once. He was able to move much faster with his wings in that awkward position.

Mahiya cheered him on, the tendrils of hair that had escaped the knot at her nape curling around her lovely face with its eyes of tawny brown, the bindi she wore in the center of her forehead a teardrop that matched the vibrant pink of her skirt. Illium, too, had gone for color, choosing a tunic of rich rust-orange that contrasted sharply with his wings.

He didn't come close to standing out, the festival was such a riot of hues.

Aodhan had gone for simple cream with gold embroidery for his tunic, paired with black pants like Illium's, but for the first time in his life, he didn't have to worry about standing out, either. The tiny mirrors so prevalent in the festival clothing turned everyone into a sparkling gemstone.

Illium looked up, and there was his Adi, watching him with a huge smile wreathing his face. That was enough of a win for Illium. He'd never force the other man to mingle so closely with so many people.

To his shock, however, Aodhan flared out his wings and glided down to the street.

As Illium watched, stumbling in the dance as he did so, Aodhan shoved up the sleeves of his tunic to reveal muscled forearms, and said, "Go slow, ladies—and Illium. I have no idea what I'm doing."

The street around them had begun to buzz the instant he appeared on the ground, for while he might not stand out as much as he usually did, Aodhan was also not known for hanging about at street level.

The buzz grew into enthusiastic cheering as the women welcomed him in with giggles and encouraging waves of the hand. Having ended up on the side across from his lover, Illium grinned as he watched Mahiya show Aodhan how to move so that he'd be part of the flow of the circle.

The rich pink of her skirts hit Aodhan's legs as she swirled, brilliant against the sparkle of him, and Aodhan just barely managed to stop from smacking the woman on the other side of him with his wing. His apology made the round-cheeked mortal clap her hands in delight, then begin to show him how to move—in slow motion.

Aodhan only grazed her with his wing this time, causing a small boy in their street audience to fall over in laughter.

Aodhan's own shoulders shook.

There was more laughter, more instruction, until at last, they began to flow in a river of color and sound.

Jason, Illium said, reaching out with his mind, *don't suppose I can dare you to join us?*

First of all, I am recording this for posterity because no one will believe it otherwise. Secondly, spymasters have a reputation to uphold. The universe will crack in two should I join in.

But then Jason did the unexpected. He vanished from sight in that Jason way of his . . . only for his voice to fill the air in a song as joyful as this celebration. It stopped Illium's heart, the beauty and pristine clarity of Jason's voice a thing that penetrated so deep that several of the people around them sobbed at the sheer beauty of it.

Mahiya's smile was luminous. "Let's give my beloved's song the dance it deserves!"

And so they danced amid the notes of a song of love and hope and heart for Princess Mahiya Geet . . . and the place she had once called home. A gift from Jason to his princess, but one that embraced each and every being who heard it. Including two warrior angels who heard in Jason's song their own love story.

They were sitting, tired but happy, on the edge of the flat roof of a fort that overlooked the town bedecked in lights, the music distant, and the stars bright overhead when Illium turned to Aodhan and said, "I got you a gift." His heart pounded, his mouth dry.

Even after a quarter of a century together, he was nervous.

Because this, they'd never done.

Sleeves still folded up and a goblet of mead in hand, a lazy-limbed Aodhan ran his wing over Illium's. "You're my favorite gift, Blue." He'd opened up his tunic partway down his chest, revealing the flare of his collarbone, the flat of his breastbone, the curve of his pectoral.

A fine metal chain lay against his skin.

Any other night and Illium would've taken great pleasure in exploring that hard body while he kissed lips that were soft only for him.

Tonight, however . . .

He held out his closed hand and couldn't find any charm or pretty words. He blurted out, "No, it's this." Opening his fingers, he revealed a bracelet of polished amber beads. The amber was crystalline but with rivers of darker shades within that took its perfection to a unique level of beauty.

It glowed in the light that sparked off Aodhan.

Aodhan had frozen at the sight, now picked up the bracelet with trembling fingers after putting the goblet unseeing onto the roof beside him. *"Illium."*

"Will you wear my amber?" Illium asked, his heart exposed.

Aodhan's hand, so strong, so careful, clenched on the beads. "Only," he rasped, "if you wear mine."

"What?"

Sliding his hand under the neckline of his tunic, Aodhan tugged out the chain on which hung a ring. He pulled the chain off over his head, removed the ring, and held it out. "Will you wear my amber, Blue?"

Illium's throat closed up, his entire being a single pulse, because as he'd spent literal years sourcing the perfect amber to resonate with Aodhan's light, it was clear that Aodhan had spent as much time making this ring. It was carved *of* amber, with a ring of metal behind it to hold the more fragile stone in place.

The design was intricate, of feathers laid atop feathers surrounding and interwoven into the symbol of infinity. "How did you make this without me seeing it?" he managed to get out instead of just snatching at the ring.

"It's good to be known as a temperamental artist who growls people away from his studio."

Illium's chest expanded in a burst of happiness that was close to pain as he held out his hand. The love of his life slipped the ring onto his finger at the same time that Illium slipped the bracelet over the strong bones of Aodhan's wrist. The amber glowed exactly as he'd imagined, lit by the luminescence that was his Adi.

His own amber settled perfectly on his finger, a deep shade that was striking against his tawnier skin. He held it close to his eye, examining the carving, which must've taken boundless patience.

Aodhan, meanwhile, was holding his bracelet up to the light, a smile curving his lips.

Illium suddenly felt silly and young and happy. Grabbing Aodhan by the front of his tunic, he hauled his lover and best friend down for a kiss that was all beating hearts and smiling lips and a certainty that this had been meant to be.

They fell off the edge of the fort.

Laughing, they broke apart, then flew high, high, higher, until they were closer to the stars than the earth, and they tangled in a kiss while Aodhan held the hover. His hair, overlong because he'd been too busy to get it cut, brushed Illium's cheek in a softness of light, while his hand was a rough counterpoint on that same cheek.

Illium loved how Aodhan kissed him, with such care every single time, even when they were caught in the turbulence of passion primal and unrestrained. Today, the kiss held a happiness and an exuberance that had them grinning at each other as they drew apart while yet entangled.

Illium ran his hand through the glittering beauty of Aodhan's hair. "I like this."

"You can enjoy it for another month before it drives me insane and I hack it off."

Illium fisted a hand in all that beautiful silk. "I could make a fortune selling your shorn locks on the black market."

"And I could pluck out your feathers one by one at night and make an equal killing."

Illium's grin only deepened. "Bet? I'll give you ten feathers, you give me enough hair for ten small bundles, and we'll see who comes out the financial winner?"

Aodhan looked at him with a glint in his eye. "No, I think I'll just catch you and pluck those feathers."

Illium bolted away before Aodhan's hands could tighten, and the race was on across the grand forts and festival-lit streets of Jaipur. People whooped when Illium swept down so low that they could've reached up and touched his wings—except he was too fast, soaring up and away before anyone could realize what was happening.

Aodhan dipped down low before flying up and around, twisting in an attempt to catch Illium by cutting him off—except Illium was a master at rapid turns and quick changes in path. Aodhan, however, had been playing this game with him for a lifetime, had a few tricks up his sleeve.

Illium didn't realize he was being funneled out over the rolling desert until he was already there—and on this landscape, Aodhan had the advantage. Because while Illium was faster, Aodhan had more endurance. So Illium went up and up and up.

Aodhan followed . . . but when Illium turned to drop down, Aodhan put himself directly in Illium's path when it was far too late for Illium to turn away. They smashed into each other with brutal force, something that would've done severe damage to angels of less power. But they were two of the Seven.

They took the blow with grunts, their wings spread as they attempted to control the spiral down to the earth. "You're a lunatic!" Illium shouted.

"That's why you love me!"

Aodhan slammed into the sand with his back, having made sure Illium was on top when they hit the earth. The impact created a dust storm that blotted out the world for a long moment, and in that moment, Illium kissed Aodhan's wicked mouth and the slope of his neck, his hands pinning the thickness of Aodhan's wrists to the sand.

Sand, gritty and fine, against his teeth, on Aodhan's skin, glimmers of silica against the faint brilliance of him, the only light out here from the stars. And in that radiance, Aodhan glowed like moonlight, lighting up his amber . . . and Illium's, too.

An entanglement of hearts in perfect sync.

Today

34

Aodhan stared out across the Hudson from his position in the trees he and Illium had planted for privacy after they first purchased this house from an angel who'd decided to relocate permanently to the Refuge. He knew what was happening, understood that Illium would be drawn to land in front of Raphael first, and he knew, *knew* that there were no two archangels less likely to do violence to each other, but still he worried.

Power altered people. It had altered even Raphael at one time. The archangel he'd known as the indulgent Rafa, then as a strong but fair warrior, had become cold and distant, a remote being who could mete out the cruelest of punishments without emotion. He'd once broken a vampire's bones with such methodical precision that the vampire had been nothing but stones in a bag of flesh.

Aodhan had been glad not to be in the city at the time, not to have to bear witness.

Raphael was no longer that man, hadn't ever regressed after he met Elena, but he was also about to lose both his first general, and a second member of his Seven.

Archangels did not always react rationally. *Dmitri*, he said, reaching out with his mind, *do you know what's happening?*

We can't see them, came the immediate answer in a voice as taut as Aodhan's muscles. *Glamour.*

Time slowed, became a river of molasses.

He's on his way, Dmitri said at last, the tension replaced by emotions far more complex. *You both remain ours, Aodhan. This territory will always be safe ground for you and Illium.*

Aodhan knew the edict must've come from Raphael, but he still didn't take a complete breath until he spotted Illium over the water after what felt like a lifetime.

It hurt going in.

And though he'd waited for this, he found himself stumbling his way back to his half-destroyed studio. Not for privacy, for the trees provided more than enough—and anyone who dared spy on a newly ascended archangel was an idiot who deserved to be blasted out of the sky—but because it was familiar.

While the man he loved beyond all reason was suddenly unfamiliar.

An *archangel*.

Illium had just become a being of such power that he could annihilate Aodhan in a heartbeat should it ever come to that.

He began to pick up broken and fallen items with mechanical numbness.

A gust of wind pulsed fine particles of debris into the air as Illium landed through the large hole in the roof and side wall that he'd created during his ascension. Falling fast, he came down on one knee, one hand braced on the floor, the dust he'd created from the speed of his landing drifting down to land on his hair and wings in a gritty coating.

He looked no different.

Then he raised his head, and in the aged gold burned the breathtaking power of an archangel.

"Does it hurt?" Aodhan asked in desperation, moving toward him in an instinctive jerk.

Illium's grin was wild and of Aodhan's Blue. "I feel high." Laughing, he rose in a fluid movement and ran to clasp Aodhan's face in his hands, haul him down for a kiss that hummed with an energy new and intense and violent in its voraciousness.

That unearthly power crackled over Aodhan's skin, down his wings, into his mouth. It was a spark everywhere they touched, tiny shocks that caused no pain but were a constant reminder that the Illium he'd always known had changed forever. But his kiss, despite the new taste of archangelic power . . . that was familiar.

His lips so soft against Aodhan's even when the kiss itself was hard and playful at the same time, his breath with its hidden whisper of sweetness, the way he liked to play with Aodhan's hair while they kissed.

Illium's eyes glowed as he broke the kiss. So did his wings. Archangels only usually did that when they were angry or powering up to strike, but Illium was afire with happiness. "Overflow," he said, showing Aodhan his forearm; power crackled over his skin. "I wasn't close enough to Suyin during the ascension to see this, but it makes sense that it takes a while for the new energy to settle."

Aodhan touched his finger to a single spark of power. It jolted him.

Jerking back his hand, he shook it out. "At least you weren't that electric when we kissed." He was trying to make a joke of it, but fear was a stranglehold he couldn't escape. They'd always said they were forever, but they hadn't understood at the time what becoming an archangel actually *meant*.

Illium was no longer the same being.

"Sparkle, you're looking at me like I'm an alien." Illium was moving around, his wings restless. "I'm still me."

Aodhan met his gaze when the other man paused for a moment. "No, Blue. We can't pretend. You're you . . . but you're also something different."

Illium's smile faded. "Whoever I am, I love you. Always have. Always will. Don't tell me you've forgotten that."

Heart tearing in two at the vulnerability in Illium's voice,

Aodhan strode across to haul the other man into his arms. "You're dazzling," he whispered. "And you're *mine*. I'll fight for you even against the power of ascension."

The sparks of energy on Illium hit Aodhan again and again, but he clenched his teeth and rode them out, Illium in his arms. "What did Raphael say?" He needed to hear it directly from Illium.

"We're allies." He looked up at the sky revealed by the hole in the roof. "Adi, I need to fly, use up some of the excess." A glance, a silent question.

"Let's go."

Aodhan wasn't surprised in the least when his lover took off like a bolt of lightning once they were in the sky, only to return a minute later at the same speed.

Aodhan kept on the same path until, at last, Illium had flown hard and fast for long enough that he could be in one place. Except, of course, he spiraled up to do a complicated aerobatic maneuver that had him flying under then over Aodhan.

Aodhan laughed. "You're an archangel! Act with decorum!"

"Hah! *Never!*"

And for that moment, it was all right—they were once again just Illium and Aodhan out for a flight.

When the two of them landed, it was in the snow-kissed mountains north of the city.

Walking to the edge of a small cliff, Illium stared out in the direction of their home. "Raphael won't push me to leave, but the power inside me tells me I have to be gone soon. It's like a cresting wave—I can never allow it to crash in the territory of another archangel."

He turned, looked at Aodhan. "That's when things go wrong; I feel it in my cells. When archangels draw blood. Too long too close together. I'd never forgive myself if I pushed Raphael to hurt me or if I did the same to him."

Worried as he was about what ascension meant for them, Aodhan's first priority would always be Illium's huge and glorious heart. A heart that was breaking at the sudden cessation of a life that had been the culmination of all his hopes and dreams. Striding over, he clasped Illium's nape and tugged him to his side while sliding his wing over those of silver blue.

It should've felt odd to do this with a being of such power, but this was Illium, the friend who'd been by his side his entire life, the lover whose back he'd stroked only this morning while kissing his nape to wake him to the glowing dawn. Illium had been smiling even before he'd opened his eyes, slumberous and beautiful. Aodhan had kissed his shoulder then, before stroking his hand down his lover's muscled arm to entwine their fingers.

He loved waking with Illium, his Blue who saw beauty in every dawn, and had not a drop of jaded ennui in him.

Illium came into the embrace with familiar grace, his head against Aodhan's shoulder.

"It's still friendly ground." Aodhan ran his thumb over Illium's pulse. "You'll always be welcome in Raphael's territory; you know that."

"But never like I was," Illium said, his voice rough. "Never again like that, Adi." His hand fisted on the back of Aodhan's tunic as he turned so their eyes met. "Everything has changed—everything but one. You."

Illium spoke on before Aodhan could respond. "More than anything else in this world, I need you to be my Adi, need you to be my friend and lover. Don't ever treat me any different, or you'll break my fucking heart."

Illium saw Aodhan's pupils flare, those stunning crystalline eyes devoid of the wary barriers he'd glimpsed after first returning home. Barriers that had kicked him in the gut, awakening fears from long, long ago.

"Shit," Aodhan said, and shoved a hand through his hair. "I'm acting weird."

That quickly, the fears retreated under a wave of affectionate amusement. Because they were them again. "A little. But you're excused. It must've been a shock to have your studio destroyed."

Aodhan squeezed his nape. "Asshole." He pressed a kiss

to Illium's hair in that way that had become a habit with Aodhan over the years, a caress with an edge of protectiveness to it that always warmed Illium from within while making butterflies flutter in his abdomen.

That he'd done it now, when Illium had just ascended, the power differential between them a gulf vast enough to absorb oceans? It calmed any worry Illium might've had.

"You do owe me a new studio, by the way." A nuzzle of Illium's temple, the scent and heat of Aodhan home in a way nothing else could ever be. "I was . . . out of balance for a short time, Blue. I worried." Huskiness in his voice. "About us. If you'd want us now that you're an archangel."

Realizing he wasn't the only one who'd been kicked in the gut, Illium pressed his lips to Aodhan's jaw. "I want you more," he said. "I *need* you more." Meeting those incredible eyes, he laid it all out in the open. "In private and in public, you're the one person with whom I don't *ever* have to be an archangel. With everyone else, I have to walk a fine line. Never you."

"You don't have to ask. I'm here." An unwavering look. "I'll also skewer anyone who dares try to take my place."

Illium grinned because this was the man he knew and loved. "As for the other . . . Adi, Ellie used to be mortal. She's still much, *much* weaker than Raphael and always will be." Elena's power had grown over the years, but she was no archangel—and, like Illium, had never desired to become one.

"Rather stab myself in the eye with a blunt blade," she'd muttered one night when the question came up during an informal dinner hosted by Honor and Dmitri.

Everyone had laughed at her answer, especially Raphael, but Illium knew it had been sincere. As had his own: "I'll join you in the one-eyeball league."

But the choice had never been his and now he had to learn to live with his new reality.

"Our power imbalance is no imbalance at all in comparison to Ellie and Raphael," he pointed out. "We're closer to

Dmitri and Raphael." The man who stood as Raphael's second had become ever more brutally strong over the years, his discipline growing apace with his vampiric power.

Aodhan blinked, thought of Elena as she'd been when they'd first met. *Such* a fragile life, so easily snuffed out. Yet she'd held her own against Raphael over and over again. Power in a relationship was what the people involved decided it should be—and as Ellie knew Raphael would never use his archangelic powers against her, Aodhan knew Illium would never use his.

"I'm glad one of us is thinking," he said, taking Illium's hand and raising it to his mouth to press a kiss to the palm.

"I'll have you know this pretty face conceals a genius brain," Illium quipped before kissing Aodhan's knuckles in turn.

Aodhan's smile came from his very core. "So, my pretty genius," he said, "where do you think the Cadre will put you in terms of your territory?" Then it hit him. "Where do you think *you* and the Cadre will decide?"

Because Illium was one of the ten most powerful beings in the world now.

"I'll find out soon. I'm guessing a meeting will be called within the next few hours."

Illium, Raphael said into his mind that very moment, *we meet three hours hence.*

Raphael gave no more instructions on the how of it because none were needed—Illium was one of the team who'd set up the Cadre's current private communications system when the technology first became available. A team of nine, one from each of the territories, Illium given the task rather than Vivek both because everyone knew Vivek was basically Raphael's secondary spymaster, and because Illium had always made sure to learn any new tech as it emerged.

Which was why he also understood the reason he hadn't received a direct notification of the meeting. He needed to be put into the system—which would occur the first time he accessed it. It likely had to do with tradition, too. Outside of exigent situations like war, the Cadre was of an age over-all that preferred the personal touch.

You are welcome to stand with me at the facility inside the Tower built for such things, Raphael continued, *but I suggest it be better that you stand on your own for this first gathering. Use the setup in the basement of our Enclave home.*

Thank you, Raphael. Illium forced himself to address the other man archangel to archangel so that he wouldn't make a mistake when they were among the others. *I appreciate the advice.* Because this first meeting after his ascension would cement his position in the Cadre in the minds of the others.

He wasn't an Ancient risen, his power long set in stone. He was a new archangel, a man all of the current Cadre had known well before he became a first general. Should he stand with Raphael, certain other archangels would see it as a weakness—and it wouldn't be just those who weren't his allies. That was the thing he'd come to understand since ascension altered the elemental structure of his being.

"I get now why archangels seem to war over nothing," he said to Aodhan. "The power inside us is a feral force that wants total dominion, and that's ready to strike at any overreach—or what it sees as overreach. It's always watching the other predators, looking for weaknesses."

Aodhan's expression was tight. "You make it sound like a being apart from yourself."

"No, it's me." Illium frowned. "And it's not. It's the me I'll become unless I fight to maintain my personality." Folding his arms, he stared down that vast internal force. "I *will* be myself, Adi. Even if I have to fight this battle every day for the rest of my life."

"Illium the Bold, Illium the Courageous, Illium the Brilliant," Aodhan said, a slow smile lighting up his face. "Do you remember how we used to make up those titles for each other?"

"You forgot Illium the Favorite." Illium grinned. "Aod-

han the Bright, Aodhan the Loyal, Aodhan the Audacious."
They'd been so proud of thinking up the last word.

"Well, I have one more for you." Aodhan cupped the side of his head, those artist's fingers in Illium's hair. "Illium, the Determined, Archangel of his own destiny."

Yesterday

35

After telling Dmitri they needed a few extra days away from New York, and receiving the second's go-ahead, Illium and Aodhan flew directly from the celebrations in India, to Africa. Instead of traveling overland, however, they flew over water, their destination the border city of Narja. Titus controlled the section of the continent below the dividing line, while Zanaya held the northern half.

At first sight of a long-range scout Illium recognized as Kwayedza, one of Titus's senior people, Illium immediately winged over. "Hello, my friend." They exchanged a forearm grip, the other man's grin a bright glow against the rich dark of his skin. "Do you know if my mother is still at Narja?"

It had been her intended destination when she left India, but as Guardian of Lumia, she could as often be found in Morocco as in the lands held by her beloved Titus. He knew the two missed each other beyond bearing when separated, but they also accepted the duty each had to the people under their care. For Illium's mother, however, her fidelity to her post had another, more visceral meaning.

"I will never again stop being Sharine—and Sharine has been entrusted to watch over Lumia," she'd said to him on one visit—when he'd acted as a courier to ferry a fragile piece of art to the place that, among its other charges, was the repository of angelic creativity.

"That Titus not only understands that," she'd said, her expression tender, "but is proud of me for the position I command, my dedication to duty? It plays an important role in why I love him so. Love should seek to make you bigger and brighter, Illium, never smaller."

It had taken Illium a long time to realize that he could never have any true comprehension of being made smaller by love—because even in the worst depths of his own anguish, Aodhan had always encouraged him to fly. He hadn't ever tried to keep Illium locked to the Refuge, to him. Illium had been important enough to Aodhan that though he hadn't spoken much after his abduction, he'd found the will to confront him about his hovering vigil.

"Don't you dare bury yourself here," the other man had growled at Illium a year after his rescue, while he continued on his long recovery.

A piercing look out of those eyes devastated by lingering physical pain. "Fly, Blue." The first time in over a hundred years that he'd used that childhood nickname. "Dazzle the world as you've always been destined to do. I'll never forgive you if you dull your shine because of me."

Illium wanted to turn, kiss the life out of his lover, but Kwayedza was replying to his question.

"You're in luck." The scout's smile cut even deeper grooves in his cheeks at the mention of the adored Lady Sharine. "If you stay on your current trajectory, you will be with her before dark."

"My thanks. And while I know you have to alert the citadel that we're on our way, could you ask them to keep it a secret from her?"

Kwayedza chuckled. "Yes, no problem. Titus has made it known that you are free to fly through his lands whenever you wish to see Lady Sharine. Aodhan, also."

"My thanks, too, Kwayedza." Aodhan exchanged a fore-arm clasp with the other man before he and Illium angled away to continue their flight to the border city.

Narja was a bustling metropolis centered around the citadel that sat on a rise at its center. It had begun life as a trading city, a center of commerce between territories, turned into a battle citadel when Charisemnon became an obnoxious—and later, an evil—neighbor, only to once more return to its original function after Zanaya took over Northern Africa.

While it was a thriving modern city of steel and glass, its streets flowing with cars and motorcycles, it had no skyscrapers—because skyscrapers were targets in a border city. The only reason the citadel itself sat high was that it permitted expansive sightlines in battle—and even the citadel had been shaped to have a massive footprint, so that it couldn't simply be knocked down. It was too heavily rooted to the earth.

Illium heard the car horns drifting up from the city as they flew through, smiled. "Narja's always reminded me of New York even though it looks nothing like it." Quite aside from the lack of skyscrapers, the streets weren't laid out in a neat grid, but in a chaotic sprawl designed to fool the eyes of winged enemies.

"It's the energy of it." Aodhan rode an air current a distance before returning to Illium's side. "It has the same vibrant heart."

"I think you're right." Having stayed high for the most part, Illium now began to descend toward the roof of the citadel.

Aodhan followed.

The lower they went, the more of the city they could see and smell and hear. A low murmur of noise that was pure life, enmeshed with the scents of food, produce, and people. Rich and layered and textured, Narja enticed with its warmth and complexity while hinting at the sleek efficiency of its infrastructure.

Titus wasn't the most tech-minded of archangels, but he

had people on his team whose job it was to stay on top of innovation. That was what made him a good archangel despite his personal preferences.

They landed to a smiling welcome from one of Titus's vampiric staff members. "Lady Sharine is in the courtyard, practicing hand-to-hand combat."

Illium had to wrench on the reins to halt his instinctive protective response. His mother was no longer a fragile being with a fractured mind. These days, not only was she the Guardian of Lumia, she was also the lover of an archangel who could be too much for even other archangels—and she had no trouble holding her own with him.

Not particularly wanting to think of his mother and the word *lover* in the same breath, Illium skated away from that thought as he and Aodhan made their way into the warm stone of the citadel. "That way"—he pointed right—"pretty sure there's a balcony there from where we can look down into the courtyard."

The citadel had an external wall, which meant the courtyard could be fully enclosed. However, the large main gates were left open for the most part. Illium didn't initially spot his mother in the huge space active with movement . . . but no, there she was, in the far right corner, the sunlight-dusted indigo of her wings held tight to her back as she circled her opponent. The two were in a more private area of the courtyard, a section surrounded by its own walls.

Her gold-tipped black hair woven back into a tight braid, she wore a dark brown tank top and sleek black pants, both similar to things he'd seen other women wear when training. No shoes, both his mother and her opponent in bare feet.

She seemed so young that it made his breath stop in his chest.

Sometimes, he looked at her and almost didn't recognize her, but in a way that made him ferociously proud of her. His mother was fully *Sharine* now, defiant and intent and a law unto herself.

She also moved with a dangerous grace that had his mouth falling open. "When did she learn to do that?"

"Is she sparring with Ozias? I can't make out the other fighter's features from here, but she has the falcon wing coloring and she's tall enough."

"Yes, that's her." Titus's spymaster—and a deadly warrior. "Knives! Why are they using knives?"

Aodhan gripped the back of his T-shirt when he jerked forward. "Do *not* make Eh-ma angry when we've only just arrived."

Illium gritted his teeth. "I can't do it. I can't watch." He promptly closed his eyes. "Tell me when they're done."

A warm chuckle had Illium barely cracking open one eye. He winced as Ozias got in a hard kick, then grinned when his mother retaliated with a punch the spymaster never saw coming. By the time the two bowed to each other to finish off the bout, he had both eyes open and a fist up in a silent cheer.

His mother's head jerked up right then, though neither he nor Aodhan had made a sound; she flew over to them a heartbeat later. "Boys! I hoped you'd detour this way!" Huge hugs and kisses from the tiny storm force of a woman who had given birth to Illium, and who had held Aodhan's hand through unimaginable pain.

She alone would always have the right to call them boys—though Illium knew she'd be annoyed with herself for the slip. Even after all this time, she took intense care to treat Illium as an adult, her son who she'd so often treated as a child during her lost years.

After she'd lavished them both with affection, she just beamed at them. "You look so happy." The champagne hue of her eyes sparkled. "What have you been up to?" Delight in her voice, along with a faint maternal suspicion that made Illium want to laugh—he couldn't really blame her for it, not after all their previous escapades.

"We snuck into Aegaeon's territory and put statues of butts facing his palace," he whispered.

Her eyes widened before she caught his twitching lips and threatened him with an invisible slipper. "I swear, you're getting worse the older you get." Her own lips twitching now, she turned to Aodhan. "I used to think you'd be a good influence, but then I realized you'd happily do things like make butt statues for him."

Aodhan's laugh was a huge thing as full of light as his voice. "I love you, Eh-ma," he said before enfolding her in his arms and wings.

Illium didn't hear what his mother said in response, but whatever it was made Aodhan's cheeks crease again before he released Sharine. "We haven't been doing mischief," he said before holding out his wrist with its amber bracelet.

Sharine's hands flew to her mouth as she looked from Aodhan's wrist to the hand Illium flexed next to it. "Oh, oh." Her eyes filled, her tears welling over as she took both their hands and just looked.

"I always knew your hearts were bound together," she said later, after she'd dragged them to the privacy of the sitting area in her and Titus's suite. "That your friendship would never break, no matter if you quarreled." She ran her hand over Illium's cheek. "But to see it come to this . . . my joy is infinite."

For a moment, as she looked at him before turning to Aodhan, Illium saw endless rivers of time in her eyes, pain upon pain, happiness upon happiness. She was changing, becoming, but Sharine, the Hummingbird, already carried lifetimes within her.

"I am so grateful to be your son," he found himself saying even as Aodhan drew her into a side hug, more comfortable with her than he still was with most people. "Your love taught me the meaning of love."

Her lower lip quivered.

"Blue has the pretty words, Eh-ma, but he says what's in my heart, too." Aodhan's voice was rough. "You helped me grow into the man I've become in a way so significant that I'll never be able to tell you the entirety of it." A kiss pressed to her temple. "Thank you for being you and for fighting to hold on to me when I wanted to forget myself."

Sharine cried again, all the while scolding them both for making her lose control even as she hugged and kissed them at the same time. "You must stay," she said when she could speak. "We will celebrate like the mortals do when they wed each other. It's not the done thing in angelkind, but Titus says I have a rebellious streak."

"Where do you think *he* inherited it from?" Aodhan said, pointing at Illium.

The dry words made Sharine laugh and Illium grin, and of course they stayed—and two nights hence, after Aodhan's parents and sister and her family accepted the invitation to join them, Sharine and Titus celebrated Illium and Aodhan in a small inner courtyard awash in flowers and lights and overflowing with food.

It was a small and intimate gathering of family, but that made it no less raucous. Especially when two of Titus's sisters joined them . . . to be followed by Naasir and Andromeda, then Raphael and Elena.

36

Illium lifted Elena off her feet with the strength of his hug. "How are you here?!"

"Lady Sharine called, and of course we were going to be here. *Everyone* wanted to come, but we couldn't abandon the territory en masse. So you'll have to hold a second celebration in New York."

As for Naasir and Andromeda, it turned out the couple had been close by.

"We went to see my parents," Andi said to him during a lull, while they were seated together sharing a plate of small foods. "I don't know quite how to be with them, but seeing this . . ." She indicated the smiling faces, the lights, the happiness. "I want to one day be in a place like this with them. Not physically, but of the heart. It might take centuries if we ever even get there, but they're not who they once were, so maybe . . ."

Illium took her hand, squeezed. "I've seen it from both sides—my father went to Sleep an asshole, woke up an asshole. But my mother . . . she was fractured, lost, and look at her now."

Sharine glowed as she danced with Aodhan—who was teasing her in that quiet, dry way of his. Illium could tell from the look on his mother's face, the way she kept pursing her lips to fight the losing battle to laugh.

If he hadn't already been madly in love with Aodhan, he'd have fallen then and there. He'd tackle his lover tonight, smother him in kisses and caresses and possibly a few bites. Because the man was bitable.

"Lady Sharine gives me hope," Andromeda whispered. "I feel as if Lailah and Cato were lost in a dream, too, and they've woken up at last. So . . . we shall see." Wariness and hope entwined.

Then there was only a wild delight, as Naasir dragged her up into a dance, snuggling her body close to his and murmuring things that made her eyes crinkle and her ears go pink at the tips.

She had a long road ahead of her when it came to her parents. All Illium could hope was that Lailah and Cato didn't let her—and themselves—down.

Tonight, however, it was another set of parents who had his attention.

Rising, he walked to where Menerva and Rukiel stood in the quietest possible corner, all but vanishing into the tree that shadowed them. Though Aodhan's parents were scholars who preferred a quiet life, Illium hadn't been surprised when they accepted this invitation. Because when it was important, and no matter their own discomfort, they always turned up for Aodhan.

Which was why Illium held them in affection, and why he asked Menerva if she'd dance with him. Pale-skinned with wings of a gold so soft, it was sunlight on water, and long golden hair, Aodhan's mother had eyes of crystalline green the same shade as some of the shards in Aodhan's irises.

"Oh," she said in a hesitant tone. "I'm not sure." A glance at Rukiel.

"You should," her equally blond mate said, his smile soft and a touch dreamy in the way of a scholar not quite present in the world. "It is our son's amber revel and his beloved asks you."

Amber revel.

Illium's mother had made up that term on the spot, and everyone had accepted it with gusto. Given the way each and every person in the citadel—from the cooks to the warriors to the scholars—had gone crazy over it, he had the feeling amber revels were about to become all the rage.

"I will be quite all right," Rukiel reassured Menerva when she continued to hesitate. "I like watching everyone." He met Illium's gaze. "Thank you for always being my son's best friend in all this world, Illium."

The gentle comment carried the weight of a father's love.

Aodhan was beside him before he could reply, having finished his dance with Sharine. Rukiel's face lit up, and that was enough for Menerva to accept Illium's invitation. As they moved in a slow dance, she said, "Rukiel is far shyer than he pretends." A low whisper. "But he loves spending time with Aodhan. We're both grateful to have a son who doesn't hold his childhood against us."

Illium smiled. "He had a wonderful childhood—I should know, I was there right beside him for every mud-splattered adventure." And for that gift, he'd forever cherish Aodhan's parents. "You understood that you couldn't give a little boy what he needed, so you let him spend as much time as he wanted with someone who could. Your generosity was an act of deepest love."

Menerva swallowed hard, looked away. But she didn't halt the dance, and when he returned her to Rukiel and Aodhan, she took her son's hand in hers and just held it. Until a small boy ran up to tug on Aodhan's pant leg. When Aodhan looked down, the chubby boy with black curls and skin of golden bronze, his wings—a deep gold with striations of bronze already too big for his body—held up his arms.

Chuckling, Aodhan reached down to swing his nephew up into the air, to the boy's giggle. Children this young were rarely ever taken out of the Refuge, but Titus had provided Aodhan's entire family with a winged escort for their journey, and Indri had spent the time being carried by warrior after warrior, his small body nowhere near able to fly that distance.

The little one's eyes were like Aodhan's just enough to tell everyone they were family. Irises that were otherwise pale green had a shattered outer ring that made the boy's gaze sparkle. Seeing them together, with Indri chattering a mile a minute at the uncle who was his hero, made Illium go soft inside.

"I was sorry to hear that there is no longer any chance of ascension for you," Menerva murmured, her fingers gentle on his forearm. "But you are so powerful already, you shouldn't worry."

Had it been someone else, he might've taken the comment as a dig, but Aodhan's parents were almost painfully sincere. It was as if they'd never quite learned the art of subterfuge. "Shall I share a secret with you?" he whispered, leaning down.

Her eyes widened. "Yes, of course. I would never betray your confidence, Illium."

"I never wanted to ascend." He winked. "If I had, I'd have had to leave Raphael's Tower, leave the Seven, and I might even have ended up in a war with Titus one day since archangels go to war for the slightest things. Ascension would've made a mess of my beautiful life."

Menerva's lips rounded. "I'd never considered that, but yes, I see. How foolish that others don't. Goodness, now you make me think about it, I wouldn't want to ascend, either—I love my life as you love yours." She patted his arm. "Never you mind, I'll get Imalia to set everyone straight. I don't know how I birthed a daughter with such a wonderful ability to speak to all the world, but that I did is not in question."

Delighted that nonconfrontational Menerva was so annoyed on his behalf, he took her hand, pressed a kiss to it. "It's all right, Menerva. The people who matter understand."

A flicker of light in his peripheral vision, Aodhan having

moved to an open area to swing his nephew around in circles that had the boy screaming with laughter and saying,
"Faster, Uncle!" while Imalia pressed her hands over her
eyes as if she couldn't watch. The boy's dark-haired father
stood beside her, one hand on her back, the other fisted in
the air as he cheered on their son.

Yes, Illium loved his life.

Most of all, he loved the man who lit it up with his starlight.

Today

37

It was clear that Montgomery had no idea how to treat Illium post-ascension. With his dark hair cut short and precise and his crisp black suit paired with a white shirt, Raphael's butler was the consummate professional. But today, when he opened the door, his face went to break out into a smile . . . then it was as if he glitched, froze.

"I'm still me, Montgomery," Illium said through a sharp stab of loss, because this would happen over and over again in the coming days and weeks. Despite his own words, he *wasn't* the same any longer, and all his relationships except for the one with Aodhan would change. It was inevitable.

"Can you ask Sivya to please make me a tray? No one told me that ascension makes you hungry enough to gnaw off your own foot." It was no lie; his body was burning energy at a rate that had led to Aodhan literally shoving food into his hands.

"I can see you losing weight in front of me," he'd said with a scowl. *"Eat."*

Illium had eaten, but was still hungry.

"The—" He caught himself, corrected. "Raphael says it

eases up after the first day or so, but I'd rather not be skin and bones at the meeting."

Montgomery's face softened. "Of course, Archangel Illium."

The address felt like a scratch on an old-fashioned record machine, an original of which Illium had kept and babied for over a century until it finally fell apart. "My thanks, Montgomery."

"Will your second be joining us?"

That question—that assumption—put his heart back together, erasing the bruise caused by their initial interaction. "No." Illium winced. "He's muttering and gathering up all the paintings I *didn't* manage to destroy when I erupted out of his studio. Shadow is muttering along with him as she pads about, sneezing in the dust."

She'd given Illium a jaundiced look, but had accepted his strokes after a careful sniff to ensure he was still the same person who'd fed her that morning. At which point, she'd begun to complain vocally to him about all the strangeness.

Illium got it; he was still reeling, too.

Now, he spread a hand over his heart. "I've promised to hand-build Aodhan's next studio. No promises on straight lines, though."

Montgomery's lips twitched, all the tension gone from his body. "I'm sure Sivya will have already prepared food for you." A smile that held deepest love for his wife's sweet, giving spirit. "I'll bring it to the meeting chamber. As you're the one who supervised its placement, I know I need not give you any instructions."

"I'd be insulted if you dared." With that light retort, Illium made his way into the house with an ease he'd never feel when it came to the home of any other archangel.

But this home that had stood for centuries after being rebuilt after the War of the Death Cascade was as welcoming to him as his and Aodhan's own home. It wasn't only because the extraordinary artwork of a skylight through which sunshine entered the central core was Aodhan's work, each tiny element done by hand—and repaired personally by him when needed. Or that the chandelier of crystal rain that hung below had been made by his mother.

Or even that the greenery that thrived everywhere held Ellie's loving touch.

It was the life he'd lived within these walls, the conversations he'd had, the laughter he'd shared, the games he'd played.

He'd spent time teasing Sivya in the kitchens until she'd put him to work cutting vegetables and making dough, and had joined in on Aodhan and Elena's continuing movie dates—though five centuries ago, he'd been banned from any commentary until the movie ended.

He'd sat with the sire in his study, the two of them going over Tower business—or just talking as they shared a bottle of mead. Because before becoming Archangel and First General, they'd been family. Would always *be* family.

As well he'd spent night after night around the large dining table with the rest of the Seven, at home in the home of his archangel and the woman who'd become one of Illium's closest friends.

The door to the secure comms room he'd helped install opened to his palm print. Heartache, bittersweet and poignant, was a weight on his chest. Shoving it to a distant corner, where it would stay until after this meeting of predators, he walked down the smooth black steps lit up by soft lighting in the walls themselves.

Raphael and Elena weren't the type to drape their home in black, but this technology required walls of a particular sleek black material that the mortal who'd invented it called *obsitru*. Given Raphael's requirements as a member of the Cadre, rather than creating a box within the basement, it had been easier to create the entire basement out of that material.

The *obsitru* was smooth and warm under his touch when he put his palm on it and, right now, quiescent. Once active, however, it would sing with the softest hum. Nothing that irritated, more like one of the old computers that used to purr in the background, a technology as far from this as computers had been from stone tablets.

The same ambient glow he'd encountered on the steps illuminated the meeting floor. Illium could've put ten circles on the floor, to mark the spot for each member of the Cadre, but it would've been a useless affectation. Quite aside from the fact that Raphael used the room for non-Cadre meetings, too, the Cadre itself had been nine when he helped install this; a defined placement would've left an obvious gap each time.

The tech was also clever enough to create a meeting circle on its own.

Taking a deep breath, Illium activated the slick touch panel integrated into the main left wall. It recognized him from that minor contact, immediately flicking to his profile . . . which had a new security setting that could've been added only by Raphael in tandem with two others of the Cadre.

Archangel.

That was it, all that was needed. Prior to today, he'd had administrator access, but even with that, he couldn't have ever spied on meetings of the Cadre. The system was built to make that an impossibility, with the entire team of builders acting as cross-checks on each other to ensure that—though the latter had never been a necessity except for the peace of mind of future archangels.

Every single person on that team was a being of integrity, and say what you would about archangels across time, the good and the bad, they were sticklers about certain things. One of which was the privacy of Cadre meetings. Not even Her Batshitness would've found it acceptable for anyone but an archangel to be privy to their conversations.

Now . . . now he was one of them.

He checked to ensure the system had changed his name over from First General Illium to Archangel Illium. He hated giving up that title, but it was no longer his, and much as he didn't enjoy playing politics, he also wasn't an idiot.

Before he could change the Cadre, he had to learn how it functioned. Good generals always did their research.

The door opened, footsteps heading down. "Archangel Illium?"

"One minute, Montgomery."

The butler waited with quiet patience as Illium finished the setup. Then he stayed while Illium methodically ate his way through the tray. Because Montgomery had been with Raphael since Raphael was a very new archangel. He understood that it wouldn't do for Illium to be seen with food nearby at this first meeting. The technology wasn't supposed to pick up random objects in the space, but they couldn't take the risk.

"My thanks to you and Sivya," Illium said after he'd eaten everything, and thrown back the glass of cold, clear water provided to cleanse his palate.

"Archangel, if I may . . ."

"Always, Montgomery."

"If anyone was to ascend, I am very glad it was you." The butler's voice was thick with emotion he rarely permitted himself to show. "But we will miss you terribly. The city won't be the same without you and Aodhan in the skies."

Illium swallowed his own thickness of emotion. "If I have a steward half as good as you, I'll consider myself a lucky man." Montgomery might prefer the title of butler, but they all knew he was so much more to Raphael.

After the vampire left—with a stiff nod that said everything—Illium set his wings and body to warrior formality, then stepped onto the main floor. "Activate."

A slight shimmer in the air at his command, and where he'd stood alone, now he stood across from Raphael. Caliane appeared within the next half heartbeat, Titus and Elijah at almost the same instant.

Alexander, Zanaya, Aegaeon, Suyin, and Marduk followed suit.

Each of them appearing as solid as if they stood in person in this circle of power, nothing akin to the flickering holograms of the first versions of the tech.

"The Cadre," Lady Caliane said, "is in session."

Her voice was clear, resonant, but the words might as well have been a gavel coming down, they held such portent.

Titus was the next to speak, a beaming smile creasing the mahogany skin of his face. "Welcome, Archangel Illium."

Illium had made a short call to his mother and Titus prior to his flight here. Now he smiled at Titus's warm greeting. It was echoed by others, several with enthusiasm, others less so—his father's muttered welcome was more sour than a lemon on the tongue.

Asshole.

"Well," Zanaya said, "that was unexpected."

Dressed in a shimmering skinsuit of a vivid indigo that left her shoulders bare, she was as stunning as always. She'd pulled her long hair, silver washed through with purple, back in a high tail, leaving her eyes to take center stage. Set against skin of the deepest night, the dark orbs that flickered with light were compelling.

"I do believe, Lady Zanaya," Illium said, "that I have the distinction of being the most surprised."

A lyrical laugh from the Queen of the Nile, but it was Illium's father who next spoke. "How did you hide the increase in your power levels? Why pretend that you weren't going to ascend?"

Illium wished he could tell the ass who'd fathered him that he'd done it to piss Aegaeon off. Despite the fact they had no relationship beyond that of politeness—which Illium had maintained because he was part of Raphael's Seven— Aegaeon had apparently been embarrassed that his powerful son had turned out to be a "dud."

Idiot asshole.

You do realize, Illium—Raphael's voice in his head, the communication between them seamless after so many centuries—*you no longer have to be polite to your father. You no longer risk starting a war between him and I . . . though I suggest you try not to start a war with him directly until you're settled.*

Illium's seething gut calmed, a faint smile on his lips as

he spoke with all the charm at his disposal, directing his words to the Cadre at large . . . except for Aegaeon. A subtle insult but one that'd enrage the man Illium had once idolized—until he'd realized that not only did his idol have feet of clay, but that those feet were rotted through.

"I thought I was the outlier in showing early signs of increasing power. I know Lady Suyin didn't."

"Just Suyin to you, Illium." The Archangel of China's smile lit up the obsidian of her uptilted eyes. "I am beyond delighted to see you on the Cadre, my friend."

He had once done her a service and she'd told him she'd never forget it. It seemed she intended to keep her promise even now that he'd become a being who could be a threat to her.

"And yes, you're right," she continued, her ice-white hair a glossy rain down her back. "While it is said that archangels do sense a rare few who have the potential to ascend, more often than not, it's a surprise."

"It was for me," Elijah said.

The Archangel of South America wore a formal high-necked suit of pale gold embellished with a darker gold that echoed the hue of his hair, his wings held neatly to his back. The suit was cut in angular panels that suited Elijah's martial nature and evoked the feel of warrior armor, but formal as it was, he had to have come from an event.

"One moment I was a general like you," Elijah added, "and the next, I was Cadre."

"First General," Caliane said with a smile. "You were a first general, Elijah, as was Illium."

Elijah inclined his head at the woman he had once called sire, his lips curved. "I stand corrected."

"We knew with Raphael." This from Alexander, golden haired and silver eyed, and wearing a cream-colored tunic with an open neck that could've come from any time.

"It wasn't simply that both his parents were Cadre that marked him," the Archangel of Persia continued. "He was a power even as a child, and he kept growing into that power. Never any hint of a plateau."

A considering glance at Illium. "You're unique in that you appeared to plateau only to smash right through that plateau after a number of centuries—but you're also the only one who came into your power during a Cascade of Death."

"Alex is right," Caliane murmured, her eyes the same piercing, dangerous blue as Raphael. "The Cascade attempted to force you to become too fast, may have disrupted your natural growth for a period."

If it had, Illium thought, then he was glad of it. He wouldn't have wanted to become an archangel any earlier. Even if he'd survived the influx of power, he wouldn't have had the entirety of his experiences of the past seven hundred years, experiences that gave him both the confidence and the maturity to stand face-to-face with other apex predators and not blink.

You've never lacked in courage, Blue. Common sense is another matter.

A memory from his youth, when he'd pushed an off-the-wall scheme far enough to aggravate even his partner in crime. The memory made him want to smile, but it was also a reminder that he'd needed all those years of life to become seasoned enough that no one could use the drop of impulsiveness in his nature against him.

Marduk, who'd remained silent and watchful this entire time, now held Illium's gaze with the disconcerting directness of his, the ice-blue of his eyes intense in that face primeval and of another time so far in the past that his world wasn't theirs. "Welcome." His voice was subterranean caverns and darkest echoes, his entire being as extraordinary today as it had been when he woke out of what had been meant to be an eternal Sleep.

Illium continued to be fascinated by the iridescent scales that covered one side of his face before flowing down his neck to his shoulder and arm, a protective armor that was all but impenetrable.

It always made Illium wonder about the world Marduk had called home.

"I sensed a ripple in the currents of the earth two days past," said the archangel, who insisted he was no Ancestor, but who had wings that shimmered with the hues of a black pearl and featured feathers so small, they were but embellishments. "But that is all. You have become in your own time."

Illium, Raphael said, *bring up territory. Stake your claim.*

Yesterday

38

A hundred years on from the amber revel that had birthed an enduring tradition among angelkind, Aodhan found himself heading back to Titus's territory. While he'd departed for this gathering from New York, Illium was coming from the Refuge, having been drafted to handle a delicate issue there. That Illium had resolved the problem without bloodshed was a testament to his way with people, as well as his growing ease in matters of angelic politics.

Aodhan's wild, courageous, brilliant Blue was growing into the skin of the general he would soon become—there was a reason Raphael had sent him on this task, and he didn't think Illium realized it. It wasn't a test. No, it was a final tempering before Illium stepped into his new role.

Another century, perhaps two, and Aodhan had no doubt he'd be not only a general, but Raphael's *first* general.

"Do you care?" a curious Izak had asked him not long ago. "That his battle rank will be higher than yours?" Because the writing was on the wall; Illium was just the best fighter anyone had ever seen. But even more, he was good at getting his people to give their best, too.

Aodhan had shaken his head. "I always knew he'd end up a general." It was Illium's dream, one he'd worked toward since childhood. Aodhan loved seeing him shine in his chosen field. Illium felt the same about Aodhan and his art—the boy who'd never been able to sit still had nonetheless had endless patience with a best friend who could sit in place for hours while doing a sketch.

Illium would practice sword drills or do push-ups but he'd never stray far. These days, he cleaned his weapons or worked on strategic security plans in Aodhan's studio while Aodhan made art.

Never had one envied the other; they were simply too different in their pursuits. That was part of what made them so good together. Illium had learned patience and the art of quiet from Aodhan, as Aodhan had learned to step outside his comfort zone and allow his wildness out from Illium.

Smiling at the memory of Illium racing back and forth across a short distance to build up his endurance, while Aodhan painted in an alpine grassland that overlooked a young mountain range, he waved at the scout who raised his hand in greeting from afar. Having been granted carte blanche to come and go from Titus's lands, Aodhan powered on, once again on a flight to Narja, the city that continued to thrive without ever losing its border heart.

Eh-ma was waiting for him on the roof, not in her warrior guise today, but in a gown of air and silk that made her skin glow, the gold-tipped black of her hair free to tumble down her back. "Aodhan." Her embrace was warm and as fierce as always—Eh-ma didn't ever hug her "boys" lightly.

"Where's my stepson?" boomed a familiar voice. "Late again? His step-grandmother will have a word or seventeen to say about that!"

Chuckling at Titus's ominous tone as Lady Sharine laughed—the sound initiating a cascade of happy childhood memories—Aodhan reached out his forearm to greet the Archangel of Southern Africa. But the big archangel hauled him into an embrace. Once, that would've been unwanted, and once, Titus wouldn't have done it. But it was

Aodhan who'd initiated the first embrace, when he and Il-lium hosted Titus and Eh-ma in their home.

These days, Titus was one of Aodhan's people through Illium and Eh-ma.

"Does the first general know you're calling her a step-grandmother?" he asked after they stepped apart, for de-spite the fact that Avelina stood as Alexander's second now, she remained the first general to her children.

"She's the boss of us," one of Titus's sisters had said with a shrug. "I mean, those are the facts."

Today, one arm around Lady Sharine's shoulders, Titus rubbed his jaw. "My mother loves nothing more than to talk about the grand dynasty she founded. At least I am not Charo or Phenie—according to the first general, they have been partnered more than long enough to have given her grandchildren by now."

He threw up his free hand. "My stalwart Phenie was so traumatized by our mother offering her advice on how to couple for the best fertility that she ran to hide in my south-ernmost citadel. As if *I* have any power over the first general!"

Lady Sharine's shoulders were shaking, her efforts not to laugh clearly unsuccessful. A snort escaped her at that moment, and then it was all over. "You make your mother sound an ogre!" She poked Titus in the hard slab of his ab-domen. "Avelina is perfectly lovely and Phenie was not traumatized but scandalized at the thought of her mother having relations!"

Aodhan loved the dynamic of Titus's tight-knit family—including the afeared and utterly loved First General Ave-lina. All of Avelina's children would battle the world for her, and Aodhan had understood why the instant he met her.

"My mother is like that with you because she's intimi-dated by *you*." Titus looked at Eh-ma's tiny form with a beaming smile before picking her up and kissing her with loud enthusiasm. "I'm so glad I have you to protect me." His dark eyes held all the love and adoration Aodhan could've wished for, for Eh-ma.

When she touched the archangel's face with one hand,

Aodhan decided it was a politic time to cough into his hand and shrug his travel pack from his back. In it was his and Illium's gift to First General Avelina—for tonight, the family gathered to celebrate the day of her birth. And that family included Titus's "stepson" and his beloved.

Having missed Illium like a limb torn from his body, Aodhan swept him into his arms when he arrived close to sundown. They could've kissed for eons, but Illium *was* almost late. So after satisfying himself with the barest taste of his lover, Aodhan pushed the other man to the bathing chamber. "Quick. I already laid out your clothes."

They had a permanent suite at all of Titus's main residences, complete with clothes and any necessities. But instead of hurrying in to freshen up, Illium hauled him down with a fist clenched in his tunic and nipped at his lower lip. "Hi, beautiful."

Aodhan blushed.

A scalding wave of molten heat.

As if this warrior with his firm lips and muscled arms, his forearms ridged with veins and his jaw a defined line, hadn't been calling him beautiful for centuries. Because it hit him the same every single time—deep inside the softest, most vulnerable core of him.

"Hi," he whispered, his voice husky. "You cut your hair." He ran the strands through his fingers.

"Only a trim." A suckling kiss of his lower lip, a tug. "Come scrub my back."

Aodhan knew he should say no, knew it was a bad idea . . . but he'd been following Illium into bad ideas for a lifetime. So it was that he found himself naked in the shower with the only man who had ever made him feel safe in a way that wasn't about outward threats but about the heart.

"You're going to get us into trouble," he murmured as he kissed Illium's back from behind while undertaking his scrubbing duties.

Water ran over both their bodies, steam rising to curl in the air.

Illium's wicked smile was visible in the curve of his cheek as he angled his head to one side to glance back. "You like trouble, Adi. That's why you love me."

Throwing down the washcloth, Aodhan gripped the other man's jaw with one hand and his hip with the other as he claimed the kiss he'd wanted from the start. The one that was open and raw and of a warrior who'd missed the other part of his heart for too many days. He could taste Illium's own need in that kiss, feel it in the tension of his body, all that taut muscle and sinew under his hands, against his aroused flesh.

Their breath was the steam now, their bodies coming flush as Illium turned . . . only for Aodhan to pin his hands to the tile of the shower wall with his own. Those beautiful, ridiculous eyelashes dripped beads of water, Illium's lips swollen from the force of Aodhan's kiss. "It's a good thing you heal fast," he murmured as he moved against Illium with teasing precision. "Or we'll never hear the end of why we were late."

"We won't be late." A glint in those pretty eyes right before he twisted with a muscular fluidity that had Aodhan pinned to the wall by Illium's body, Illium's strong hand between them moving in a rhythm that turned both their breathing harsh. "We'll. Be. On. Time."

Passion unbridled burned between them, their bodies going rigid as Aodhan's playful, powerful lover took them over the edge hard and fast with knowledge born of centuries of loving.

"Told you so," Illium whispered huskily in the aftermath, pressing a kiss to Aodhan's jaw. "This wing commander gets the job done."

Aodhan cuddled him close, his smile affectionate and heart tender. "I missed you." Illium was the light in his world—his life always lost color when his Blue was gone, his paintings never as vibrant.

Illium, a man who Aodhan knew would one day be a first general akin to Avelina, put his head on Aodhan's shoulder, his body lax against Aodhan's, but his wings held with warrior perfection because it was second instinct. Aodhan stroked his back, got kisses on the neck for his trouble, and wanted nothing more in life.

They just barely stumbled into the dinner on time. Illium managed to close the front placket of his black suit as they reached the door to the formal dining chamber. That suit hugged his chest and thighs and everywhere else and was made of a thin material that acted as armor.

This one, however, had been embellished with silver scrollwork down one side to make it clear he wasn't declaring battle, but being a respectful guest and wearing his best. Aodhan reached out to settle the other man's hair with his fingers, while Illium made sure Aodhan's traditional tunic-style suit, the color a pale gold, was sitting properly.

"Illium!" Charo, tiny and dazzling and a whirlwind, flew over from where she was talking to the twins, Nala and Zuri, to hug Illium so hard, it should've been impossible for such a small woman.

"You'll break me, Charo!" Illium protested but he was lifting her off her feet even as he did so, and pressing a kiss to her rounded cheek. "So," he whispered, "any signs of grandchildren yet?"

"I will *murder* you if you bring up that subject in front of my mother," Charo threatened.

Aodhan didn't hear the rest, because Isiel had come over to tell him all about a young artist whose work he thought Aodhan would appreciate. He felt it when Eh-ma and Titus walked in, caught their welcome of Illium out of the corner of his eye.

And he most *definitely* felt it when First General Avelina stepped into the room. Amber-eyed and not much shorter than Aodhan, the woman who'd birthed five of the people in the room—including an archangel—was a deadly warrior with skin of onyx, wings of rich cream swirled with honey, and a mass of curls that she usually wore in fine braids, often with bronze threads woven into them.

She'd let her hair out for tonight, her precision-separated black curls a glory against the forest green of her simple ankle-length sheath. Simple, that is, until she moved and the material flowed around her like water, displaying a stunning black-on-white print from this region.

Aodhan was both fascinated by the fabric, and itching for his sketchpad.

He'd drawn the first general in her favored leathers, but never in this avatar—power unleashed in a way most unexpected in one of the most dangerous fighters in the world. He tried to memorize everything he could about her in this moment, but she moved with rapid fluidity to greet Eh-ma as Eh-ma did the same, and theirs was the greeting of two strong women who were both comfortable in their power and felt no need to flex it.

Aodhan caught a breath. *I'm going to paint this scene*, he told Illium. *The Hummingbird and First General Avelina, second to Archangel Alexander. They are extraordinary.*

"Tito!" Avelina looked to her son, then turned her cheek, pressing a finger to one.

Titus—wearing armor similar to Illium's but in bronze, with a hummingbird in flight detailed over his shoulder—bent to kiss her as directed, as if he wasn't the archangel and she the angel. Because in this room, there were no titles except those of family. Here, Titus was "Tito," Avelina's youngest child and the petted and spoiled little brother of four strong-willed older sisters.

The conversation was joyful and chaotic over dinner, and despite their oft-avowed "fear" of the first general, her children weren't afraid to speak their minds and push back against their powerhouse of a mother. Avelina had raised all five to be vibrant and unique personalities. Their lovers and partners were either as animated, or as tranquil as water, just flowing in and out.

It worked, the gathering a mix of people who just clicked. That included Aodhan and Illium.

"Illium." Avelina pinned Illium with her gaze. "I hear you are to be made a general. Why am I the last to know?"

Illium's lips kicked up. "I'm afraid you've been misinformed, First General. I am a wing commander and, being in only my seventh century of life, unlikely to be considered for the position of general for some time yet."

A vee between Avelina's eyes, the merest flicker in her gaze, before she reached for Aodhan's mind. *Every single senior warrior in the Refuge is saying this.*

Raphael will be the one who decides was all Aodhan said, and Avelina left it at that. Because while they were family, they were also loyal to two different archangels and in the court of a third. It was complicated and beautiful and Aodhan was delighted to be a part of it. But nothing delighted him more than having his Blue by his side, listening to him reply to Avelina with a charm and wit that made the first general's eyes fill with humor, or Charo's with warmth, Eh-ma's with a pride echoed in Titus's gaze.

Illium was extraordinary.

And he was Aodhan's.

Today

39

Illium, bring up territory. Stake your claim.

Standing face-to-face with the most dangerous people in the world, Illium took the advice of the archangel who had never once let him down. "I think," he said, "we must talk territory before we go any further."

"Do you still wish to Sleep, Marduk?" Caliane asked in response. "There's no need of it if you do not. We are now ten for the first time in centuries."

"A full Cadre," Suyin murmured, and Illium realized she'd never had that luxury, her reign having started with nine archangels—and of those nine, three had been injured enough to be out of commission for an extended period. Add in the poison Lijuan had left behind in China, and the start of her reign had been brutal.

"I would experience this, Marduk, but only if you wish it," she said. "I know you didn't want to be awake in the first place."

Marduk's smile was opaque, but he turned so that his more human side faced Suyin. "My consort has only been awake but a heartbeat. We spoke prior to this meeting, and she's amenable to remaining a touch longer to further explore this new world."

When the entire Cadre seemed to sigh, Illium gained a glimmer of understanding of what it was to rule with a partial Cadre. He'd come into the meeting assuming he'd take over Marduk's territory—the Pacific Isles—in a simple transition, but now, they had to discuss territorial boundaries.

"The easiest path," Caliane said, "would be to go back to the boundaries of the last full Cadre."

Illium didn't even think about it; he used subvocal commands and a hand gesture to throw up a map of the world from the last time the Cadre had been complete for a significant period.

The time of Uram, Archangel of Blood.

"You must teach me how to do that, my young stepson!" Titus boomed.

"Of course I will, honored aged stepfather," Illium said with a grin that matched Titus's. The two of them had been playing this game ever since Titus and Sharine became one, and they both found it equally hilarious.

Today, however, in this context . . . *Did Titus just make it crystal clear that he is my ally and I am his?*

Yes. He also took the chance to aggravate Aegaeon while having plausible deniability.

Illium looked down for a moment as he fought not to snort with laughter. *I should've remembered archangels can be petty.* But this petty, he could get behind. Because while he and Titus had nothing akin to a father-son relationship, they had a far deeper and genuine bond than the absolute nothing that Illium shared with his father.

Keeping his outward mien sedate, he nodded at the territorial markings on the map. "It looks like what was once Uram's territory is now being governed piecemeal, with parts of other territories being truncated or artificially elongated to provide the cover."

The land area involved—which included all of Russia—was too vast for such a reign, which meant all the archangels in the vicinity, including his father, had to have been pushing themselves to ensure the residents there knew they were under the oversight of one of the Cadre.

Sans that awareness, vampires who didn't have iron control over their bloodlust would begin to slip, hunting mortals until the affected parts of the world turned scarlet in an inexorable tide. Because bloodlust was infectious once it began—as if seeing their fellows lose control flipped the switch in others who were susceptible either by dint of youth or a lack of discipline.

Charo had told Illium the story of a time when three continents drowned in blood. Since she was Charo of the Tales, and had a tendency to mix fact and fiction in her stories, he'd taken it with a grain of salt—until she'd sent him a copy of the relevant historical record from the Archives.

> *. . . and I stood in a sea of blood, the bodies that floated by torn effigies and the screams that filled the air a haunting of insanity.*

Yeah, bloodlust wasn't a threat to take lightly.

Lady Caliane frowned as she examined the territorial map. But when she spoke, it wasn't aloud. A private message for him appeared in the air in front of him. Startled that she knew how to use that aspect of the technology, he quickly read what she'd spoken at a subvocal level after using her personal codes to alert the system that this appear only to Illium.

I apologize if I overstep, Illium. But as well as being the treasured son of my closest friend, you were a loyal and steadfast first general to my son, and so I would watch out for you in this.

If you take this territory, you will be next to Aegaeon. Is this what you wish? I have come to love India as my own, but I'm willing to shift if you wish—no archangel should have to start his reign next to such a . . . contentious neighbor.

Touched by the generous offer, Illium also knew he could never accept it. Each and every member of the Cadre would know why Caliane was making the move, and it would be seen as a declaration of weakness on Illium's part.

I thank you from the bottom of my heart for your grace and generosity, he replied as privately. *But Aegaeon is my problem and I'm unwilling to subject any other to it. Perhaps if I irritate him enough, he will go into Sleep.*

Caliane's expression remained unchanged, but he got the sense of laughter in her eyes. *Well, I think meetings of the Cadre from this point on are going to be most intriguing.*

"I am in accord with Illium," Marduk said aloud right then, having been examining the map with dragonish focus. "That landmass needs to be a single territory, not chopped up in pieces. That it's held stable for this long is a testament to all of you who have added parts of it to your own lands."

Elijah agreed with him, as did Suyin, Zanaya, and Alexander—the last of whom had borne the heaviest load when it came to ensuring stability in that region. Illium knew that Alexander had managed it only because he had the backup of both his consort, Zanaya, as well as his ally, Titus.

Aegaeon said nothing, which was the best that could be expected.

Raphael chimed in with his agreement last. Illium knew the sire had waited this long because he couldn't be seen to be leading Illium.

"So we are agreed?" Caliane, who seemed to be in charge of running the meetings—a state of affairs with which Illium had no argument—looked around at each archangel in turn, received a nod.

Eyes ancient and wise landed on Illium. "The territory is yours, Archangel Illium. When will you take it?"

Grief was a lonely nocturne in Illium's heart even as he spoke. "If Raphael permits my intrusion a touch longer, I will take three days in this city, to put together a small squadron of my own. Then I'll fly to my lands."

"I have no disagreement with the time needed," Raphael said. "You are my welcome guest."

"I'll withdraw the instant you reach the border," Alexander said with his usual adherence to protocol, then sent Illium a private message.

That all of the Ancients appeared to have learned how to utilize that bit of tech told Illium that meetings of the Cadre might be far more fun than he'd believed. It also made him wonder how many other little conversations were going on around him. No doubt they did this mind to mind during an in-person meeting.

If you need intelligence about the people in your lands, Alexander had written, *I will give it to you. Because of the fragmented nature of the territory over the past centuries, it has its problems—but there are a number of honorable and strong angels and vampires there who you may wish to utilize. Others are poison and should be ejected.*

Unspoken was that Illium would have to win those he wanted to his cause. It wasn't unusual for a huge turnover in personnel when a new archangel came in, a change that arose from both ends. The new archangel wanting his own people in positions of power; the present team unwilling to serve under a new leadership.

Unlike a newly awake former member of the Cadre, however, Illium had no historical team who'd fly to him after resigning from their current posts, but that was an advantage, too. The last time anyone had had the chance to join a fledgling court had been with Suyin, roughly seven hundred years in the past.

I thank you for the intelligence already given, he responded to Alexander, because the Archangel of Persia had just alerted him that some of those powerful people would be loyal to Aegaeon.

You may thank both my consort and my second. Avelina calls you family, and Zanaya believes you will be trouble. Since she is trouble herself, she is predisposed to like you. A wry glance at the Queen of the Nile, who was even now smiling sweetly at Aegaeon.

Hates him with the passion of a thousand suns, Raphael filled in for Illium on the mental level when he saw Illium take in the interaction. *I don't know the genesis of their enmity, but she takes every opportunity to stir things up. I'd be surprised they've only had minor skirmishes in the past centuries except that I know we were all exhausted post-war, especially in ruling long term with only nine. That changes with you in the mix.*

It was yet another insight into how an underpowered Cadre drained archangels. *I am warned.*

Even as he spoke, Suyin said, "I'm not so very far from you, Illium, and I have rebuilt my lands to the point that I can lend you squadrons should you wish. We shall call it a small repayment for the many months of your life you gave to me as a warrior when China was at its most damaged and dangerous."

"Then I accept, Suyin," Illium said, because she'd been careful to couch her offer as an exchange rooted in honor.

He also knew beyond any doubt that he could trust her and her people.

Unbeknownst to anyone else in this space but Raphael and perhaps Caliane, Illium and Aodhan had visited China with regularity over the years. Not only to see Suyin and witness the healing of the land Lijuan had brutalized, but to meet with Jinhai, the broken, twisted boy with clipped and scarred wings they'd discovered in the snow.

Suyin had grown into her power, had a steel core, but she'd remained honorable throughout in a determined repudiation of the monster her aunt had become. As for Jinhai . . . his wings had grown back strong and undamaged, but his mental journey would be longer, far longer.

"I would offer you the same," Caliane said. "You have but to make the request. It'll be good to have a solid territory in that region again."

The conversation ended soon afterward, all the archangels blinking out of the meeting room one by one. Groaning, Illium shook off the tightness across his shoulders and down his spine. He wondered when it would end, this sense that he was playing at a game of power. Would there ever come a time when it would feel natural? When he wouldn't have to consciously plan his words, or analyze those of others?

Upstairs, Montgomery had a veritable feast waiting for him. The butler had laid it out on the table in the library, where Illium had eaten a thousand casual meals, and Illium could've kissed him for it. It would've been a blow to the fucking heart had Montgomery decided on the main dining room. That was for guests, not family and friends. And *never* for Illium alone.

Sitting down, he began to fuel himself—and wasn't the least surprised when Raphael took a seat opposite him not long afterward. "Well done, Bluebell."

Not pointing out the slip of his nickname—it made him feel normal, at home—Illium clanked his tankard of mead against Raphael's. "You know what I realized?" he said after swallowing his current mouthful. "That I have more friends on the Cadre than not. Most through you, granted, but Suyin, Titus, and you are friends I hold on my own."

"Yes." Raphael leaned back in his chair. "The only real problem you have is Aegaeon, and possibly Alexander."

"Alexander?"

"He's calmed down since my time, but it'd be wise to be wary. He's a very old angel, and while he appears settled since he and Zanaya became consorts, you're a brash new archangel on his border."

"He offered to give me intelligence about the people in my territory. Should I trust him on that?"

Raphael raised an eyebrow. "If he said that, then yes. Alexander doesn't play those kinds of games—if he's going to come at you, it'll be out in the open. How did you win him over? I'm fairly certain he only tolerates me even now."

Illium grinned. "Zanaya thinks I'm trouble—and of course, I am Avelina's favorite grandchild."

Raphael's shoulders shook, his grin reaching his eyes just as there was a stir at the doors to Illium's back. Striding in past him, Elena drew back a chair beside Raphael, sat, then glared daggers at Illium. "You *ascended*!"

"I know. I know. Not my fault." Pushing her favorite pastry in her direction in mute apology, he said, "But now you have an excuse to visit my side of the world."

Dressed in black hunter leathers that hadn't changed much over the centuries except for becoming closer to soft armor in the protection they provided, the near-white of her hair in a braid, Elena tore off a bite of the pastry. "I am not going to forgive you for this," she said, and pastry abandoned, got up again before walking out through the external doors.

Raphael, his expression tender, watched her leave. "Go," he said to Illium. "You can still be her Bluebell for one more day."

After that . . .

Throat choked up, Illium shoved back his chair and went after Elena. She wasn't on the lawn, but he knew where to find her. Her greenhouse had been renovated and repaired countless times over the years but it remained true to the vision she'd always had of it—there was a sense of age about the structure, the iron of it weathered and curved, the curlicues that Aodhan had designed a few hundred years ago the gentlest touch against the glass, which let in all the glorious light that made her plants thrive.

She'd tested out trailing grapevines on the outside but that had blocked too much of the light, so her outdoor growing area was behind the greenhouse, and she took great care to keep the glass free of lichens and other growth. The passage of time meant that the glass was no longer as shiny as it had once been, but the patina just made it lovelier.

Opening the door after taking a deep breath, he walked into a humid warmth rich with the earthy kiss of life as familiar to him as the scent of paint and clay that was Aodhan's studio. The banana palm in one corner groaned heavily with plump yellow fruit, while just-ripe mangoes, their skin red blushing into green, hung on another tree in the opposing corner.

Elena crouched on the floor by the mango tree, working on the underplanting. Her wings lay on the grass floor of the greenhouse in a show of midnight and dawn that rippled with bursts of wildfire, her braid reaching her lower back.

Aware that she knew he was there, he sat down next to her, his wing overlapping hers. And he began to weed and remove dry or old leaves as she'd taught him over the years.

The two of them worked on that bed for a quarter of an hour before she looked at him and said, "I will *miss* you." Her voice trembled, her gaze ashine.

He closed his hand over hers, their fingers entwining. "If you don't visit me at least ten times in the first year, I won't talk to you for a century."

Making a wordless sound, she leaned her head against his shoulder, her hair a glow in his vision that reminded him of Aodhan. When she spoke, however, it wasn't with anger but with the worried love of a friend who'd been with him through multiple seasons of life. "How are you feeling about it?"

Sitting up, she looked at him with eyes of silver-gray that no mortal would ever possess. The Cascade's mark on Elena had taken time to emerge and settle, but it was there in those eyes that were just a *touch* too silver to be gray, and in the wings that crackled erratically with fine threads of wildfire.

But when it came to Elena, the external didn't matter, had never mattered. It was her heart that made her—and that heart was proudly, defiantly mortal. She'd stayed true to herself through the very alteration of her being. So would he. He *would not* contort himself to fit some ordained vision of what it meant to be Cadre, would not lose himself.

"I . . ." He took a breath, released it. "Much as I didn't want ascension, I know it was time. It's right—I feel it. This is who I was meant to become."

Elena ran her fingers through his hair. "Just . . . stay a little bit Bluebell, won't you?" A whisper.

"Not a little bit, Ellie." Grinning, he rose to his feet and offered her his hand. "I plan to be *all* Bluebell. The Cadre will learn to deal."

Lips curving, Elena allowed him to haul her up. "I expect great things," she said in a voice portentous. "So, Pacific Isles?"

"Oh no. I'm taking over the territory next to the asshole."

Elena's eyes widened before she gripped the front of his combat tunic and hauled him close. "Don't you dare start a war with him. I mean it, Illium." A glare. "He's an *Ancient*, and you're still wet behind the ears. I swear I will come over there with my knives and pin you to your damn throne if I get even a *hint* that you're trying to start a war."

"A throne?" Illium made a humming sound. "I hadn't thought about that." He rubbed his jaw. "Maybe Aodhan will design me one that'll go down in history as the throne of thrones."

Elena groaned.

40

Among the many things he and Aodhan had to do to prepare for the departure to their new territory was find people to take over duties that were too personal to simply trust to those who were already in the roles—if the role even existed in what had been a territory ruled piecemeal for centuries.

That included the steward who'd be handling Illium's "court" at the start. Later, once he was established, the same person would become critical to the smooth running of his household. His own Montgomery, in other words—because the butler handled far more for Raphael and Elena than was apparent on the surface.

"Knock, knock."

Dulce jumped up from behind the sleek glass of her desk to run over on clear sky-high heels. Only to halt. "Wow." She physically swayed, the motion causing the changeable fabric of her close-fitting suit to fluctuate from purple to blue to deep citrine. "That's some power you have pulsing off you."

"Side effect of ascension. Raphael says it'll wear off."

"I hope so, because I can't hug you like this." A pause.

"Is that still allowed? You're Cadre now." Her eyes widened, as if the knowledge was just sinking in. *"Fuuuuck."*

"You have no idea." He grinned, relieved that Dulce was herself with him. "I have an offer for you."

A raised eyebrow, the gemstones she wore over the curve of her left cheekbone catching the light. "You want me to set up a club in your new territory?"

"You can if you want," he said, because she was damn good at it, had an entire empire of entertainment under her belt. "But you said you're starting to grow bored."

She made a face. "Not bored so much as unfulfilled. I've mastered this business, have pots of money, need a challenge—but I have no idea what that might be."

"Be my steward," Illium said.

Dulce's lips parted, her forehead furrowing below the sleek asymmetrical cut in which she wore her hair this decade. "What does that mean?"

"We say 'steward' because it's the traditional term, but it effectively means head of operations. To start with, you'd be in charge of creating then managing the 'household' team at my version of the Tower, whatever that ends up being. You'd have full control of all processes to do with maintaining the back end—ordering everything from food supplies to organizing necessary repairs to hiring the staff."

Seeing she was listening, he continued, "It might sound simple, but Dulce—full disclosure—it'll probably run you ragged. Especially now, as we gear up. Along with all the operational work, I'd need you to be my eyes and ears on the ground, to weed out the bad actors and spies who'll no doubt try to weasel their way in.

"You'd also be in charge of long-term preparation to ensure we can survive if hemmed in by enemy forces." He folded his arms. "I'm not planning to start a fight with anyone soon, but I need to be ready." One of Montgomery's most important tasks was to make certain the *entire* population of the Tower could survive for a solid block of time if the enemy cut off their supply lines.

"As my steward, you'd also be handling incoming contacts alongside Aodhan—people who'll be applying to join my 'court,' so to speak. He'll handle the martial angels and vampires, and any senior scholars, with you dealing with the rest. I need people I trust to help filter incoming staff, and I know you have a laser eye and even better instincts. Even if you don't want the full steward role, I'd like you to take on recruitment."

Dulce was quiet for a while before she said, "I'd basically be managing the needs of hundreds of people on a daily basis and—once you're established—ensuring your base runs so smoothly that everyone forgets I'm there? Like Montgomery?"

"I knew you'd get it." Most people only ever saw Montgomery as a butler because that was how he liked it; everyone senior in the Tower, however, well understood that he was one of them. The vampire was a quiet, thoughtful presence at all strategy meetings, not only for his expertise in the practicalities warriors often forgot when focused on battle, but because he spoke for the entire non-martial population of the Tower, too.

The big difference was that Montgomery had started with fewer duties than Illium was throwing at Dulce—but Dulce was older and far more experienced at management than Montgomery had been at the time he began. He'd grown with Raphael's team, while Dulce was coming in as a woman who'd been a formidable CEO for centuries; she was looking to be stretched, to have to think fast on her feet.

"If I decide to have a separate residence at some point," he added, "I'd ask you to manage that, too." Illium trusted her without question; Dulce had never lost her defiant streak of honor, no matter that she'd walked in the gray most of her near-immortal life. "If, after trying it out, you don't like the position, I won't hold you to it—but I need you to sign on for the first full year if you do want to try it."

"Not asking for much, are you?" Dulce's lips curved. "The answer is yes, I'll be your steward. I can't think of anything more interesting than helping to set up an archan-gel's home base. If nothing else, I'll have bragging rights for eternity."

"What about Ezra?" he asked, referring to her husband—a chef as a mortal, he hadn't lost anything of his love of food or cooking even after his Making and owned a five-star restaurant in the city; having been there many times, Illium well knew his skills. "I'd welcome him on my team."

"Are you kidding? He's been trying to get onto the Tower kitchen team for decades, but no one ever leaves, so there are no openings!"

"Tell him I need a head chef—he'll have full autonomy to put together a team." To know the food he and his people would be consuming came from trusted hands? It meant a hell of a lot. Because while angels were tough, they weren't invulnerable; poison might not kill them, but it could make them sick and weak.

A beaming Dulce said, "Fuck it," and, taking a deep breath, crossed the distance between them to embrace him. "It's like electricity crawling over my skin." She shuddered before breaking away, but they were both grinning, excited about the future to come.

In the days that followed, however, Illium tasted as much sorrow as excitement. Especially when it came to saying goodbye.

Vivek, with whom Illium had worked side by side con-stantly over the years, gave him a manifesto he'd prepared at insane speed; it was a guidebook on how Illium should set up his own surveillance and spy network. He also flat-out refused to say goodbye. "I'll see you again," he said in a tone of voice that Illium couldn't quite decipher.

Nisia, the healer who'd patched him up more than once, scowled even as she hugged him tight. "At least you're all but indestructible now."

Janvier, Ashwini, Izak, Sam . . . so many of the people he loved and called friends, the latter two angels he'd watched grow from fledglings. One a senior wing commander now, the other nearing his own promotion to that role.

He'd been their teacher once, flown with them under his wing, and now they almost crushed him with the force of their hugs.

"City won't be the same without you, *mon ami*," Janvier said with the affection of long friendship, while Ashwini stared at him with eyes that saw too much and made a face.

"No," she said firmly. "Irritating Aegaeon for funsies is not a good idea."

Laughing, he accused her of being in Ellie's pocket, but as she hugged him, she whispered, "I see a dazzling horizon for you, Illium, a life extraordinary. As long as you're not stupid enough to be derailed by old anger."

He allowed the words to settle deep within—because Ash, like Cassandra, rarely said words she didn't mean.

Montgomery and Sivya, both trembling with the force of their emotions, gifted him a photo of the entire Tower family from a decade earlier, when they'd tumbled into a shot together after a celebration. An old-fashioned still, it captured lifetimes of friendship and happiness.

The goodbyes weren't tough just for him—Aodhan was leaving everyone behind, too, would be missed as badly. But the other man shook his head when Illium voiced that. "I can come back, stay for long periods if I wish. You, my Blue, never can." A cupping of Illium's cheek. "Let them focus on you, let them cherish you. You've been the heart of the Seven and Raphael's Tower for centuries upon centuries."

There were so many more people he knew and loved in ways he hadn't understood till this moment of parting, so many more people he had to see before he left. But the worst goodbyes came toward the end.

All of the Seven not based in the city managed to make their way to it before his departure.

Galen hugged him so tight that Illium could barely breathe.

Jason whispered intelligence about his new territory in his ear.

Naasir, feral and loyal, had eyes that shone wet as he grabbed Illium's face and growled, "I will come into your territory whether you invite me or not."

His own throat rough with emotion, Illium said, "Bring your cubs and Andromeda. I expect you to help establish my reputation as an archangel with wild and unsuitable friends."

Naasir's embrace was a huge thing full of the love he held for the child angel he'd once known, and the man who'd become his battlemate. "I will come," he promised, the tiger's stripes in his skin. "I will make your enemies fear your friends."

Dmitri and Venom, based in New York, said their goodbyes in the final hour before Illium flew from this city that had pulsed in his blood since the day he'd first come to it. Venom's grip was that of a warrior, forearm to forearm, and though his viper's eyes looked unflinching and hard, the truth of his emotions was in the fact that, though his throat moved, he didn't speak.

Heart raw, Illium somehow found his own voice. "Visit me," he said to this friend, as he had to all the others. "I'll need people I trust more than ever."

A curt nod before Venom drew back . . . but then he returned to embrace Illium, his speed that of the viper in his eyes. "I'll miss you, you blue asshole." Words ground out in a harsh whisper.

"Will you watch over the little bakery in Harlem?"

"You know you don't have to ask."

Then Venom was gone, and Dmitri was there. Like Naasir and Raphael, he'd hauled a child Illium out of many a scrape, and now tapped him on the cheek with an open hand. "I always knew you'd get into trouble. I just didn't think you'd join the Cadre to do it." His eyes glinted. "Stay safe, Bluebell. And know that no matter how far you go or how much you grow, you'll always be one of the Seven. We'll never let you go."

The words were the best gift the other man could've given him.

He embraced Dmitri with the love of the child he'd been, primal and free. The vampire returned his embrace with as much affection.

"You know who Aodhan and I think should join you, Venom, Jason, Galen, and Naasir," he said when they parted. "We've said for half a millennia that he's our shadow eighth."

Dmitri nodded. "It's too soon. Maybe in a few decades, we'll be ready to make it official. Trace would say exactly the same if you asked him. He also likes that he's not a 'giant Seven-shaped target.'"

Illium laughed, but it hurt. Trace was handling the Refuge stronghold so the others could come to New York, and as a result, Illium wouldn't see the suave vampire who'd often been his accomplice in dares neither of them should've accepted, until Trace could visit his new territory. Illium had no Refuge stronghold of his own due to the passage of years since there'd been ten in the Cadre, and setting one up wouldn't be his priority for some time yet.

"Naasir's firstborn cub has informed me that he's aiming to join the Seven when he's of age." Dmitri rubbed his forehead. "The Ancestors help us all."

Illium's chest heaved. "You have near to at least half a century yet." Naasir's cubs were maturing at a faster rate than other immortal children, but they weren't much more than toddlers at this point. "Fuck, I want to be around to see that."

"Our friendship will endure." A vow from the man who'd been the first of the Seven, the one who had always been their leader. "You'll never be left out in the cold." A squeeze of his shoulder. "Go, Illium. Do us proud."

Then came the hardest goodbyes.

Elena grabbed his face, her tears silent. "Don't start a war with your father," she ordered again before pressing her cheek to his, her arms around him.

"I won't . . . yet." Lifting her up when she shifted to scowl at him, he spun her around one last time. Because he was an archangel now, could never again be her Bluebell as he'd been for century after century.

Arms tight around his neck, she laughed and cried and,

when they broke apart, gave him a blade. Her smile was wet. "Look after it. I want it back the next time I visit."

He slipped it into an upper arm sheath. "I'll treat it as a treasure."

He looked to Raphael, his power recognizing another of its like . . . and his heart recognizing the man who had raised him into the man he was today. Their embrace was silent and deep, and when Illium drew back, Raphael reached to his back to withdraw a formal sword with an intricate hilt, centered on which was a single large stone the blue of Illium's wings.

The blade gleamed sharp and silver-blue.

It was unquestionably the work of a master craftsperson.

"I had this made for you a decade ago. To gift to you when you reached your next half century." Midnight strands of hair brushed the other archangel's cheek as the wind blew past. "Now, I give it to you as a gift on your ascension."

Removing the sword he already wore, Illium handed it to Elena, who promised him she'd ship it over with the rest of his belongings. Then he accepted the sword Raphael held, his chest so tight that it was a pain terrible.

All he could do was slide the sword into the simple scabbard on his back while fighting the rock of tears in his heart.

Then, unable to bear it anymore, he stepped off the roof with one last backward look.

Raphael stood watching him with eyes that blazed with pride and love, the archangel's hand tight around his consort's. Elena's unbound hair was a pale banner, the sword in her hand glinting in the sunlight.

Aodhan rose up beside him from where he'd gone to make his own goodbyes to those in the Tower. He'd already spoken to the remaining five of the Seven and to Raphael and Elena. They'd made that decision together, that they'd make their farewells alone, say the private words they needed to say.

Today, they didn't speak until they were far out over the water, Manhattan but a memory on a distant horizon. *Adi?*

It hurts, Blue. Fractured words. *I thought I'd be all right because I'm not an archangel. But I'm not.*

He held up his wrist: a bracelet of smooth wooden beads encircled it, each of intricate detail. *Naasir made me this.*

Illium wasn't surprised. Aodhan and Naasir had been close from the time Aodhan was a child. As Naasir had put it, "a grown-up one-being and a cub one-being." Two unique individuals who understood what it was to be different.

There had been other gifts for both of them, but as with Illium, what affected Aodhan worst was that they'd said a final goodbye to their friends. When they returned, it wouldn't be as members of Raphael's Seven, but as guests.

Ellie says we'll still have movie nights, use the meeting technology so that we're side by side on our favorite sofa.

Illium's heart ached. *Am I invited?*

You remain on probation. A harsh exhale. *Jason sent me a mass of intel. Dmitri and Venom have told me to contact them at will if I have questions about setting up a Tower or a court, whatever you decide. Galen—*

It's okay, Adi, Illium said when Aodhan abruptly broke off, as if he couldn't form the words anymore, even in his mind. *We can talk later.* He held out his hand and Aodhan took it to spin into him, the two of them sharing a hovering embrace for a long moment before they spread their wings and carried on, riding the winds farther and farther from the place they'd called home for the vast majority of their lives.

The one bright point was that Illium hadn't had any trouble finding a squadron's worth of warriors to come with him. He'd actually ended up with two full squadrons made up of highly experienced warriors.

A unit of vampiric ground fighters was also joining him in his new territory.

Raphael could've made all three stay in New York simply by asking—he was their liege and they were loyal. Instead, he'd accepted their resignations at once.

"I would you have a trusted group at your back from the very start," he'd said to Illium. "It may be that your own version of the Seven will grow from these units who have fought side by side with you for centuries." A hand squeezing Illium's shoulder. "Losing two squadrons and a ground unit is a small price to pay to know that you'll enter your territory surrounded by friends."

The squadrons had flown ahead, because both Illium and Aodhan were faster flyers. They'd catch up an hour or two out from the border of their new territory. The vampiric ground unit was already in the air, their flight having taken off earlier that day.

I couldn't do this without you, Illium said. *I'd be lost.*

You'll never be without me. I asked Jason to spread the word that I'm quite psychotic under my sane exterior and will decapitate anyone who tries to jockey for my position as your second.

Illium bit back a smile. *Who's annoyed you?*

Dmitri told me that several strong angels and vampires reached out, wanting to know if the position of your second was open. Obviously, they're utter imbeciles to even ask the question, so you didn't need to be informed about them.

Illium burst out laughing, the grief of goodbye overtaken by sheer delight. Because Dmitri and Aodhan had been right—the people who'd asked that question weren't people he wanted on his team. Anyone with a single brain cell in their head knew that the position hadn't ever been open.

It was always going to be Illium and Aodhan.

Yesterday

41

Illium was in Dmitri's office talking to him about a security upgrade when Dmitri's entire system flashed red with an urgent message from a priority sender. "Shit." Dmitri's heart kicked as he opened it. "Bluebell, Operation Cubs is in progress. Initiate the agreed protocol."

He barely heard Illium's "Whoop!" as he raced out of his office. *Honor!*

I'm just picking up a crossbow, she said. *Heading out to assist on a hunt for a vampire who's given in to bloodlust.*

Pounding straight into the weapons locker at the end of the hallway, he picked her up and spun her around. The leather of her hunting gear soft and pliable under his palms, her muscles fluid and strong, she placed her hands on his shoulders and laughed. A tattoo of translucent green wove over her right cheekbone, the semi-permanent art that altered patterns throughout the day one of the few things Honor liked about this century's fashions.

"What's got into you?" she said when he stopped spinning and put her down.

"Healers have told Andromeda to prepare."

Honor thrust the crossbow in her hand straight back into its holder. "I'll ask Ellie to cover for me while you drive."

"I have it under control!" Illium called out as they exited the weapons locker. "I'll brief Venom when he gets back, and I'll tell Ellie she's needed by the Guild!"

Dmitri shot the other man a wave of thanks before he and Honor sprinted onto the platform for the elevator. The protective gravity rings spun up around them in a split second, the trip down to the garage so fast that they barely felt it.

Their bags were already in the vehicle, had been since the day Andromeda and Naasir had reached out to ask them to be there for the birth. The jet had also been on standby for the past week, even though they were a month out from the birth.

"Keir did say it could happen early," Honor said as their vehicle raced out of the city in silence, Dmitri having put it in auto mode for maximum speed. "They're prepared." Her tone was jittery.

Dmitri's hand squeezed the steering wheel, even though he'd willingly given up a measure of control of the sleek red vehicle. Still a Ferrari, one born in this century, complete with technology so advanced that it wouldn't even have been a dream to the farmer Dmitri had once been.

"They're prepared," he echoed. "We'll get there in time." He knew the couple needed them—and they needed to be there for the two.

Naasir had been in Dmitri's heart since the day Raphael brought the feral little boy to the Refuge, and in the time since Andromeda had become Naasir's, she'd also become an integral part of Dmitri and Honor's family.

Though Andromeda's relationship with Lailah and Cato was far better than it had been during Charisemnon's reign, some wounds while healed, couldn't be forgotten. Andromeda might never be at a place where she wanted the two by her side at such a vulnerable moment in her life—though she'd made it clear that once she'd given birth, her parents were not just welcome, but lovingly invited to visit.

Lailah and Cato, meanwhile, treasured their daughter's willingness to allow them to be a part of their grandchildren's lives. The two were yet on their own journey toward true peace, but had seemed genuinely happy the last time Dmitri had seen them.

"What if it happens before we reach them?" he found himself saying, remembering the second time Ingrede had given birth—how fast it had been, too fast for the midwife to get there. It was Dmitri who'd caught the slippery body of his newborn daughter in his arms, his heart thunder and tears running down his face.

She'd been so small, their Caterina, such a fragile life that had never had a chance to bloom.

"Hey." Honor's hand on his, his wife seeing right through to his soul. "Remember what we said."

If I got a second chance, don't you think our babies must have, too?

Swallowing hard, he squeezed her hand, his lover who had fought death itself to come back to him. "Yeah."

"As for Andi, she's got Keir and Jessamy with her," Honor reminded him. "Neither she nor Naasir wanted us there too early." A scowl in her voice. "Andi said our hovering added to Naasir's might make her homicidal."

Dmitri grunted. "I don't hover."

"Neither do I," Honor said right before she laughed. "It's possible we're a *wee* bit protective, but who wouldn't be? No one even knew if they'd be able to have children together."

Nobody had been able to predict what might happen when the only known chimera in the world mated with an angel, but Dmitri had hoped, knowing how much Naasir ached for "cubs." Keir had also been hopeful, because while Naasir did drink blood, he was no vampire. He was a whole different species, a true immortal akin to angelkind . . . and he had once been a feral boy who'd ingested the heart of an Ancient.

"I ate my enemy and it made me strong," a young Naasir had told Dmitri once, his teeth bared. "I'm not sorry."

Dmitri had shrugged. "Me either. Good job."

Wings of blue in his peripheral vision, a sparkle of light from the other side of the vehicle that was going at speeds that turned the world into a blur. Two more warriors he'd known as children, grown until he could no longer see them as children. Funny how that had never happened with Naasir. Dmitri saw the warrior, but he also saw the boy who'd liked to linger on high shelves, just waiting to pounce on his unsuspecting prey, the boy who'd once eaten the school's bunny.

And the boy who'd run out to greet him, shouting, "Dmitri! Dmitri!" until Dmitri's heart broke from the memories of another boy who'd run into his arms. But catching Naasir's pelting form, holding this living, breathing child close, it had healed him as much as it had healed Naasir.

"We have an escort."

Said escort kept them company all the way to the airport that housed the high-speed jet. The flat, triangular vehicle with no apparent seams and no wheels was as different from the planes of yesteryear as those planes had been from blimps, but the verbiage stuck.

Getting out of the car after the system inside brought it to a smooth stop, he pointed at Illium. "Look after her. One scratch and I'll pluck your feathers."

"You better send us photos!" Raphael's first general yelled as Dmitri and Honor ran onto the tarmac to enter the jet.

Once inside, Dmitri looked out through the sleek windows that appeared black from the outside to see Aodhan leaning on the other side of the red bullet of the car, the light of him dazzling as he waved . . . and his happiness even brighter.

Their Sparkle had come back piece by piece.

He wasn't who he'd once been, wasn't the boy who'd sketched a shirtless Dmitri eating an apple one lazy afternoon, but that was all right. Dmitri was no longer the farmer who'd courted Ingrede, either, but he was no less for it.

The flight felt endless no matter its speed, their nerves taut. It was at times like this that he almost wished the scholars who insisted that transportation by teleportation was a viable future goal weren't as deluded as the alchemists of the past.

He'd have loved to jump onto a platform, only to reappear in the Refuge.

Too bad the experiments had never managed to progress beyond fresh vegetables. Which had come out black and dead on the other side no matter what, until only a rare few scholars continued to pursue the goal. Privately, Dmitri believed they were doomed to failure—because they were working with incomplete information. No one had ever been able to explain the energies that created archangels and forced Cascades after all.

Their world was no easy calculation, its mysteries fathoms deep.

Today, he kept himself busy by communicating with Venom on issues about which he hadn't had the chance to give his second-in-command a briefing.

Honor, in contrast, read books that she'd downloaded onto her phone. A small and transparent sheet, it folded up to fit even the most miserly pocket, but many people had gone even further a century ago and begun to embed the phones into their palms.

When a few angels attempted the same, their bodies had thoroughly rejected the idea. Their healing ability meant the embed became uncomfortable as scar tissue built up around it—and for angels on the more powerful end of the spectrum, their body extruded the intrusion after a matter of days at most.

Vampires had the same problem, though to a lesser extent. As a result, the physical phone would never die, whether worn on the wrist or carried in a pocket. Even mortals were switching back. A genius inventor had created a brain implant phone that connected to the eyes—and, contrary to all predictions, caused a mass exodus away from embedded tech.

Turned out brain embeds were a step too far.

"Take my flesh, take my blood," a poet had written, "but do not seek to take my last refuge, my final quietness."

When Dmitri glanced over to see what Honor was reading, he spotted imagery from a book about baby angels.

He knew she'd already read that book at least five times, but his heart aching, he let her be.

The trip took an eternity and they weren't done even once the jet landed. Because there were no suitable landing areas in the Refuge itself.

Which was why Dmitri had stored his silent phantom of a motorcycle in a warehouse at the landing strip.

Neither one of them breathed easy until Dmitri stopped the motorcycle on the edge of the Refuge. When they glanced up, it was to see a grinning Naasir crouched on a large boulder above them.

The chimera pounced.

"How is she?" Dmitri asked after hugging the wild child become a man who was such a huge part of his heart.

"In the Medica, growling at everyone." Naasir beamed.

Releasing Dmitri, he lifted Honor off her feet with his embrace, then nuzzled against her as he always did. With the affection of a child, though in strict terms, Naasir was older and stronger. When Honor petted his hair, Naasir leaned into it, turning his head so she could press a kiss to his cheek.

"Andi says she feels as big as a house," he told them afterward, "and that everyone is annoying, and she wants to bite their heads off."

Dmitri couldn't imagine sweet, warm Andi doing anything of the sort—but then again, she was mated to Naasir. There was definitely mischief in her bloodstream, and more than a streak of the primal.

"Come!" Naasir led them to the gentle beauty of the building that housed the Medica. Rebuilt after the quakes that had shaken the Refuge to ensure it remained solid from the foundations up, it was a single-story structure that hugged the rugged landscape, full of windows and skylights that let in the mountain light and allowed patients sweeping views, but that could be blacked out by curtains and technology should the light make sleep difficult.

Andromeda was in the wing for birthing mothers. In effect, it was a wing for any *one* birthing mother at a time. With angelic fertility so low, it was rare for there to be more than one woman in there at a time. Even after the Cascade, pregnancies had rarely coincided so closely. But the wing still had four separate rooms, just in case of a baby boom.

Andromeda's was on the very edge, and featured huge wraparound doors that allowed the light to pour in—and crucially, could be opened so that an angel didn't feel pinned inside. Or so a wild creature like Naasir wouldn't feel trapped.

It also faced the part of the Refuge where it was understood that no one was to fly without permission. The area was private to the Medica, with Refuge residents giving it a wide berth, so that any angel who wished to give birth under the piercing mountain sky could do so in privacy.

Even the youngest of them capable of flight knew of the no-fly zone. Those same young ones would often be the first visitors after Keir announced the restriction lifted for a period. They'd fly in and peer from beyond the glass, all unwieldy wings and excitement.

Today, the doors were wide open to the biting spring air. Andromeda stood framed in them looking not out at the view, but at the door from the main part of the Medica . . . as if waiting for something or someone.

Her face both lit up and wobbled the instant she saw Honor.

She went to move toward her, but Honor was already there, her arms around the other woman. Andromeda was far older than Honor in years, but age didn't work the same in those who had once been mortal as it did in those born immortal. And Honor, while she'd stopped aging when she became a vampire at twenty-nine, held an inner age Dmitri alone truly understood. Her maturity was that of a woman far beyond her years.

She cupped Andromeda's shaky face. "Look at you, you gorgeous glowing creature."

"I'm huge," Andromeda whispered on a sobbing cry, her

emotions all on the surface and her curls wild. She clung to
Dmitri's hand when he reached it out to her, while Naasir
rubbed her back. "And now I'm crying. *Again!*"

Nuzzling her, Naasir murmured something Dmitri didn't
hear, but that made Andromeda sniffle back her tears and
turn her face into his chest. After she was steadier, Dmitri
caught Naasir's eye, and the two of them stepped out onto
the rocks, so that Andromeda could talk to Honor.

Because sometimes, a woman needed a mother's advice
and comfort, and for Andi in this moment, Honor held that
role. At first, their bond had been through Naasir, but over
the years, Dmitri and Honor had both formed their own
relationship with her. How could they do anything but love
the woman who loved Naasir with all her fierce heart?

"How are you doing?" Dmitri asked Naasir when they
were distant enough that they couldn't overhear the two
women.

Naasir walked to stand on the far edge of a cliff, the
wind blowing back the thick silver of his hair. "Scared." A
single rough word as he glanced back at Dmitri. "She . . .
they . . ." His throat moved.

"I know. They're everything." He hugged his arm around
the younger male, tugged him close. "It'll be fine. She's too
tough for anything else."

"Yes," Naasir said, a growl in his tone—but he didn't
pull away. "Will I be a good father, Dmitri?"

Memory crashed into Dmitri, of Naasir asking him another question that had destroyed him: *Am I a person, Dmitri? Will you be sad if I die?*

"You'll be the best," Dmitri said, his voice raw. "Trust
me. I know exactly who you are."

Naasir shuddered, sighed. "I didn't know I could be this
happy-scared."

"It's wild, isn't it?"

Naasir knew about Misha, about Caterina, about Ingrede.
He'd come upon Dmitri as a youth, while Dmitri held a
painting of his lost family, his tears locked hard and painful
in his chest, and somehow, even though Naasir had still

been more feral than not, he'd known that all Dmitri needed at that moment was to be loved. So he—the boy who was ever in motion—had sat nestled against Dmitri's side until Dmitri was ready to speak.

When he was, he'd told Naasir stories of his little boy and little girl, and of the wife who had been his soulmate. Even so young, Naasir had understood loss. Naasir, too, had been wounded by grief. He hadn't been afraid or scared or uncomfortable at hearing of Dmitri's own loss.

Rather, he'd seemed fascinated that Dmitri had sired a baby girl, his eyes going wide when Dmitri explained how Caterina had fit into his hands and how she'd cried for her papa to rock her to sleep. "Only Papa could get her down," he'd said, the precious moments spent with the little girl he'd intended to spoil and cherish spilling over into words.

Naasir had smiled at the stories of Misha's mischief, asked for more, and for the first time in eternity, Dmitri had found joy in speaking of his boy, who'd always run pell-mell toward him when Dmitri returned home from the markets, and who'd once tried to hide in the cart with the vegetables so he could go to the market with his papa.

Now, the boy who'd listened to his stories of his family needed him to stand as his father, and Dmitri would do so with pride. His job here today was to be whatever Naasir needed him to be, while Honor's was to be the same for Andromeda.

Which was why Dmitri stood guard outside when the contractions turned urgent, while Naasir and Honor stayed in the birthing chamber with Andromeda and the healers. They might be in the safe haven of the Refuge, but Naasir's primal heart needed to know that Dmitri, dangerous and deadly, watched his family's back at this vulnerable time.

Only then could Naasir let down his guard and just be in the moment.

The first shocked cry came far faster than Dmitri had expected, with angelic birthing often taking well over a day or more. That cry was thin but strong. It was followed by a second . . . then a third.

All different tones. All different children.

Because Naasir, their primal chimera, had managed to do the impossible—he'd sired not a single child, but *three* at once. Triplets were so rare in angelkind that this birth would go down in history, talked about for centuries if not longer.

That wasn't the only thing that made this birth momentous, of course. These were the only children ever born of a chimera and an angel. Not even Keir had any idea of the form the babes would take. Winged chimera? Born vampires who needed blood but could also process food and weren't prey to bloodlust? Beings unique?

It was all an unknown.

The only certainty was that Naasir would love his cubs with primal joy. As would Dmitri.

"Dmitri." A crying Naasir opened the door . . . and against his bare chest, he held three tiny babes with skin as brown as his own and wings so fine, they were translucent.

Dmitri touched a gentle finger to the head of each before Naasir handed the children over to the healers, for they had been born too young and would need a little extra care. They would, however, remain in the room with the new parents.

Naasir watched them like a hawk, while an exhausted Andromeda beamed from the bed, where Honor had already helped her become more comfortable, and the healers buzzed around, as excited for the births as the entirety of the Refuge.

Later, after things had settled, and Andromeda and the babies were sleeping, while Honor spoke with Jessamy and Keir in the corridor outside, Naasir turned from his babies to Dmitri and whispered, "I'm not a one-being anymore, Dmitri." A rough tremor in his voice. "I have cubs like me."

Dmitri looked down at the children, saw the faint ripple of stripes under the skin of one before it settled back to a smooth deep brown. "Not just one, but three." He squeezed the other man's nape. "At this rate, you'll have a whole squadron by the time you're done."

Naasir looked down at his boys. All three of them. "Do you think they'll fly?" he asked, curious and unworried. "I never flew and didn't mind, but they have things that look like wings. Maybe they'll want to fly and be sad they can't."

"They'll fly," Dmitri confirmed. "Their wings look so fragile because they were born early. I've seen it before."

Naasir prowled to gently nuzzle his sleeping mate. Smiling in her rest, Andi turned toward him.

"They're like both of us," Naasir whispered proudly even as he stroked Andi's hair, petting her in that way of his. "We made them together. *Our* cubs."

42

A massive group of the senior Tower crew, including Elena and Raphael, crowded into Venom's office to look at the three-dimensional images Dmitri had sent through of the newborn cubs. The images were so lifelike that it was tempting to reach across and try to gather up a tiny newborn in the hand.

"They look about the size of beans," Illium said with a worried frown. "Is that normal?"

Aodhan spread his wing partially over his lover's—only partially because there were too many people around the desk for any further movement. "They're not quite that small. And yes, it's normal—Indri was bigger, but he was full term and a single baby."

"To have more than one child in a single pregnancy is rare among our kind," Raphael added, "but I watched over one such pair during my time standing guard in the angelic nursery, and they were much smaller than the single births."

Aodhan could well see the sire holding watch over their

most vulnerable. Even during the period when he'd turned cold and heartless, he'd never once been anything but kind to children.

"Their wings." Elena pressed her hand to her heart. "They're so fine, almost invisible."

"They'll fill in," Nisia reassured her. "I ministered to another child born with wings that undeveloped." The healer glanced over at Illium. "Doesn't seem to have stopped him."

No, Aodhan thought, nothing could stop their Bluebell. "Is the Refuge in an uproar?"

"Complete chaos," Venom confirmed, while Holly stood next to his chair with her hand on his nape and her face glowing with utter happiness; she and Naasir were tight. Not the same way Naasir was with the rest of the Seven. They had their own—very sibling-like—relationship.

"Dmitri called earlier," Venom continued, "and he says that while people are being very good and giving mother and babes the peace they need, everyone's bursting out of their skin and the gifts are piling up. One old one has declared it a harbinger of good luck for the next eon."

"I wouldn't argue with that," Raphael said. "Children are a gift, and today we've been gifted three bright new lives."

The archangel glanced at Ashwini. "What say you, Ash?"

The hunter with a gift for prophecy tucked her long dark hair behind her ear to reveal a dangling earring in reds and oranges. "That they're babies," she said sternly, hands on her hips. "No one should be dooming them with portents."

Instead of laughing, they all stayed silent, because she was still looking at the images and there'd been a tone in her voice they'd heard before. Ashwini was no seer, not in the angelic sense, her ability a wholly mortal thing that she'd brought with her into vampirism, but when she picked up a glimmer of the future, it came true more often than not.

Her lips kicked up. "Don't assign them rooms too high

up in the Tower when they start to visit—even though they will be able to fly, they'll climb down the walls just because."

Janvier chuckled, his hand on his Ashblade's lower back. "That sounds like exactly how I'd expect our Naasir's cubs to behave, *cher*."

Aodhan had the feeling the hunter had seen far more from the way she was staring at the images, but since her smile had only deepened, it was nothing bad, and that was all he needed to know.

"Have they chosen names?" Vivek asked from his spot beside Nisia; he, no doubt, was wearing an invisible earbud to stay on top of his intelligence network, but his eyes were on the infants.

"No news yet." Venom wrapped his arm around Holly's waist. "With a librarian and Naasir for parents, I can't even imagine what they'll choose."

The answer came the next day at nightfall: Misha, Nasien, and Izar.

"Nasien and Izar, I understand," Illium said at the news. "Izar means 'star' in the old language of Euskara, and Nasien is close to Naasir's name while being different enough that it won't cause confusion." He flared out his wings as they walked onto a Tower balcony, closed them back in. "Why Misha, though?"

Aodhan thought of a time long ago, a time of pain and shadow. And of a grief shared. "Naasir would've wanted Dmitri to name his firstborn and so, I think, would Andromeda." It was as close as he could get to telling Illium without breaching that confidence.

Dmitri wouldn't mind, but it wasn't Aodhan's place to decide that.

And Illium's heart, it was big enough that he understood at once. "It's a great name. All of them are. Links to their past and to love while giving them futures of their own." He glanced at Aodhan, the moonlight a caress of silver that outlined his profile. "Shall we gift them a Naasir-appropriate item?" Because first general though he might be, he remained Aodhan's wicked Blue down to the bone.

Aodhan laughed, his universe as dazzling as the lights of Manhattan. "Let's save *that* for when they're toddlers and can drive their parents crazy with their toys."

Today

43

The sun was bright overhead, the sky clear as Illium and Aodhan continued their flight to his new territory.

"Dmitri told me the rules of being an effective second," Aodhan said aloud when they swung close enough to talk, the wind having died down. "The first one is to protect your archangel from idiots."

Still laughing, Illium said, "Adi, do you think we have to follow the rules?"

"I was joking. There aren't any official rules for seconds."

"No, not that. I mean rules in general. About archangels."

Aodhan glanced over. "What are you plotting?"

"Well, who made the rule that once you become an archangel, you can't truly maintain friendships that have endured through time—even if those friendships are in the team of another archangel?" He scowled. "I don't ever plan to be Raphael's enemy, so what does it matter?"

Aodhan thought about it. "Right now, you have to follow the rules because it's about appearance, about ensuring others see that you have your own power. That's another thing Dmitri told me—sometimes, seconds have to advise their archangels to play the long game, as new archangels tend to be temperamental."

Illium scowled. "I'm not sure I like your new advisor on all things second," he said, no force in his tone—because Aodhan could find no better mentor. "He really told you Raphael was temperamental as a young archangel?"

"I can neither confirm nor deny," Aodhan said piously. "That was a private second-to-second conversation."

Yet, even as the two of them bantered, the sadness lingered, and when they landed for a break on a remote uninhabited island, they sat in silence while eating the food that Venom, Sivya, and Montgomery had packed for them.

When they did speak, it was about the people they'd left behind.

It wasn't until the final break before reaching Illium's new territory that they shifted focus and began to discuss those who might be enticed to join Illium's team.

"You've already had several good approaches," Aodhan told him as they sat on an isolated atoll, stunning white sands falling into an azure ocean. "I'm handling it, creating a short list. Dulce's doing the same on her end, and talking to me when she's not sure about credentials or reputation. There's some I know you won't be interested in off the bat."

Illium didn't question him on those calls—if anyone knew him, it was Aodhan.

"Oh, and Indri's on his way." Aodhan smiled. "He gave Marduk notice the instant he heard of your ascension. Told me that he expected me to exercise my powers in the pursuit of nepotism."

"Excellent. Saves me having to steal him." Aodhan's nephew had grown into a whip-smart warrior-scholar who would be a vital asset.

"I forgot to tell you," Illium added, "just before we left, I called Navarro and asked him to consider joining me as my interim first general. My plan is to lure him with a temporary post, then slowly make it permanent." After a long time in Raphael's forces, the highly respected angel had spent the last century as a trainer in the Refuge.

Aodhan chuckled. "Excellent choice. Let's hope your lure works. I can't think of a more stable head to have in that position."

"Do you think we'll have any trouble filling all the positions?" Illium played a piece of polished jet through his fingers—Aodhan had balanced it perfectly to his hand.

"No. Being at the ground floor of a new archangel's territory is exciting. And Blue, you keep making friends everywhere you go. Xander's already told Alexander that he's sent through a request to join your team."

Illium raised an eyebrow, recalling Raphael's advice regarding the Ancient. "Alexander won't like losing his grandson."

"No, Xander has his approval—Alexander knows as well as anyone that you don't stifle warriors as strong as his grandson. This is an opportunity Xander might not have again for centuries, perhaps even millennia.

"It matters even more because Alexander's court was settled even after his waking, as so many of his people returned. Xander's never experienced a new court, much less the work it takes to build it."

"I'd be glad to have him at my side—he's one hell of a commander."

"You have any hesitation on his loyalty?"

Illium shook his head. "Raphael told me Alexander isn't two-faced and he's been a huge influence on Xander. Plus, Xander was fostered with Titus—we both know he's as honest and openhearted as they come. And Rohan was an honorable man." Xander's father had died at Lijuan's hands, but he'd held the line to the last.

"Yes." Aodhan nodded. "Built of honor, all three of them."

"If Xander vows loyalty to me, he'll hold it even against his own—but I don't intend to allow it to ever come to that." Illium might enjoy irritating his asshole father, but he wasn't planning on picking fights that could degenerate into war, no matter if the archangelic power within him pushed for aggression, for total dominion. Because that way lay megalomaniacal madness of the kind that had consumed Lijuan.

"There's another applicant you might not be expecting." Aodhan drank from the bottle of water between them. "Vivek."

Illium snapped his head toward his lover. "I'm not poaching from Raphael and Elena." Because not only was Vivek Jason's right hand, he was also part of Ellie's Guard. "I can't believe you'd even consider it."

"He's over seven hundred years told, and spymaster-level experienced, but he'll never be Raphael's spymaster. That's Jason's position, and Vivek wouldn't even think of jockeying for it." A glance at Illium. "The spymaster position on your team, however, is wide open. And unlike all the other courts who've approached him over the years, Vivek *wants* to be part of yours."

"Adi," Illium began.

"I already spoke to the sire," Aodhan said, before wincing. "To Raphael. I have to make that a habit or I'm going to get both of us in trouble."

"Don't worry, I'll be right there beside you." The only difference was that the power inside Illium stirred each time he thought of Raphael, and it was a quiet warning not to slip. "What did he say?"

"That he knew it was a distinct possibility the instant you ascended. Vivek went to him twenty-four hours later." Arms on his raised knees, he looked out over the water. "The s—Raphael is willing to let him go. Losing both you and Vivek at the same time will be a hit to the Tower's tech arm, but you've both trained enough people that it won't create a dangerous hole."

"And Ellie?"

"You know she'd send her entire Guard with you if it would make your life safer," Aodhan chided softly. "Vivek says she all but pushed him out the door the second he started telling her what he wanted to do. 'Of course it has to be you, V. I thought you'd never figure it out!' That's what he said she told him."

Illium would fucking miss Ellie.

"To have Vivek with us would make the transition a hell of a lot easier," he admitted roughly, torn between his loyalty to Raphael, and his instinctive loyalty to the people of his new territory. Because that was what it meant to be Cadre—to spread your wings over those you claimed, keep them safe.

"I'll talk to Raphael myself," he said after watching the waves roll in to shore for several long heartbeats, the crashing sound of the ocean a quiet thunder. "I have to act like an archangel with another archangel, no matter how weird it feels."

"You should talk to Elijah, too, after things settle down," Aodhan suggested. "He was Lady Caliane's general once, and now they stand on the Cadre together."

Nodding, Illium pulled out his phone. While the communications device had undergone multiple iterations after the invention of this flat rectangle as thin as paper that could be folded up and put away in a pocket, this was the one that had eventually stuck. Sometimes, he'd realized over time, technology hit the perfect balance between form and function, and entered a long stasis period.

"No signal." Not a surprise at this remote location in the middle of nothing but ocean and more ocean. Angelkind had blocked the expansion of connectivity even when it became possible. Some swathes of the world, they'd declared, deserved to remain free of any interference, even by so amorphous a thing as a signal. "I'll call Raphael the minute I can—because if Vivek is coming with us, then I want him in on the ground floor, so he can set up the right systems from the get-go."

Aodhan rose, stretched out his wings. "Agreed." Arms up, he flexed, and for a moment, Illium was stunned by him, as if he hadn't been waking next to him for hundreds of years. But what struck him most was how fucking lucky he was to have a best friend and lover whose loyalty was absolute and unquestionable.

"I couldn't do this without you," he said as he got up, the words husky. "You know that, don't you?" His lover had a way of not seeing his own importance not just to Illium, but to the world. His art had changed futures, opened closed hearts, brought beauty in the most terrible times. "You make me braver because I know I always have you at my back."

A bemused smile as Aodhan closed his wings back in. "What brought this on?" He nuzzled Illium's temple, running his fingers through Illium's hair. "The way you look at me . . . of course I know what I am to you." A kiss to his cheekbone. "I also know I'm not good with compliments, but don't ever think I don't hear yours, hold them close."

"Do you ever resent it?" Illium asked, his chest tight. "Not being able to devote all your time to your art?" Because the demands on Aodhan were only going to get worse going forward.

Shifting so he could look Illium in the eye, the other man shook his head. "No, never. If I did, I wouldn't have picked up a sword to train with you in the first place." He pressed his forehead to Illium's. "Stop worrying, my darling Blue. I've made my own decisions all my life, and each time the urge to create art hits, I find a way."

A kiss hard and firm. "Right now, I can think of no greater art than the creation of your rule. A blank canvas, beloved mine. What shall we paint on it?"

"A damn legend," Illium said with a smile that was a touch shaky with all the emotion roaring through him. No one had warned him that becoming an archangel would dredge up every emotion he'd ever had, swirl it around in his gut, then punch him right in the softest places in his spirit.

Aodhan's chuckles cut through the morass, anchoring him to the astonishing now. "Well, Illium, Archangel of

Legend, I have another suggestion for you." His eyes went to the extraordinary sword on Illium's back.

Illium cocked his head; he'd been considering the same person, but—"She's a weapons-maker not a weapons-master."

"Only because that's what she prefers—but she's fully trained in how to handle all the weapons she makes. The knowledge in her head is probably in line with Galen's when he took on the role of Raphael's weapons-master," Aodhan argued before digging out a handful of dried meat from his pack and handing it to Illium.

"A weapons-master has to fight, yes," he continued, "but they have to be strategists and long-term thinkers most of all. First generals lead troops into battle, but it's the weapons-masters who make sure the first general has the troops and the weapons to make that possible. Weapons-masters are the forge of a battle force."

Illium chewed on the jerky as Aodhan dug out more for himself. "You think she'll go for it?" The vampire who'd forged the sword Raphael had gifted Illium was someone Illium called a friend true, but despite her visceral connection to the Tower, she'd never given any indication that she wished for a more active martial role.

"No way to know unless you ask. Zoe might decide she likes the challenge."

Zoe Elena Haziz-Grange was now heading toward completing her seventh century as one of the Made, but Illium remembered her as the chubby-cheeked mortal child of Elena's best friend in all the world. He'd played with little Zoe back then, had shared a drink with her as she grew, and had helped her navigate the tough years after her transition to vampirism.

It hadn't been a true choice, not as he'd have wanted for her, but it hadn't been a thing of pain or violence, and Zoe had navigated it with her usual wit and grace. "Ash says she's still going despite the insanity-inducing malformation in her brain—and that these days, she's usually only insane

on Tuesdays," she'd said right before her transition, "so
I've got nothing to worry about. Only a tiny aggressive can-
cer. Pfft."

Knowing who Zoe's mother was, Illium guessed that
she was the one who'd asked Ashwini to talk to Zoe. Because Sara Haziz would've known about Ash's medical history; her hunters had trusted her to the bone, had turned out
for her in their hundreds when the time came.

Sara had been carried to her final resting place, beside
Deacon, the weapons-maker she loved and who had taught
Zoe all she knew, by an honor guard that included Zoe,
Ashwini, and the consort of the Archangel of New York.
But that day, she'd been just Ellie, Sara's best friend and a
woman whose heart was broken into a million pieces.

"I know it was what Sara wanted," Ellie had said to Illium days later, while they sat on the Tower roof looking
out at the sparkle of the city. Her voice had been hoarse
with all the tears she'd shed and her eyes swollen because
even angelic healing couldn't keep up with her grief.
"She never wanted to live forever. Neither did Deacon. I
still hate that they're gone. I'll never again have a friend
like Sara."

Illium, with Lorenzo and Catalina forever a part of him,
had needed no further words to understand her grief. What
he'd also understood was that Ellie's statement said nothing
about her incredibly fierce and loving relationship with her
sister and fellow hunter, Eve. Elena had always been—and
always would be—Eve's big sister, no matter that Eve was
centuries into being a vampire.

Sara and Elena, by contrast, had begun and ended as
equals.

Ellie had taken a shuddering breath that night they'd
talked. "Zoe's doing better than me. She told me she always
knew they'd go together, and they did, didn't they? Within
a month of each other. Even though she's a vampire, she has
a faith that's a song inside her—she believes with all she is
that they're together beyond the veil."

A hard swallow. "I've decided to follow Zoe's lead, imagine Sara and Deacon young and vibrant, hand in hand as they live a thousand adventures together."

Zoe and her "aunt" Ellie remained family true and forever, their love for each other so deep that it shimmered in the air around them when they were together.

Today, Illium said, "I always figured she'd join Ellie's Guard if she was inclined that way."

"Ellie's overprotective of her." Aodhan handed him more food.

The man couldn't help looking after Illium, and Illium adored him for it.

"To her, Zoe is forever the child she first knew—Sara's precious baby girl." Aodhan took a drink from his water bottle. "Zoe loves her, but being on Ellie's team would drive her crazy. Ellie's the same with Sam, but Sam's so good-natured that he just rolls with it. Zoe's more fiery, more like Ellie herself. They'd slam heads, then both feel bad about it."

"Yes, I can see that. Explains why Eve refuses to become an official part of her Guard, too, even though we all know she'd decapitate anyone who dared hurt Ellie." Of the six daughters sired by Jeffrey Deveraux, only two walked in this time, and they were linked by bonds of loyalty and love unbreakable.

"There's a reason Titus refuses to let his older sisters near his court in any official capacity." Aodhan scowled. "Older sisters can't help themselves. Trust me, I have one— she just today told me I looked 'tired and cranky' on a call, and that she's sending me treats via angelic courier."

Illium laughed, continuously delighted by the relationship that had grown between Aodhan and Imalia over the centuries. "I'll ask Zoe," he said, decision made. "What about Eve? Do you think she'd consider it?"

Aodhan took a moment to think before nodding slowly. "It's worth reaching out to ask. She'd make one hell of a ground commander in battle."

"Let's do it," Illium said. "I'd much rather start my court with people I know and trust, even if some of them only decide to join for a temporary stint." He made a face. "I don't want an *actual* court. I want something like the Tower."

Shifting to face him, Aodhan gripped the side of his neck. "You'll do it. You'll build something strong and beautiful because that's who you are. A builder. A rescuer. A lover." All heart, that was Aodhan's Blue. So much so that Aodhan worried what being an archangel would do to him— because archangels had to make decisions dark and terrible over and over again.

Turning his head, Illium kissed his palm. "The power fuels me, but one thing I understand now," he said. "I knew Raphael valued his Seven, but after ascension, I truly *get* the depth of his need for us, for Elena."

He looked out over the ocean. "An archangel is an island of aloneness in his power—without friendships that endure, without love, that's where the madness comes. Because the aloneness?" Eyes that glowed locked to Aodhan's. "It has the capacity to build and build and build until it eats away all light, leaving only darkness in its wake."

Fear gnawed at Aodhan, for the stark horror of what Illium was describing. And while Aodhan would never understand what it was to be Cadre, a being so removed from angelkind as to be another species altogether, he knew one thing. "I *love* you." He kissed Illium with every ounce of the fury of his emotions. "I have loved you all my life in one form or another, and I will love you the rest of my existence in ever more complex and potent ways. But I will always, *always*, love you. You'll never be alone."

Illium's wings began to glow with the same primal energy as his eyes. "I know," he whispered, twining his hand around Aodhan's neck to kiss him with passion slow and sweet as his power thrummed through Aodhan's bones.

It sang of his Blue. Still *his* Blue, no matter that he was now archangel of an entire territory. Be that they could,

Aodhan would've lingered in that kiss, in that moment forever, but when they drew apart, they lifted off without discussion. Because right now and for the foreseeable future,
Illium's territory had to be the priority.

"What will you call yourself as your official archangel
name?" he asked once they were in flight.

"My mother suggested Illium, Archangel of Mischief." A wicked grin. "She also told me not to pick a fight
with Aegaeon the Asshole until I'm settled enough to handle it."

"Eh-ma told *me* to smack you upside the head should
you start to go in the direction of picking a fight."

Illium's laughter was wild and delighted. "She's the most
important being in angelic history, you know that?"

Aodhan asked the question with his expression.

Illium lifted up his hand and began ticking things off.
"Mother of an archangel. Consort to an archangel even
though she refuses the title. Best friend of another archangel. Foster mother to yet one more archangel."

He lowered his hand. "She sits in the center of countless
streams of power, and she handles it all so effortlessly that
no one sees how much she holds in her hand. If she called,
I would come. Raphael would come. Caliane would come.
Titus, of course."

"She's the right person to hold all that power."

"Yes." Illium dove down, flew back up, his pleasure in
flight untrammeled. "As for my name, I don't know yet. I'll
just be Archangel Illium until I see my territory. Raphael's
first name wasn't the one he holds now, remember? New
York didn't exist on his ascension. He was Raphael, Archangel Destined. He never used it himself, hated it—but it
was how people started referring to him."

"I'd almost forgotten that." He and Illium had been so
young then, children who'd tagged around behind their patient Rafa.

Now, as they flew on, they talked of the past, laughed
over memories, were solemn in thoughts of friends and

warrior compatriots lost and energetic in their discussions of those they intended to approach to join their court.

"Because it will be *ours*, Adi, your voice as important as mine." A starburst of golden light as Illium threw power up into the air. "Now, let's go make trouble."

44

Illium finally got a signal on his device two hours out from his new territory. The call went through without a hitch, Raphael's face appearing on the screen. "Illium?" A frown. "What is it? A problem?"

The instant protective edge to Raphael's tone made his heart ache. "Aodhan told me about Vivek's request," he got out through the roar of his emotions.

"Ah." A faint smile. "I wouldn't lose him, but fact is that most vampires of his strength and expertise would've already long flown the nest to experience other territories, other ways of life, if only for temporary periods.

"He's only stayed this long because, first, it took considerable time for him to heal completely from his spinal injuries, second, he couldn't find any other court that he both liked and that would encourage him to do the complexity of work he does at the Tower, and third, his intense loyalty to Elena."

"Elena's Guard should have someone like that on it," Illium argued.

"But not at the extent of clipping his wings." Raphael

gave a gentle shake of the head. "Elena has always told Vivek that when he needs to fly, he's to go. You know her, Illium. She'd never tie Vivek in place when his Making was about freedom."

Illium nodded. "No, she wouldn't do that."

Raphael held his gaze. "Quite aside from his wanderlust, Vivek's brain is astonishing and needs to be fed. You're the first opportunity he's had to leave and still end up where he wants to be." A smile. "It helps that he knows you'll let him do whatever he wants and will, in fact, enable him to rise to even greater heights."

"You and Ellie, you're both sure?"

"Yes. Even Dmitri left once. A time before your birth. While he returned, I don't think Vivek ever will, and Elena and I couldn't be happier for you, Illium, that you'll have a spymaster of his caliber."

"Then will you do me the favor of telling him to pack his bags and get to my territory asap?"

"He'll be on a plane today. You know he won't be coming alone?"

"Lady Katrina is welcome in my territory." Illium grinned. "Even Jason says she has a way of knowing things no one else knows." Vivek's lover was a vampire old and with all kinds of murky connections.

At first, Aodhan said after the call ended, *when I heard about Vivek and Katrina, I thought she'd eat him alive.*

Pretty sure Vivek was offering himself on a silver platter to be eaten. With sauce. Illium had seen the way the other man looked at the mysterious owner of the Boudoir. *But they're a good team, aren't they?*

An unexpected but excellent team, Aodhan agreed. *What businesses do you think she'll set up in your territory?*

Who knows? With Katrina, it could be a weapons clearinghouse, a club decadent and exclusive, or a guild of assassins. Her only loyalty is to her people—and Vivek's at the top of that list, so as long as Vivek is loyal to me, we'll have her cooperation and occasional assistance.

A crisp wind, its fingers riffling their hair. And in the distance, the first smudge on the horizon that was land.

Illium took a deep breath, looked at Aodhan. "Ready?"

"With you? Always."

Grinning, Illium raced forward, Aodhan by his side.

45

Vivek had spoken to Katrina before he'd approached Raphael about leaving the Tower. No matter the roaring need inside him to go with Illium, be part of an adventure unlike any other he might ever encounter, he wasn't about to jeopardize his relationship with the only woman in the entire world who had seen into every corner of his soul and loved all of him.

Including the old shards of bitterness that had faded with time but would never be erased. Because a man couldn't simply forget that he'd once been a child abandoned by his family. A child who couldn't move, couldn't defend himself. That child had grown into a man who was now a fully trained and lethal hunter with an extraordinary life, but he never denigrated the emotional pain of the person he'd once been.

It had helped shape him—including the need for fidelity that was so important to him.

So, that night, in the midnight hours after Illium's ascension, he'd lain with his head in Katrina's lap in the moonlit confines of their lush bedroom while she sat up in bed. She'd been running her fingers through his hair with one hand and answering messages from one of her business managers with the other.

Most of his Kat's businesses came alive only at night.

He knew why she preferred the night, understood that he wasn't the only one with shards of bitterness lodged in his innermost psyche. As he'd been a helpless boy once, Katrina had been a young woman with no way to keep herself safe.

"Kat," he'd said after she put down her phone.

"What is it, lover?" Her head shifting so that he could see those pale feline eyes, her hair a midnight curtain around them, and the strap of her scarlet nightgown falling off one shoulder to expose the plump curve of her breast.

"Damn but you're gorgeous. My brain just short-circuited."

A husky laugh. "You say such things."

Each and every word was true. Vivek would never get over the fact that she'd chosen to be his all these years. She would never wear his amber, unable to accept such a physical symbol of locking her life to another's, but Vivek didn't care. He knew his Kat. She'd murder anyone who dared separate them—and he loved her enough to tend to her wounds as she did his.

"What do you think about moving territories? I know you have so many businesses here—"

"Lover," she'd interrupted, "I have businesses everywhere. I've only stayed in New York all this time because it's your home."

Shifting so that he could sit up, face her, he'd stroked her hair back from that astonishing face that had become even more otherworldly in the centuries since they'd first found each other. No one would ever mistake Kat for mortal. The golden cream of her skin was too flawless, the pink of her lips perfection, the pale green of her eyes a rare hue no mortal would ever possess.

But in bed, her hair tumbled and her breasts curving

over the lace of her nightgown, she was an earthy goddess. "You wouldn't mind?" he'd asked. "Because I won't go without you. Nothing in my life is as important as you."

A softness to her that Vivek knew he alone was privileged to see. "Your open heart terrifies me," she'd murmured, leaning forward to brush her fingers down his chest. "And no, I wouldn't mind. Where are we going?"

That she'd just accept such a huge move without hesitation—and without any foreknowledge of what exactly he planned—simply because it was what he wanted, it destroyed him. His Kat didn't say as many words of love as he did, but he had no need of them. To have this dangerous power of a woman trust him with such completeness? It said everything.

"I'm going to ask for the position of Illium's spymaster."

A sharp inhale, those feline eyes acute with attention. "You do keep life interesting, Vivek."

Now, mere days later, he stood on distant soil, Katrina's hand in his. She had long been a creature of decadent gowns, but did alter her fashion on rare occasions. Today was one of those. She'd chosen wide-legged black pants paired with a silken shirt the same shade as her eyes; cuffed at the wrists, it was tied at the neck with a bow.

"Good style," she'd told him more than once, "never falls out of fashion. What is the point in being immortal if I cannot choose my desired apparel from across time?"

He thought her striking in everything she chose to wear.

She'd put her hair into a sleek roll at the back of her neck for today, wore a stylish and wide-brimmed black hat over it. Her eyes, however, were still his Kat's eyes—sharp, taking in the activity around Illium's chosen base command, her mind cataloguing all the information for later use. She'd have made an excellent spymaster herself had she ever had the inclination.

"That one," she said to him now, nudging her head toward a strawberry-blonde vampire who stood talking to an angel holding a box of supplies. "She's clever but faithless. Damaged too young—has near-to-no capacity to trust. But she won't betray Illium."

Vivek looked at his lover, smiled. "Is she yours?"

A curve of the lips. "We met after the damage. I did what I could, tried to give Ana a chance at a better life, but I couldn't erase the scars."

The blonde turned away from the angel then, her eyes landing on Katrina and Vivek by chance. Her steps speeded up and she was almost running by the time she reached them. "Lady Katrina!" A smile so huge, it exposed her fangs. "I didn't know you were in the territory! Do you know the new archangel?"

"Yes," Katrina said after she'd embraced the other vampire with warmth and care. "Archangel Illium is to be protected from those who would shake his rule."

Vivek wondered what Illium would say to the knowledge that Katrina had wrapped him up in her protection. If he knew Bluebell, he'd grin and consider it an unexpected gift.

The blonde's eyes widened. "I understand, Lady." A glance at Vivek, a genuine smile, her eyes sparkling. "I'll cut off your head if you ever harm her." Turning, she walked away to continue with her duties.

"As I said," Katrina murmured, "damaged." A sigh. "But far better than she once was, so we will take that as a win."

Lifting her hand to his mouth, he pressed a kiss to her knuckles. "Thank you for looking out for my friend." Because no matter if he had ascended, Illium remained Vivek's friend. Nothing of their Bluebell's heart had changed in the ascension—he'd seen that firsthand in the shine in Illium's eyes when he'd said goodbye.

"He's important to you," Katrina murmured before looking back at the activity in front of them. "Go start your setup as I know you're itching to do. I'll join you in our assigned apartment later. After I take care of some business, I'll track Ana down and discover where the gray runs in this city, find us a place to call home." She didn't ask if Vivek would join her at that home, for it wasn't a question that needed to be asked.

Vivek and Katrina were as interlinked as Illium and Aodhan. Where one went, so would the other, their amber an invisible but unbreakable thread. "Till tonight," he said, his blood buzzing with anticipation.

"Vivek," Katrina said, her eyes brilliant even under the slant of her hat. "Spymaster to Archangel Illium. Yes, that has quite the nice ring to it." Long fingers brushing his cheek. "You will make Illium the envy of all the Cadre."

46

Illium's new territory had countless ancient structures and long stretches of desolate lands, along with the glittering spires of modern cities. What it didn't have—and that became immediately clear—was a strong sense of cohesion.

This was a territory that had been fragmented for centuries. Some of its people were fiercely loyal to the archangel who'd watched over them in years past, while others were excited to be part of a territory under the control of a new archangel; still others were scared about the same.

Vivek was already making up lists of senior people who could be trusted, and others who had a question mark over them. Anyone associated with Aegaeon, Illium had asked to leave the territory as soon as he arrived. Well aware of the tension between father and son, none had argued, and he'd been sorry to see a number of them go—they were good people.

But even if Aegaeon was a shit father, he was a good archangel overall, and there was too high a risk that his people would continue to be loyal to him. No doubt Aegaeon's spymaster had sleepers embedded in the territory, but that was to be expected. Dulce had already seen signs of other loyalties in people applying for positions in Illium's court.

On the flip side, Illium wasn't exactly blind when it came to knowledge about the other territories, either.

"I've already started creating our own spy network," Vivek had said smugly soon after his arrival. "Jason and I made a deal to pass on anything useful to each other as long as it doesn't affect the security of our archangels—Raphael knows about it, too. Since I've always had my own contacts quite apart from Jason's, it works. Plus, Kat's network is vast and labyrinthine—and she likes you."

The latter was a coup indeed. Lady Katrina was a law unto herself, but from what Illium had seen over the centuries, while she might choose to live in the gray, she'd never once backed anyone who chose to do evil. He also had the feeling that Vivek didn't grasp the depth of his influence on his lover—because Katrina looked at him the same way he looked at her.

Having decided to set up his temporary base in a tall silver spire that overlooked a sprawling and green city, Illium had acceded to Vivek's request to take over the basement. "You sure you don't want more light?"

"No, this is perfect for when I'm in the Spire. I'll be traveling a lot as part of my duties." The hunter, lithely muscled as a result of his Guild training, still had sharp facial bones, but was no longer rail thin as he'd been for so many years.

Not only had he put on muscle, but he'd been able to exercise his hunter-born instincts after his spine healed to the fullest extent. "I no longer have to use half my mental strength to contain the urge to hunt," he'd told Illium at the time. "I never realized how hard I was always working to not give in to the urge—if I *had* given in while paralyzed, I'd have gone insane. The freedom is dizzying."

Before Vivek took on the travel duties that were a natural part of a spymaster's role, however, he had to set up his complex technological network. "We each have our strengths. Tech is mine."

While Vivek got down to that, and Aodhan juggled myriad duties, Illium had undertaken a flight across his territory. His aim had been to take the pulse of the region, discover its strengths and weaknesses, judge the current state of the population—and let them see that they were now under Illium's wing.

It had been a long and intensive task.

At last, he stood once again at the top of the Spire—as everyone had taken to calling it—and considered his next move. Situated on a hill, the Spire dominated the landscape. But more importantly, it gave him and his team a clear line of sight in every direction.

He'd learned the value of that in the war against Lijuan, would never forget it.

As it was, the more time he spent in the Spire, the more he liked it. It fit him far better than any of the castles or citadels or palaces in the region. He'd grown into adulthood in a time of considerable change, had helped Raphael's Tower become the most state-of-the-art court of any in the Cadre. Now, he intended to take that crown for himself.

Already, he had a team working on a system that would create a sonic shield around the Spire in case of attack.

As for aesthetics, the building was sleek and aerodynamic, with the required balconies set into the building itself rather than jutting out. Any railings on the higher floors had already been removed. Cosmetic changes could be made later. First, they had to get the basics right. Not only in the building but in personnel.

Smiling as he saw a clear bullet of a vehicle hover to a stop above the entrance path to the Spire, he flared out his wings and stepped off the edge of the roof.

Zoe was standing on the path by the time he landed, her pack beside her, while the vehicle had taken itself off to the garage under the building. Lean but muscled, her black curls currently contained in two braids, one on either side of her head, she wore rugged pants in a brown fabric that hugged her legs and was likely to be fine armor, along with a simple black vest top that left her arms bare and exposed a strip of her belly.

A metallic tattoo ran down her temple, flowed across her cheek, the bronze and silver of it arresting against the brown of her skin.

Around each wrist was a bracelet of hammered metal, a set that Deacon had fashioned for her on her Making, and that Illium had never seen Zoe without. Inset into the left bracelet was the diamond from Sara's engagement ring and a shard of dark metal that had once been part of Deacon's favorite sword, while the bracelet on the right bore a message written in her mother's curving hand in a code the two had developed when Zoe was a teen.

Illium knew what it said only because Zoe had told him once: *Live your wild, baby girl. We love you more than the moon and all the stars. ~ Mom and Dad*

Sara and Deacon would be incredibly proud to see who their daughter had become.

"Are my eyes deceiving me"—having removed her sunglasses, Zoe squinted as she looked up—"or is your entire building electrified?"

"Shield midprogress. Sadly the sparks will disappear once the system is up and running." He held out his forearm. "Welcome."

Zoe clasped his forearm . . . and sucked in a breath. "Whoa. You're waaaay more buzzy than Raphael."

"You should have seen me right after ascension." His power had felt as if it floated at the top of his skin, just ready to leap out. "Nice tattoo."

"Removable—new tech I'm test-wearing for a friend. He wants to see how long it lasts on vampires." She shifted her head so the metallic colors caught the light. "Neat, huh?"

"Your mom would've had a coronary."

Zoe grinned. "She would, wouldn't she?" Lifting the bracelet with Sara's diamond in it, she pressed a kiss to the metal. "Then she'd have researched the hell out of it and come with me while I had it done to make sure they did it right. So, Archangel Illium. *In. Sane.*"

"You have no idea." Illium kept being surprised by the new power that danced in his veins. "I'm very happy to have you with me, Zoe."

"A century," she said, as firm as her legendary mother. "That's the trial period. If I don't like it, I go back to being a weapons-maker."

"Agreed. Your priority task is to build me an armory." He'd been a first general, could handle strategy and other logistics while she focused on that.

Zoe nodded, all business.

"And by 'build,'" he clarified, "I don't mean you specifically. Your time is too valuable and I want you to save that energy for the weapons you decide need your expert touch."

"It'd be too slow if I did it all anyway."

"You have a ton of buildings to choose from—we've acquired this entire area." He'd made sure any affected residents had been relocated to even better homes in locations they chose because it would've been a bad omen to start his reign by kicking people out and leaving them unhappy. "Aside from any personal weapons owned by my squadrons, you're starting from an inventory of zero."

Zoe's mouth fell open, her eyes shining. "Are you serious? *All* of it?"

"No one's officially ruled this as one territory for centuries." Illium shrugged, hands on his hips. "Uram's armory is long gone, and the archangels who looked after each of the discrete areas have withdrawn their people and weapons. So yeah, all of it."

Even as her expression turned gleeful, she frowned. "How vulnerable are we?"

"Raphael says the Cadre has an unofficial understanding that it's bad manners to attack an archangel in the first century of his rule. Still happens now and then, but no one on the current Cadre is out for my blood."

Aegaeon might be enraged by Illium's rejection, but he was also too prideful to attack his son—at least at this early stage. "We need to be up and running by the end of that period, but I'd prefer it if we hit an earlier deadline."

"I'll have us sorted in a year." Zoe waved a hand and only then did he notice that her nails were painted a glittering black. "The pretty weapons can wait; we have to be practical. Does Lady Katrina still like you?"

"She's here, with Vivek—my new spymaster."

"Well, damn, that should speed up the timeline even further. Woman has connections everywhere even if she hasn't been in the weapons business this century." A crisp nod. "I'll get you up and running. Leave it to me."

So he did. As he left others to their tasks while being aware of the bigger picture, and keeping his focus on building up their squadrons and ground crews. It wasn't about readying himself for war, but about having the forces to deal with any uprising in his own territory—especially the vampiric kind.

Illium also made it a point to speak one-on-one with any senior vampire or angel in his territory who wanted to join his units. He did the same with the applicants from outside his territory after Aodhan created a short list.

They'd had a massive influx of applications.

"Color me surprised," Elena'd said dryly when he mentioned it on a call. "Of course all those people who've interacted with you over the years, who know that you're both smart and fun to be around, want to work with you. Oh, and Jason said he's hearing courtiers whispering about going to your territory to attempt to catch your eye."

Illium had groaned. "I'm going to off-load that handling to Dulce." He had no room in his Spire for courtiers, but some of them could turn vicious if insulted, so Dulce would have to find a way to keep them calm but out of the way.

Dulce rolled her eyes when he warned her what was incoming. "I know how to deal with snotty old immortals. I'll handle it."

In better news, a suspicious Navarro had accepted the interim first general position. "Do you think I was born yesterday?" he'd muttered on arrival, even as his eyes scanned the lists of Illium's current forces. "You have every intention of seducing me into a permanent role."

Illium had grinned. "Of course I do. You know you're going to love it."

Aodhan, as his second, meanwhile, handled all other details of setting up a functioning center of rule and liaised with everyone from Navarro, to Dulce, to their new head of administration—an angel who'd resigned his position in Elijah's court to join Illium's.

Vivek had been able to confirm that there were no hard feelings there, the transfer expected, given the age of the angel and the opportunity for a more senior role.

One unexpected but very welcome transplant was Laric, who was now the healer in charge of setting up the infirmary in the Spire, and building up a team around himself. Andreja had come with him, of course, with Navarro rapidly drafting her to a lieutenant role under him.

So it went.

A number of scholars had also relocated to Illium's home base, their task to chronicle the beginning of his rule. As a favor to Jessamy, Aodhan made sure they had the access they needed without getting underfoot. His parents had actually applied for the post but been declined because their expertise was in a different area of scholarship. However, Menerva and Rukiel were excited to visit once Illium and Aodhan had more time on their hands.

Aodhan's own chosen center of operations was an entire floor high up in the Spire that offered a three-hundred-and-sixty-degree view when the blinds were up. "It can double as your war room," he told Illium. "For now, I just like the light."

Aodhan was thriving in that light, angels flying in and out of that floor as he sent them on their tasks, or they reported back. A number still had difficulty looking at him even though the glass was treated so the light didn't blaze off him, but everyone they'd chosen to join their staff was in awe of his skill.

"This will work," Illium said after his return from a flight to quell a small stirring of vampires who'd gotten the bright idea that a busy and brand-new archangel meant they could go off the leash and start a bloodthirsty game of hunting mortals without attracting attention.

They had learned differently, as those who'd witnessed their punishmet had learned that their archangel could be ruthless when lines were crossed. Still, Illium knew he'd be putting out such idiotic fires for a while yet. His hold on the territory would be built over hundreds of such interventions and actions that taught his people that they could trust him, look to him for protection.

Fear, too, was an important factor. Like Raphael, Illium didn't intend to rule with fear. However, he did need young vampires, and any others with violent urges, to dread the wrath of their archangel enough to toe the line. Once things stabilized, Navarro and other senior members of Illium's team could handle such matters, but for now, it had to be him. He had to personally deal with every incident, burning both his power—and his intention to watch over them— into the minds of the populace.

It was going to be exhausting—but it was exhilarating, too.

He took Aodhan's hand as they stood on top of the Spire that night, while the stars glittered overhead, and their city sprawled out gently in all directions. The lights were muted, lush green rooftops dominating until they overlooked a thriving low forest.

"Ellie will love it here," Aodhan murmured, his mind clearly on the same path as Illium's. "This entire place is like the Legion's tower."

"Yes." Its green heart was part of why Illium had chosen this small city at the center of his new territory as his home base. Built atop an ancient city that had been all twisting lanes, and strange avenues, it had kept that rich depth of character even as it walked into century after century.

Power attracted power, so the city would grow, but he would ensure it never lost itself.

Aside from the Spire, there was a small grouping of high-rises in the distance, but even those buildings had been designed to be nourished by the rain and energized by the sun. That made Illium's chosen base an anomaly in its hard exterior, but that suited him. No matter how the world advanced, vampires continued to be driven by blood and angels by power.

They needed to respect the Cadre.

A stabbing pain. "I'll miss making mortal friends," he said. "I can no longer walk into bars and bakeries and just pull up a chair." No matter what, however, he vowed in that moment, he would not permit ascension to steal from him the part of his heart that understood and cherished mortals.

Aodhan didn't tell him that he was wrong, that nothing was stopping him from carrying on as he'd always done. He understood that an archangel occupied a different stratum of existence, that for him to make mortal friends would just put those friends at risk. Instead, he said, "This is only the beginning, Blue. Once you're settled, your reign solid, that's when you can start changing all the rules."

His wing slid over Illium's.

"Adi?"

"Hmm?"

"You know you're my consort?"

47

Aodhan didn't stiffen or send him a shocked look. "I was expecting a grand proposal. Now you've gone and shattered all my dreams." Words so dry, they could've ignited a forest fire.

Illium threw back his head and laughed, then spun the other man around to kiss him. Aodhan was smiling, his words laced with amusement when he spoke into Illium's mind. *Of course I know, you idiot. But I'm not sure it's good politics to announce it.*

Scowling, Illium drew back. "Why not?"

"When was the last time you heard of a second who was also a consort?" Aodhan raised an eyebrow. "Consorts are protected in battle even when they're warriors. A second can *never* be protected, because his strength is yours."

He held up a hand before Illium could speak. "And aside from some outliers, archangels don't consciously attack consorts or target them. You pronounce me your consort and your second at the same time and it'll screw up the entire system."

Illium folded his arms across his chest. "It's not like everyone doesn't already know we wear each other's amber." Aodhan's bracelet glinted as if in agreement.

"Yes, my darling," Aodhan said with tenderness, because he knew his lover. Archangel or not, Illium's heart could be hurt—and Aodhan could hurt it most of all. "But you know the games of the Cadre. They can all accept that I'm yours and you're mine, while politely ignoring that in favor of my title as second."

Illium's lip curled up in a snarl. "I *refuse* to play this game."

"You have to." Aodhan went toe to toe with him because that was his job as both Illium's consort and his second. "You can't destabilize the system. Not yet. Not when you're so new as an archangel. And Blue? I don't need a title to know who I am to you." Grabbing one fisted hand, he pressed it to his heart. "I *know.*"

Illium's jaw worked. "One hundred years," he said. "Then, I'm adding you to my sigil. We're one, Adi, and we'll always be one. I don't care if people want to pretend otherwise. I won't."

Aodhan exhaled. "One hundred years," he said, accepting the compromise. Because he knew that obstinate look; Illium wouldn't back down any further. "And you don't have an official sigil yet."

"Yes, I do. You already drew it. So when are you going to show it to me?"

"You drive me crazy." Glaring, Aodhan cupped Illium's face, kissing him with love and tenderness and affection. Because while he wouldn't carry the title of consort, he'd never hide what they were to each other, what they'd been to each other for centuries.

Illium's anger hadn't totally retreated when the kiss ended, but the wicked glint was back in his eye. "Did you plan for it to be a surprise?"

Aodhan squeezed his nape. "I swear . . ." he muttered. "You're infuriating."

Releasing Illium's nape, he reached into his pocket and withdrew the sigil he'd begun to work on in his mind the instant after Illium's ascension. Since sigils were black for the most part—for only a rare few archangels had the gift of burning their sigil with color—he hadn't been able to work with Illium's signature hue.

Instead, he'd thought of all the pieces of his Blue, and decided on the image of a shooting star, but one that spiraled up in a bolt of dizzying power, not down. The detail was in the spiraling bolt—it was made up of innumerable other tiny stars. "All the hearts loyal to you," Aodhan said. "All the people who love you because you know how to love so hard."

It was a stylized design, crisp, clean lines with nothing fussy about it. "I can change it if you don't like it," he said when Illium was silent. "I have other options, I just—"

"Hush, you beautiful, talented man." Illium's order was tender, his hands careful as he took the sketch lit up by the glow coming off Aodhan's hand. "Is this how you see me?"

"As bright and generous and a gift?" Aodhan nuzzled Illium's temple. "How can you not know that after all these years?"

Illium leaned into him, running his fingers over the lines of the sigil . . . until it suddenly glowed a vibrant blue. Lifting his hand, Illium did something in the air that Aodhan couldn't quite follow . . . and the sigil glowed vivid Illium-blue against the night sky over their city, big and bright enough to be visible for miles.

Wonder and delight in Aodhan's breath, his heart thunder. "I should've known you'd find a way to stamp your mark on it beyond any doubt."

"Figure out how you're going to incorporate yourself into it as my consort when that ridiculous century is over."

Aodhan threw his arm around Illium's shoulders. "You're cute when you're mad."

"I am going to strangle you," Illium threatened . . . right before he smacked Aodhan in the back with his wing, sending him tumbling off the roof.

As Aodhan yelled in surprise, Illium said, *Illium, Archangel of Patient Vengeance.*

His laughter lit up the night as above his city glowed a sigil of stars countless . . . and Aodhan's laughter joined his, theirs an infinite symphony of two.

The Guild Hunter series continues
with Elena and Raphael . . .